E. M. Kkc

The Triumph of Mars

Ships of Britannia

Book 4

ISBN: 9798442536300

PublishNation
www.publishnation.co.uk

Contents

List of Locations

Chapters
I
II
III
IV
V
VI
VII
VIII
IX
X
XI
XII
XIII

Author's Note
Acknowledgments

List of Locations

Octapitarum Promontorium – St David's Head, South Wales

Malvadum – Ilfracombe, Devon

Meridianum – Plymouth, Devon

Lon – River Lune, Lancashire

Abona – Sea Mills, near Bristol

Luguvallium – Carlisle, Cumbria

Portus – Portsmouth

Noviomagus - Chichester

Mona – Isle of Anglesey

Vectis – Isle of Wight

Isle of Manannan – Isle of Man

Hibernia – Ireland

Norvegia – Norway

Gaul – France

Eboracum – York

Verulamium – St Albans

Londin/Londinium – London

Dubris – Dover

Isles of Sillina – Isles of Scilly

Kernow – Cornwall

Britannic Ocean– English Channel

Mare Germanicus – North Sea

Oceanus Hibernicus – Irish Sea

BRITANNIA

PICTS

CALEDONIA

MARE GERMANICVS

GAELS

HADRIAN'S WALL

LVGVVALLIVM

LON

ISLE OF
MANANNAN

EBORACVM

OCEANVS
HIBERNICVS

MONA

DEVA

LINDVM

LETOCETVM

HIBERNIA

OCTAPITARVM
PROMONTORIVM

GLEVVM

VERVLAMIVM

ISLE
OF THE
DEAD

ABONA

AQVAE
SVLIS

THAMESIS

LONDINIVM

DVBRIS

MALVADVM

PORTVS

DVRNOVARIA

ISCA

NOVIOMAGVS

ISLES OF
SILLINA

KERNOW

VECTIS

MERIDIANVM

OCEANVS
BRITANNICVS

GAVL

KRJB

I

The grim faces ranged around her Great Cabin told their own story.

Maia's gaze flitted to each one, seeing the signs of shock which no stoicism could mask. She tried not to think about the one who was missing; Magpie, whose poisoned corpse had been put into spelled stasis in her deepest hold until such time as she might make landfall and he could be decently buried. Few Mages were buried at sea. Raven had explained to her that their connection to the land ran too deep.

Her Admiral – no, her King now that his nephew was dead – was seated at the central table outlining their position. His niece, the Princess Julia, pistols thrust through a wide leather belt naval-style, flanked her uncle with the Agent, Milo, in the background as always. The elaborate gown and hairstyle had gone, in favour of more practical garb. Disappointment hovered in the air as the Admiral broke the bad news.

"I'm afraid to say that fewer Ships than I'd hoped have openly declared for us. Many of them have been deliberately kept in port, and I fear that they're being held hostage. This includes the *Victoria*."

Maia remembered the new Flagship's announcement of plague, and wondered if that too had been part of the meticulously planned coup to bring Britannia under the sway of Marcus and his perfidious allies. At the moment, she wouldn't have put it past them to have arranged the whole thing. Of those Ships that had pledged their allegiance to King Cei Pendragon, most were well away from Britannia and out of danger. She was glad that her friend, the *Patience* had been one of them, but others were too afraid to speak out. She had the feeling that many of them were biding their time and waiting to see what would happen.

"Some did manage to escape, Sire," Leo pointed out. Outwardly, her Captain remained steady and self-composed. Only Maia knew how he secretly cried in the dark for the loss of

1

his friend. In contrast, Julia's grief at her brother's assassination had turned quickly to a cold rage and thoughts of revenge.

Maia wondered whether anyone else saw the momentary flicker as her Admiral was addressed by his new rank. The fact that his rival was his own son surely made the title even more of a curse.

"Too few," he replied, shortly. "I know from experience that Ships tend to take the long view. Kings come and go, yet they remain. Many Captains won't commit themselves, or risk their crews."

"Lapwing did say that if I didn't comply, I would be forcibly detached, weighted and sunk," Maia said. "I don't blame them for being cagey."

"And the others won't return until all this is sorted," Raven agreed. "Would you leave a safe berth in the Empire, or the New Continent?"

Pendragon frowned. "Has there been any news of the Fae? If we had intelligence that they were on the move, it would give everyone a different perspective."

Raven shook his head. "They won't show their hand until the very last second. The country would rise against them. No, as far as the general populace is concerned, we're all dead."

Pendragon glanced down at the charts spread before him.

"We need to take stock," he said firmly. "I doubt that there are many on land that we can rely on. We have limited information, but we must act on what we have. Our mere existence is a threat to the Usurper and that is what we must maintain at all costs."

There were murmurs of agreement.

"May I suggest that we regroup off the Isles of Sillina?" Raven offered. "We'll be in a better position there."

Pendragon and Leo exchanged glances, then the older man nodded.

"A good idea. *Tempest*, inform our allies to proceed to the designated co-ordinates with all speed. We'll have part of the Fleet at least and we may be able to muster reinforcements from the Empire and the New Continent. When the Fae decide to move, we need to be within striking distance. Any questions?"

The Master Mage's whispery voice cut through the stillness. "The slave girl, Sire. Do you wish me to question her further?" Pendragon's dark eyes hardened. "Yes. She may be able to furnish us with something. After that, she'll be dealt with publicly."

Maia knew what that meant. This would be her first on board execution, but she doubted that it would be her last.

"Aye, Sire."

Again, Maia sensed the Admiral's brief discomfort. Sometimes she could swear that she was more in tune with him than with her Captain.

"Very well. You all have your orders. Dismissed."

The men saluted and left to resume their posts, only talking amongst themselves when they were out of the cabin. Leo gave Maia the co-ordinates and she busied herself in adjusting her course northwest, towards the small group of islands that lay in the Atlantic Ocean off the coast of Kernow. Soon, only her Admiral and the Princess remained in the cabin. She left them, flowing upwards to join Leo and a silent Sabrinus as they scanned the morning horizon for any sign of danger.

*

Milo followed his old master down into the darkness of the orlop deck, the deepest place in the vessel, where the treacherous slave, Melissa, was imprisoned. They found her sprawled on the wooden planks, weighed down with heavy iron fetters. The lamplight reflected off sullen eyes from which all hope had fled.

"This is your last chance to speak under your own volition," Milo told her. As a slave, she could be compelled by magic and she knew it. Any secrets would flow like spilled wine, regardless of her intent.

Melissa chewed her lip.

"I don't know anything." Tears began to well up, but it seemed that some defiance remained.

"Tell us what Lapwing told you," Milo continued. He crouched down, to look directly at her. "Were your actions your own, or were you compelled?"

He saw the brief flare of hope. If she thought there was any way to escape her fate, she'd surely take it.

"He used magic on me!" she blurted out. "I had no choice! I was possessed!"

If he hadn't been an experienced Agent, her expression of innocence might have fooled him but, just for a second, there had been a look of calculation as she weighed up the odds.

"I see," he said, his tone sympathetic. "Of course, we'll have to confirm this."

He stepped back and Raven spoke. Immediately, he could sense the spell spiralling out to encircle her in its grip. Melissa writhed weakly, the chains rattling as she tried to resist.

It didn't take long for her to condemn herself utterly.

*

Tempest's voice echoed through the vessel, ordering all hands to assemble. Her crew hurried to comply, forming up amidships to witness the end of the would-be assassin. It only took a short while before the space was filled with upturned faces, all eyes fixed on the poop deck and their Commander.

Julia, attended by Latonia, took up position next to her uncle. Her new slave had a bandaged shoulder but was otherwise unharmed. She'd acted with commendable swiftness and Julia felt nothing but gratitude towards the girl. If it hadn't been for her warning, Julia knew that Melissa's attempt could have succeeded, sending her to join her brother in the Underworld.

Everything felt unreal. There was no chance of making it to Gaul now, even if they could have counted on King Parisius's help. The way would already be blockaded. Marcus couldn't take the chance that a rival to his stolen throne would slip away to muster forces against him. The grief for her murdered brother had hardened, like metal armour around her heart. Beside her, the King watched impassively as the girl was dragged out. The only sounds were the wind and waves as the company stood in silence to witness justice being done.

A rope was brought out and flung over a yardarm, the end held by a team of marines ready to hoist the unfortunate slave aloft. If she was lucky, she would choke quickly. Osric stood impassively by with the noose, ready to slip it around her neck. The chains had been removed, but her hands were bound. Melissa's eyes swept the vessel, seeing nothing but implacable judgement. There was no sympathy here. She started to struggle, forcing her captors to drag her over to where she would meet her fate. All eyes turned to Pendragon, who gave the nod. Melissa sagged, fainting, as one of the men bent to secure her ankles.

Suddenly, she kicked out, catching him on the jaw and wrenched herself free, setting off at a run.

"Where's she going to go?" Pendragon said wearily, frowning at the negligent marines.

Crewmen dashed to cut off her progress and *Tempest* belatedly cast ropes in her direction, but Melissa was already at the rail. The condemned woman didn't hesitate, hurtling past startled crewmen and throwing herself over the side to disappear into the frigid depths with a splash.

Osric barked an order.

"Shoot her!"

Julia knew it would be a miracle if the woman managed to swim to shore with her hands bound. The marines rushed to the rail, weapons raised. Death by musket ball would be better than swinging from the yardarm and slowly strangling.

A bell chimed below, followed by another, then another. Danuco, the Priest, shook his head at Leo's questioning glance, but Raven spoke first.

"It's the kraken alarm!"

Leo's shout was drowned out by the crack of musket fire and bursts of sulphurous smoke whipped away in the wind.

"Reload!"

Julia struggled to keep her balance as the deck pitched. *Tempest* was acting as quickly as she could to change course, hoping to avoid the creature's grasp.

Suddenly Melissa reappeared, catapulted from the waves as a huge geyser spewed from the surface, legs flailing wildly as her body spun helplessly in mid-air. Beneath her, a vast grey shape erupted from the depths, revealing a gigantic maw lined with razor-sharp teeth. A tentacle shot up, whipping around her as she fell and giving her enough time for one final scream before the monstrous cephalopod gulped her down in a single mouthful. An enormous eye regarded the Ship curiously before the creature submerged once more, its hunger assuaged. As it disappeared, the alarm bells gradually ceased their jangling, one by one. The monster had moved incredibly swiftly.

"That's that, then," Raven remarked, whilst Pendragon's thunderous expression boded ill for the unlucky escort.

"It is now," Julia answered. She stared down at the ripples, relieved that it was all over. "At least we won't have her corpse stinking up the rigging. She got what she deserved for her betrayal."

The marines holding the rope hovered uncertainly, until the Ship's Priest stepped forward.

"It was the will of the Gods and a fitting punishment," Danuco announced. The men cast him grateful glances. They were dismissed and promptly retreated below, no doubt to get a thorough chewing out from Osric, the will of the Gods notwithstanding.

As the crew dispersed to their posts, Leo approached her, eyeing her weapons.

"I take it you know how to use those, Highness?" he asked.

Julia arched an eyebrow at him. "I certainly do. Frequent target practice helps."

"Are they loaded?"

She met his gaze directly.

"Oh yes."

"Very wise. And you've got your guard dogs."

He jerked his head to where Milo and Latonia were standing at a respectable distance. That made her smile.

"I suppose I have. Well, no marriage for me, then."

"Or not yet."

She felt her face harden. "Or ever, I hope."

To his credit, Leo hid his surprise. "Then unless Marcus produces an heir, or the Admiral divorces and remarries, that's it for the Pendragons."

Julia frowned as the realisation hit home. She'd always assumed that Artorius would marry and secure the next generation. His death complicated matters in more ways than she'd thought.

Leo continued, "Surely Parisius will be even keener to marry you now? Your child could inherit two thrones."

"Then he'll have to come to our aid, won't he?" she answered, thinking that it was unlikely. "If the old fool had any sense, he'd have appointed a successor by now and married me off to him to secure his line."

"From what I've heard, he'd rather die and leave his kingdom in a mess for the Emperor and the Imperial Governor to sort out. It wouldn't surprise me if conflict's imminent there as well."

"Wonderful," she sighed. "In the meantime, we're off to the Isles of Sillina. What are they like?"

"Small, with a mild climate. We'll be striking out across open water and going as fast as possible. There'll be a chance to re-provision, but I don't know what the Admiral has in mind after that."

"It's strange to think of him as the King," she admitted and he nodded in agreement. "I think we should take our chance on land," Julia continued. "Surely people know Marcus is lying through his teeth? Some of the legions must be loyal."

"That's the problem. Communications have been disrupted, something we didn't think possible, and you can be sure that the enemy is monitoring them. Making landfall will be very dangerous."

Julia bit back a curse, staring at the waves tumbling from the bow in a froth of white and green as *Tempest* piled on the speed.

"Maybe the Gods can help?" she offered, hopefully.

"We can only ask," he acknowledged, following her gaze. "But we can't make burnt offerings and attract hostile attention. Smoke can be seen for miles out here."

The Ship stood to one side, eyes fixed on the course ahead and her features showing no emotion. Julia knew that she was on full alert. A few small sails dotted the sea; merchantmen plying their trade and nothing to cause alarm, but even so they steered clear.

"Perhaps you should go below and rest," Leo suggested. Julia came to a decision. It was getting a little chilly and she could do with strengthening her armoury of spells.

"Good idea." She left him on deck and headed down to the Mage quarters.

Time to learn something new and, with only one Mage left, she suspected that her more unconventional talents would be needed sooner rather than later.

*

Londin was the best bet, Caniculus decided. It was somewhere he could keep his head down and his ears and eyes open. Like most Agents, he had various bolt holes around the city and enough coin squirrelled away to keep body and soul together while he weathered this particular storm. The idea of two would-be monarchs clashing was not a pleasant one, and he felt that he'd already been caught up enough in current events. If Londin became too hot, he could always head off to Verulamium, or even further north to Eboracum if things became desperate.

He'd disguised Excalibur in a rough pack made from a couple of blankets hastily grabbed from the stables and packed with straw to pad them out. They would do service as a bed roll as well. To be honest, he hadn't a clue what he was going to do with the sacred weapon, or why he felt the urge to hide it. It had seemed like a good idea at the time, he supposed, even as he cursed himself for a fool and tried to put as much distance between himself and the villa as humanly possible. A swift horse would have helped, but he couldn't risk being seen and heard galloping away from the scene of the crime. It was better to casually walk away and blend in with the nearest crowd. He trudged onwards through a patch of woodland, knowing that if he was correct in his bearings he would soon reach the main thoroughfare.

Although the light was failing, he was more than happy to see that the road up to Londin was still busy. Vehicles of all descriptions passed by, everything from lumbering carts pulled by oxen, to swifter private carriages. There were plenty of folk on foot as well, so it was easy to join the flow of traffic. He briefly considered taking one of the regular horse omnibuses, then dismissed it. They were generally reliable, but a little warning voice told him to steer clear and he knew from experience that he disregarded it at his peril.

At least he wasn't on a Ship in the middle of nowhere. He hated the sea.

After a couple of miles, he stopped to buy some food from a roadside trader, together with a measure of ale in a disposable pot. It would see him through the night, as he didn't want to risk finding an inn. Caniculus didn't think he'd been spotted but he wasn't sure.

He rid himself of his speechstone at the first opportunity, tossing it unobtrusively into a small river as he crossed a bridge. The tiny plop was masked by the rumbling of cart wheels. Running water was a sure way of messing up the Potentia in the spelled device, so if they wanted to track him now, they'd have a job. Whoever was in charge now could take that as his unofficial resignation letter. His only regret was that he wouldn't be able to talk to Milo again; that was if his friend wasn't with his speechstone at the bottom of the ocean. So, the *Tempest* had gone down with all hands? Then again, could anybody believe Marcus, the lying toad? He relieved his feelings by spitting into a bush to show his contempt for the man.

Night was drawing on fast and he knew that he'd have to find a place to rest. Stumbling around in the dark wasn't really an option. Perhaps he could find a warm barn? Failing that it would be a small campfire and a sheltering tree. Fortunately, it wasn't raining and he had a thick cloak, plus his purloined blankets.

Caniculus scanned his surroundings. There was a smaller road, barely a track, leading off to his left into a patch of forest. Would that be a better path to take? The sound of shouted orders and the tramp of many feet made the choice for him. He could see the standard in the distance, the eagle's wings outstretched against the darkening sky and the yells as carts and people did their best to get out of the way of the advancing legionaries. He couldn't see who they were, but he would bet that they weren't friendly. He decided it was best to make himself scarce and headed off into the trees, ducking under low branches. There would be good cover and he could find somewhere to camp out for the night before resuming his journey in the morning.

The remaining light dwindled as he trudged along, heading roughly north-east. There were a few dwellings and signs of small farms in the distance, but he walked by quickly, glad that

9

the way was deserted and the spring weather was fine. He was just about to disappear quietly into a denser patch of vegetation when he came to a small crossroads. Two hooded figures were standing having what seemed to be a conversation, one male, one female. He pulled his hood up quickly hoping to slip by unnoticed, when the man hailed him.

"Greetings, friend! You're out late!"

"A good evening to you both," Caniculus replied courteously, while trying to hide as much of his face as possible. He was unremarkable enough, though Milo frequently compared his long features to those of a particularly miserable hound.

"Where are you off to this time of night, so far from home?"

Something in the stranger's voice set the hairs on the back of his neck to rise and he started to reach for his dagger.

"There's no need for that, Little Dog." The woman's voice was low and echoed with Potentia. He'd heard it before, outside the villa as he'd watched Artorius' body bleed. To his horror, he realised that the pair standing before him weren't human.

"Lord, Lady," he said, through a suddenly dry mouth. His heartbeats sounded loud in his ears emphasised by the eerie silence of the woods.

The man threw off his hood to reveal a smooth young face and dark, curly hair. His eyes were bright in the dusk, glinting with little points of light. The woman remained concealed, though he realised that what he had taken for a tall stick was in fact a spear.

"We have a task for you, faithful Dog," the man said, a half-smile playing on his lips.

"Yes, Lord?" Caniculus said, though it came out as more of a squeak.

"You're Milo's friend, are you not?"

The Agent nodded, praying that his legs wouldn't give way.

"I've met him," the young man said. "I helped him with a job he was on west of here." He turned to his companion. "A light spot of grave robbing," he added.

"Grave robbing? How did you explain that to our Uncle Hades?" She sounded amused.

"Oh, it was sanctioned. I'm a good boy and do as I'm ordered," the youth grinned back.

"Well at least it wasn't cattle stealing this time."

"Oh come on. That was just the once and I was only a child. I made up for it and Apollo forgave me in the end."

"Humph." She didn't sound impressed, but she did remove her hood. Gleaming grey eyes fixed on Caniculus. "I suppose I'd better tell him what we want him to do, before he falls over," the God remarked. "It's been a long few days, has it not?"

"It has, O Swift One," Caniculus answered, trying to lock his knees to keep them from trembling. Was he expected to kneel before them?

"See, I knew he'd recognise me – unlike most mortals," Mercury said.

"It was only because I called you a cattle thief," his companion sniffed. The God rolled his eyes.

"As I was saying, before Athena here interrupted me, we have a task – no you don't have to kneel, though we might be better sitting down –,"

"No time," Athena interjected. Caniculus wondered whether she was Minerva as well, not to mention Sulis and several other Goddesses.

"Rufus mainly worshipped me as Athena, so that is who I am now," she told him, divining his unspoken question. "I could not prevent his death, but I can avenge his murder. He was brave, true and devout. I am permitted to tell you that the Twelve have turned their faces from Marcus."

So, the battle goddess of the Greeks was an enemy of the Usurper. It made Caniculus feel a lot better about his situation. You didn't mess with Athena; look what had happened to the Trojans.

As if hearing his thought she smiled, though there was nothing of humour in it, rather the fierce grin of a she-wolf.

"Caniculus, you are charged with two tasks. The first is to go to Londin and do what the Sword tells you to do. You have already felt its power of compulsion."

So that was the reason he'd grabbed it. It hadn't been his idea after all.

"Your second task is to pass information to the true King."

11

The Agent felt his jaw drop. So, Cei Pendragon wasn't dead after all!

"The true King, Lady? I don't know how I can do that."

"He's got a point," Mercury observed, or was it Hermes? Caniculus had the feeling that the name didn't matter. "He can't mind-speak on his own. Nor can he sneak into the palace unobserved, unless he has magic."

"Magic?" Caniculus squeaked again. "I'm not a Mage!"

He looked from one to the other in desperation. Athena nodded.

"True, and your face is already known. You will need help."

"So, in time-honoured fashion," Mercury announced. He produced a bulky, cloth-wrapped object from under his cloak and offered it to him with a flourish. For one awful second Caniculus thought it was the Gorgon's head, but then the God burst out laughing. Even Athena's mouth twitched.

"It's a helmet. Gods' sake man! Did you think we'd give you the deadliest weapon in the world?"

Caniculus accepted the bundle speechlessly, unwrapping the material. The helmet was made of bronze, close fitting with a nasal guard and looked extremely old.

"What does it do?"

"Try it." Mercury was clearly enjoying himself. "It does still work, I hope?" he asked his companion.

"Yes," Athena replied. "Hephaestus does good work and Perseus had no complaints."

"But that was ages ago," Mercury pointed out.

Caniculus regarded each of them for a moment, then lowered the helmet over his head. Immediately everything was sharper, every detail of his surroundings clear through the growing dusk. The trees around him faded to translucency and he could see through them to the woods beyond. Deer moved in the depths and small animals rustled in the undergrowth. Everything was revealed and nothing was hidden. Startled, he lifted the helmet off again.

"Do you think it'll be useful?" Mercury asked cheerfully.

"Definitely, Lord," Caniculus said. "It's an Agent's dream, though hardly the latest fashion. I'll attract attention."

"Really?" said Athena. "Put it on again and hold out your hand."

Caniculus did as he was asked, raising his hand in front of his face. He wiggled his fingers. Yes, it was there. He just couldn't see it, though the sense of its location remained.

"The Helmet of Invisibility!"

Mercury nodded. "That's the one. Perseus used it to kill Ceto and rescue Andromeda. I happened to find it lying around and thought it might come in useful one day. It's the only one in existence and we'll want it back, so don't break it, sell it, or trade it in for a villa in the country."

"Because *you* would," Athena remarked.

"I would not! The very thought!"

She gave him a withering glance, then turned back to the overawed Agent.

"This will help, but you'll still need your wits about you. It's proof against magic as well, but don't push your luck too far. Report back to your friend Milo."

"How?" Caniculus asked.

Mercury tossed him a familiar stone, still complete with its armband.

"You dropped this. Don't worry, it can't be used to track you, but now you can remain in contact with the King."

"Is Milo with the King?"

Mercury's smile widened. "He is indeed. He's highly favoured."

Great. He gets to bask in the royal favour while I get a... he broke off the thought, aware of whom he was dealing with, but Mercury was laughing again.

"Oh, he hasn't got it easy, I assure you. In fact, friend Milo is having a very testing time!"

Caniculus didn't quite know what to say to that.

"I pray that you both favour him, O Mighty Ones," he said at last.

"You ask for your friend and not yourself," Athena said in approval. "You are indeed a faithful hound. Now, go. Do your duty to your Gods, King and Country."

Caniculus bowed low and when he straightened up they were gone. Off to his right, a fire was already burning in a small clearing, its cheerful light flickering like a welcome beacon. He moved over to it, grateful for the warmth. The unnatural stillness was gone and the normal sounds of the evening woodland had resumed once again. If it hadn't been for the solid weight of the helmet in one hand and the speechstone in the other, he would have thought it all a dream.

At least his path was set. He would reach Londin the next day and take things from there. He decided to call Milo immediately, secure in the knowledge that it was safe.

<Dog to Ferret!>

There was a pause, then a cautious acknowledgement.

<Dog? What's happening?>

<Are you still at sea?> Caniculus didn't want to commit himself.

<Yes.>

<Did you know that Artorius has been murdered and Marcus has taken over? He's announced that the *Tempest* is sunk and everyone's dead.>

He sensed the indrawn breath. <We know that Artorius is dead and Marcus has seized the throne. We didn't know the rest.>

<Oh yes, Marcus is lying through his teeth to get the population on his side. We're in the middle of a coup here and I don't know who to trust. That swine Macro murdered Senator Rufus in cold blood as well.>

<What?> Milo couldn't disguise his ripple of shock, and at that moment, Caniculus knew with relief that whatever was happening, Milo had had no part of it, even though the Gods had vouched for him in their own way.

<Rufus drew his sword and challenged Marcus to state his innocence on his cousin's corpse. It bled, right there, in front of everyone. Macro slit his throat from behind. He'll be purging anyone who supports his father. Look, I haven't got time, but the Gods aren't pleased. If you're with the Pendragons, for Gods' sake take care. He'll be after them too.>

<It's sorted,> the grim reply came. <Lapwing tried to kill them and suborn the *Tempest*. I beheaded him myself.>

Caniculus muttered an oath. <Look, I've been given a mission.>

<By whom?>

The Agent bit back a laugh. <You wouldn't believe me if I told you. I have to take something important somewhere and spy on Marcus for the true King, reporting back to you so you can tell Pendragon. I ditched my stone, but I was given it back. Still, I don't think it'll be safe to contact anyone else, least of all Favonius.>

<You take care too, Dog. And be warned. There's Fae involvement. I don't think Favonius would ever support that, so he's probably already dead. This is too well organised for him to be left alive.>

<And if he is, he won't know who to trust, either.>

They exchanged mutual curses. The Chief Agent would have been handy in this crisis.

<Contact me when you can,> Milo Sent.

<I will, when I have more information. Otherwise, probably not.>

<Understood.>

Caniculus broke the link. He knew he could rely on Milo, but he was too far away to do anything here. That the true King lived, together with the Princess, was one positive thing and surely Marcus couldn't keep the lie of their deaths going for long. Furthermore, if the Usurper expected his father to capitulate, he was wrong on that score too. There would be a reckoning.

He snorted to himself as he gathered more wood for the fire. The helmet gleamed dully in the flickering firelight and Caniculus had the uncanny feeling that it was watching him.

It seemed that both he and Milo had their challenges ahead. In his own case, he'd have to complete the tasks the Gods had set him, or die trying.

As for Excalibur – what more would it demand of him? He dreaded to think of the answer.

II

It was late afternoon when Maia sighted land. The Isles of Sillina rose as dark splotches on the horizon and she instantly felt a small measure of security. The islands were populated by hardy, independent folk who would have no truck with a far-away usurper. A king on their own doorstep would be another matter entirely. Even so, Pendragon was proceeding carefully.

<Anchor offshore,> he instructed her. <We need to get the lie of the land.>

Maia did as she was ordered, scanning for any signs of her sister Ships, but she seemed to be alone for the moment and she couldn't open up a wide link to see if anyone was about. It would be easier as they approached. She only wished that her friend and mentor, the *Blossom*, was able to join them, but the old Ship had been in Portus and was probably even now under guard. The thought of Captain Plinius being in danger and maybe even arrested was not to be borne, but what could she do?

The King and Leo joined her on deck.

"Any signs of the Fleet?" Pendragon asked.

"No, Sire," she replied, "but from their last reported positions, most should join us within the next three days."

He pressed his lips into a tighter line. "Let's hope we have enough time," he said at last. She could already sense the tension on board. Leo shot her a glance.

<He's bearing up well, but I fear for him.> Her Captain's voice slid into her mind. Leo had largely recovered from the siren attack, but she noticed that he still favoured his ankle and carried himself stiffly. He'd be scarred for life, much as she had been before she shed her mortal flesh.

<We'll take care of him,> she Sent back. He gave her a barely perceptible nod, before turning his attention to the land.

"Sire, is it possible that there's a welcome committee there already?"

Pendragon took a deep breath. "I doubt it. It's a long way to Londin and the Usurper had planned for us to be dealt with. I can only hope that his source of intelligence dried up with Lapwing's death. He might be suspicious, but will know nothing for certain, least of all our whereabouts."

"True," Leo acknowledged.

The Usurper. How much easier it was to turn his son into something faceless and nameless.

"Permission to take a party ashore and spy out the situation," Leo said.

The Admiral frowned. "I'd rather you stayed here, plus you're not back to full fitness. Send Mr Amphicles with a party of marines to get as much information as possible and secure the co-operation of the locals."

They fell into discussion of numbers and possible outcomes. Maia left them to it and cast her gaze around her vessel. The youngest members of her crew were frightened by the sudden change in their fortunes and she was doing her best to reassure them. Maintaining morale was an important part of her duty. Danuco was already over by her altar making offerings to the Twelve, plus anybody else who might be listening, and the steady sound of his chanting drifted over on the breeze. She wondered whether he was including her aunt in his petitions. If only Pearl would appear!

She searched the skies in vain, hoping that her sister would make contact before too long. Until then, she'd just have to wait, but surely she could turn the Tempestas' abilities to her advantage? Pearl could travel faster than any of them and over longer distances. If she could persuade her to spy for them and report back, it would be something concrete to rely on instead of guesses and whispers.

She checked out the Mage quarters. Raven and Julia were deep in conversation, the woman's head bent over an ancient scroll as she fired questions at her mentor. Maia couldn't help feeling a small stab of jealousy. Julia didn't know half as much about Raven as she did. Hadn't she been inside his head, reliving his life through his eyes? How many people could say that?

She chided herself immediately; Raven was perfectly correct to train the Princess, and it was nothing more. Why did she feel so possessive of the ancient Master Mage? Was it because they had shared so much?

Maia turned her attention elsewhere, annoyed with herself. With everything that was going on, she didn't have time for pettiness. She resumed her duties, looking for anything out of place, whilst unable to dismiss the nagging fear that events were whirling like Charybdis, out of her control.

*

The sun was long past its zenith over Portus and the harbour had begun to settle down after the bustle of the day. *Blossom* was chatting idly over the Ship link, when Plinius's voice sounded in her head.

<We're off ashore to dine with my new Lieutenant. I'd be grateful if you could somehow detach Heron from that whatchamacallit he's working on. By force if necessary.>

She groaned quietly to herself, knowing her Mage would be reluctant, but decided not to give him the option of backing out.

"Heron."

"I'm busy." His muffled voice echoed hollowly from where his head was jammed into the whatchamacallit's interior. *Blossom* thought it looked like a mechanical winged fish that had been messily eviscerated on his worktable.

"It's bad manners to decline the invitation."

"But I'm not nearly finished!" he complained, pulling himself clear and gesturing at the tangle of wires and parts.

"It can wait until the morning. It's only fair that you get to know young Manius, as you'll be working with him for the foreseeable future. You never know," she wheedled, "he might be interested in mechanical things and it'll give you the chance to tell him all about your latest inventions."

Heron thought for a moment, his bushy eyebrows raised, before finally surrendering to the inevitable.

"Oh all right! I'll go for you, though I wish officers wouldn't move just as soon as I've got used to them! I suppose this can wait until tomorrow. Where am I going?"

Blossom rolled her eyes. She'd already told him at least three times; he was just being awkward. Still, she was nothing if not patient.

"The Mermaid. Plinius has booked their small dining room for the evening."

Heron smacked his lips. "I hear they do a nice lobster there."

"Among other things."

"I'll just finish up."

"Well, don't be long. And change that robe!"

He pretended to be affronted. "See how I'm bullied, Sobek! No rest on this Ship!"

The mummified crocodile fixed to the wall didn't respond, but *Blossom* blew her Mage a raspberry.

"Isn't that beneath your dignity as a Ship?" he demanded.

She blew another one, even louder, just to annoy him.

"You're worse than that damned parrot," he muttered, as he finally gave in and went to wash his hands and change his oil-smeared robes.

"It will do you good," she replied. Sometimes, when he was obsessed with one of his pet projects she had to remind him to eat, and he'd got worse since Robin's departure. An evening ashore would benefit everyone.

<Mission accomplished,> she Sent to her Captain, <but try to get him to talk about something other than machines and devices, if you can. Poor Manius.>

The young man was keen, but Heron could wear down even the most enthusiastic listener.

Plinius's amusement filled the link. <If the lad can cope with Heron, he can cope with anyone. I haven't the heart to tell him that this is the final test before he starts.>

<Well, if he snaps and starts throwing punches, you can definitely say he's failed,> *Blossom* retorted. Her only reply was a snort.

After a wait for Heron to get organised, the little party, consisting of himself, Plinius, Manius in his brand new lieutenant's uniform, and Campion finally reached their destination. Heron had already taken the opportunity to monopolize the conversation, when a commotion along the waterfront caused *Blossom* to snap to attention immediately. Shouts and curses echoed off buildings as the rhythmic sound of marching feet grew ever louder. She was focusing her vision to see what all the fuss was about, when the *Persistence* raised the alarm.

<All Ships in Portus! I can see legionaries and plenty of 'em, heading our way!>

Legionaries? They weren't usually about in this city, unless Ships were taking them to war abroad. It took enough time and energy to deal with sailors and marines without adding landsmen to the mix. A thrill of warning ran through her; something bad was about to happen, or she wasn't a three-hundred-year-old Ship.

<Plinius, we have trouble.>

<What's happening?>

<Soldiers are coming.>

Just then, the *Peridot*, one of the smallest Ships, squealed in alarm.

<They're taking my Mage!>

She opened the relays instantly, allowing the other Ships nearby to see through her eyes.

"What are you doing?" *Peridot* demanded. The soldier in charge saluted her.

"Orders, ma'am. You're confined to port and your Mage has to come with us."

"Whose orders?" she snapped, moving closer to the man. To his credit, he only flinched a little.

"The King's, ma'am." He produced a paper, which she snatched from him. *Blossom* and the others read it with her. He was right. They were collecting Mages.

"What's all this?"

It was the *Peridot*'s Captain.

"New orders, sir, from both the Admiralty and the Collegium."

The Captain read the paper, his face paling. "I understand," he said, slowly. "*Peridot*, call him on deck."

<What can I do?> *Peridot* pleaded with her sisters.

<You have to obey.>

That was the *Justicia*, anchored further up the coast. *Blossom* realised that the Royal had been listening in and waiting for this very moment. What was she up to?

As they escorted a startled Linnet off the vessel, other Ships began to raise their voices in protest. *Blossom* Sent an urgent message ashore.

Plinius! Heron has to run! They're taking Mages, by order of Marcus!>

An oath shot through the link as Plinius passed on the information. <He seeks to cripple us for his own ends. Feign ignorance of Heron's whereabouts and stall them. Have they boarded yet?>

<They're about to.> She couldn't refuse the request that was bellowed from her gangplank.

<We're on our way. Good luck!>

Her first instinct was to tell him to run too, but she knew that she needed him here. Captains weren't killed lightly.

The lead soldier, a Centurion by his insignia, stamped up on to the deck, to be met by glares from the men on watch. His men followed after him, faces set. She didn't think that they were entirely comfortable around Ships. It was something she could use to her advantage.

She rose from the deck like Venus from the waves, wearing her best smile.

"Gentlemen. How may I assist you?"

The man licked his lips nervously. Good, he'd heard the stories.

"Ma'am. My name is Centurion Salvius, Third Legion. I've come for your Mage. By order of the King."

She raised a polite eyebrow. "Indeed? The Third Legion? We must all obey the King. I assume you have the correct paperwork?" He couldn't fail to hear the edge to her voice and, as she had surmised, didn't realise that every Ship in the harbour had seen a copy already through the *Peridot*'s eyes.

"Yes, ma'am." He pulled it from his uniform and handed it to her. She took it graciously and pretended to read it.

<Plinius, has Heron gone?>

<He has. They'll never catch him, the wily old fox. He vanished before our very eyes.>

She permitted herself an internal sigh of relief, before handing back the papers.

"I would be delighted to assist, but I'm afraid that he's currently on shore leave."

The Centurion stared at her for a moment.

"We'll have to search your vessel."

She regarded him coolly. "Do you doubt my word?"

He sidestepped the question. "Is Captain...er," he checked a list, "Plinius, aboard?"

"He's also ashore."

And that was all the man was getting out of her.

"I must follow my orders, ma'am," he said at last, signalling to his men. They immediately headed for the companion ladders to search below, when an ear-splitting shriek made them stop and stare upwards. It was followed by a stream of invective as Cap'n Felix sighted the invaders.

Her crew grinned behind their hands.

"I must apologise for the parrot," *Blossom* said sweetly. The Centurion scowled.

"Get on with it!" he ordered his men. If they'd been apprehensive before, the avian menace's curses unsettled them further, but they hurried to obey. *Blossom* followed, leaving Salvius gawping after her, to reappear in the Mage quarters.

"Don't touch anything," she ordered the startled legionaries. "It might explode."

The soldiers had a cursory look around and rapidly headed back on deck. If it hadn't been so serious, she would have laughed at the looks of superstitious fear on their faces.

"I hope you're satisfied, Centurion." He ignored her, rounding on his men.

"Did you search everywhere?"

"We checked the Mage quarters, sir. There was nobody there. It's all empty." The soldiers stood to attention whilst Salvius fumed.

"All right. We'll check ashore. Where's your Captain?"

Blossom resisted the urge to brain him with her *tutela* bouquet. Few people knew that the Ship's official symbol wasn't simply there to look pretty.

"My Captain is dining at The Mermaid, along with my Adept and my first officer."

"And your Mage?"

"I really have no idea."

He glared at her as Cap'n Felix let rip once more, insulting not only their appearance, but their parentage and amorous intentions towards various farm animals.

"I'll bid you a good evening, ma'am," the Centurion said, through gritted teeth.

"Good evening, Centurion Salvius."

A large thump from below made him pause. "What's that?" He stared at her accusingly.

The rasping click of claws on wood made *Blossom* sigh. She checked the Mage quarters.

"I'd leave now if I were you, Centurion."

As she had feared, Sobek was on the move. The ancient crocodile had roused himself from his dormant state and torn himself from the wall. His grinning snout was already emerging from a hatch,

Salvius opened his mouth to ask why, then his eyes bulged from their sockets. The soldiers were already fumbling for powder and shot.

"Don't even think about it," *Blossom* snapped. "He's the avatar of a God. I haven't got a Priest on board to placate him, so don't do anything stupid."

Hands left weapons, reaching instead for protective amulets as the great crocodile passed by, scaly feet scraping the planks and eyes glowing with ancient power. *Blossom*'s crew gave him a wide berth, muttering prayers in supplication.

"Where's it going?" The Centurion's jowls quivered as his eyes tracked the reptile. *Blossom* seized the opportunity to discomfit him even more.

"He's probably going to tell the Gods what's happening. My Mage has many friends in high places."

Sobek had reached the rail. He paused, then heaved himself up and over in one agile movement. The last glimpse of him was his serrated tail slithering over the side as he plunged into the murky water of the harbour and disappeared from view. Necks craned to follow his progress, but the ripples faded outwards with no sign of the avatar. *Blossom* hoped that he had followed Heron to wherever the Mage had gone to ground. One thing was definite; anyone trying to capture him would come up against more than mortal Potentia. She turned her attention back to Salvius as Plinius came striding up the gangplank to confront the legionaries, Manius and Campion in his wake. The Centurion had already collected himself as Plinius approached.

"Captain Gaius Plinius Tertius, HMS *Blossom*."

The Centurion saluted. "Centurion Julius Salvius Barbus, Third Britannic Legion. As I've just explained to your Ship, I'm here on the King's business. You are to be held in port until further notice. Where is your Mage?"

Plinius regarded him stonily. "Visiting friends ashore."

The Centurion nodded, his mouth quirking up at one corner. He knew that he could do nothing to catch Heron now. "Understood. It seems this bird has flown. You and your crew will remain on board and my men will be stationed here, for your safety. Decurion! Please escort the Captain below."

"I formally protest this treatment," Plinius said, calmly. "My Ship and crew are loyal to the Crown."

The Centurion smiled without mirth. "Of course you are, Captain, but there are others who are not. I repeat, it's for your own safety."

<It means that he won't shoot us all out of hand,> Plinius Sent.

<I know. Give the word and I'll –,> *Blossom* began.

<You'll do nothing!> he ordered. Unease and not a little fear leaked into his tone. <Not yet, anyway,> he added, quietly. <Let's go along with this for now and see what happens.>

<It's happening to every Ship I've spoken to, and not only here in Portus,> she told him.

Aloud, the Captain said, "Very well, Centurion. I'll need some crew on deck to continue maintenance work, cleaning and the like. The usual things we do in port."

"You can have six."

The crew went below in silence. Cap'n Felix had flown to Scribo's shoulder and was bobbing in agitation. *Blossom* hoped he wouldn't start again, as she wouldn't put it past Salvius to have him disposed of.

"Scribo, keep him quiet!" she hissed in the crewman's ear. The man's head jerked once and he whispered to his pet. It was only when they were below that the parrot's favourite oaths floated up, complete with an obscene rhyme. Centurion Salvius ignored it.

"My compliments Captain. Continue to comply and no harm will come to yourself, your crew – or your Ship."

<Steady, old girl.>

Blossom reined in her mounting anger but if looks could have killed, the Centurion would have been a smoking heap of ash. He shouted an order and several legionaries took up positions, first bolting the hatches so that her crew couldn't escape.

<He doesn't realise that you can open them with a thought,> Plinius Sent, adding aloud, "I understand, Centurion." <Damn him to Tartarus! How dare he threaten you!>

<He doesn't know much about Ships,> she retorted. <That's an advantage. Where are the marines?>

<Confined to barracks, or so the word is in Portus. People are afraid.>

<And so they should be. I can't see this ending well.>

"Thank you for your co-operation," the Centurion was saying. *Blossom* watched as her Captain, Manius and Campion went below, escorted by their guards. Manius stared straight ahead – no doubt following his Captain's orders, but Campion threw her a worried glance as he passed.

"Hang tight!" she breathed in his ear. "Plinius will think of something."

The Adept's lips moved silently.

I hope so.

She did too.

*

As the sun set over Sillina, the King received better news.

"The islanders are with us, Sire," Amphicles reported back. "They can already see that what they've been told is a pack of lies."

"Our mere presence says that," Leo agreed.

"Yes, but it also means that he'll soon know where we are. Communication goes both ways," Pendragon replied. "We must be on our guard."

The landing party had been welcomed as emissaries of the Crown. All knew of Artorius's death, but not what had really occurred and King Cei was being hailed throughout the small archipelago as the rightful monarch, backed up by the local temples and their Priests. Being mainly reliant on the sea, their loyalties were to the Ocean, including Neptune and his family, plus other, more local Gods and Mer-Lords.

"I'll host the local nobility tomorrow night," Pendragon added.

"They've offered to hold a banquet in your honour, Sire," Drustan told him.

"You're better off staying here, Sire." Raven was adamant. "Who knows what dangers lurk ashore?"

Cei clearly didn't like it, but was forced to agree.

"I'll hold audience here tomorrow, after Magpie's funeral, to be followed by a banquet on board."

Osric met Maia's eyes and nodded briefly. The Captain of Marines would be on full alert and all visitors would be thoroughly checked.

"They're sending supplies over, as much as they can afford to give us," Amphicles continued. "There are rumours of blockades to the east, though merchantmen are being allowed through. One merchant captain has reported an unusual number of Ships in harbours and anchored off shore as he passed. This is his last port of call before returning to Gaul."

The lieutenant was trying to make a point and it wasn't lost on Pendragon.

"Maybe it would be safer to send the Princess with him," Raven stated. "We'll shortly be on a war footing and the future of the dynasty rests with her. It's in Parisius's interests to keep her safe and show her all honour."

"Marry her off quickly, you mean." The King suddenly seemed undecided, as if loath to let his niece out of his sight, and Maia didn't blame him. Still, a conflict was no place for Julia, even if she was a half-decent Mage, though she suspected that the first battle would be getting the Princess to go along with the plan. She watched in apprehension as Pendragon summoned Julia to his quarters to inform her of his decision.

She was right.

"I'm not going."

The King raised a conciliatory hand.

"It would be better for all concerned. You know that my first priority is keeping you safe. You'll be able to slip through the cordon and make your way south."

"And can you trust this vessel's captain?" Julia demanded. "How do you know that he won't hand me straight over to Marcus?"

For a split second, Maia thought that the Admiral would shout back, but the moment passed.

"Good Gods, you wouldn't be alone! You'd have every protection I could afford you and Raven tells me that you have a few tricks of your own as well."

The Princess wasn't mollified.

"I have Potentia and I intend to become a Mage, not a royal wife. Divorce Severina and start a new family. You're young enough."

His jaw worked as he sought to control his emotion. "You know it isn't that easy; plus I would have to survive for a good number of years until any heir came of age. You're Britannia's best hope."

The words *if only your father had lived* hung between them, unspoken.

Julia turned away and stared at the deck above her. "You know that Parisius is no good," she said quietly. "I'd need another husband – someone strong enough to come to your aid and father children. Wouldn't it be better to ask the Emperor to choose one of the Gallic princes? Or," she swallowed, "open negotiations with the Alliance?"

Pendragon's eyebrows shot up.

"You can't seriously consider marrying a barbarian!"

"Oh, Uncle! They're almost on a par with us now and growing stronger every day. We need some new blood, not worn out, inbred, decadent Empire royalty. At least they're not soft!"

"Absolutely not." The King's tone was pure ice.

"Think!" she urged him. "They have no love for the Hibernian Fae either and have powers and deities who would help if they thought that they could strengthen ties with Britannia." Maia

27

could hear the cold calculation in her voice. "If I have to be bargained away, let it mean something!"

Pendragon stared at his niece, aghast, then abruptly turned and lowered himself into a chair.

"Gods above! How have we come to this? Look, even if I agreed with you, we're in no position to open negotiations. The treaty with Parisius is signed and sealed. We can't go back on our word now. The Usurper has no such understanding, which puts us at an advantage. Parisius might send military aid."

Julia snorted, "And he might not. We're on our own here, even if the Gods favour us. I'd rather have arms, men and Ships, though I personally think that this battle's going to be won on land. There must be some legionary commanders loyal to you, surely?"

"I'm trying to get messages through," Pendragon told her. "There are some who won't bow to Marcus that easily, but it depends what they've been told."

"All the more reason to strike now!" she urged him, her eyes fierce. "There are two Pendragons here and you have the rightful claim. Gather your forces and attack. Once the people realise they've been lied to they'll rise up, you'll see!"

Pendragon rubbed a hand over his face. "Maybe. I fear that you have more faith in the people than I have, plus Marcus will have taken control of every armoury he can get his hands on. Also, a population panicking about foes with supernormal powers isn't the best material for an army. How will they be equipped and fed? The logistics are against us."

"So you'll sit and do nothing?"

He gave her a sharp look. "No. But we must be cautious and not charge into anything headlong. We must plan and prepare. Only then can we have a chance of winning anything back."

Julia stood, hands on hips, frowning. Maia could see that the Princess was impatient to act, but she had to agree with her Admiral.

"I still think I should stay with you," Julia told him, her face resolute.

"I could command you to go," her uncle said.

Julia stared at him. "Have you spoken to Raven about this?"

"He suggested it."

The shock of betrayal flashed across her face.

"His priority is the same as mine – to get you to a place of safety. I'm sorry, Julia, but it's my command, both as your uncle and your King. Pack what you can. I can send the rest of your dowry when all this is sorted."

Her mouth opened, but no words emerged. Then she mastered herself and sank down in an elegant curtsey.

"Your Majesty."

He could only watch, tears welling in his eyes as she swept from the cabin. It was only when she was gone that he put his head in his hands and wept silently. Maia withdrew, knowing that nothing she could say would make anything better now. She opened a link to Raven.

<The King's told Julia to pack. Are you sure it's for the best?>

The ancient Mage was on deck, the afternoon breeze teasing his wispy hair into fluttering threads.

<It can't have been an easy conversation.>

<It wasn't. He had to command her.>

She heard him sigh. <Needs must.>

<But it isn't right! Maybe if he knew what she was capable of –>

<It doesn't matter. I'm sorry, but for the present her worth lies in marriage, not Magecraft. It's what was agreed. Julia can take care of herself, believe me.>

<So why can't she stay here?> Maia felt that someone had to take the Princess's part.

<All our eggs in one basket? Bad idea. I'm sorry, Maia.>

He leaned on his staff, bony fingers clasping the smooth wood, immovable as any stone.

Angered, she broke the link. Leo wasn't much help either, though in fairness there wasn't any way he could countermand the King's orders.

<I hope they send Milo with her,> he said. <He's a useful man to have around and can hold his own in a tight spot. Raven can disguise her somehow. She could pass for a boy, I suppose.>

Maia nearly pointed out that she already had done, but didn't feel it was her place. Down in the cabin, Latonia was sorting through trunks full of clothes and other belongings. Julia was pacing up and down, biting her lip and scowling, whilst the slave shot her looks of concern. Maia came to a decision.

"Princess, I'm so sorry."

Julia paused, her eyes ranging around the cabin, so Maia descended from the quarterdeck and formed her Shipbody on the bulkhead. Julia swung to face her.

"I've no choice. Again," she said bitterly. "Don't they see that I can fight? This wouldn't be happening if I was male!"

"Your uncle loves you and wants to keep you safe."

She met the full force of Julia's glare. "*Et tu, Tempest?*"

"Oh come on," the Ship pointed out. "I'm hardly stabbing you in the back. It's a reasonable thing to do. You can get to work in Gaul. Wrap Parisius around your finger and get him to send troops."

Julia stopped pacing. "It's an idea," she conceded.

"Besides which –,"

"I know, he probably won't last the year! Everyone keeps saying that. Knowing my luck, he'll live till he's ninety."

Maia shrugged. "If he dies, you could always return at the head of an army."

She could tell that the idea appealed. "Like Queen Boudicca, ready to avenge my family."

"Quite."

"It's a nice thought, but I doubt they'd let me. It's my fear that the new ruler would come to an arrangement with my perfidious cousin, may he rot in Tartarus for all eternity."

"He might be deposed by then."

Julia flung up her hands and resumed pacing. "It's all 'might' and 'maybe'. The only certainty is war!"

Maia decided the argument had just become circular. "And so it's best you're out of it."

Her only reply was a groan. It was only then that Maia realised that she was the object of scrutiny. Teg the monkey's beady little eyes were watching everything with great interest from his new perch in the corner.

"I see your pet has a new berth."

Julia cast the creature a negligent glance. "I'm not keen on him, but I didn't want to leave him in a cage and I don't want to take him with me. Do you know anyone who wants a monkey?"

Maia immediately felt sorry for the poor little thing. "I thought you were using him as a food taster?"

"He won't eat everything he's offered. I need a human for that, so I'm telling Latonia to try my food first."

Maia watched the slave as she continued to pack whatever her mistress would need, knowing from her own experience that Latonia's bag would be a lot lighter. Technically, slaves had no possessions at all. Maybe Julia would free her for saving her life, but considering the circumstances that wouldn't be for a while.

"Are you sure there's nobody else on board we need to watch?" the Princess continued.

"Not to my knowledge," Maia replied. "If there are any more spies they're probably keeping their heads down. I wouldn't be surprised if they try to escape to shore, but I haven't lost any crew so far."

"That's good. Where do you think you'll go next?"

Maia considered this for a few moments. "I think it depends on what intelligence we have. I know the King fears invasion from the west."

Julia shuddered. "The thought of Fae involvement makes my skin crawl. I could never abide all that romantic 'swept off one's feet by a Faerie Prince' rubbish. They're bad news, and if my cousin thinks he can get the better of them he's more of a fool than I already thought. There's no way he could have planned all this by himself."

"We know he's had help," Maia pointed out.

"To think he was arranging my brother's murder, whilst all the time pretending to love him! I can never forgive him for that. I won't be happy until his head adorns Londin Gate, right next to his supporters'!"

Maia could only agree. "I can ask around about Teg," she offered.

"Thank you. I really think my uncle would like him. He was a present from Artorius after all, so he will have sentimental value."

Maia had the impression that Julia didn't have a sentimental bone in her body. Latonia's quiet voice broke the silence.

"I've finished, Highness."

"Good." Julia sighed. *Tempest*, could you please inform my uncle that I'm ready?"

"I will, Highness. He's been busy hand-picking your bodyguard."

"And arranging payment for the merchant captain, I imagine. I hope he has a fast vessel. I'll see you on deck."

Maia bowed and left the cabin, simultaneously opening her link to Leo, who greeted the news with relief.

<Thank the Gods she knows her duty.>

<Well, she could hardly refuse a direct command, could she? A bit like me.>

<Or me. It's not only women who have to follow orders.>

<I suppose so. She wants to give her monkey to the King.>

Her Captain's surprise came through the link. <Doesn't she like it? They're very fashionable.>

Maia just laughed at him. <A princess doesn't follow fashion – she sets fashion.>

<I'm no expert.>

<Men's fashions? What about monkeys?> She formed up next to him, amused to see that his face was bland even though he was joking.

<I think it would depend on the man.>

Maia was just about to give another riposte when she realised that something was climbing up her flanks. She could feel long fingers and toes gripping the wood as whatever it was hauled itself higher and higher.

"Captain, something's coming on board," she said urgently.

"Hostile?"

"Unclear." As she spoke, she alerted both Osric and Raven. She felt their acknowledgement and was about to give the general alarm when Danuco hurried on deck.

"It's the Lady Sillina," he explained. "She's curious."

"Wonderful," Leo muttered, adding to his Ship, <order an honour guard.>

Maia did as she was bid, noting his less than thrilled reaction with interest. Had they met before? Marines formed up on deck with a clatter of weapons and the crew stood warily to attention, their eyes darting nervously around the deck, waiting for the appearance of the Goddess of the Islands.

A clawed hand appeared over the rail, dark and close-furred like the skin of a seal, followed immediately by the rest of the immortal. Her shape was limned in a strange phosphorescent light, like something from the depths, haloing her sleek head and huge liquid eyes. She regarded the assembled humans with interest, swinging her legs over and landing lightly on the deck. Maia admired the necklaces she wore around her neck and skirt of shells and coins, clearly made from previous offerings.

"Hail, O Sillina, Lady of these Isles!" Danuco intoned.

The Goddess gazed at him curiously, then fixed her eyes on Maia. Her flat nostrils flared as she sniffed the air.

"Greetings to you," she said in a human voice. Maia was surprised, expecting to hear a voice more like those of the Mer People. Sillina was different, more mammalian and less like a fish. She strolled around the startled crew, her adornments clicking and jingling against each other, examining each man in turn. When she got to Leo she smiled widely, showing wickedly sharp little teeth and longer canines.

"Well, if it isn't my old friend Valerius Leo! And what are you doing on this fine new Ship?"

He saluted smartly. "I am her Captain and we are about the King's business, Lady," adding to Maia, <Where's the King?>

<On his way,> she Sent back.

Sillina's eyes widened. "The King? I heard Artorius died and his cousin ascended the throne?"

"Marcus is a Usurper. His father is the rightful heir."

"Ah!" Sillina frowned, just as Pendragon appeared.

"Greetings, Lady of the Isles." He bowed. "I am King Cei of Britannia."

Sillina's eyes fixed on him and she inclined her head in return.

"King Cei, or should I say, Admiral Pendragon? It is many a year since last we met."

"It is, ma'am. I was but a young officer then."

"And now you're older, but thus it is with mortals." Her eyes narrowed. "But what of this King Marcus who sits in Londin? There is much talk of him."

So this immortal was well-informed, unlike many of her kind. Maia could tell that she was used to dealing with humans.

"My son is a usurper, ma'am. He murdered my nephew, the rightful King, and claimed the throne unlawfully."

Sillina hissed her displeasure.

"You're going to reclaim Britannia."

"I am, Lady."

She regarded him thoughtfully.

"Well, good luck. You'll need it," she said carelessly. "Things are waking that have been sleeping for a long time. I should know, I'm related to some of them." She smiled again, her sharp teeth gleaming white. "You'll have a battle on your hands."

She looked over at Maia curiously, then turned to face Leo, staring at him in anticipation.

"Please accept this gift, Lady," he said hurriedly, gesturing to Sabrinus, who presented her with a small silver box. She opened it and sniffed the gold within, then delicately picked out the coins, lifting them up to admire the sheen they gave off in the light.

"I like these," she said. "Pretty." She gave them an appraising look. "I take it that's all on offer?"

She smiled winningly at the Captain, who spread his hands in seeming regret. "Alas Lady, I have other more pressing responsibilities at the moment."

Sillina pouted. "Then I must be content with these...for now. But, as you have given generously, I will tell you some news. There is another Ship coming from the east. A big one."

"Do you know which one?" Leo asked.

She tilted her head coquettishly. "Let me think. She's new as well. *Regina*. Yes, that's right. Other Ships follow her."

"Thank you for warning us," Leo said, outwardly calm, though Maia caught his sudden stab of alarm. Sillina smiled again.

"I wouldn't want anything to happen to you, my dear Captain, would I now? Not since..."

She broke off to trail a claw lightly across his cheek.

"How could I forget, my Lady?" Leo said, smiling. What had happened between them?

"Alas, I can't detain you – this time," she said regretfully, "but I'm sure we'll meet again."

She leaned forwards and kissed him full on the mouth, before breaking off with a sigh.

"Until then, farewell!"

She winked at Sabrinus, who blushed, then swayed over to the rail, coins and shells clicking and jangling around her. A final wave, then she dived smoothly back into the inky water and disappeared.

Pendragon cleared his throat. "All hands, back to your posts. All officers, war meeting. We must decide on our next course of action. Mr Sabrinus, take command. *Tempest* will keep you updated."

Osric quietly marshalled his men and the other sailors resumed their watch, but not without some mutterings and surreptitious glances towards their Captain. Danuco sidled over to Maia, who was smothering a grin.

"We're fortunate that our esteemed Captain has met the lovely Sillina before. She can be capricious."

"She was certainly pleased to see him."

"Wasn't she just!" He raised his eyebrows at her and she bit her lip before she started giggling.

"Now, now. We shouldn't speculate."

"No, of course not. She looked very happy and I don't think it was just the gold. If we pass this way again any time soon, I think the Captain should be prepared for a sneaky visit."

<*Tempest*, we would value your input,> came the call from the Great Cabin.

<On my way,> she sent back, leaving the Priest with a knowing smirk on his face.

Below decks, Pendragon was sitting at the head of the table, listening to Leo.

"The *Regina* is a formidable threat. I'd say we're equally matched and it's unlikely that she'll be ready to give quarter."

"Even if we were prepared to accept it," Pendragon cut in, crisply. "Furthermore, we have certain advantages, our esteemed Master Mage for one."

"I'm both flattered and alarmed that you have such faith in me," Raven replied. "Unfortunately, I'm the only Mage we have and you can be sure that the *Regina* will have picked up reinforcements by now."

The silence that met his remark was proof enough that he spoke the truth.

"Our own reinforcements should arrive very soon," Leo pointed out. "It won't be long before we rendezvous with the *Diadem, Imperatrix, Leopard, Farsight,* and the rest. Perhaps we should risk communications?"

Pendragon considered this for a moment.

"*Tempest,* can we ascertain their exact position?" he asked.

"I daren't open the link," Maia warned him.

"No, but I have been given to understand that you have another way of communicating." His eyes flicked to the Master Mage. "I must warn you, gentlemen, anything you hear now is to be kept strictly confidential. Raven, if you would care to enlighten us?"

Maia could only stare at him in alarm. What had her Mage told him?

"*Tempest* has a gift of direct communication with certain parties," Raven began. "It is part of her Potentia. I believe that she can Send to friends without having to use the Ship link. Is that not so?"

He turned clouded eyes to her position on the bulkhead and she suddenly became very aware of all faces turning to her, their expressions eager.

"Er, yes. On occasion," she stammered. "I hadn't really thought about it."

Maia noticed that Leo looked hopeful, but inside she knew that he was a little hurt that she hadn't confided in him.

"She was ordered not to divulge this to anyone," Raven said, which made her feel better. "The extent of her ability is not yet known, but it should give us an advantage in the current situation."

He tilted his head, as if to say 'over to you'. Maia switched her gaze to Pendragon.

"It is as the Master Mage says," her Admiral agreed. "Now is the time to use this gift. *Tempest,* which Ships can you contact in this way?"

"I can speak to *Patience* and *Blossom,*" she confessed. "I haven't tried it with any of the others. It's best if I have a bond with them first." She felt oddly reluctant to mention her link to Raven.

"Try the *Blossom*," Pendragon ordered. "She's docked at Portus and will know more of what's happening than the *Patience*, who's coming north. I doubt she'll be supporting the Usurper. Still, don't give anything away about our current situation, just in case."

"Aye, Sire."

Maia tried to block out the hopeful expressions and reached inside herself for the tenuous thread that she'd mentally marked '*Blossom*'. The picture that sprang into her mind was of a braided twist of vivid pink that she always associated with her old mentor. *Patience*'s was a calm ribbon of shimmering blue and she set that aside for the present. It helped if she visualised picking up the thread and running it through her fingers, ready to pull as if she were hauling the Ship closer to her on a rope.

<*Blossom*, can you hear me?> She Sent a whisper of power through the line. The reply was immediate, but tinged with suspicion.

<This is *Blossom*. Who is this?>

<It's me, Maia.>

The suspicion vanished, warmth and concern taking its place.

<Good Gods! You're doing your mind trick again. It's just been proclaimed on shore that you were lost with all hands. Of course, we Ships didn't believe a word of it. Where are you?>

<I can't say,> she Sent regretfully. <Orders. Look, I need information. What's happening in Portus? Are you all right?>

Blossom's sudden rage flooded her mind. <I'm not going anywhere and neither are the others. We were boarded by legionaries and our Captains and crews are being held hostage against our good behaviour. Heron managed to escape, but the other Mages were taken ashore and we don't know where they are. Their speechstones were taken, too. Plinius is being held under guard in his cabin. They're on the *Persistence* right now.>

Maia listened in horror as *Blossom* reeled off a list of captured Ships. She'd hoped that more would be free to act. The information only confirmed what all of them had already realised.

<This was planned well in advance!>

37

<Oh yes. It seems the swine thought of everything,> *Blossom* said in disgust. <What does Admiral Pendragon, I mean the King, order? I take it he's there with you?>

<He is,> Maia confirmed, simultaneously relaying *Blossom*'s information. <Stand by.>

"Holding Ships hostage? Outrageous!" Hawthorn muttered.

"Tell *Blossom* that she is to free herself by whatever means possible, and that goes for her sister Ships as well," Pendragon commanded.

<I'll do my best, Sire,> her friend replied.

Maia relayed *Blossom*'s answer directly.

"It's to be presumed that Marcus has control of the Collegium, as well as the legions and it's also telling that he's used soldiers, not marines. Raven, do you think that Bullfinch has allied himself with the Usurper?"

Raven shook his head. "I don't know. I think it's more likely from Lapwing's actions that he's been replaced, if not killed."

"Can you find out?"

"Not by using the usual methods, especially if everyone's had their speechstones taken. I'm afraid that Mages have come to rely on them too much."

"Then use an unusual method." The King was in no mood to delay. "Do it now."

Raven bowed and left.

"What of the *Regina*?" Pendragon asked Maia.

<Last I heard, she was heading west at a rate of knots,> *Blossom* replied. <I wish I could speak directly to the Admiral, but I have the feeling that communications are being monitored somehow. I don't know which Ships I can trust and I know for a fact that some are reporting on others.>

Maia could scarce believe it. <Surely not!>

<How else could the enemy be one step ahead of us all, unless they had help? I wouldn't trust *Justicia* right now, that's for sure. Wait. Something's happening with *Persistence*. Her crew are being forced on deck and I can hear shouting.>

Even as Maia relayed it, the need for more information overrode her sense of caution and, before she knew she'd done so, she'd seized the thread and willed herself to see through *Blossom*'s eyes. There was a startled reaction from the other

Ship, then *Blossom* allowed Maia in to share her space just as she had done so many times before. The familiarity was such that Maia had to remind herself that her body was no longer lying suspended in her old cabin.

Maia pushed the thought away and concentrated, aware that some mechanical part of her was continuing to report to her officers.

The *Persistence* was in the next berth. Her vessel was almost identical to *Blossom*'s and Maia knew that they'd been constructed at about the same time, thus it was easy to look over and see what was happening on deck.

Scuffles had broken out and sailors were being restrained by men in the red uniforms of the Britannic Legions, not the usual blue coated marines.

"You can't do this!" A man shouted and Maia could see that it was *Persistence*'s Captain. He was struggling between two soldiers, desperate to get to his Ship. At first, Maia couldn't understand why the *Persistence* wasn't going to the aid of her crew, until she saw the glint of metal at their throats.

"One move from you and they're dead," the officer in charge informed the Ship. "You've been pronounced guilty of mutiny against the Crown and will be dealt with accordingly."

The *Persistence*'s screech echoed clearly both across the water and through the Ship link.

"I *am* loyal to the Crown, yer pox ridden sons of whores! Long live the true King, and not that kinslayin' serpent in Londin! May the Furies rip out 'is guts!"

<What did she do?> Maia asked *Blossom*.

<She called on all Ships in Portus to rise up against Marcus.>

<What will happen now?>

<I don't know. Nothing good.> *Blossom* opened a link to her sister. <*Persistence*! This is futile! Think of your crew!>

Maia saw the other Ship shake her head.

"I ain't bowing before traitors!" she bellowed.

Movement to one side made *Blossom* cry out a warning.

<Behind you!>

Persistence caught the axe as it was about to fall, lifting her attacker off the deck. Her *tutela* of a leaping salmon morphed into a sword in her other hand, skewering the unfortunate man as he dangled.

"Now!" she screamed.

Chaos erupted as almost every rope on the vessel came to life, looping around the armed intruders to pinion arms and legs. Sailors fell, their bodies pushed aside as the legionaries began to fight for their lives. Sudden sharp cracks and clouds of smoke told of pistols and muskets being fired, but soldiers were vanishing under piles of equipment or being hoisted high up into the rigging, to be hanged from the topmost spars. All was confusion, then *Persistence*'s Mage burst on deck, firing spells. How he hadn't been rounded up with the rest, Maia couldn't imagine.

Blossom came to a decision, the strength of her determination burning through the link. She would not leave her sister ship to fight alone. An answering echo from Plinius signalled his agreement.

<We fight!>

Following her sister's lead, *Blossom*'s pretty bouquet became a cutlass as the old Ship threw back her head and howled in defiance, her ropes slithering across the deck like kraken tentacles. Her deck crew grabbed the unlucky men's muskets, turning them on the redcoats restraining the *Persistence*. The blasts of gunpowder and the stink of sulphur was followed by furious yells as the *Persistence*'s men fought off their captors. *Persistence* herself was laying about her with sword and axe, spurred on by her rage and the need to defend her men.

Blossom left the quarterdeck, materialising in her Captain's cabin. The two guards standing over Plinius went for their swords, but they were no match for one angry Ship and they were smashed into bulkheads before they knew what was happening. Plinius leapt to his feet.

"We have to get out of the harbour," he said urgently. "Will your shield be enough to stop cannonballs?"

"Let's find out," *Blossom* replied, her teeth bared in a fierce grin. Now two decks were full of struggling men fighting above the dead and the wounded. Maia prayed, casting her words into the heavens in the hope that somebody friendly would hear them.

"O Gods, you who favour our cause. Come to their aid now, I beg you!"

Persistence had weighed anchor and had already begun to drift away from the harbour wall, piling on sail as fast as she could, her Captain and crew fighting by her side. Plinius had ordered *Blossom* to follow her lead and helped himself to a brace of loaded pistols from one of his captors. There was nothing calm about him as he shot first one soldier, then another who tried to restrain him. His Ship was slashing at her assailants, smashing them to the decking which was already running red. Maia left her to it and slid into the vessel to assist, operating the capstan to raise the anchor as she had done so many times before. Now the *Blossom* began to glide after the *Persistence* as her sails came into play.

Suddenly, a freshening wind began to blow from the land, pushing both vessels further out. Maia's heart lifted.

<Thank you, Mother!>

The two Ships raced for the harbour mouth, picking up speed as they went. Maia was relieved to see that the sailors were getting the upper hand, but at great cost. Bodies hung from their rigging like ghastly banners.

A roar announced that the hatches were open and the remainder of two very irate crews poured on to the deck, quickly overwhelming the remaining landsmen. Of those, some were tossed over the side, whilst the others were dispatched to Hades without further ado.

<*Persistence* 'ere! We've got to make a run for it. Can you raise a shield?>

There was already a purple shimmer forming around her vessel.

<I can. Try to steer clear of the batteries,> *Blossom* answered. <They'll be firing on us as soon as we're in range.>

Her sister Ship's reply was a string of profanities as she dealt with the last of her invaders. *Blossom* stood in the midst of carnage as the crew scrambled to man her defences.

"Status?" Plinius called to her.

"We've not much powder," his Ship answered, "and I think *Persistence* will be the same. <They removed it,> she added to Maia. "I'm raising a shield now."

41

Maia felt the Ship struggle without her Mage and added her strength to *Blossom*'s own. A flare of purple surrounded them instantly.

"*Tempest*, report!"

She must have fallen silent and Pendragon was impatient for details. She quickly explained events.

"And you are there with them, not just observing?"

"I'm lending my strength to *Blossom*. *Persistence* will have to take her chances."

"It may not be just cannon fire. If they have Mages stationed there, there may be fire bolts too."

Maia focused her divided attention. Both Ships were keeping to the deepest channel and she could see the open ocean waiting for them. They would have to skirt the island of Vectis before they were truly unobserved. Meanwhile, they would be forced to pass within range of the land defences.

<Let's hope we caught them unprepared,> *Blossom* said, moving to her Captain's side. Maia was relieved to see that Plinius was unharmed, but he surveyed the disarray with horror before turning his gaze upwards.

"Are they dead?" he asked, squinting at the limply hanging soldiers.

"Yes," *Blossom* replied. "We don't have the manpower to keep them captive, besides which they killed my men."

Maia heard the steel in her voice. The crew had been murdered in cold blood whilst helpless prisoners and that could never be forgiven. She was glad that some, like Hyacinthus and Big Ajax, had been transferred to her, but there were familiar faces amongst the dead.

Campion was checking the wounded. "Sir," he said quietly. Plinius moved to his side, but it was clear that there was nothing to be done for some.

"May the Gods welcome them to Elysium," he said. "They fought bravely."

"We'll grieve later," *Blossom* answered, ever practical, casting a glance at where the dark bulk of one of Portus's forts squatted on the coast. "Any second now."

She was right. Maia spotted the plumes of smoke spurting from the bastions a second before the sound reached her.

"Prepare for incoming!" Manius shouted.

Blossom's surviving crew raced to load the guns with whatever powder they had.

"I daren't lower the shield," the Ship reported.

"The guns must be a last resort," Plinius agreed. "I want speed rather than firepower. It won't have much effect anyway."

Splashes off the sinistra side gave the gunners their range. The next shots wouldn't miss. Ahead of them, *Persistence* was pushing through the water, sails stretched taut. Maia sent up a quiet prayer and felt the wind strengthen in answer. *Blossom*'s structure creaked and groaned as it was stretched to its maximum tolerances.

"The Gods are listening!" Plinius shouted to his crew. "They're sending a favourable wind!"

Maia wondered whether Aura, her mother, had called in support of her own. Surely this was one of the Four Winds that had come to her aid? Any stronger and they would have had to shorten sail, but there was just the right amount to propel them at speed without tearing the canvas.

More booms echoed across the water, but the two Ships were already moving out of range. A couple of cannonballs hit the shields, but their impetus was already weakened so they did little damage. *Blossom* cursed as the Ship link opened.

<*Persistence*, *Blossom*! Return to port immediately, by order of the Admiralty!>

It was Blasius Cadogus. So, Albanus wasn't alone in turning traitor. Either that, or the Senior Admiral had just thrown in his lot with what he perceived as the winning side. Maia wondered how many other Admirals had capitulated and who had refused. The latter would be either dead or locked up by now, their earrings forcibly removed. It would have to have been done without the Ships' knowledge, as they were former Captains and loyalty ran both ways. Even as it crossed her mind, *Persistence* echoed her sentiment.

<What have yer done to Helvius, yer thrice-cursed cowardly dog?> she rasped down the link.

Cadogus refused to rise to the bait.

<*Blossom*! Talk some sense into your sister. Return to port and you will be forgiven!>

<She asked a valid question, Admiral,> *Blossom* snarled. <Personally I don't trust a word you say and neither should any of us. You support Marcus the Murderer, may he rot! Long live King Cei!>

The link broke and Maia sensed *Blossom*'s satisfaction. <That told him!> she Sent.

<Aye, sister. You gave 'im what for!> *Persistence* crowed.

Behind them, the land faded into the distance.

<What now?> *Blossom* asked.

<Head to the Isles of Sillina,> Maia told her.

<Maia? Is that you?> Plinius had heard her thought.

<It is, Captain. Thank the Gods you're safe. I'm with the King, anchored off Ennor, the biggest island. We await other loyal Ships there.>

<Relay to *Persistence* and set a course. My compliments to Captain Instantius,> Plinius instructed his Ship. *Persistence* received the news with pleasure and adjusted accordingly. Soon, both ships had skirted the island of Vectis and were heading west into the Britannic Ocean and freedom.

<It's a shame we couldn't get more Ships to come with us,> *Persistence* grumbled.

<They're afraid,> *Blossom* replied. <You took a great risk, sister.>

<Hah, so did you! I thought yer were going to stay put.>

<So did I.> *Blossom* admitted.

Both Ships were in mourning. Many good men had died to pay for their freedom and, as soon as there was time, their bodies would be committed to the deep.

<We never got a cannon shot off,> *Persistence* observed. <Not that I've much powder. You?>

<Removed. They couldn't risk us fighting back with full stores, could they?>

<I'm reporting back to the King,> Maia told her friend. <I'd better get on with it, but I'll be in touch.>

She wasn't speaking through the Ship link, so *Persistence* was unaware of her, though it was interesting that Plinius had picked up on her presence. She wondered whether she could also communicate with him directly. It would be something to try out later.

<We're on our way.> *Blossom* confirmed.

<Have a care for the *Regina*,> Maia warned her <and any other Ships who've been turned. See you soon!>

Gently, she loosened her grip on the thread she had been holding so tightly and let it fall back into its place. The sense of *Blossom* vanished and that of Leo and Pendragon grew, as they discussed all that they had learned.

At least part of it was bearable.

*

Just over an hour later, Maia sighted a familiar vessel.

<*Tempest* to *Patience*!> she Sent, glad that at last she wasn't alone. She could just spot another vessel coming up over the horizon too, larger and flying the Imperial Eagle as well as the Britannic Dragon. It was the *Leopard*, hastening to join her King.

The Ships exchanged greetings, keeping communications to a tight distance and wary of eavesdroppers.

<*Farsight, Unicorn, Cameo, Diadem* and *Imperatrix* are on their way,> *Leopard* reported. <Others would join us, but they're being held in port or their Captains don't want to commit themselves. I know the *Victoria* is helpless and under guard.>

<Has anybody been in contact with the *Regina*?> Maia asked.

<Last I heard, she'd declared for the Usurper and was heading west, but she seems to have vanished.> *Leopard* said, her tone dry.

<I fear for the *Victoria*.> *Blossom* was worried. <*Regina*'s ambition is limitless. Being named Flagship could be the least of it.>

Maia heard her with dread. Tullia's mind had been swayed by something, otherwise she'd never had gone through the trials to become a Ship. Somehow, she didn't think that the promise of becoming the Flagship would have been enough.

<Who knows?> *Patience* said, though Maia could tell that her friend shared her misgivings. Of all of them, the two of them knew the girl who had been Tullia Albana the best.

<How's the King?> *Leopard* asked.

<Discussing re-supplying,> Maia said. <We need more powder and ammunition if we're to fight and *Blossom* is without her Mage. Somehow *Persistence* hung on to hers.>

<I'd heard that all other Ships in port, unless they declared for Marcus, have lost their Mages,> *Leopard* answered. <Thank the Gods we were at sea. *Tempest*, you have two, right?>

Maia was forced to explain what had happened.

<My condolences,> *Leopard* offered. <You have Raven. I have Tern and *Patience*, you have…?>

<Sandpiper.>

<Any use?>

<He's very nice, but I've hardly been in a battle yet. He's extremely good at defusing diplomatic situations,> *Patience* said. *Leopard* snorted.

<I think that any current negotiations will be settled with cannon, not words. Tell him to brush up on his attack spells. We're not going to escape this without a fight, unless the Gods strike Marcus dead.>

<We can only hope,> Maia answered, thinking that the Gods were more likely to sit back and enjoy the battles from their lofty viewpoint. She checked on the Great Cabin. Pendragon, Leo, Sabrinus and Raven were poring over charts. The thought of going into battle against sister Ships made her feel queasy, the lack of a flesh body notwithstanding. The images she had seen in the *Augusta*'s mind of broken bodies and smashed vessels didn't make her eager to experience the same thing in reality.

A signal from shore told her that Drustan and Amphicles were returning with a boat load of powder kegs that they'd obtained from somewhere. The islands did have small forts for defence – they must have commandeered some of the supplies, unless a merchantman had been intercepted and persuaded to part with its goods. It was a pity that Marcus would have vast supplies stored on land, enough to equip the Fleet three times over. All he had to do was order transportation.

She stared at the peaceful scene. Ennor looked beautiful in the spring sunshine; even the sea was in a benevolent mood, little wavelets casting reflected glints of light from the afternoon sun. Seabirds called overhead and little boats plied their trade or fished placidly in the calm waters. It was hard to believe that they were heading for all-out conflict.

At least she was no longer alone and the others would be here soon. Then they could start to plan for war.

III

Caniculus awoke to a riot of birdsong. It had filled his dreams for some time, but he'd resisted its call until the clamour was such that he knew it must be nearing dawn. He heaved himself out of his cocoon of blankets, knowing it was best for him to get his feet on the road before the sun appeared above the horizon.

The fire was mostly reduced to crumbling ash but he managed to coax the few tiny embers that remained back into a semblance of life, just enough to warm himself and get the morning damp out of his bones. He'd saved enough food for breakfast and, as he chewed, he reviewed his options.

There was absolutely no question of ignoring the assignment the Gods had given him. Looking back, the encounter seemed to be something out of a dream. Of all the Agents they could have picked, naturally it just had to be him. It couldn't have been his friend Milo, or even Foxy, who was always boasting that he was descended from Mars through his grandmother. He'd always suspected that the man was talking a load of rubbish. No, the Fates had decreed that it was time for poor old Caniculus to be dropped into the cesspit. Again.

He eyed the innocent-looking cloth that wrapped the Helmet of Invisibility, wondering idly if it magically expanded and contracted to fit the wearer, or if he really did have a head that was the same size as Perseus's? The thought of putting it on again made him feel sick with both dread and excitement. If he lived through this he'd really have something to boast about.

The fire was burning itself out now, so he kicked soil on it and rewrapped his pack, tucking the helmet into the shapeless mass of blankets alongside the Sword. Not many people would be hauling one magical item up to Londin, let alone two, and it could be disastrous if someone decided to rob him. A brief glance about assured him that he was alone, so he hefted his bundle and set off towards the nearest road. All tracks led somewhere and he had the feeling that this one would bring him back to the main thoroughfare. Too bad the Gods hadn't seen fit to provide him with Perseus's winged sandals as well; he could have saved himself sore feet and worn shoe leather.

He consoled himself with the fact that it wasn't raining, and strode off.

After about half a mile, the track ahead of him widened and he saw that he was coming to the Via Londinium. This would take him straight into the heart of the City, and Caniculus was relieved to see that it wasn't busy at this time of the morning. Most of the carts would have made their way up to the gates through the night so they would be ready to get their produce inside as soon as they were opened. He could have kicked himself as he realised that if he'd kept going he could have got a lift on one of them. He'd done that before. Then he remembered that the Gods had left him a fire, so they must have meant for him to get some sleep.

Raised voices and the sound of cursing caught his attention. As he drew closer he saw that there was a laden cart in the ditch, with two men straining to replace a damaged wheel. They were attempting to use a stout branch to lever it high enough to prop it up, but it was taking both of them which meant that there was nobody to shove the support underneath. The older one, a grizzled chap and a farmer by his clothes, was using an extensive vocabulary of swear words to describe the cart, the wheel, the day and the situation they were in. Caniculus was impressed as the torrent of frustrated rage continued unabated.

"You feculent pox-ridden piece of useless worm-eaten –!"

The man's eye fell on Caniculus and his face lit up with hope.

"Greetings, stranger! Do you think you could give us a hand? We've been stuck here this past half hour, with not a soul to help!"

Caniculus grinned and hastened to add his strength to the lever. The younger man gave him a look of pure gratitude as they heaved down on the branch together. The farmer quickly slipped a block of wood underneath the cart and hoisted the repaired wheel on to the axle before securing it with its peg. He grunted in satisfaction as he moved back to survey the result. Further down the verge a large brown mare regarded them with curiosity before continuing to crop the grass with enthusiasm, as if knowing that her enforced break would soon be over.

"There it is!" The farmer wiped his sweaty hands on his tunic before offering one to Caniculus. "Surely the Gods heard our prayers to send us such a strong fellow as yourself! Son, go and get the horse."

They were certainly hearing something Caniculus thought, remembering the stream of invective, but he smiled in return. Perhaps the Gods were taking pity on him after all.

"Are you heading up to Londin?" he asked as the youngster backed up the carthorse into the shafts, clucking at her encouragingly.

"We are indeed," the farmer replied, "though that blasted wheel's cost me time, and time is money as they say. Want a lift?"

"Most kind," Caniculus replied.

The man waved a hand. "Ach, it's the least I can do. We kept thinking someone would come along but it's been quiet. Good job I was able to fix it, or we'd be in more trouble."

Caniculus peered into the cart which was filled with stacked wooden crates.

"Finest lettuce," his new friend said proudly. "In great demand too, but the fresher it is the better, and it's not getting any fresher sitting in this damned ditch. Hop up and we'll be off."

Caniculus climbed up and the farmer took the reins, snapping them and calling to his mare. She set off at a brisk trot, the iron rimmed wheels rumbling loudly over the smooth cobbles. The red-faced son sat quietly beside his father, picking at a rough spot on his hand. Neither of them seemed inclined to ask about his business, being intent on getting to market as quickly as possible, so Caniculus just enjoyed the ride. It wasn't as good as tearing along on a fast horse, but it beat walking. In the meantime, he could sit and think about how he would get into Marcus's inner sanctum, magic helmet or no magic helmet.

The journey took less time than he hoped for and it didn't seem long before they were joining the line of traffic waiting to be admitted through one of the great triple gates. It stood open, as it did from dawn to dusk to welcome the people of the Empire into the largest and most prosperous city in Britannia. Caniculus stared up at the painted statues in the niches, their worn faces covered in a layer of grime like so many of the buildings and most of the people. Black banners were draped over much of the structure as the city mourned its slain king.

"Better late than never," the farmer said. "I hope we can still get buyers for this lot so late in the day." He reined in his horse and waited patiently in the queue. Caniculus decided that it would be a lot quicker to walk through one of the smaller archways reserved for foot traffic.

"Thanks for the lift," he said.

"Don't mention it! I hope your business here is successful."

"Yours also."

Caniculus jumped down from the cart and headed off into the crowd. There were a lot more polismen around than usual, checking vehicles and generally watching comings and goings, so he strolled along in a nonchalant yet purposeful way. Just one more anonymous visitor to the metropolis. Despite his misgivings, he felt his spirits lift at the familiar sights. All the noise and commotion made it much easier to blend in and this was his city, the place of his birth and full of crowds, unlike the countryside where every stranger's face stood out like a beacon.

He mulled over his options as he paused to relieve himself in one of the public urinals; after all it was his civic duty to help local businesses. Nothing would go to waste and that included waste. The launderers and tanners would receive his offerings via hidden pipes. A deep shaft in the road surrounded by busy workmen indicated where they were building the new sewage system, started by the old King. Caniculus made a note to get a plan as soon as he could. Tunnels meant another opportunity to escape and he was all for that, even if it meant wading through the dark, and the filth of over half a million people. Now, where to start? He could hardly stroll up to the palace and hope that his helmet would protect him, added to which, after his days of travel, the guards would probably smell him coming.

That reminded him: he definitely deserved a bath, and he'd get all the local gossip. Caniculus had his favourite bathhouses but he'd be known there, so he opted for one he'd not been to before. There were plenty to choose from in this city. He skirted the Forum, avoiding all the public buildings and staying well away from the House of Agents, favouring the back streets and alleyways that criss-crossed the major arteries instead. The

Romans had laid out a grid plan, but there were plenty of shortcuts if you knew where to find them, and he'd made a point of memorising the layout of the city as a whole. The alleyways were narrow and he often had to turn sideways to avoid people carrying baskets or even wheeling small handcarts, but they knocked time off his journey and tended to be darker because of the overhanging buildings. Space in Londin was at a premium and it paid to make the most of every square inch, so that meant building upwards.

The bathhouse was medium-sized, with a sign declaring it to be dedicated to Mercury. A crudely carved statue of the God stood above the door to welcome patrons, who would mostly be travelling businessmen. Caniculus reckoned that, having met the God in question, he might be on safer territory than if he went to one of his usual haunts. Inside it seemed clean enough and the doorkeeper took his coin without question, pointing to the locker room.

"Do you have keys?" he asked the man, a wiry snub nosed slave with a shock of white hair.

"No, but if you tip Brutus he'll keep an eye on your stuff," the oldster informed him. "Just a bath or do you want company?"

Caniculus was tempted, but thought better of it. He didn't have time for anything other than to get clean.

"Just a bath," he said and the man nodded.

Brutus was a huge Germanic type, with heavily muscled arms and a watchful attitude. His scarred face remained impassive as Caniculus gave him a good tip to look after his bundle. The man had the look of an ex-gladiator: too battered to stay in the ring but obviously able to do security jobs. Caniculus decided the money was worth it. Lots of people had their possessions nicked in places like these, and he really didn't fancy explaining to angry Gods why he'd lost two important magical artefacts.

He undressed hurriedly, grabbed the toiletries provided for clients and went on through to get the first decent bath in more days than he cared to think. Several rooms later he was relaxing in the *caldarium* pool and listening to the general chatter from the men around him, who mostly seemed to be merchants and local traders.

"I'm looking forward to the week of the Games," one man announced, a swarthy man with elaborately curled hair. He sounded Eastern from his accent, maybe Aegyptian.

"I can't stay that long. My vessel sails tomorrow," another said, with regret.

"That's a pity," the first one said. "You'll miss the celebrations, not to mention the food and wine. They'll be sacrificing most of the day and the Priests are handing out the meat to ticketholders. Bulls, cows, pigs and sheep, or so I hear. There'll be wine in the fountains too."

"Just my luck," grumbled his companion, "But my family is looking forward to it. They've signed up for a ticket, so they might get something."

A local. Caniculus moved a little closer, nodding pleasantly to the two of them.

"Forgive my interruption, friends, but I've been out of the city. Did you mention Games?"

They clearly weren't averse to company and the local man hastened to explain.

"You've arrived back at the right time. King Marcus has announced a whole week of Games, food distribution and a general holiday."

The Easterner nodded eagerly.

"It'll be a sight all right. Not to be missed. Rumour is that he's staging a sea battle in the new amphitheatre and an exotic animal fight, though we don't have the details as yet. It all starts in two days!"

Caniculus pretended enthusiasm.

"It's to celebrate his accession then?"

"Sort of," the local replied, "and to honour the late King, his father and his cousin, the Princess. You've heard that they are dead too?" Caniculus nodded. "Artorius is being buried first, then the celebrations will begin. Out with the old and in with the new, if you see what I mean."

"Yes," Caniculus replied, adding casually, "He'll want to be crowned as soon as possible. It's a dreadful shame how his father and cousin were lost at sea as well. Very strange. Rumours can be so unkind."

The other men exchanged uncomfortable glances.

"Of course, some people will say anything," Caniculus continued and his companions relaxed slightly, but not without first looking around to see who was within earshot.

"Well, I wouldn't know about that," the local said carefully. He shot the Agent a wary look. "It was terrible news alright." They'd obviously heard something, but were unwilling to discuss the matter. So, there was plenty of unease after all. Marcus was counting on the time-honoured tradition of bribing the populace with lavish spectacles and free gifts.

"Exotic beasts you say?" Caniculus steered the conversation on to less controversial ground and felt the atmosphere lighten. "Lions, tigers and such I suppose."

The Easterner smiled. "Ah, my friend, possibly not. The word is that there will be something truly extraordinary, not often seen in the Empire! But," he spread his hands in a cascade of water drops, "we'll have to wait and see."

Caniculus grinned back. Games meant that the city would be busier than usual and it would be easier for him to move in the shadows. The attention of all would be directed to whatever they could get from the open hands of the Usurper.

"I count my good fortune but lament yours," he told them, with a look of sympathy for the local merchant. "I'll be sure to go early to get a good place. I'm not missing this!"

Although he would have liked to stay longer, Caniculus was unwilling to leave his bundle for longer than he absolutely had to, so he heaved himself out of the pool and finished in a hurry. He retrieved his belongings from its shelf and exited on to the street, feeling cleaner and more civilised than he had in a while, and strode off towards his next port of call.

*

It was time for Julia to depart. Maia watched as chests and trunks were packed with essentials, though it was still more stuff than she'd seen belonging to anyone in her entire life. The Princess stared at the pile.

"I think that will be enough, Latonia. We may have to travel fast at the other end and I don't want to be overburdened."

"Yes, Highness. It is as you say, but the Gauls mustn't think you a pauper." The slave held up a couple of jewelled necklaces and some gold chains. "I can tuck these inside one of your pockets."

Julia chewed her lip. "All right. They can be used as bribes, or converted to cash if necessary, I suppose."

The rubies, diamonds and emeralds winked in the light. Maia was glad they weren't moonstones, remembering the cursed necklace with a shudder. She left them to their packing and turned her attention to the Great Cabin, where Pendragon and Raven were meeting with Julia's potential saviour.

Arrangements were being made with the owner of the merchant vessel, who also happened to be its captain. Pendragon was interviewing the man personally, with Raven by his side, and a careful mix of inducement and veiled threats were serving to ensure the man's obedience and discretion. As she listened in, he was being assured that there would be a similar reward waiting for him at the other end, as King Parisius was eager to claim his Britannic bride, whoever ended up holding the throne. Negotiations concluded, the man left after many protestations of loyalty.

"She'll be as safe as we can make her," Raven remarked.

Pendragon ran a hand over his face and stared down at his desk. "I hope you're right. Do you think that Marcus would kill her out of hand?"

The Master Mage raised an eyebrow. "Based on past experience, yes, though it's possible that he would force her into marriage to legitimise his claim. It's been done before."

Pendragon snorted. "He'd be in for a shock if he tried. No, the best thing is to get her to Gaul immediately." His eyes unfocused as he concentrated and his voice came over Maia's private Ship link. <Tempest, tell my niece that she must be ready to depart.> His gaze cleared once more. "Come on, old friend, we'd better go and say farewell."

The Ship's boat would take the Princess to the quayside, where the merchantman, a sturdy little vessel by the name of the Cornucopia, was waiting to greet her. From there, it would be a trip across the open sea to the continent.

Julia was standing on the deck wrapped in a cloak, her cheeks reddened from the breeze. From a distance she looked normal enough – there were none of the trappings of royalty here – but her eyes were troubled as she gazed towards the shore. Behind her, men passed luggage down into the boat. Latonia stood to one side looking unhappy, whilst next to her Milo waited, his stance alert. Pendragon had specifically ordered him to go with the Princess as an added protection.

Maia watched the little group with concern. She was torn between wanting the Princess to stay with her and knowing that she'd be safer away from any potential conflict. This was no formal leave-taking with cannon salutes and banners, such as she had got at Portus, only a quiet exchange of goodbyes and best wishes for each other's safety, uncle to niece.

"May the Gods watch over you and bring you safe to harbour," the King said.

"You, also, Sire," Julia replied, with a formal curtsey. "May you triumph over our enemies."

Maia had seen many families saying farewell to their loved ones amid tears and a lot of fuss. This was nothing like that, with not even a hug. It seemed strange to her.

"Oh, uncle, I've left my monkey on board. Will you look after him? I called him Teg, after the ugly sailor."

A flicker of surprise crossed Pendragon's face as he quirked an eyebrow. "Teg, eh? He might be quite handsome for a monkey, unlike his human counterpart! The men like their little jokes, but I doubt it's complimentary to a poor old sailor." He turned to Maia with a questioning look. "I take it that there are no restrictions on the creatures?"

"No, Sire," she said, deciding that she wasn't going to let slip to the crew that Teg had a smaller and hairier namesake.

Pendragon gave a wry smile. "That makes a change. Yes, you can be sure I'll see that he's well cared for."

So he did like monkeys. Teg would be fine as long as he was fed regularly and it wasn't as if there was any close bond between him and his owner.

"Send word when you reach land," he said and she nodded. "Safe journey, and may Neptune watch over you."

There would be several sacrifices to that end. Danuco, plus the island's Priests, would be kept busy until word came through that Julia had arrived safely.

The King helped his niece over the rail and watched as she was lowered into the boat. Milo climbed down the side, as did the accompanying marines. Latonia waited patiently for the chair to return for her so that she could follow her mistress. Soon, they were all aboard and Maia got the order to send them to shore.

"Well, that's that," he remarked to Raven. "Keep me posted."

"Aye, Sire." The company bowed as Pendragon strode off back to his cabin. Leo was on the quarterdeck scanning the horizon and his Ship went to join him.

"They aren't very demonstrative, are they?" Maia said. Leo shook his head.

"No. It's part of being royal. Of them all, Artorius was always the one who showed any reactions to things."

"I hope she'll be all right."

"Me too." His eyes flicked sideways. "Any news on the other Ships?" Maia concentrated.

"*Blossom* and *Persistence* are a couple of hours away. *Unicorn* is almost here and the rest aren't far behind."

"Good. The quicker they arrive, the better."

The boat was almost at the quayside now. A few locals had stopped to watch, but it was thought best that nobody knew of the Princess's departure. Who knew how many spies Marcus had? It was valuable information and they couldn't afford for it to leak out to unfriendly ears. Julia and her party would board the vessel immediately, just in time to slip away with the evening tide. Maia could feel that it had already started to turn. The weather was set fair, so if all went well, they would have a smooth voyage.

She could see them disembarking on to the quayside and beginning to move towards the merchantman, which was drawn up alongside. Then, without warning, a young Priest ran towards them, his robes flapping and a look on his face that told them all he was the bearer of bad news.

*

57

Milo wasn't unhappy with his new assignment. He had no wish to be embroiled in a sea battle or two, and he would be of more use on land guarding the Princess. Also, there were a few magical tricks he could teach her to supplement her growing armoury of spells. All in all, Julia was as well-protected as they could plan for. The rest was up to the Fates. Milo hoped that they were feeling more charitable towards her than to her unlucky brother.

They had just got to land, when he was alerted by sudden movement. A Priest was making a bee-line for them and Milo automatically interposed himself between the stranger and the Princess, who hadn't noticed his approach. The marines formed up alongside him as the Priest stopped, panting and red-faced.

"I need to get a message to the King," he gasped.

Milo wondered why he hadn't Sent to Danuco, before remembering that the Priest was ashore, procuring a sacrificial bull.

"You can tell me," he said quickly, taking the man to one side and pulling out his Agent's badge. The man nodded.

"We've just had word. King Parisius of Gaul is dead."

Sharp intakes of breath from the nearby marines told him how unwelcome that news was. *Merda!* Why couldn't the old fool have lasted another couple of months? This changed things and not for the better. Gaul would be in uproar, unless the old man had finally named a successor.

"Keep everyone here," Milo snapped at the marine sergeant. The man nodded and barked an order at his troop. Milo activated his speechstone as he watched them form up around their little group.

<Milo to Raven.>

<Yes, Milo?>

<Parisius is dead.>

There was a moment's silence, then a muttered oath. <Bad timing, but it could have been worse. You'd better come back aboard.>

Julia had noticed the exchange and pushed past one of her guards. "Milo, what is it?"

He told her, noting that fact that she couldn't hide her relief. She really hadn't wanted to go to Gaul.

"We're to return to the *Tempest*."

She nodded. "Understood."

Her face was composed, but he'd have bet that she was quietly offering thanks, even if her situation had become even more uncertain.

Shortly, the luggage was being removed from the *Cornucopia* and Milo was having a quiet word with its captain, who wasn't displeased that he wouldn't have to carry his dangerous passenger after all. A new price was decided on to keep his silence and clasped hands sealed the deal.

Milo was handed his bag by one of the crew and made his way over to where the *Tempest*'s boat was waiting.

"That was a short trip," the sergeant commented. He cast a glance towards the bow, where Julia and Latonia sat huddled for the return journey.

"Too right," Milo answered.

"What now?"

"Who knows? She can't stay here."

Even the sunshine had disappeared as the evening approached, the lowering clouds threatening rain and the promise of darker skies ahead.

*

Caniculus hurried along until his surroundings became even more familiar and buildings he'd known from childhood came into view. He could smell the river now and the warehouses that held his family's goods, brought from all over the Empire to please the populace and turn a healthy profit. He knew that the whole tribe still lived above the shop, father, mother, uncles, aunts and a whole rabble of cousins, all working to get orders filled and please their patrons. It was a world he'd turned his back on many years ago to go into government service. He'd never regretted it; despite the long hours and moderate pay, it still beat what he'd left behind.

It was best to slip in quietly, so he went around the back and used the side gate rather than the one into the main yard. The smell of animal dung lying in piles ready for collection hit his senses first, followed by the noise.

Most of the cages and crates were full. A camelopard regarded him inquisitively from under its long eyelashes as it chewed on a leafy branch, and several varieties of exotic birds bounced and chirruped in their aviary. From what he'd seen of the dung piles, there were several elephants in stock as well as a variety of other species. Business seemed good. The roar of a large cat echoed off the brick walls, but so far he'd seen nothing unusual.

"Well, if it isn't my errant nephew Brocchus! Welcome!"

A lanky older man bustled into view wiping his hands on a cloth. His broad smile showed Caniculus that he was pleased to see him.

"Uncle Baro! I was just in the area and thought I'd pop in," he explained. "Is Pa about?"

"He's up at the new amphitheatre, taking some animals in for the Games," his uncle told him. "We've got massive orders to fill, so we're working flat out. Every venue in the country wants to stage their own events, so nearly everyone's off shipping animals to all quarters. We've had to turn down work it's been that busy, though we've provided stuff where we can. It's been a madhouse."

"Now you know why I switched professions," Caniculus grinned. "Where's Ma then?"

"Feeding the elephants. I'm glad they're going tomorrow as it's costing us a fortune. Come on. She'll be happy you're here. It's been a while."

His uncle was right. It had been a few months since he'd had the leisure to call round. He made his way through into the cavernous interior of the animal sheds to find his mother.

"Valentina! Look who I found!" his uncle called into the shadows.

The woman, throwing bushels of hay into the eager grasp of three large elephants, didn't bother to turn round.

"Not now, Baro, can't you see I'm busy?"

That was his mother all over, waspish when stressed.

"No problem, I'll come back another time," Caniculus said loudly, laughing when she spun around.

"Brocchus! Oh! Come here and hug your mother!"

He scooped her up easily – she was half his size – and enfolded her in a big hug. She smelt of sweat and grass, testament to all the work she'd been doing. She looked tired too, he thought, noting the dark circles under her eyes.

"You look well," Valentina observed, subjecting him to an intense gaze. "You must excuse the state of me. We haven't had time to spit around here. Your father and brothers are up delivering the stock for the upcoming Games. The new King is really pushing the boat out for these and ordinary stuff just won't do. Aulus and Caius will have to stay up there to make sure that the animals are treated properly. We can't have them dying before they make their appearances, can we? Now, you can help me finish this and then we'll go and have something to eat. You must be starving!"

He smiled, her words making him almost feel that everything was normal again, and helped heave the final bunches of branches into the pen.

"There's a good boy. Baro, you come too. You haven't eaten since breakfast and we should grab the chance while we can."

"I'm up for that," his uncle replied. He wasn't married, and was like a second father to Caniculus and his siblings.

"Are Balbus and Silo around?" Caniculus asked. The yard was unusually empty of people. He was normally up to his neck in relatives, especially his other uncle and eldest cousin.

"Yes, they're with the special," Baro told him. Caniculus raised his eyebrows.

"A special, eh? What is it this time? There are rumours that Marcus has ordered something different."

Baro's weather-beaten face split into a broad grin.

"We've surpassed ourselves this time for sure," he teased. "She's a beauty all right, though she nearly took my head off when I caught her. Good job I got the dosage right and could sedate her quickly. I only got back the day before yesterday."

"Back from where?" his nephew asked as they made their way to another shed, set apart from the others.

"Cappadocia."

"I thought you had more of a tan than usual. You've not been here all winter, then?"

"No, thank the Gods, though it got pretty cold where we were. There were reports of a sighting and the locals wanted it gone, so our scouts went out and I followed on as fast as I could with a bigger team. I can't remember the last time we got one of these."

"One of what?" Caniculus asked impatiently, but his uncle refused to be drawn.

"Come on, but you'll have to be quiet. We're feeding her a concoction of valerian, catnip and camomile to keep her calm, but she's still dangerous."

Baro carefully opened a smaller door set into the larger double ones and slipped inside. Caniculus followed him into the dark interior and waited for his eyes to adjust. The smell hit him immediately, rank and sharp like a lion, but more intense and with overtones of something that he didn't recognise immediately. Reptile?

Dim shapes appeared in the darkness – two men. One was shovelling dung into a bucket, while the other stood ready with a long lance. They were clearly taking no chances, but it was the creature lying sprawled on the floor that grabbed his attention. His eyes travelled from the huge paws with their retracted claws, up the legs to the muscled lion body, then on to the three separate heads that sprang from the single neck. All six eyes were closed in sleep as the great beast dozed. A thick reptilian tail curled round its flanks.

Lion, goat and dragon, or more properly, big cat, horned caprine and scaled lizard. If he hadn't been well-trained he would have gasped aloud, but no sound escaped his open mouth as it dropped in amazement. Several thick chains were fastened around the creature's legs to iron plates and bolts set into the floor.

The man with the lance cast him a look and he saw that it was Silo. Five years younger than himself, his cousin had taken to the animal trade like a duck to water, and was taking over more and more of the day-to-day running of the business, along with Caniculus's brothers, Aulus and Caius. Silo's father, Balbus, was busy clearing up after the great beast. The latter finished his task and gathered up his equipment, making no sudden moves that might startle the animal. Both men moved slowly and carefully away from the animal and retreated to where Baro and Caniculus were standing. Silo indicated with a jerk of his head that they should get outside. He was the last to leave, lance at the ready in case there was any trouble, but the chimaera slept on, oblivious.

Once outside in the fresh air Caniculus exchanged greetings and congratulations with his family.

"Valentina's made dinner," Baro said.

"Excellent. We'll wash first though," Balbus said. "We take it in turns to muck the creature out and I have to dispose of this." He hoisted a bucket.

"Where do you put it?" Caniculus asked curiously.

"Oh, the Adepts pay handsomely for it because it can be used for various cures. I wouldn't like to put it on the roses. Nasty stuff!"

Caniculus agreed with him. "Still, extra profit, eh?"

"Indeed!" Balbus laughed, "And you can believe we're charging a fortune for it."

The two men went to wash at the courtyard pump and Balbus tipped the dung into a sealed container. Caniculus wondered what it cured, then decided that he'd be better off not knowing. It might put him off medicine for life.

Inside, his sister Nessa had laid the table and was decanting food from various pans and kettles. Caniculus went to give her a hand and she gave him an arch look as she passed him a dish of stew.

"Hello, Brocchus! What brings you here?"

"Aren't I allowed to come and visit my family?" he replied. He noticed that she was pregnant again. This would be her fourth.

"We haven't seen you for a while," she pointed out.

"Work," he said shortly. "You know I'm often posted away and it's been very busy lately. I can't stay long now."

"I suppose the new King has you running about." She leaned in closer. "They're saying that an evil spell killed Artorius and sunk the *Tempest*. Mother's been in tears. Funny how Marcus is the only one left, isn't it?"

He shot her a look of warning as he took another dish.

"Don't even think about it, sis. People have disappeared for saying less."

"But that's what everyone's saying –,"

"Don't. Don't gossip, don't even speculate and don't believe everything you hear."

"It's true then?"

He refused to answer, turning away to where the places at table were filling up. A small pair of arms grabbed him from behind, followed quickly by another.

"Hey! Not while I'm holding plates!"

"Children! Stop that!" Valentina reprimanded them. "You can play with your uncle later."

The children giggled and went to stand at the table. Soon, all were tucking into the meal.

"Marcus is going to have the chimaera as his centrepiece," Baro told Caniculus. "He's ordered pegasi as well, to re-enact Bellerophon's slaying of the beast."

"But didn't Bellerophon only have one?"

"Well, yes, but that wouldn't be much to look at, would it? It's going to be more spectacular with several of them, and if any are killed there'll be more as back up."

"They must be paying the riders a fortune," Balbus said. "I wouldn't do it. We'll have to stop dosing her up beforehand or she won't react."

"Is it to the death then?" Caniculus asked.

"I believe so, though it seems like a waste. I suppose if she manages to kill all the pegasi they might use her again."

"I want to see the fight!" a small voice piped up. Valentina laughed.

"No, you're too small to stay in the arena all day."

"Aw! I'm not!"

"Yes you are, Melitus," Nessa told her six-year-old son. "And you'd need the latrine just as it got exciting."

The adults laughed, much to the annoyance of little Melitus, especially when his sister Velibia joined in.

Much of the conversation then turned to family matters and how the business was prospering, what with so many royal occasions lately. Caniculus was relieved that he wasn't questioned in any depth. His sister didn't bring up the subject of politics again, though more than once he caught her sending worried glances in his direction. It was good to be back with his family, though he wondered if he would ever see them again, especially his father. The old man had never really approved of his choice to become an Agent of the State, but over the years he had become more used to it. He would rather have kept his second son in the family trade, but Caniculus had had enough of animals, savage or otherwise, and didn't intend to spend the rest of his life hunting them down for profit.

Hunting men was much more interesting.

He'd debated whether to turn to his family for help, as the last thing he wanted to do was to put any of them at risk. The Department would have been alerted when he stopped reporting in, but he had to be in Londin anyway and he might never get another chance. With luck, Marcus wouldn't get to hear of his whereabouts, but he couldn't count on it. He could feel the accustomed lump of his speechstone, warm against his skin and shuddered slightly at the thought that a God had touched it.

"My brother's woolgathering." Nessa's voice cut through the murmur of conversation.

"Oh, sorry. I've a lot on my mind," he explained.

"You're not in any trouble are you?" his mother asked, her eyes worried.

"No, no. Nothing like that," he said hastily. "Just busy, that's all."

She appeared mollified, but he knew that she wouldn't rest until she got to the bottom of what was up with him. He'd have to make sure that she didn't get wind of what he was planning to do.

*

Caniculus awoke in darkness. For a moment, he couldn't remember where he was, then memory returned. He was back in his old room under the eaves of the family home. He knew that he couldn't stay there long, but surely he'd get away with just one night. After that, he'd have to plough ahead and take whatever chances he could, telling his family to deny all knowledge of him, and to disavow him if necessary to protect themselves.

Something had woken him, but he couldn't tell what. He lay still, ears straining to catch the faintest of noises.

There it was again. A low, metallic hum, almost mechanical in its intensity, as if some sort of machine was operating in the background far away. He sat up, puzzled. They weren't near any of the big foundries or other factories, as that would upset the animals. So what was it?

His eye fell on the cloth-wrapped bundle he'd placed on the floor next to his old bed. It was coming from there.

Caniculus swung his legs out of the bed and eyed the package dubiously. It had to be either the helmet, or the Sword and he had a nasty feeling that he was about to find out. He took a deep breath and undid the material, tugging at the coarse cloth until the contents came into view. It was only then that he saw the Sword. The helmet was as it had always been, but the weapon glowed softly, even through the scabbard, casting a yellow radiance around the room. He took a second to marvel at it.

"What do you want of me?" he whispered.

Before he could stop himself, he'd picked it up. It felt warm under his fingers.

*

The harbour lights of Ennor were twinkling now, answered by the lamps of the Ships anchored off shore. *Leopard*, *Farsight*, and *Cameo* had arrived from various points of the compass as dusk had fallen, ready to pledge their allegiance to the rightful King. *Blossom* and *Persistence*, helped all the way by the powerful wind, had appeared shortly afterwards, battered but determined. *Persistence* still bore several grisly trophies in her rigging, though *Blossom* had already relinquished hers to the sea.

<Her Captain will persuade her to give them up, eventually,> *Blossom* told Maia. <She's a fierce one in battle! I should have known that she wouldn't give in easily.>

<I'm just glad you're here,> Maia Sent. <*Diadem* and *Imperatrix* are on their way, too. That's three Royals.>

<True. I think the *Victoria* would have joined us, but there's no chance of that, the state her crew are in. She'll be swarming with soldiers, too. Don't tell me that the plague was all chance either!>

Maia felt safer surrounded by her sisters, even though they were few.

<Poor *Victoria*! How many do you think will support Marcus?>

Blossom thought about it. <Fewer than he hopes. Many will stay put, especially if they're abroad. A lot depends on what their Captains think, and I don't know how many were approached. Plinius wasn't, but then again I'm only an old training Ship, so they probably discounted me.>

<More fool them then,> Maia shot back.

She sensed her friend's grin. <True. I've still got a few battles left in me, though I really hope it won't come to that. We've never fought each other, except in the odd case when a Ship has needed to be constrained, and never in war. Northmen, yes. Plenty of them.>

<Constrained?> Maia wanted to know more.

Blossom sighed. <It happens, sometimes, when Ships grow old and start to fail, like the *Augusta*. Occasionally their wits wander. I heard a rumour of one that turned pirate along with her Captain many centuries ago, but I don't know if it's true.>

<If it is, the Navy wouldn't want people remembering that," Maia said. "Some might go mad, like the *Livia*.>

<Yes, but it's very rare and usually never that extreme.>

Maia didn't want to think about fighting other Ships.

<We could go to the New Continent and get more support,> she said. She thought it was a good idea. Marcus had too many advantages at the moment and they were bound to need more troops.

<I don't think we can,> *Blossom* told her. <Pendragon can't let his son get too entrenched. Also, it would take weeks. Suppose we got back and found the place overrun with Fae? What would we do then? The land would already be lost.>

<We might have to fight our sisters and he has to fight his son,> Maia said. There was nothing good about their situation.

<And Old Parisius is finally dead. No more marriage for Julia, at least not yet. The nephews have petitioned the Emperor to decide who takes the crown of Gaul, though I expect it will be the Governor who recommends the next king.>

<She could marry the victor.>

<It will take too long. Diplomacy moves slower than a three-legged tortoise. He'll have to think of another use for her.>

Maia was tempted to tell her friend that Julia could be very useful, but it wasn't her place to give away the Princess's secret.

<I know he's working on something,> she offered. Pendragon and Raven had been closeted together far into the night, discussing strategy and where to find allies but when she'd tried to listen Raven had blocked her from doing so, against naval protocol. She thought it odd and was slightly hurt at the thought that he hadn't trusted her, but knew that it must have been on Pendragon's orders. What was so sensitive that she wasn't supposed to know about it?

<He'll have a plan,> *Blossom* said, confidently. <Speaking of plans, here's the *Imperatrix* now. *Diadem* is close, plus some smaller inanimates as well. Things are looking up!>

Maia tried to feel optimistic, but the dread that hung over refused to dispel. It wasn't long before they were hailed by the senior Royal.

<*Imperatrix* to the Fleet! Greetings!>

The Ships responded. Maia watched as the great Royal hove into view. She hadn't had much to do with the *Imperatrix*, though she was familiar with her Shipbody from the statues that had been in the hall of the Portus Academy. She tried not to think of them coming to life during her trial and berating her for being unworthy.

<*Diadem* to the Fleet.>

So, the other Royal was in her sister's wake. Maia was a little in awe of this Ship, though she'd been friendly enough when greeting her new Royal sister.

<*Diadem* was the first Ship I ever met,> she told *Blossom*. <She was stationed in Portus waiting to be installed, along with the *Swiftsure*.>

<Oh yes, I remember that,> *Blossom* said.

<As do I,> another voice cut in.

<Greetings, *Diadem*! You're here!>

<Nearly. Give me a few minutes. It's bad luck about Parisius, isn't it?>

<I don't think the Princess is complaining,> *Blossom* observed.

<No,> Maia agreed. <Talking of the *Swiftsure*, I haven't heard her lately and I've not seen her at all.>

<She's off New Roma these days, glaring at Northmen,> *Blossom* said. <She's the oldest non-Royal, you know. You can bet that she'll be keeping an ear on things, but there's not much she can do at the moment.>

<I take it the King's asleep?> *Imperatrix* cut in.

<Yes. He was up very late,> Maia replied.

<Inform me immediately he wakes.>

There was an edge to the other Ship's voice that alerted Maia. What could she have done to annoy the *Imperatrix*? They'd hardly ever spoken. She wondered whether this was one of the 'hoity-toity' Royals that the *Jasper* had spoken of. She certainly sounded like something was bothering her.

<What have I done?> Maia asked *Blossom*, privately.

<Nothing. That's her all over. I'll bet that she wants Pendragon to name her as lead Ship and transfer to her. She won't like that he's chosen to stay with you.>

Maia eyed the dark bulk of the *Imperatrix* and decided that her vessel was bigger than the older Ship's, for all she had seniority.

She settled down for a night of catching up with her friends. The *Imperatrix* and her jealousy could wait until the morning.

*

It was almost dawn when Milo woke with a start. He was back in his cubby hole aboard *Tempest*, his role as a servant resumed since the Princess wasn't going anywhere for the moment. He'd been in a deep sleep, but now he was fully awake.

Someone had been calling his name. He rubbed his eyes and looked around, but all was quiet. Had it been Raven? He dismissed the idea instantly. He could have sworn that it was a woman.

"*Tempest*," he whispered. The answer came immediately.

"Yes, Milo?"

"Did you call for me?"

The Ship sounded puzzled. "It wasn't me and, before you ask, the Princess and Latonia are asleep."

Milo shook his head. "I'm sorry. I must have been dreaming."

She laughed quietly. "Go back to sleep. Everything's fine."

He thanked her and lay back down. It was only then he realised that whoever had been calling him had used his real name. He stared into the night, his heart thumping, before settling down once more.

It must have been a dream after all.

IV

Morning brought uproar to the streets of Londin. Caniculus was dragged from sleep by excited voices and the sound of running feet.

His first thought was that one of the animals had escaped. He threw off his bedclothes and hurried down to lend a hand, hoping that he wouldn't find an angry chimaera prowling around with some unlucky passer-by dangling from its jaws.

His mother was standing in the yard, talking to a female neighbour, their faces alight with excitement.

"Ma? What is it?"

She broke off to answer him.

"You'll never guess what's happened!"

He stared at her in confusion. "Has something escaped?"

She waved a hand at him. "No, no, nothing like that. There's a sword stuck into a stone in the Forum!"

Caniculus stared at her in horror. "A sword? In the Forum?"

"Yes, yes!" the neighbour squealed. "It's jammed into a column and nobody can budge it!"

"Er, right." He left them to their chatter and returned to his bedroom.

The helmet lay on the floor next to the blanket it had been wrapped in, but the Sword was gone. It was only then that he realised that he was already dressed and he knew for a fact that he hadn't gone to sleep in his clothes.

The damned Sword had used him! A faint memory surfaced of something glowing, but it slipped away when he tried to snatch at it. No, there was nothing there. Chagrin combined with a surge of relief – at least it was out of his hands now. He could only pray that he'd been unobserved when he'd disposed of the dratted thing.

Thinking of praying reminded him to go and pay his respects to the Household Gods before breakfast. He was just on his way down, when more raised voices sent him into the street.

71

An agitated crowd had formed outside. He'd just joined it, craning his neck over the sea of heads for a better view, when he felt the ground heave beneath his feet as if something heavy was shifting underground. Had there been an accident with the new sewers? For a second the world seemed to tilt, making him put out his arms for balance while around him passers-by gasped and shouted. Cries of alarm came from the houses as their occupants rushed out of doors, staring around wildly.

"*Chasmatias!*" one woman yelled.

"Don't be daft!" another replied. "They don't have earthquakes here like they do abroad."

"They have them in Italia," her neighbour said.

"Well, we're not in Italia. They have tremors up north, but not here. It's something else."

Everybody held their breath, but the movement wasn't repeated.

"A sign!"

The cry came from the doorway of a small temple. Mercury again, Caniculus noted.

"The Sword of Kingship has returned! It speaks! The Gods proclaim the arrival of the true King!"

A young Priest staggered into the street, arms raised to the heavens and a look of rapture on his face. The crowd muttered in alarm.

"Someone shut 'im up, or the polis'll be 'ere soon an' then there'll be trouble," one man insisted.

The Priest continued his speech undeterred, this time addressing them all directly. His eyes were wide and strangely blank.

"The murderer will be cast into the Stygian depths! The Gods see all and they have turned their faces from him. Hail the true King!"

Two burly, uniformed men pushed through the growing throng of onlookers. City polismen.

"What's this?" one demanded, glaring at the Priest.

"He's having a funny turn is all," a young red-haired woman insisted. They ignored her and grabbed the young man.

"You can't be talking like that! You'd better come with us."

"You serve a false King!"

The polismen frogmarched the Priest away, still shouting that the true King would come and save them all. Caniculus watched in horror. The man was clearly Godstruck: you could tell from his glazed eyes that he was in divine thrall and speaking the truth.

"Poor Carbo! What will happen to him now?" The woman who had tried to defend him burst into tears. "He wasn't himself, anyone could see that!"

An older man, probably her grandfather, judging by the red hairs among the grey, tried to console her.

"I don't know what we can do, love. Perhaps they won't hurt him because he's a Priest."

Caniculus doubted that. The man would be fortunate if he got out of prison in one piece. As an Agent, he knew all too well that people could be made to disappear quietly and without fuss. He offered up a quick prayer on Carbo's behalf to Mercury and any other Gods who might be listening.

A young boy ran up, red-faced and panting.

"Have you heard? Excalibur's appeared in the Forum!"

"So it is Excalibur. That's what Carbo was talking about," the old man said, shaking his head. "This means trouble, for sure." He took the sobbing woman by the arm and led her inside. Caniculus heard the mutters from the others and saw that a few people had already walked away, probably to see the miracle for themselves. So that was why the Sword needed him.

Would this make his task of spying harder, or easier? One thing was for sure, he'd better get on with it immediately, before worse befell Londin than a possessed Priest and the sudden appearance of a magical sword.

*

The Londin Forum was packed. Word had spread fast and a seething mass of people had squeezed into every available space to gawk at the latest attraction. The noise was deafening.

Caniculus had grabbed a hasty breakfast and joined the throng, hoping to get a glimpse of what was happening. He felt safe amongst so many people and wanted a quick look before carrying out the next part of his plan. True to form, it seemed that the whole of the city had turned out to view this historic

73

appearance. He squinted in the light to see where the sword had ended up.

"Where is it?" he asked the man next to him, who was also scanning the area. "Can you see it?"

"No...yes! There it is!" The man answered, pointing. "Look at the Basilica!"

Caniculus turned his attention to the large and impressive government building that dominated the Forum. Now he was looking more closely, he could see the cordon of City Polis keeping people back. The sword was sticking out one of the massive central columns, above head height, its jewelled hilt glittering in the sunshine as if winking at the crowd.

He couldn't stop a burst of laughter. What had he expected? It seemed apt, somehow.

"It looks funny," his neighbour said. "I thought Artorius the Great got it from some magic rock in a wood?"

"Yes, it does look strange," Caniculus said, still laughing. Others joined in.

"Marcus'll have to stand on a ladder and give it a tug," another snorted.

"He can try," someone else chimed up. "But only the rightful King can pull it out."

The little group exchanged knowing looks.

"He'll be in trouble if he can't."

There were several murmurs of agreement.

"They should let everybody have a go. We could queue up."

That provoked more laughter.

"Why, do you fancy being King?"

"Oh aye. I'd like that. Beats being a shopkeeper."

Caniculus left them to their speculation and set off back home. The sword was Marcus's problem now. Any delay in proving his claim would fatally undermine him and lead to further unrest. Now it was time for Caniculus to start on the next part of his plan to fulfil his Gods-given obligations. The Sword had provided the distraction he needed, now the rest was up to him.

He slipped back inside the atrium, pausing to open the doors of the little shrine and murmur some prayers of appeasement to the Lares and Penates that protected his family line and household. These small Gods would be watching his every move and, he thought ruefully, he'd need all the help he could get. The back of his neck prickled and a shiver ran up his spine as he prayed and lit the tiny cone of incense.

"Forgive me for bringing trouble here," he whispered. "I serve the Gods and my King."

Go. Now.

The whisper was just on the edge of hearing.

A tiny rustle and flicker of movement in the corner of his eye told him that something was about, and no wonder. It was one of the little Gods of the Household giving him a warning he couldn't ignore. He'd been a fool to come home.

Back upstairs, he shoved a few things into a bag and unwrapped the helmet. The dull bronze gave no indication of its origins, though he fancied that some form of intelligence lurked in the empty eyeholes. Caniculus swallowed hard and put it on.

*

It was dawn and the late Aprilius mists cloaked the calm waters of the harbour. Maia could see the looming shapes of her sister Ships emerging into the early light, pennants and colours hanging limp in the still air.

Pendragon's voice snapped in over the link.

<Tempest, I'm expecting a visitor. Inform me the moment you see a Longship. He's called *Wolf of the Waves* and he's carrying the Alliance Ambassador.>

A Longship? She acknowledged him automatically, straining to pierce the lightening gloom for any hint of the spirit-driven vessel. She hadn't had anything to do with their former enemies as yet. It appeared that diplomacy had been going on behind the scenes, even as King Cei had been gathering his forces and reaching out for support.

<Tempest to *Patience.>*

Her friend answered immediately, *<Patience* here. Good morning!>

<Good morning. I've been told to look out for a Longship. Can you see anything?>

<A Longship? Fancy that! No, nothing yet.>

75

<I've just been told too.> *Leopard's* cool tones advertised her presence in the link. <Do you know which one it is?>

<It's called *Wolf of the Waves.*> *Leopard* gave a coughing growl.

<That one! I know him. We've had run-ins in the past. He's one of the oldest Longships, older even than the *Augusta* was. Their Ship spirits keep going forever, it seems. What's he here for?>

<Diplomacy.>

Other Ships started to comment amongst themselves and Mia could hear old *Persistence* grumbling in the background about barbarians.

<If they're going to support us, you can be sure they'll want something in return,> *Leopard* continued. A sensation of raised hackles crept down the link. There was definitely something about this particular Longship that set her fangs on edge.

<Down, girl,> *Diadem* cut in. <Just because you sank his vessel –.>

<And he repaid the favour!>

<Still, let's be polite, shall we? That goes for your crews, too.>

<We've already been told.> A sulky *Persistence* didn't sound happy about it. <I agree with *Leopard*. Them scurvy savages are only out for what they can get their 'ands on.>

Maia left them to their bickering and extended her awareness to its limit, searching the open sea. Longships were generally smaller than second-rates, but moved swiftly and silently. Their design had largely kept up with the Empire's: gone were the clinker-built, oar-driven galleys that harried the coasts of Britannia in centuries past, replaced by sleek, three-masted vessels built for speed and stealth. They were never to be underestimated and relied on numbers to defeat their enemies, like sea-going wolf packs, as many Ships like the *Leopard* had discovered to their cost.

There. Something alien impinged on her consciousness on the very edge of her range, but approaching rapidly. Maia realised that she wasn't sure what to do. If it had been another Ship, she would have hailed them as a matter of course.

<Leo, I'm sensing something and it's not one of ours. What should I do?>

Her Captain was making his way up to the quarterdeck as he replied. <Hail him as you would any other Ship. He's used to us and will respond. It will seem strange, or so I'm told.>

She took his advice as the presence grew sharper.

<This is His Majesty's Ship *Tempest*. Please identify yourself!>

There was a second of empty air, then Maia's mind was filled with a sudden flood of impressions.

See you/moving towards/intention non-hostile/meeting along with a sensation of rough fur and the sharpness of teeth. She gathered herself and quickly withdrew from the link. Leo was right. This was a very different kind of communication.

<He's approaching,> she warned the others, whilst simultaneously alerting Pendragon and Leo.

<I can smell him,> *Leopard* growled. Old enmities died hard.

The sunlight was strengthening now, burning away the last wisps of vapour and revealing the scene in its entirety. The *Wolf of the Waves* was slipping into the shelter of the harbour like a racing thoroughbred. His vessel was low in the water giving him a predatory look, unlike the high-decked Ships, and she could see his crew on deck as he prepared to come alongside her. Maia's own crew were staring back, though they were keeping their comments to themselves, as per orders. The older sailors clearly had no love for their former opponents and there were sideways glances and surreptitious mumblings to rival *Persistence*'s curses.

Now that he was close, she could make out the guiding spirit that gave the vessel its name. His Shipbody was situated at the prow, looking ahead of his vessel. Unsurprisingly, he had taken the form of a running wolf, black as bog oak though larger than any flesh and blood animal. Strange, sinuous patterns coiled down the length of his body, creating an almost stylised version of a creature with pricked up ears and gaping jaws. As if aware of her scrutiny, his head turned towards her, a red tongue lolling in the parody of a smile. She sensed his curiosity at their first meeting.

A shrill whistle and the thudding of feet sounded across her decks as her crew formed up to greet the Ambassador. She noted that Leo was in his best uniform, ready to escort the man down to where the King would be waiting to receive him in the Great Cabin. First impressions counted, and it was vital that they obtain his goodwill.

The *Wolf of the Waves* drew up next to her, so close that a plank could be laid from his vessel to hers. She could no longer see the spirit from her place on the quarterdeck, but she was still conscious of him, as a walker in the forest is aware of something menacing lurking nearby. She was impressed by the sheer energy he projected, and wondered whether it might be something she needed to learn for herself.

Activity on the Longship corresponded with movement on her own vessel as crewmen adjusted the gangplank to allow easy access to the Ambassadorial party. Bearded faces stared up at her rail with frank curiosity. A few of them grinned when they saw her looking and Maia itched to draw forth her dagger. As it was, she made sure that her silver mask gave away nothing, her eyes sliding over them in a show of indifference.

"Attention!" Osric bellowed, as the marines snapped into formation, muskets at their side. The sailors stood in the background, wary eyes watching every move. Down below decks, Hyacinthus was assuring Sprout that no, Northmen didn't eat human flesh, unless it was cooked first. Monkey suppressed a snigger, until Musca glared at the pair of them.

"Give over," he growled.

She resisted the urge to laugh and turned her attention back to the *Wolf of the Waves*.

Two figures emerged on to the Longship's deck, negotiating the gangplank with confidence. Leo and Sabrinus stepped forward as one took the lead, striding up to meet them. It was only when they stepped on to her deck, that Maia saw that they were both female.

"Ambassador Gudrun, daughter of Estrid, welcome aboard HMS *Tempest*," Leo said formally. He must have been briefed by Pendragon, Maia thought. "Allow me to present my second in command, Lucius Albanus Sabrinus."

Sabrinus also saluted and the Ambassador inclined her head. "Gentlemen." Was it Maia's imagination, or did Gudrun's eye linger on Sabrinus, as if knowing whose son he was? "This is Bodil, daughter of Hild, my Shieldmaiden." Stiff nods were exchanged.

<She means bodyguard,> Leo explained to Maia, sensing her puzzlement.

Gudrun was dressed conventionally enough in a tunic and cloak of fine wool, augmented with large gold brooches and intricate jewellery. She was tall for a woman, able to look Leo directly in the eye, with greying fair hair plaited in an elaborate style close to her head. She had to be in her fifties, but moved with grace. She didn't appear to be armed, unlike her dark-haired companion who bore daggers attached to a belt slung around her hips over scale armour and leather trews.

Bodil's stance was relaxed, but her eyes missed nothing and Maia had the impression that she was constantly on the alert. She was reminded of Milo in the way the woman held herself.

"We'll keep your weapons to one side for you," Leo told her. "You have our assurances of safe conduct."

Bodil's eyes slid sideways to Gudrun, who gave her a short nod, causing the woman to pull the daggers from her belt. She walked over to the rail and rested them on the deck before straightening up and giving Leo a challenging glare.

"Nobody will touch them."

"As you wish," Leo replied, adding mentally to Maia, <You'd better come forward to be introduced.>

Maia had been standing further back and now took the opportunity to glide forwards across the deck to her Captain, ensuring that she was tall enough to tower over the two women. The Ambassador's face showed nothing but polite interest, but Bodil's eyes flickered, as if in appreciation.

"My Ship, *Tempest*," Leo said.

"Ah, the newest one." Gudrun smiled, lines fanning out from her pale eyes as her gaze took in the latest addition to the Britannic Royal Navy. "Most impressive, as is your vessel."

"Thank you, your Excellency," Maia replied.

"And loyal, too. That is always a good thing." The Ambassador stated smoothly, her unaccented Latin bearing a sting, nonetheless. "Please lead the way, Captain. There is much to discuss."

The small party trooped below, where Pendragon was waiting to greet them. Sabrinus remained on deck with Maia, who immediately divided her attention to watch their progress.

So, the Ambassador was a woman. Interesting. There was no way that a country nominally under Roman rule would allow that. She wondered whether it had been deliberate, although Gudrun looked as though she was more than equal to the challenge. It certainly made a change. Some of her crew had been surprised too.

"Their women are different," Caphisus was saying. "They have female dux and such – call 'em Jarls. Scary, eh?"

"They scare me," Teg replied, pulling a face, which got a laugh from his fellows on the gun deck. Maia thought it made him look even more like his namesake, Teg the monkey.

"Still, I'd rather 'ave 'em on our side, right lads?"

"Too right," Hyacinthus said. "Even if their Ships give me the shudders."

"Are they all wolves?" Sprout piped up.

"Nah. Sometimes they're stags or serpents. Saw a dragon once."

"They can be bears," Batacarus agreed. "Always animals, never humans. Don't know 'ow they do it and they won't tell. Different Gods, you see. They sacrifice people, too." He shuddered at the thought. Human sacrifice had been forbidden in the Empire for centuries.

Down in the Great Cabin, the courtesies had just been concluded. The main players were sitting at a round table: Pendragon, Raven, Leo and the Ambassador. Bodil and Milo were standing behind their respective charges. The servants poured drinks, then were dismissed. Maia was surprised to see that Julia wasn't present and quickly checked on her whereabouts. The Princess was in her cabin and, from the look on her face, very unhappy to be there. Latonia was preparing her hair to take the royal tiara. The rest of her finery was draped on the bed, ready for her transformation into the Royal Princess.

Meanwhile, Pendragon was thanking the Ambassador for agreeing to meet.

"Forgive me for getting to the point, Ambassador, but we haven't much time. I'm sure you are fully aware of the current situation."

"The coup? Yes. As you will appreciate, your Highness, my government is watching developments with interest."

"Naturally. Are you also aware that Marcus instigated my nephew's murder?"

Gudrun regarded him levelly.

"Do you have proof?"

"A witness, currently in hiding, plus the Gods gave a sign. The King's body bled when Marcus placed his hand upon it and not before."

Her mouth twisted. "Your Gods have spoken?"

"They favour my cause."

She nodded, slowly, her eyes hooded.

"Your son wants you dead."

Pendragon's face became granite. "Yes. I have reason to believe that he has a hidden agenda and is being used by unfriendly powers."

"Gods?"

"Major Fae."

Gudrun's eyes flickered wider. "You believe they are planning to return from Hibernia?"

"We do."

"Forgive me, your Highness, but again, do you have proof of this?"

This time, Raven answered.

"There has been enemy action in Londin. A government Agent was almost killed by a Fae construct summoned by a spy, who was subsequently captured and interrogated. Both the King and the Princess have survived plots to assassinate them on this very Ship. All the malefactors were put to the question and confirmed Fae involvement. Believe me, the creatures are on the move."

The Ambassador nodded. "I can see how you are alarmed," she replied, "but how will this affect the Alliance?"

"If the Fae get a foothold in Britannia it will affect trade, not to mention putting a serious dent in the population. I doubt that any treaty would survive. Your people would lose business, and

81

those that have settled here will be forced to return to their ancestral homes. Just because your Alvar have been driven underground doesn't mean to say that you could cope with ours."

"Alvar?" Leo queried.

"Fae that harried the North in times past."

Gudrun considered his words.

"It's true that we would not want anything to jeopardise the new-found peace between our nations," she said at last. "My government is still debating the implications and I will have to report this new information. However, my King has instructed me to begin negotiations on your other proposal."

Maia's ears pricked up. Other proposal?

"I do not offer this lightly," Pendragon said. "In return, I hope that aid will be given if called for. After all, my niece will be the heir to the throne once the Usurper is dealt with."

"She will," Gudrun agreed. "Marriage is always the best way to seal a treaty. However, and forgive me for speaking bluntly, there is the possibility that you will fail to win back your throne and Marcus will produce other heirs."

She gave them both a challenging look, secure in her government's upper hand.

"Then there will be blood ties between two thrones," Pendragon answered her. "You win either way."

She raised an eyebrow.

"Or a double-edged sword. Still, as I said, King Harald is willing to negotiate for your niece's hand in marriage to his son, but the matter of military support must be debated by the Althing when next they meet."

"I understand, though I would urge speed. There will soon be a new King of Gaul."

The threat was implicit. *I could still marry her off there.*

Gudrun smiled. "I'm sure that the Emperor will announce his choice soon. I understand that most of the candidates are already married?" *It would take too long to arrange a new marriage for her.*

"At present."

Maia listened, fascinated as much by what wasn't being said as what actually came out of their mouths.

"Then, Your Highness, please permit me to report back without delay for, as you say, time is pressing."

"Indeed. Please return to dine with us this evening. The Princess Julia will be in attendance."

Pendragon rose, signalling the end of the audience. Gudrun bowed, then paused.

"I am honoured, Your Highness. There is one further thing I have been instructed to say. The Council will take heed of your own laws. If Marcus should remove Excalibur, he will be regarded as the legitimate ruler of Britannia."

Pendragon stared her down. "If he should do so, I'll kneel to him myself."

The Ambassador bowed again and left, accompanied by her shadow and Leo as escort.

<Tell me when she's gone.> Pendragon ordered Maia. Despite his usual iron control, an undercurrent of rage, grief and frustration churned through their link.

Maia dutifully watched as the two women returned to their vessel. Bodil swaggered over to the rail and retrieved her daggers without incident. It was only when the visitors were back aboard the *Wolf of the Waves* that she signalled to Pendragon, who collapsed into his chair and put his head in his hands.

"I need information! Jove's beard, that damnable woman knows more than I do!"

Raven helped himself to the untouched wine. "So, the Sword of Kingship has activated. I wonder where it's turned up now."

"Everyone knows except us, apparently. We must find out."

Raven put down the glass and smacked his lips.

"Milo, time to contact your friend."

The Agent shifted his stance. "Understood, sir."

Milo's gaze travelled inwards as he activated his speechstone. On deck, Leo and Sabrinus were conferring, with many a glance towards the Northmen; Julia was pacing in her quarters, half-dressed despite Latonia's pleas, and the atmosphere in the Great Cabin was brittle and tense.

<*Imperatrix* to *Tempest*.>

Maia sighed to herself and responded. What did the Royal want now? She'd already demanded a better anchorage, forcing several smaller Ships to move and had made it clear in no uncertain terms that she was very unhappy that Pendragon hadn't rushed over to her immediately, as she was the senior Royal present.

<What's happening? You should relay to the rest of us, to keep us informed, you know.>

Maia was tempted to tell her to mind her own business. She promptly widened the link to include the other Ships; she wanted witnesses to the *Imperatrix*'s demands.

<The King has met with the Ambassador,> she Sent.

<And?>

<There is to be a formal dinner tonight.>

The other Ship's annoyance radiated through the link. <Aboard your vessel, I suppose.>

Maia felt her patience fraying. <It will be as the King commands,> she Sent.

And if you don't like that, you can take it up with him!

Imperatrix broke the link in a huff.

<What's got into her?> she asked *Blossom*. <She's being offhand, if not downright rude.>

<Take no notice. At least she's on our side, even if she is a pain in the arse.>

<Another hoity-toity Royal, as *Jasper* put it?>

<She's not usually this bad, but she's unsettled and that often brings out the worst in people. Ships are no exception.>

<And because I'm the youngest, she thinks she can throw her weight around,> Maia sniffed. <I'll only take so much!>

<Like I said, ignore her,> *Blossom* insisted. <You've more to think about at the moment than a disgruntled Ship.>

Maia observed the activity aboard her vessel. Small boats were coming alongside bearing provisions and there was a general air of purposeful activity as preparations were being made for the evening.

<You're right about that,> she agreed. As she ended the chat, Maia wondered if Julia already knew what her uncle had planned for her.

*

<Dog. It's Ferret.>

The reply came back instantly.

<How are you?>

<Fine. Look, I need information. What do you know of Excalibur?>

<Ah, that. Yes. It's currently stuck into a column in the portico of the Londin Basilica.>

Milo almost gasped out loud.

<How did it get there?>

<Everyone's saying it's magic. Swords like that have a will of their own, you know.>

Milo knew from long acquaintance that his friend wasn't telling him everything, but perhaps that was the wisest course. He would have to withhold facts too.

<Has the Usurper tried to pull it out yet?>

Caniculus laughed. <What do you think? Not bloody likely. There's a large crowd waiting for him to fail. Rumour is he'll have the whole thing moved, stone and all, but that will take a while or the whole front will come crashing down.>

<Whoever stuck it there knew what they were doing.> Milo doubted there was a more public place in the whole of Britannia. <You wouldn't know anything about that, then?>

<No, of course not.> His friend was definitely holding something back.

<Hmm. The Usurper must be wetting himself with fear.>

<Probably. Best not stay on too long.>

He had to admit that Caniculus was right. <I agree. Look, if there's anything else, contact me. We need to know what's going on and we're, shall we say, out of the way.>

<Got you. Oh, by the way, the local gossip is that Marcus killed the rest of his family with an evil spell. Thought you should know. Take care, Ferret.>

<You too.>

Milo broke the link to be met with an air of expectation. *Tempest* was nowhere to be seen, but he knew she'd be listening in.

"I made contact, Sire. Excalibur is jammed into the portico of the Londin Basilica, daring the Usurper to come and pull it out."

Pendragon's eyes widened. "By whose agency?"

"Nobody knows. Also, rumour is saying that Marcus used an evil spell to kill King Artorius and sink us."

Raven cut in. "He said Excalibur. Is he sure?"

Milo cast him a puzzled look. "Yes. The King's sword. Everybody knows what it looks like."

"And he wouldn't dare try to remove it in plain sight," Raven mused. "It could destroy his claim instantly."

"But it's too dangerous for me to attempt and the same will apply to Marcus," Pendragon said. "Nor can he just leave it there."

"My informant thinks he'll try to move it to a private place."

"And switch it with a replica, if I know him."

Raven shrugged. "That's what I'd try. However, I think he'll have difficulty. Once the Sword is lodged it refuses to budge, or so the legends say."

Pendragon frowned. "Legends and rumours. That's all we've got to go on here." He gazed off into the distance, as if picturing the scene hundreds of miles away. "I don't suppose you could portal me in so I can grab it?"

Milo looked at the Master Mage hopefully. It was an idea.

"I wish, but it will be well guarded. You'd be killed before you could take a single step in its direction. No, I have the feeling that we're going to have use a less direct method."

"Fight our way through, you mean?"

Raven spread his hands helplessly. "Be assured, Sire, I'm already searching for allies, both on land and sea."

"Then it's war. Albanus and his Ships will try to stop us making landfall and we can't hide here forever. We'll get this evening over with, then we'll make sail. I'm calling a meeting of all Captains immediately to discuss strategy. *Tempest*, inform your sisters."

The Ship's voice sounded in the cabin.

"Aye, Sire."

Pendragon turned to him. "You have my thanks, Agent Milo, for this and everything else you've done for your country."

Milo bowed. "I know my duty, Sire."

Pendragon nodded. "I wish I had more like you. Carry on."

The Agent left, returning once more to the Mage quarters. As he nodded to various crew members, he pitied the person who'd be explaining the King's plan to Julia. He didn't think that she'd take the news well.

*

Caniculus broke the link to Milo and surveyed the view of the tradesmen's entrance to the palace. There were the usual couple of guards making cursory checks of comings and goings but apart from that all seemed quiet. It was easy with the helmet to slip inside in the back of a cart laden with amphorae. The wine was the good stuff judging from the stamps on the seals, probably for the parties Marcus would be holding to celebrate his accession. He would have to show himself open-handed, though what was here was many times better than the rough vintage given away to the populace. Caniculus would have to be careful that his passing left no trace. Footprints suddenly materialising in the dirt would be a cause for suspicion, if not outright alarm and he intended that nobody should know of his presence.

He jumped down from the cart as it trundled inside, secure in the thought that dry stone wouldn't give him away, and dodged into a storeroom that led to the kitchens. He'd been right. The place was swarming with servants and slaves preparing the most luxurious of dishes, using ingredients from all over the Empire and beyond. The smells of spices and rich sauces made his mouth water as he tried to work out how to get across the floor without cannoning into a dozen sweating cooks and kitchen boys.

The heat from the charcoal stoves mingled with the blast from iron ranges and open fires, all funnelled up into huge chimneys overhead. Every face was fixed in concentration as their owners chopped, mashed, poured, stirred and arranged dishes in elaborate nests of flowers and pastry. Others hurtled around the floor in some strange dance of their own, carrying prepared dishes away and shuttling fresh produce in like demented ants. Caniculus was just wondering whether he should have taken his chance climbing over the wall to the gardens, when an opening presented itself.

Something was burning.

"Jove's bollocks! I told you to watch it!" The irate cook grabbed a potboy by his scruff and started beating him with a wooden spoon, probably the one the lad should have stirred the sauce with. The boy's yelping caused all heads to turn in his direction and left a path clear for Caniculus to scurry across, praying that he wouldn't run into anything. From here, he could get through to a back corridor that gave him access to every quarter of the palace.

He sent up a silent prayer to Mercury as he felt the cool air of the passageway hit his face. It was a relief after the steamy fug of the kitchen, and he thanked whichever Powers were listening that he'd bothered to memorise the layout of the twisting warren that was backstairs at the palace. The public rooms and private suites might be the grandest in Britannia, but here was the domain of those who served, scuttling like ants in a nest to attend their masters and mistresses. It wasn't long since he'd been one of them, rooting out any who sought to harm the Royal Family or the Engine of State. Now the times had changed and he knew just where to go.

A few more turns brought him to the service door of the audience chamber, concealed behind a tapestry. He could hear raised voices beyond, so he applied his eye to a split in the door and listened, grateful to whichever past Agent had surreptitiously widened a crack in the oak. It gave him just enough of a view into the room beyond.

The Usurper was standing on the steps that led to the throne. Flanking him were two guards, with others ranged about. Facing him was a trio of figures. Caniculus strained to make them out. One was in Mage robes, the other two were nobles. Interestingly enough, the Mage wasn't Bullfinch, but Kite, one of his lackeys.

"How did it get there? You said it would be found!"

Marcus hurled his goblet of wine across the throne room, adding the clatter of metal to his shouts. Red wine sprayed across the marble walls like arterial blood.

Several slaves, standing quietly behind the guards, flinched at their master's fury. The three figures before the throne remained immobile.

"Well?" the young man spat. His normally pale face was flushed.

"We have been searching night and day, Sire." Kite spoke evenly, his thin mouth pressed into a tight line. Pale brown eyes stared past a beaky nose and long grey hair, plaited with charms and feathers, flowed down over the robes of Prime Mage. His cheeks and forehead bore faded tattoos which gave him a savage look, quite unlike his previous inconspicuous persona. Caniculus realised that now he'd taken over Bullfinch's office, there was no need for him to hide his true self and he clearly revelled in his outlandish appearance. As for Bullfinch, he'd most certainly been done away with.

The other two figures, both conventionally dressed as high ranking nobles, watched unblinkingly. Caniculus didn't recognise either of them, but his sixth sense screamed a warning. There was something inhuman about their stillness.

Marcus threw Kite a look of disgust.

"I knew there'd be trouble when we couldn't find it. How in Hades did it get to Londin?"

"We presume that it has its own way of doing things, Sire. It is a magical artefact, after all."

"I know it's a magical artefact!" Marcus's voice rose as he advanced on the Mage. "And now I'm going to have to go and pull it out of the bloody stone, aren't I? Suppose it won't let me?"

"It will, Sire," Kite replied, seemingly unfazed by all the drama. "We will announce that there will be a formal removal soon."

Marcus rolled his eyes and paced back and forth. "You're missing the point. What if I *can't* remove it?"

Kite looked smug. "You *will* pull the sword from the stone, Sire. In public."

The emphasis stopped Marcus in his tracks. He broke into a grin. "Then everybody will see that my claim is legitimate, not my father's. This will give us the excuse to bring everything forward and have the funeral immediately to get it out of the way. I take it you've arranged the details?"

Kite nodded. "The body has already been disposed of, Sire. Nobody will know."

"Good." From the look of relief on Marcus's face, Caniculus knew that he wouldn't want another chance for his cousin's corpse to accuse his murderer. Having a coffin filled with weights would solve the problem right there.

He turned to the silent watchers. "What have you got to report?"

One spoke. His voice carried a faint, unsettling echo inside the helmet and Caniculus shivered. He'd been right. Whatever this creature was, it wasn't born of woman.

"The first vessels are prepared, Sire. They await your command and a fair wind."

Marcus seized on his words. "Not all of them?"

"Alas, Sire, but we feel it better to make a cautious beginning. There is still opposition to your rule and, until this is dealt with, we must be careful."

Marcus clearly didn't like the answer, but he nodded. "We've come this far, so I suppose it would be foolish to take risks now. I agree. Make preparations."

The creatures bowed and Marcus waved a hand to dismiss them. Caniculus watched as the pair glided away into the foyer. Even their movements seemed unnatural. Meanwhile, Marcus had turned to Kite.

"What of the Collegium?"

"Dealt with. Those who would not join us, even with inducements, are imprisoned or dead. Some may yet come to their senses, but the ones who don't will share Bullfinch's fate."

"And Favonius?"

"He's gone. We think he escaped to Gaul, but we've found a successor. Any missing Agents are being rounded up as I speak."

"Good. I'll leave it to you. What of these mad Priests spouting off in the streets?"

Kite shrugged. "They'll be irrelevant when the people find they have new Gods to worship. The foreigners' power will wither and die and the Twelve will be forced to retreat back to the continent. In the meantime, your rule will be consolidated, our friends can reveal themselves and the new era will begin."

The Mage's absolute confidence seemed to reassure Marcus.

"What do we do with my father and his fleet? I hear they're gathering off Sillina."

Kite's smile grew wider. "And yours is preparing to meet them. They have few Mages. We have many, plus a Flagship with special armaments and something to fight for. Should he decide to rebel, he doesn't stand a chance."

"Excellent. Sort it out, including the matter of that blasted Sword." As Kite bowed and turned to leave, Marcus added, "Oh, and see to the slaves, will you?"

"As you command, Sire. They will remember nothing."

A flick of his fingers and Caniculus felt a wave of Potentia wash through the room. It broke on the helmet like a collapsing wave, leaving him unaffected, and he released the breath he'd been holding. Mortal Potentia wasn't up to Divine standards, for which he was incredibly grateful. Now he understood why the Gods had ordered him here; this wasn't just a matter for mortals.

Olympus was gearing up for war.

He watched as Marcus threw himself on to the throne and stared into the distance. Caniculus left him there, retracing his steps and cursing his stupidity. He had to report back to Milo and check on his family immediately.

*

The coast of Ennor was filling up with craft of all shapes and sizes now. Word had trickled out that this was where Pendragon was, and his allies were coming to his aid, not all of them Ships. Maia counted several inanimates, their crews prepared to risk everything to support their King. A cold, inner part of her scrutinised them carefully – should any Ship be forced to detach, taking one of these vessels could be an option. Not ideal, to be sure, but better than being totally helpless. Channels of Potentia would have to be forced, but the wood could be bent to their will.

She turned her mind away from the horrific scenes of destruction she had witnessed through the *Augusta*'s eyes. The thought that it might be Britannic Ships who could be smashed to pieces by their own sisters wasn't to be borne, and she could only hope that the others felt the same way.

She focused on the Mage quarters, where Raven had entered and was speaking to Polydorus. Maia immediately eavesdropped.

"...on your guard. If there are any spies aboard, this would be an ideal time for them to show their hand. Use the device."

The Greek nodded, his dark eyes filled with worry.

"I shall do so. I have it here with me." The man patted his tunic and Maia caught a glimpse of something circular through the material. Some sort of amulet? Maybe it was similar to the one that had enabled Milo to fight off Lapwing's paralysis spell.

"Good."

"Do you require anything further, Master?"

"No, no. Go and eat. You won't have time later when the place is swarming with Northmen and the Gods know who else. We shall all have to be on our best behaviour."

Polydorus pursed his lips and disappeared off to the galley to find provisions, leaving the Master Mage standing alone in the cabin.

"I know you're listening in, Maia."

She formed her Shipbody on the bulkhead and folded her arms. "And if I wasn't, I'd have been alerted when you called to me."

He grinned wickedly. "I win, either way. So, are you ready for this evening?"

She pulled a face. "It has to be done, I suppose. Poor Julia. Who's going to tell her?"

Raven tilted his head, one cloudy eye fixed unerringly on her position. "Her uncle, of course. Do you think he's the sort of man to let somebody else weather the storm?"

She bit her lip. "No. He'll tell her. How will she take it?"

He took a deep breath. "Equably, I think. It's hardly going to happen immediately. Running Marcus's inevitable blockade will come first. How many Ships are on our side?"

She ran through each name for him, starting with the Royals. He grimaced. "Not nearly enough, unless some remain impartial and I can't see that happening when their crews are in danger."

Maia agreed with him. She wouldn't have been able to stand by and watch her men being hanged either.

"What other options do they have?"

He shook his head. "I don't know. I've put certain things in motion, which I hope will benefit us, but there are worrying signs. Tell me, how did you find Ceridwen?"

The sudden change of subject took her aback for an instant.

"The High Priestess of the Mother?"

"Yes."

Maia thought carefully.

"*Blossom* told me to ask you about her."

"Why?"

"Ceridwen didn't exactly hinder me, but she did say that I could stay in the forest and become a Priestess. I knew I couldn't and I assumed that it was all part of the trials. There has to be temptation, hasn't there?"

There was something about his intentness that was a little alarming. What did he know?

"Did *Blossom* mention her daughter?"

"The girl that failed. She didn't want to become a Ship and shouldn't have been forced."

"You're right, but there were good reasons at the time."

Maia glared at him. "Really? Well that worked out well, didn't it?"

He crossed to a table and poured himself some wine.

"True."

"What happened to her?"

He took a swallow. "Lost in the forest. Nobody knows her fate for sure."

What wasn't he telling her? "You doubt her loyalty? What could she do?"

Even as she asked him, Maia remembered that the High Priestess had access to the Grove of the Mother. "She wouldn't exhume our bodies, would she?"

"No, no," Raven assured her. "That would be defying the Mother and she wouldn't dare do that. The *Livia* was an exception. Also, Ships are sacred and there aren't enough of you as there is."

"What, then?"

"Oh, I don't know. I think I'm getting paranoid in my old age. I saw a change in her after her daughter was taken that's all, and I haven't heard from her lately."

"Perhaps she's keeping out of it," Maia proposed. "I would. She'll want to keep her people safe until all this is sorted out."

"That must be it," he said, rallying himself. "I expect she was just testing you." He switched the subject again. "Are you ready for the Northmen – and women?"

She decided to let the previous subject drop. "I think the women are scarier than the men. Ambassador Gudrun is remarkable."

"Oh yes. Don't underestimate them. Have you spoken to the Longship?"

Maia remembered the strange Sending from the *Wolf of the Waves*.

"Sort of. It was all emotion and intent. No words. I haven't tried communicating back. I could tell he was curious about me." She laughed. "He did everything but sniff my stern!"

Raven smiled. "You're new so he'll want to learn about you. You should try talking to him the same way, though I don't recommend actually sniffing. Think of sniffing!"

She tutted at him. "Really! I'm not a dog – or a wolf."

"Pretend." His grin widened. He was enjoying himself now.

"Perhaps I should throw back my head and start howling?"

"Or grunting. Or roaring. Seriously, practise talking to him. He's very old and very wise. He's seen more than any Britannic Ship living, and we want to get him and his fellows on our side. With any luck, we'll be working with them soon."

Maia considered the prospect. "Or fighting them, if they decide to throw in their lot with Marcus. Do you think he'll be able to pull out the sword, like Artorius Magnus did?"

Raven shrugged. "A murderer who has lost the favour of the Gods? I sincerely hope not."

"The Olympian Gods. We both know there are others."

His smile vanished. "I know," he said softly, "and some that were once worshipped as such. Keep praying that the new ones are stronger and the old Powers don't return."

"And if they do?"

"Then it'll be time for you to seek other shores, and pray they don't follow."

V

Caniculus was just coming to within sight of home, when he spotted Silo lurking in a doorway. This meant trouble. He ducked into an alley, making sure he was unobserved before removing the helmet and wrapping it in a piece of cloth he'd kept with him for that purpose. His cousin spotted him the second he emerged and beckoned him over.

"Thank the Gods!" Silo's face was flushed. "Three polismen are looking for you, plus some other man we think's one of your lot. Pa sent me to try and catch you."

A lead weight dropped into Caniculus's stomach. "What did you say?"

"That you were here, but you'd gone, we didn't know where. It was too risky to say otherwise." His cousin's blue eyes fixed imploringly on his face. "What do you want us to do?"

"You know nothing."

Silo's face crumpled. "It's to do with the King, isn't it?"

Caniculus grimaced. "As I said. It's too dangerous." He was struck by a sudden horrible thought. "Did they search?"

"Yes, but they were just looking for you. I legged it out the back while Pa and Auntie distracted them."

Caniculus swore. They'd be bound to have the place under surveillance now. He'd thought he might have had more time. "Look," he said. "Have you any money on you?"

Silo dug around in his pockets and pulled out a handful of coppers. "A bit."

"Good. Go and buy something, anything. You were sent out on an errand. Act surprised if they're still there when you get back. And remember…"

"I know nothing."

"Right. Off you go. Don't worry about me. Tell Ma and the family I'll be fine."

Silo opened his mouth to object, but Caniculus gave him a shove. "Go on! And don't look back!"

The younger man gulped, then set off walking purposefully towards a baker's shop, leaving Caniculus fearing for his family's safety. He was consoled by the fact that they couldn't have anything concrete on him. He'd gone to ground as soon as he'd witnessed the murders at the villa and dropped out of sight, but his continued absence would have made them suspicious by now.

He waited for a couple of minutes, but it appeared that Silo hadn't been spotted and followed, so he popped on the helmet once more and allowed the crowds to carry him back towards home. As he arrived, voices drifting out through the huge double gates stopped him in his tracks.

"...already told you. He was here, but he left at first light."

That was Baro. Another voice answered him and Caniculus felt his hackles rise.

"So you say. Did he speak of where he was going?"

"He's an Agent, as you well know. We don't ask and he doesn't tell."

His uncle was standing hands on hips facing a man Caniculus knew as Foxy. Except it wasn't. He didn't know how he knew, but something was off. Some inner voice was screaming at him that something else was there, wearing Foxy's face like a Saturnalia mask. Perhaps it was the helmet warning him, as the disguise was clearly enough to fool everybody else.

Three polismen came out of the building, followed by an irate Valentina.

"Just this woman and some kids, sir," one reported.

'Foxy' stared at Baro for a while longer. "If you see him, tell him to report in immediately. Believe me, it's in his – and your – best interests if he does."

"I'll tell him," his uncle replied, returning the stare. "Now, if you don't mind, I've got work to do if the King wants his animals ready in time for the Games."

A clanking of chains and a hissing roar issued from the nearby shed. The chimaera was getting restless. Caniculus bet that it smelt whatever was standing nearby.

The polismen twitched and looked to their leader, but he already was striding hurriedly away. So, whatever it was didn't like the thought of being too close to the hybrid? Interesting.

Caniculus filed that piece of information away for later. The polismen scuttled after the fake Foxy like eager ducklings. His uncle's mouth twisted into a sneer as he watched them go. Valentina went to stand at his side, her lips moving almost silently. Caniculus read her words with the skill of a trained Agent.

"I hope Silo managed to warn him."

Just then, his cousin strolled through the gate, a loaf tucked under his arm. Valentina opened her mouth to question him, but Baro gave her a warning nudge.

"Good lad! You got the bread then. Just in time for a snack."

He took his sister-in-law's arm and guided her back inside. Caniculus rested his head against the stone gate posts and cursed his own stupidity once more. The consolation was that his family was well-regarded and necessary to the King's plans – for now.

Satisfied that all was quiet, he crept across the yard and into the living quarters. Valentina was sitting at the table wringing her hands, whilst Baro and Silo tried to console her.

"Oh, I wish we were all here and Novius and the boys weren't at the amphitheatre! Are you sure he got the message?"

"Yes, Auntie," Silo said. "He'll be fine."

Caniculus forced himself to retreat out of the door. He'd already made what could have been one disastrous error. Another could prove fatal.

It was time to report in, then get back to work.

*

Maia guided her boats across the harbour. They contained various island worthies, including the local High Priest, the Prefect and a few landowners. All of them were delighted to be invited to dine with the King aboard his newest Ship, despite the threat of war being brought to their shores. It appeared that they had a lot of faith in the power of their resident Goddess to protect them should the worst happen.

"It wouldn't surprise me if the whole archipelago has hidden protections," Raven told her. She turned to look at him, surprised that he was on deck, instead of waiting with the King below.

"What are you doing up here?"

He leaned on his staff. "It's easier to think up here. I hate to be confined. There'll be no escape for the next few hours when's everyone's on their best behaviour and trying to resist the urge to knife each other under the table."

She couldn't help but smile. "Isn't that what diplomacy is? Talk first and hopefully not kill anybody?"

He snorted. "I suppose so. How's our friend the *Wolf?*"

"I've not sniffed or howled, yet. I still don't see how I'm supposed to talk to him though, when he's so alien."

Raven raised an eyebrow. "*You* should be able to talk to anything. Try."

She scowled at him. "It's bad enough talking to the *Imperatrix*. She's in a snit because Pendragon's not aboard her."

"She's in for a long wait, then. He can't stand her."

Maia giggled before she could stop herself. "Really?"

"Oh yes. He knows what she's like. He knows all his Ships after nearly forty years of thinking about little else. There's no way he would ever choose her as his Flagship and the sooner she comes to terms with that, the better. The only person who doesn't realise that is her. Believe it or not, the *Justicia* is worse."

"I haven't had much to do with her either," Maia admitted. "Perhaps it's just as well and anyway, she's on the other side." She decided to change the subject. "Talking of the others, have you heard anything else?" she asked him.

"About?"

"Anything. Marcus, the Fae."

"Only whispers. I know that the Gods are speaking out against Marcus, but people are disappearing up and down the country. Any opposition is being dealt with and those who swear fealty to him are being lavishly rewarded. It's a bad combination. There are those who don't give a fig who sits on the throne so long as they profit by it."

Maia thought back to her own miserable life as an indentured servant. Had it mattered to her who ruled? She'd have been in the same position no matter what and couldn't have cared less.

"That's true," she admitted. "Still, when the Gods speak, people do well to listen or everyone suffers."

"That's the way of it, especially with the Olympians. They're, shall we say, direct in their dealings, but that's the Greeks and

Romans for you. All straight lines, see, regimented and proper. Black and white. Civilised and barbarian. But this is Britannia. Here there are borderlands, spaces between the light and the dark where old powers lurk and the Gods are not so easily swayed. You've been in a couple of those places yourself."

"The Grove of the Mother?"

"That's one. The Forest at the Heart of Albion."

"That's why you're worried about Ceridwen," she blurted out. "You think she'll ally herself with these old powers."

Raven stared blindly ahead, his face shadowed against the lamplight.

"It's possible. Speak nothing of this."

The boats had reached her flanks now and it was time to welcome her guests.

"What will we do if she turns against us?"

His voice was a whisper in the growing darkness.

"Don't be afraid, Maia. We have allies of our own."

She was about to demand more information when Leo's voice came over their link.

<*Tempest*. Is everything ready?>

<Aye, Captain. The Sillinians are coming aboard now, then it will be the Ambassador's turn.>

Raven had already set off to take his place at the King's side and she watched him go, a frail figure swathed in his grey robe. What wasn't he telling her? She supposed she'd find out soon enough.

Maia switched part of her attention to below decks, where Julia was preparing to take her position at her uncle's side. A gracious expression was already fixed to the royal features, though Maia knew that inside she was seething. She had to admire the Princess's poise and elegance, no doubt instilled over many years of training.

Latonia lifted the heavy tiara, set with winking diamonds and huge, lustrous pearls on to the carefully-arranged hairstyle. More jewels adorned her fingers and throat, as befitted the only female of the line of Artorius Magnus. Her dowry alone would give King Harald an incentive to give her sanctuary.

Maia switched her attention to Pendragon, as Milo appeared at the door of his cabin.

"Sire, I've news," he called. The expression on his face left Maia in no doubt that it wasn't good news, either.

"In here." Pendragon led the way to a smaller cabin. "What have you heard?"

"Caniculus has reported back, Sire. He observed Marcus meeting with others in the palace. Kite is Prime Mage now and controls the Collegium. Favonius has fled, so the Agents are compromised. There were two others there that he swears weren't human and he thinks that they're using shapeshifters."

"And the Sword?"

"They're planning on having the Usurper remove it."

Pendragon looked thoughtful. "Surely they know he won't be able to?"

"He appears to think it's a certainty, Sire. They also have intelligence as to our position and are gathering their forces. Fae vessels are standing by, probably to transport their forces across from Hibernia, but they're not rushing. Several are definitely prepared to sail."

A quiet knock heralded Raven's appearance. Milo quickly repeated the information.

"We should stay clear of the Britannic Ocean, Sire," the Master Mage offered immediately. "Marcus's forces would overwhelm us. We must draw out his supply chain to its limit."

The King grimaced. "And ours, too, though you're right that we'll have more support in the West. What do you suggest?"

"It's unlikely that we can stop the Fae vessels, but we must prepare to meet the enemy fleet and I'd prefer it to be at a site of our own choosing."

"I'll think on it. In the meantime we have to get this evening over with. If necessary, I'll send my niece to the Alliance immediately, under promise of safe conduct."

"She could go to ground in Kernow," Raven replied. "I have contacts there."

Pendragon compressed his lips, undecided. "We'll see what the Ambassador suggests. It would be fatal if they threw in with the Usurper whilst she was held by them. I know there's the risk of her being used as a bargaining chip whatever happens, but this seems the safest option we have left and I refuse to believe that

Marcus can remove the Sword. I favour your last suggestion, if Harald says no. We can keep Gaul as an option too."

"Very wise, Sire."

<Tempest,> Leo Sent. <Tell the King that the Sillinians are waiting to meet him and the Northerners aren't far behind.>

Maia thanked her Captain.

"Sire," she said aloud. "Everyone's ready."

Pendragon took a deep breath and adjusted his robe. He looked every inch a king, Maia thought, though she could tell he'd rather be wearing his usual naval uniform.

"Let's get this over with, then we'll sail with the morning tide."

He exited, returning to the Great Cabin and the waiting dignitaries with a show of regal confidence that belied the dread that Maia knew he was feeling inside.

*

The banquet seemed to be going well. Maia was on constant alert for anything untoward, as were Osric and his marines, fully-armed and scanning the horizon. The sun had sunk away to the west, leaving only the tiniest line of pale light before that, too, disappeared into darkness. Maia had ignited her lamps and was comforted by her sisters' answering gleams bobbing across the inky water. All of them were more subdued than normal, fearful of what the coming days would bring and there was none of the usual light-hearted banter and gossip that they usually shared. Even the *Imperatrix* had fallen silent for once. Maia was obliging them by relaying the banquet for those who wanted to see through her eyes.

<Patience to *Tempest.>* A little voice sounded across the link, the range pitched for her ears alone.

<Tempest here,> she replied quietly.

<Nobody's talking,> her friend said wistfully. <How's it going at your end?>

<Oh, they're all busy eating and drinking,> Maia answered. <The real discussions will happen when the King and the Ambassador withdraw, which should happen shortly. They've a lot to talk about.>

<So, we sail in the morning. Any clue where we're headed?>
<No. I think the King will tell us at the last minute, so that word doesn't get out. The Gods alone know how many spies there are here.>

Patience was shocked. <Surely they've all been rooted out?> Maia had to disagree. <I wouldn't bet on it. Marcus has to be getting his information from somewhere and it isn't possible to interrogate everybody. It could even be one of the Northerners, or someone here on the islands. There are always folk ready to make money that way.>

<Even at the risk of getting caught?>

<Oh yes. Did you know that some Fae can change shape?>

<No, really? The Gods can, of course. They love to appear as mere mortals.>

Maia thought of how many times she'd been fooled by Mercury and couldn't help but agree.

<You're right there. It's a horrible thought, but I know that Raven can tell, so perhaps your Mage can too. I don't think they'd get away with it here, but on land who knows? We'll have to make our move soon. Have you got all the provisions you need?>

<Mostly, though we could all do with more powder and shot. There wasn't much on the islands – or not enough for all of us, so we'll have to find another source.>

<And that means a larger port. I doubt we'll go east.> Maia pulled up a mental map of the country. There were the forts at the mouth of the Fal in Kernow, but that would mean heading back into danger. <If I were the King,> she said, slowly, <I'd head up the northern coast, towards Abona and the mouth of the River Sabrina. There's not much there, for sure, but we'd be in striking distance of the Silurian coast and the supplies they could provide.>

<But nearer to the Fae.> *Patience* objected.

<All the better to intercept them if necessary, though I think they'd land further west.>

Every scrap of myth and legend she'd ever read was whirling in her head as she sought to make some sense of it. The trouble was that nobody remembered the last great battles, not even her ancient Mage. All the ones that fought the Fae were long dead

102

and much of their knowledge with them, despite what various chroniclers had written. That oversight was returning to bite them now. Had their ancestors really thought that the Fae were gone forever? Probably. Arrogance was one thing the old Romans had had in vast quantities.

<I hope you're right and we don't meet up with them. I wonder what weapons their vessels have. Not cannon, surely. They can't stand iron.>

<They'll probably rely on magic,> Maia told her, grimly, <but I'll ask Raven. I expect he'll know.>

<What's really worrying me is the thought that we might have to face our sisters,> *Patience* admitted. <I can't believe that Ships will fire on Ships. Surely it won't come to that. They can't make us fight if we refuse and I don't see how they can support Marcus.>

She was right. It was against everything they believed in and had trained for.

<We'll have to wait and see,> Maia replied. She signed off, regretting the fact that they had no good news to share, but all the while, a little thought was hovering at the back of her mind like a persistent itch.

Were the other Ships really prepared to turn on their own sisters?

*

Naturally, there were speeches.

Julia ate little. It was her job to promote her uncle's cause by being gracious and charming to the prominent locals, whilst all the while keeping an eye on the Alliance Ambassador. Gudrun's piercing eyes were weighing her up, much as a cautious farmer checked his livestock though Julia had to admit that the woman was discreet in her observations. Her shadow, who had been introduced as Bodil, daughter of Hild, had taken up position behind her mistress's seat where she had a good view of proceedings.

Julia didn't quite know how to take the two women, though a part of her was grateful that her fate wouldn't be decided solely by men, even though her uncle and the distant King Harald would have the final say. A small part of her wished that she'd been born in the Northern lands, where women were valued for much more than the advantages they could bring to their family. Empire custom and practice meant that they were largely seen as potential wives and mothers. She'd have liked to walk the streets freely, weapons at her hip and with the knowledge that she was free to use them. Instead, she couldn't remember a day when she hadn't been constantly reminded of her exalted position and her duty to the Crown.

She upbraided herself, whilst putting on an attentive face as a local Senator droned on about yearly yields. She had tasted freedom, however briefly, when she'd been Little Owl. It had made such a change to be respected for her abilities, rather than for which family she belonged to. She quelled the sudden urge to wave a hand and have the dishes before her erupt into the air.

"Thus as you see, Highness, our profits have increased lately with the expansion of our port facilities and the increasing trade to the New Continent."

The Senator paused for breath, a satisfied expression spreading over his features like oil.

"I am *so* pleased to hear this, Senator," Julia answered, her fantasy evaporating. "Please be assured that His Majesty intends this to continue. He will defend your ancient trading rights and privileges in this area."

The man nodded, but Julia sensed his uncertainty. It was obvious that they had his full support for the moment. It was hard to argue otherwise when a heavily-armed battle fleet was anchored on your doorstep. When they sailed it might be a different prospect, but that problem would have to wait. If she'd been in his position she'd have been cautious too, as her cousin currently had the advantage and everybody knew it. It was a relief when her uncle struck up a conversation about harbour taxes.

When Gudrun turned to her, she was ready.

"Trade is our lifeblood," the woman observed.

Julia knew that this was yet another test she had to pass.

"Indeed, Ambassador. It is in all our interests to nurture it and I am aware of the consequences to both our peoples should it be disrupted."

Disruption was the least that would happen if Marcus had his way. Britannia would be torn from the rest of the Empire, there would be a mass exodus as people fled the Fae and the land would be plunged back into savagery. The ancient Romans had thought it to be the Land of the Dead, shrouded in mist and barely accessible – *Terra incognita*, like the interior of the New Continent, haunted by strange monsters and Gods that fed on blood and death.

"You favour this marriage proposal, then?" Gudrun asked her.

"I favour whatever supports my people in the face of this danger," she replied. It was an interesting question. Gudrun would surely know that she would obey her uncle.

"Of course." The Ambassador inclined her head. Julia decided to go on the offensive.

"Tell me of King Harald. I hear his father, King Haarkon, was a man of great renown as a warrior."

"Indeed," Gudrun replied smoothly. "King Harald is mighty, as was his father, though these times are more peaceful and he has only lately come into his crown. He is a wise ruler and generous to his friends."

So far Gudrun was only saying what was expected. He could be the most feckless ruler in history and she would shower him with compliments, though Julia knew that the man had a brain in his head, having negotiated the peace treaty that benefitted his people.

"I hear he is a man of middle years."

"He is forty-six and in the prime of life. Young Prince Haarkon is the same age as you, an excellent son and a credit to his ancestors."

That remained to be seen. Julia shied away from the thought of a lusty young man and concentrated on the present.

"And if my uncle and King Harald approve the match?"

Gudrun smiled. "Then, Highness, you should be wed as soon as possible. Be assured that, whatever the outcome of this contest, you will be treated with the respect due your rank."

What she meant was that the soft and helpless little princess mustn't be afraid of the big bad Northerners. Also, any child of hers would have a claim to the throne of Britannia.

"I would expect nothing less," Julia replied, allowing a little steel into her voice. There was a flicker of acknowledgement in the woman's eyes.

"It seems that we understand each other, Highness."

"I'm sure we do."

And, Lady Ambassador, you have absolutely no idea what I am capable of.

*

Maia had taken up position against a bulkhead, on the King's orders. He wanted his Ship visible to all, so she'd had to break her usual rule of being absent during meal times, something she thought she'd inherited from *Blossom*. There were twenty guests, all dressed in their best clothes, busy talking, drinking and picking at the dishes on offer. In deference to the space, they were seated on chairs rather than reclining on couches, with the King at the head of the long table.

The Princess and the Ambassador were sitting opposite one another and it seemed like there was some verbal sparring going on. Maia listened in, quietly chortling to herself at the Ambassador's words. They were clearly designed to calm a nervous bride, but she rather thought that they were only succeeding in putting Julia's back up.

<That woman doesn't know what she's getting poor Prince Haarkon into,> she Sent to Raven, who was also listening in from his place further down the table.

<And I'm praying that she'll keep it to herself, unless forced otherwise,> Raven replied.

<Wouldn't her Potentia be an advantage to her children?> Maia asked him. <It might reduce the dowry.>

Raven chewed thoughtfully.

<It would endanger her further. If her abilities became common knowledge, Marcus would stop at nothing to try to kill her a second time. If he thinks she's helpless, she has a chance to be used as a game piece in the future.>

<If he has a future," Maia said, loyally. <The crew are placing bets as to the day the Admiral pulls the sword out of the stone. Nobody thinks Marcus will do it.>

106

<Being seen to do it is as important as actually doing it,> Raven retorted.

<But if he removes it from the Forum, isn't that admitting that his claim is false?>

<We'll have to wait and see.>

Something was unsettling the ancient Mage, but she knew that it would be fruitless to press him further. She watched him enviously as he helped himself to some candied fruit. She still missed eating.

<I think we'll be ordered north,> she told him. He raised an eyebrow in her direction.

<We are somewhat backed into a corner here,> he agreed. <Running to the New Continent is out of the question and the ports to the east will be blockaded. We need to put some distance between us and the renegades but we can't allow ourselves to be boxed in. He might aim for Abona, where we can get supplies, then take us back into open water. Alas, I fear we're only postponing the inevitable.>

Maia regarded him, glad that her Shipbody precluded physical feelings of nausea.

<Surely the Gods themselves will openly condemn him?>

<Who knows? If they're going to do something, they'd better do it quickly. They have the whole of the Empire and beyond to concern them, not just this small group of islands. Don't put your faith in Divine intervention, Maia.>

<It's not like you to give up so easily!> she shot back at him.

<I'm just being realistic. Speaking of Gods, have you heard from your sister lately?>

Maia had to admit that she hadn't.

<No, but I hope she'll pass by soon.>

<Well, if you see her, tell her to keep watch for trouble from the east. There's no point in having an advantage if you don't press it.>

<I'll do my best.>

The event was coming to a close and Maia was ordered to ready the boats. The King seemed satisfied, thanking each guest personally, but nobody was fooled.

The coming days would be the turning point and if Pendragon didn't prevail, everybody knew he was doomed.

*

Eventually, the guests departed and peace reigned once more, Maia was doing the customary check of her vessel after the change of watch, when the strange stillness in her second-in-command's cabin drew her in. Sabrinus was sitting motionless at his desk, staring at the bulkhead. Writing materials lay scattered around, as if he'd started a letter then abandoned it to fix on something unseen.

After a couple of minutes she became concerned as he showed no inclination to move, nor had he called his servant to ready him for sleep.

"Sabrinus," she whispered He started, blinked and ran a hand over his face.

"Yes, *Tempest*? Am I required?"

Of course he would ask that. He was nothing if not conscientious, but the serious young man had turned into one driven by an almost fanatical approach to his duty and Maia had to admit to herself that she was worried about him. Asking to be referred to by his last name was only part of the guilt he carried for his father's betrayal. She hastened to reassure him.

"No. I was just a bit worried about you. Are you feeling well?"

She tried to put it as tactfully as she could, not wishing to cause him to lose face. Still, if he couldn't talk to her, who could he talk to? Sabrinus swallowed, clearing his throat.

"I'm fine. Just a little tired, that's all." He glanced down at the mess on his desk and smiled without mirth. "I was going to write some letters, then I remembered that I don't really have anyone to write to. I don't know who's on which side anymore."

His head drooped a little, before he remembered his rank and straightened up.

"You need to sleep," she insisted and he nodded.

"I wish I could, but I can't stop thinking about everything. Now my father and Tullia are both traitors I feel somehow adrift, as if cast away in an open boat."

"You have us," she reminded him. "You have me."

She partially emerged from the wood to face him.

"I have my duty. I think it's the only thing keeping me going."

"Both the King and your Captain think very highly of you," she said. "I think you should talk to Leo. He's been betrayed too, you know. Artorius was his best friend."

"I always knew my father was ambitious." Sabrinus's face clouded. "He chose me above my mother, did you know that? She had difficulties during my birth and he ordered the Adepts to save me, whatever the cost. He was desperate for a son. Tullia is my half-sister from his second wife, Lavinia. My stepmother's as ruthless and ambitious as my father and I expect she's pushing him on to ever-greater heights of treachery."

So, Tullia was only his half-sister. It explained a lot. Maia had the feeling that young Sabrinus hadn't had a particularly happy childhood, with his mother dead and a stepmother whose sole intention was to supplant him in his father's affections. She knew from personal experience that Admiral Albanus was a persuasive and wily operator, always several moves ahead in the game.

"Your father might not know everything that's going on," she answered. Sabrinus snorted.

"Don't you believe it! He'll have been in it from the start, head down and plotting with Marcus and his evil cohorts. I was offered my own Ship, did you know that? I could have gone straight to Post-Captain and it was only when I threatened to leave the Navy altogether that I got this position. I wouldn't serve under Silvius either. I never liked the man. In a way I pity my sister, having to cope with him."

"He seems like a cold fish," Maia agreed.

"That's only the half of it. He'll be only too happy to back up the Usurper on the promise of the return of ancestral lands that King Julius took off his grandfather."

"Everyone seems to have been promised something."

"That's how they work. I've seen enough of it, even though I've been at sea for over ten years now. I was the youngest midshipman in the fleet. My father was so desperate for my promotion that he couldn't wait to be rid of me."

He focused on her face, his eyes fixed earnestly on hers.

"You mustn't doubt my loyalty. I know what some of the crew are muttering behind my back, that I'm my father's son and must be reporting to him. I swear I'm not."

"I know you're not," she hastened to say, "but you should really talk to somebody."

She checked the Captain's cabin. Leo was still up, reading at his desk in his shirtsleeves. Honestly, did none of her senior officers intend to sleep tonight?

Sabrinus spread his hands, helplessly. "What can I say? 'Please believe me, I'm not a traitor?'"

Maia quietly opened the link to Leo.

<Captain. Sabrinus needs to talk to you. Now would be good.>

Leo answered immediately. <I'll come to you.>

He threw on his coat. "Victor? Fetch me the brandy and get yourself to bed. I may be some time." His servant obliged.

"Nobody believes you're a traitor, Sabrinus. You're an excellent officer and would be a dutiful son, if your father was worthy of the title."

The knock was subtle. Sabrinus shot her a puzzled look.

"Enter."

Leo's head appeared. "No, don't get up." He waved the bottle. "Have a drink with me. *Tempest*, you can stand down now."

She withdrew quietly. She'd done all she could, but she'd have to keep a very close eye on her first officer over the coming days. Truly, Albanus didn't deserve the young man, just as Pendragon didn't deserve his slimy offspring. If only they'd been switched at birth!

She sighed at the vagaries of fate and went to keep Drustan company during his watch.

The next morning brought an overcast sky and a persistent drizzle that shrouded the islands in a cloud of mist. The crews of each Ship went about their duties with a subdued air as they readied themselves to weigh anchor and set sail. Even the usual chatter on the Ship link had stilled, as everybody waited to see what the new day would bring.

Maia watched the activity aboard her counterpart as he made ready for departure. The Longship had taken the chance to resupply, even as they had. The islanders would be busy making money and already various small merchant vessels had been drawn to their location, lured in by the prospect of quick sales. Leo and Sabrinus were on deck supervising preparations, their coats covered by oilskins and collars turned up against the wet. Raindrops pattered from their hats as they tilted their heads. Neither seemed much the worse for their late night and Maia fancied that Sabrinus seemed a little more at ease.

"They'll want to make money while they can," he remarked. "Though they'll be happy to sell to both sides."

"Profit is king," Leo observed, "and always will be. There won't be much call for luxury goods at this rate. Everything's going to Hades."

Sabrinus nodded. Maia was relieved that her swift action had had a positive effect and brought the two young men closer together. Pendragon, too, had taken a special interest in the young officer, both men brought together by the treachery of the ones closest to them.

"I wish to the Gods that he'd been my son," the King had confided to Raven, with only Maia as witness. "That faithless wretch Albanus doesn't deserve him."

"We cannot choose our parents, or offspring," Raven had replied and Maia knew that he was thinking about his own parents, fooled long ago into thinking that their son was dead, instead of hideously transformed and cursed with longevity beyond the lot of ordinary mortals.

She hadn't been able to do much for the Princess either, though Julia was putting a brave face on the situation. Meanwhile, Leo was scanning the water as if searching for something.

"Looking for somebody?" Maia asked her Captain, innocently. He lowered the telescope and regarded her before his face broke into a rueful smile.

"I can't keep anything from you, can I?"

Maia grinned at him. <Well, sir, I would have been remiss in my duty if I hadn't noticed the presence of a certain Lady aboard very late indeed last night, though I have to admit that she was most discreet.>

Leo flashed her a grin. "A gentleman never tells."

It was true that Sillina had slipped aboard like a shadow, not leaving until first light.

<As long as you don't fall asleep on watch,> she Sent, archly. <Did you get any sleep at all?>

111

<Who, me? I'm indefatigable!>

Maia refrained from comment, contenting herself with exchanging knowing looks with Sabrinus, who'd certainly got the gist of the conversation even if he couldn't be party to it. It broke the tension and she was glad of it, especially when she heard Pendragon talking to his niece.

"It's agreed. You're to marry Prince Haarkon at the earliest opportunity."

Julia regarded her uncle steadily. The time for tears and complaints were over and both of them knew it.

"How am I to get to Norvegia?"

"You'll leave with the Ambassador aboard the *Wolf of the Waves*. He'll see you there safely. We'll accompany you as far as we can, but then you'll continue north as we move eastwards up the Sabrina to Abona."

"I'll make ready," Julia replied and Maia instantly knew that she had to make more of an effort to contact the Longship. She concentrated her thoughts and found the channel that he'd used before.

<*Tempest* to *Wolf of the Waves*.>

The reply was immediate as his presence entered her mind, together with the accompanying sensations of alertness. She could almost see the wise old eyes and lolling tongue as he grinned back.

Black paws skimming white wave crests. So that was how he thought of himself. She replied in kind.

Dark clouds, stormy sea, jagged lightning. A burst of surprised approval greeted the image.

<Greetings to you,> he responded.

So he could use words. It had been some kind of test, and apparently she'd passed.

<Greetings, ancient one.> *A great tree, hoary with age.*

<You are very young,> he replied. *An oak sapling thrusting up through the forest floor towards the light.* It made her smile at the contrast.

<I am indeed.> She added a tiny raincloud above it, watering the little tree.

<Just so. I am to take your Princess to my King in Norvegia.>

The image of a lean man in the prime of life appeared in her mind, a gold circlet embedded with jewels resting on his fair hair, and she knew that it was Harald. Behind him, high mountains fell abruptly to the sea.

She paused, but he continued. *Julia guarded by a great black wolf.* <I will care for her. She will marry the Prince and have many sons and daughters.>

Maia Sent agreement, quashing any doubts she may have had, adding children to the picture. Some had fair hair and some black.

<I wish them both long life and happiness.>

<As do I.> She had the sensation of a wet nose pushed against her in friendship. That was definitely sniffing, so she responded in kind, whilst reminding herself never to tell Raven. As they touched noses, she Sent *sunlight on calm seas.*

<I wish this to be true,> *Wolf of the Waves* answered, <but I know this.>

Dark skies, rough water. Maia could smell smoke and hear the battle cries of warriors as cannons spoke and wood splintered. It was something the Longship knew all too well.

<Kill the evil ones!> *Wolf of the Waves* told her fiercely. <Destroy your enemies!> *Bodies floating amid the blood. A surge of triumph and shattered hulks sinking to the depths.* <Fight with honour!>

She felt her courage crystallise at his words, answering with an image of her Shipbody, storm in one hand and sword in the other, bearing down on her enemies.

His howl rose into her mind, echoing through their bond and beyond, summoning others whose wild snorting, neighing and roaring admitted her into the company of the Northern Fleet as they banded together in support. A surge of emotion swept over her and she found herself answering with a crack of thunder that rolled over the distance between them.

The cacophony fell away at last into silence. Maia knew that another thread had been drawn out between them, this one consisting of scales, fur and hair woven into a sturdy braid for her to call upon. The Althing, the Alliance equivalent of the Senate, might not have decided whether to support Pendragon, but the Longships abhorred the murder of the rightful king in such a cowardly and dishonourable way. She Sent a burst of gratitude and respect that they should allow her to partake in their hallowed bond, and felt their acknowledgement.

<You are different, not like the others,> *Wolf of the Waves* told her, his astonishment seeping over the link. <You understand? I have met many, many Ships before.>

As he spoke, a picture of the *Leopard*'s face appeared and she felt his admiration.

<She says you're an old enemy.> Maia made the face snarl, together with the familiar coughing growl.

<She hates me!> His laughter was contagious. <I'll show you. Hey! Big kitty!>

The *Leopard*'s acerbic tones broke into the link.

<What do you want, you disgusting smelly creature?>

The Longship's mirth only grew. <Beautiful kitty. So fierce. Admit that you love me!>

The Ship cursed at him. <In your dreams!>

<We sank each other!>

<And I'll do it again!> she snarled happily. <Savage!>

Wolf of the Waves yipped at her, beside himself with glee.

Maia quietly retreated, leaving them to their protestations of love and hate. She didn't know who was enjoying themselves more, lupine or feline.

<Oi, you two! Keep it down!>

Persistence's shout almost drowned out the noise.

<There they go again. Every time,> *Diadem* chipped in. <It's all "I hate him" until they actually meet up.>

Maia and the other Ships dissolved into laughter. Only the *Imperatrix* remained aloof, muttering to herself about 'impropriety', which was somehow even funnier.

<It's called fostering international relations!> *Unicorn* announced, which brought forth a spate of cheering and shouts of encouragement.

The crews of the Britannic Ships were carrying on as usual, but the Northmen were grinning and making lewd gestures. So, they had more of a link with their Ships. Perhaps it went both ways.

She truly did have a lot more to learn about the life of a Ship – or a Longship for that matter. Just as she was thinking about that, Raven cut into her thoughts. He sounded irritated.

<What's going on, Maia?>

She smiled to herself. <Oh, I'm just pressing my advantage like you told me.>

<Humph!> He broke the link but, she reasoned, some things were definitely not for the ears of Mages. One thing was for sure; her dearly bought Power of Mind would have many more uses than she'd dreamed of if she could communicate with Longships as well, and in a language that they could understand.

*

Latonia fastened the heavy cloak over her mistress's shoulders, securing it with an elaborate gold and amber brooch, a gift from her intended father-in-law. Julia had accepted it graciously, along with half-a-dozen other small items that Gudrun had produced as tokens of the Norvegian King's regard. More gold and amber swung from her ears to form a matching set as she surveyed the cabin that had been her temporary home.

"I think that's it," she told Latonia. "Time to go, I suppose."

"Yes, Highness."

Truly, Latonia was a woman of few words, unlike her previous slave. She pushed the thought of the dead Melissa from her mind, knowing that she would be given more attendants on arrival at her new court. Her first duty there would be to practise her Nordic, though hopefully most of the nobles would speak Latin. The King and his son certainly would.

"Latonia, have you got enough warm clothes?" she asked. The woman looked startled for a second, as if unused to anyone asking after her welfare, then bobbed her head.

"Yes, Highness. Master Milo gave me these."

She went to a bundle and drew out a thick jacket and a cloak. Julia realised that she'd seen the clothing before. It made sense to re-use the items. Melissa certainly no longer had any use for them.

"Good." She made a mental note to thank the Agent for his kindness towards her maid and upbraided herself for not thinking of it first. Come to think of it, she knew hardly anything about Latonia, and would have bet on her being a traitor before Melissa. The betrayal still hurt, despite all her efforts to forget.

"Come on then. Let's see what a Longship is like, shall we?"

Part of her was quite to excited to find out, whilst the rest of her dreaded the end of her journey.

Latonia shot her a dubious look before following meekly out of the cabin and up to the deck, where Milo was waiting to accompany them. Her uncle had wanted to send marines, but Gudrun had refused. Two servants were all King Harald would permit and even then they might be sent back when she had been delivered. Julia would be expected to owe her allegiance to her husband and his people as soon as they were married. King Harald would not allow for possible spies in his new daughter's household.

She stepped forward, curtseying to her uncle, as Leo and his crew saluted. Danuco had already sacrificed to Juno, Neptune and Diana on her behalf, so the Olympians had hopefully been placated. There was no excuse for her stay any longer.

A haunting call sounded from the water and the Priest hurried up.

"The Lady Sillina is here, Sire. I suggest that the Princess offers gold as thanks for her hospitality."

Pendragon nodded and Leo directed two men to the replenished strongbox to fetch more tribute. The islands were small, but there were innumerable rocks and many dangers. In light of this, quite a few sailors had already made small offerings. The Goddess clearly enjoyed receiving gifts, so hadn't strayed far from the fleet.

"She's done well out of us," the King murmured to Leo, with a knowing look. The Captain tried to look innocent.

"Aye, Sire. She never lags behind when it comes to offerings."

"Of all sorts, it seems."

Pendragon's mouth twitched and Julia saw a hint of red creep up from the Captain's collar. She had to look away to stop herself bursting into laughter and didn't dare meet her uncle's eye. She wondered if the amorous Sillina had ever approached a young

Prince Cei as well; if so, she would have been sorely disappointed.

The crewmen returned, bearing a pouch of gold and a heavy chain; rich gifts for a useful ally that ensured that she would be well-disposed towards them in the future.

Julia took them and moved to the rail.

"Hail, O Sillina, Lady of the Islands," she called, her voice carrying over the water. "Please accept these offerings in thanks for your gracious hospitality!"

A head broke the surface, huge eyes staring upwards in anticipation, followed by a torso as the Goddess rose from the waves. Julia cast the gold in her direction, the shiny metal flashing through the air to land with tiny splashes and instantly swallowed by the green-grey ripples. Sillina dived to fetch them, emerging in a sheet of water. She ran the chain through her fingers, then looped it over her head.

"Your generous gifts are accepted," she called back, grinning. "In return, I will tell you that the other fleet is massing at Portum Meridianam."

Julia's stomach lurched. That was far too close and everyone knew it.

"We thank you, O beneficent one," she replied. Sillina's grin grew wider. More gold sparkled on her arms and Julia recognised Northern work. The Captain of the Longship had not been remiss in ingratiating himself either. Sillina had indeed benefitted from her offer of aid.

Sillina waved and blew them all a kiss, before once more descending into the deeps. Julia returned to her uncle's side for a final farewell.

This time, he kissed her, whispering, "I'm so proud of you." Then, for the ears of all, "Safe journey to your new husband. May the Gods smile on your union."

She forced back the tears as she gazed into his eyes, so like her own, wondering whether she'd ever see him again. To onlookers they would appear cold and distant, but now that her brother was gone and her cousin turned traitor, all they had left was each other.

"You will always have my love and loyalty, Sire," she said firmly.

"And you, mine," he assured her, his eyes full of warmth.

Everything suddenly seemed too vivid, as if each sense was stretched to its fullest. The grey sky, threatening rain; the cries of the seabirds. Even the gusty breeze on her cheek, sharp and smelling of salt and seaweed combined with the odour of tar and hemp from the vessel served to imprint this moment on her brain, as if suspended in time. Then she turned away and the feeling was gone.

As she passed *Tempest*'s Shipbody, Julia paused.

"Thank you for everything," she said. The Ship's black eyes fixed on hers.

"I wish you a safe journey, Highness." Then, the Ship's voice sounded privately in her ear.

"I'll do my best to look after him, don't you worry."

Julia gave her a little smile in return.

The crew cheered as she walked across to the *Wolf of the Waves*, her head held high. The Ambassador was waiting for her, along with a man she assumed was the Captain.

"Welcome aboard, Princess Julia Victoria," Gudrun said. "May I present Captain Thorgrim Ranulfson?"

The Captain bowed. His black beard was divided into plaits, as was his hair, though his eyes were the bright blue of cornflowers.

"Highness. My Ship and I will do everything in our power to protect you and give you a good voyage."

His Latin was good, if rougher than the Ambassador's, but she didn't doubt his sincerity. One cheek was marked with a tattoo and he wore a leather coat, the colour of oxblood, over a woollen tunic. Gold glinted at his neck.

"Thank you, Captain Ranulfson. My compliments to your Ship and crew."

"Please come with me and I will show you to your cabin," the Ambassador told her.

Julia forced herself not to take a last look at the deck of the *Tempest*, instead keeping her eyes firmly fixed on the Ambassador's back as the woman led the way below.

The first thing she noticed was the decorative carving. It looked as if the very wood of the vessel was alive, animals and foliage tumbling over and through each other in a riot of bright colours. *Wolf of the Waves* had a very different feel to the *Tempest*, as if his vessel had been grown from a seed rather than built.

"This is a much different vessel than you're used to," Gudrun said, guessing her thoughts, "but we hope you'll be comfortable."

Julia was glad when they came to an open door and what would be her home for the journey. It was about a third the size of the one she'd enjoyed on the *Tempest*, but bigger than Little Owl's quarters, so she couldn't complain. Her personal luggage was already stacked in a corner ready for Latonia to unpack, and the bed was hung ready. The small amount of dowry she had with her was stowed in the hold, with the promise that the rest would be delivered as soon as possible. She'd brought her own sheets, covers and pillows too, so there would be something familiar. Latonia scurried inside and began the task of making everything ready. Milo entered, cast his eye about and stood attentively to one side.

"I'll leave you to settle in, Highness. Your man's cabin is adjoining, through there." Gudrun gestured to a door. Milo immediately went to investigate. It was a much smaller cabin, meant for a servant. Naturally, Latonia would sleep in her cabin to attend her mistress at any hour. A thought struck Julia.

"Has Captain Ranulfson given up his cabin for me?"

"He has," Gudrun replied, "though it is no hardship for him."

Julia nodded. It was only to be expected. "I hope he will not be deprived of it for too long."

"Indeed, Highness."

When Gudrun had left, Julia took a deep breath and turned to her two companions.

"Well. That's that. We'd better settle in. Milo, thank you for helping Latonia. I feel safer with you here, I must admit."

Milo bowed and smiled. "I'm glad I was allowed to come. I know something of Northmen."

There it was again. That niggle of familiarity. How many times must she have passed him in the palace without really noticing him? He was a master of unobtrusiveness that was for sure.

"Have you everything you need?"

"Yes, Highness. I'll give Latonia a hand, shall I?"

"Please."

Latonia looked a little more cheerful as she and Milo started to open the various chests and drag out bedding. Julia went to rummage through another.

"Oh, Highness. I'll do that!"

Julia turned to meet Latonia's anxious expression.

"You've enough to do," Julia replied. "I may as well sort through this."

Besides, she knew which trunk contained her pistols and two very handy daggers. She wanted them with her as soon as possible, to complement the one she had tucked down her garter. Being forced to wear a dress had its compensations. It wasn't long before she unearthed the case and was examining the weapons under Milo's admiring gaze.

"Very nice. May I?"

She handed him one and he inspected it carefully.

"Only the best, eh?" He handed it back with a wolfish grin.

Latonia had her back to them and she was about to say something about *special defences* when Milo's eyes narrowed and he shot her a warning look.

"I'm sure that the Longship will be more than able to protect us," he said.

Of course. She'd forgotten that the *Wolf of the Waves* would always be listening, just like any Britannic Ship.

"I have faith in his abilities," she said, for his benefit. She sneaked a quick peek around to see if he would materialise as *Tempest* had done, but nothing popped out of the bulkheads.

"I believe the Northern Ship Spirits stay at the prow," Milo said.

"I bet some of the Britannic crews wish our Ships would too," Julia replied, wryly. At least she wouldn't have to worry about some huge wooden wolf appearing without warning.

"You're right, Highness."

The noise on board the Longship had been increasing steadily over the time she'd been in there, but it was only when the cabin swayed abruptly that she realised what was happening.

"We're moving!"

120

Julia rushed to the porthole. The glass was thick and wavy, but she could just make out Ennor and the *Tempest* falling away behind them as the *Wolf of the Waves* picked up speed and headed out of the harbour. Latonia squealed as the vessel listed, changing course.

The view was even blurrier now, but not only because of the imperfections in the glass. This time, Julia couldn't stop the tears as all she had ever known slowly vanished into the grey distance.

"All Powerful Jupiter, King of Olympus, grant my uncle victory and keep him safe," she whispered.

Where she was going, though, it wasn't Jupiter she would be expected to pray to.

*

The *Wolf of the Waves* wasted no time in setting sail and heading on his way with all speed. He might be smaller than her, Maia observed, but what he lacked in size, he more than made up for in speed. She reached for the special thread that linked to him, marvelling at its texture.

<Safe journey!> *Black wolf speeding over still water towards high mountains.*

<Fight well, sister!> *Storm clouds building, enveloping the ocean.*

She broke the link, feeling elated that he had called her sister. Even if they were to find themselves on opposing sides at some time in the future, she felt closer to him than she did to many of her fellow Ships, as if the link was somehow stronger. Had the *Livia* ever spoken to him in this way, she wondered? Maybe, sometime in the future, she might ask him.

Her thoughts turned to Julia.

<Mother! If you can hear me, give them a favourable wind and a smooth passage,> she prayed, watching as the Longship vanished into the far horizon. A swirl of silver in her rigging caught her attention and a familiar voice answered her.

<*Sister! What are you doing?*>

Pearl had returned.

<Waiting for the order to sail,> she replied.

<*Are you going to fight a battle?*>

<Probably. Unless Marcus chokes on his dinner, I can't see any way out of it.>

<I agree. Mother tells me that the Old Gods are on the move.>

<Old Gods? Do you mean the Fae?>

Pearl thought for a moment. *<The ones that ruled here before. They have no thought for humans save as cattle or sport. Mother remembers them.>*

This wasn't the news Maia wanted to hear, but she knew that she had to get as much information as possible. Her sister had helped her in the past and even though her understanding of mortal affairs was limited, she could at least report on what she saw.

<Can you tell me where they are now?> she asked Pearl urgently.

<They have vessels too, crossing the sea from Hibernia. I counted nine of them and there are more being prepared.>

Maia stifled a curse. <Are they near the coast of Britannia?>

<About halfway,> the Tempestas told her, swirling idly about her mainmast. Some of the crew had spotted her and were pointing. Amphicles was shading his eyes and looking upwards. If Pearl hung around longer, there would be more questions being asked. She quietly alerted Raven, sending the alarm through their link.

<How far are they from here?> she questioned. She had to get more accurate intelligence and her sister's vagueness wasn't helping.

<To the north.>

<Off Demetae, or Gael territory?> Pearl radiated confusion and Maia knew that she couldn't push her much further. She tried a different tack. <Would it take me long to sail there?>

<No, I don't think so. It's not very far north.>

Never had Maia felt the gulf between them more than she did now. It would just have to do.

<Thank you, Pearl. Please thank Mother too. Can you go and see where they are now?>

Regret sighed through her sister's tone. *<I'm sorry, but I must go south now, on an errand for Boreas. I just wanted to talk to you.>*

<And I'm glad that you did,> Maia replied sincerely. <Please, if you hear anything else, can you let me know somehow?>

<*I'll try!*> Pearl promised. <*Mother is with you.*>

It was a nice thought, but Aura couldn't communicate with her at all. Maia couldn't even remember hearing her voice before her mother had been forced to abandon her at the Foundling Home. It was ironic that she could remember almost everything else that had ever happened to her from babyhood, yet nothing of the one who had borne her remained in her memory.

<It's a comfort to know she's there,> she told Pearl.

The Master Mage cut into the link.

<Your sister's here?>

<Pearl's just going.>

Even as Maia finished the thought, her sister streaked upwards like a ribbon of silver and vanished into the clouds. Several crew members watched her go and Amphicles cast Maia a questioning look.

"Anything to report?" he asked her.

"Just a friendly Tempestas," she replied. "I'll make my report to the Captain now."

The young officer nodded and resumed his watch as the crew made ready to weigh anchor. They were making sail very shortly and heading north-east around the Kernow Peninsula, as she had surmised they would.

<So?> Raven asked.

<Nine Fae vessels have set sail from Hibernia and are crossing to Britannia as I speak.>

He paused for a moment as the news sunk in. <Unwelcome, but not entirely unexpected,> he said at last. <Position?>

<About halfway. I couldn't get any more out of her.>

Raven sighed. <I suppose it's too much to expect her to be able to use our reference points.>

<She says that there are more being prepared as well.>

Raven came to a decision.

<You'd better get down here. We need to tell the King and see if this changes anything.>

Maia obliged and flowed down into the Great Cabin, to find Pendragon, Leo, Sabrinus and Raven conferring. Danuco hurried in, his face creased with concern. As their link to the Gods, his input was essential.

"It seems that we're trapped between Hades and a hydra," Pendragon stated grimly. "Do we go north and engage the Fae, or stick to the original plan?"

"We might have more chance against the Fae, Sire," Leo urged him. "Nine of their vessels are no match for our fleet."

"Don't underestimate them," Raven warned. "Also, if we can manage to engage them and use all our powder, what will we do when the enemy fleet comes up from behind? You can be sure that they have lines of communication open."

The King looked from one to another, his face bleak. "We have no way of knowing their exact position. Our helpful Tempestas was too vague, alas! If they take the shortest route, they'll end up north of the wall among the Gaels. If they leave from the south, they'll land somewhere near Octapitarum, in Demetae country. I wish we knew where."

"She did say that it wasn't too far," Maia told him. "I think the southern route is more likely."

"And it would be easier for them to strike at the heart of Britannia," Pendragon agreed. The others watched him carefully as he pondered the matter, staring down at the charts spread over the table. Ultimately, the decision would be his and all knew that he had little time to make it.

"The Master Mage is correct," he said eventually. "As much as it pains me, it would be a fruitless endeavour to head north and hope by some miracle that we can intercept the Fae. The threat of the Usurper's fleet is more pressing and we know it's heading here."

He looked up, his steady eye meeting each of their faces in turn.

"I suggest that we sail up to Malvadum to take on extra supplies, then turn and meet them on the way back. We may be able to glean some intelligence on numbers in the meantime that will better prepare us for the battle. Any thoughts?"

He glanced at Leo, who looked worried. "Suppose there's nothing available at Malvadum? They might have been ordered to empty the stores."

Pendragon spread his hands. "If they have, they have. It will buy us more time, at least. Maybe the Gods will send a storm and push them back."

Maia heard the unspoken thoughts – *or wreck a few*. It was not a pleasant thing to contemplate, but would be better than a pitched battle, Ship against Ship.

"I agree, Sire," Raven added. "Hopefully, the enemy fleet will expect us to make our stand here and our departure might throw them into confusion."

"Unless their spies are better than ours," Pendragon replied. "I fear that they are. Still, we must make the best of it. Communications are indeed our main problem, especially in regard to our potential allies. Danuco, have you any messages for us?"

"The Gods have stated their preference, Sire," the Priest replied, "And they favour our Ship. More than that I cannot say at this time."

This was it. Maia knew she had to say something.

"Sire," she began, suddenly self-conscious as all eyes turned to her. "I may be able to help a little there."

Pendragon gave her a quizzical look.

"How so?"

"I may be able to talk directly to Alliance Longships. I found this out with *Wolf of the Waves* when he accepted me into their link."

Pendragon's eyebrows shot upwards, but Raven smiled.

"This is surely unheard of?" Leo said in astonishment.

"No," Raven replied. "There is a precedent. I have known of one other Ship who could communicate using their methods."

A chill beyond the physical ran cold fingers through Maia's Shipbody. So, she had been right.

"Ah," Pendragon said, slowly. "You must mean..."

"The *Livia*. Yes. When she tried to claim Maia – *Tempest* – she passed some of her abilities on to her through the link she shared with Captain Valerius."

A range of emotions flitted across the King's face.

"And when were you going to tell me this?"

"They are as yet unproven, Sire. This latest facet has only just emerged, isn't that correct?" Raven fixed Maia with his clouded eyes and she nodded.

Pendragon suddenly rose. He seemed happier, all of a sudden. "Then we must take advantage of this. *Tempest*, keep me informed of my niece's progress northwards. Furthermore, if you are able to call upon aid, Divine or otherwise, I suggest you do so with my blessing." He seemed about to say more, then changed his mind. "Inform the Fleet. We sail directly the wind and tide allow."

"Aye, Sire," Maia replied. She regarded his hopeful face with a feeling of guilt. How could she tell him that she could only pray and hope that her mother was listening? Jupiter's ruling had been final. She would never be able to contact her directly, or receive an answer in return. To try to do more was more than her life was worth.

She was as dependent on the whim of the Gods as anybody.

VI

Julia stood on the deck of the *Wolf of the Waves*, gazing out across the choppy sea. To the west, the last of the sun's rays glinted on the water but she could see that Helios's chariot was plunging into a sullen cloudbank that presaged incoming bad weather. She drew her cloak more firmly around her shoulders, wishing for a swift journey on one hand, and that it might last forever on the other.

Milo was standing respectfully to one side, on guard as always.

"It looks like we might be in for a bit of a blow," she remarked. He moved a little closer, as the wind was rising and snatching her words away.

"It does indeed, Highness," he replied. He didn't look happy at the prospect. "I'd rather it was coming from any other direction."

She turned to him, noting his creased forehead as he squinted into the failing light.

"Do you think it might be a problem?"

"Possibly. It's a natural direction for this time of year."

She had the impression that he was trying not to worry her. "I'm quite aware of what lies over there. Do you think *they* might be involved?"

"I don't know, Highness." So there wasn't any more information. They were both aware that he had to be careful of what he said, in case the Longship was listening in. It wouldn't do to actually confirm the fact that he was a trained Agent.

"Have you ever been to Norvegia?" she asked him, not wishing to dwell on the thought of hordes of vicious Fae.

He shook his head. "No, though I know plenty of Northmen through business dealings."

She flashed him a quick grin, understanding what he was getting at. "And how did you find them?"

He shrugged. "Much like us, though they usually have their ancestral weapons close to hand somewhere. They like to drink, sing songs and they're skilled craftspeople. They worship their Gods – and ours if necessary, and worry about their families, trade and the state of the world just like anybody else.

"So not bloodthirsty savages then?"

He laughed at her expression. "Not all of them, though they like to tell tales of war and heroism too. You have read Homer haven't you, Princess?"

She pulled a face. "Naturally. Battle after battle and warriors behaving like spoilt brats."

"Well, there you go," he agreed. "Not much difference really. I've not heard anything bad of King Harald or Prince Haarkon, if that's what you mean."

She sighed. "Well, that's good to know."

"It's a shame you can't practise your own set of skills," he continued. Both of them knew that the Longship would notice any use of Potentia immediately and report it to his Captain. Both she and Milo had been very circumspect, so as to give no cause for alarm; besides which it was always good to have a surprise up one's sleeve for emergencies.

"It is. I was just moving on to more interesting stuff as well."

"Perhaps when we get to Norvegia you could take part in some weapons training. They actively encourage young women to learn to defend themselves and some, like Bodil, make a career of it."

It was an interesting idea, but she doubted whether they'd let her. "I'll ask, but I have the horrible feeling that they'll want me married and producing heirs as soon as possible."

Just because she'd accepted her fate didn't mean that she desired any of it.

"I'm sorry," Milo said quietly. "It can't be easy and I know your wishes don't lie in that direction."

He was a very perceptive man. Despite her natural reserve, she felt that she could tell him more than any other, save Raven and her uncle. Cei had also been forced to marry for the sake of the dynasty. Her brother had never understood her reluctance.

"My uncle, too," she said. "It would have been so much better if he'd had the chance to follow his heart, then he'd never have sired that poisonous worm."

Milo was silent for a while. "Things don't always work out as we'd like, Highness," he said at last, "especially in matters of love."

She glanced at his impassive profile. So, he hadn't been lucky either.

"Haarkon's the same age as me, unlike poor old Parisius. That's something, I suppose, whether it's a bad or a good thing."

"Is there someone else you'd prefer?" he asked, looking at her with frank curiosity.

She pulled a face. "No. I'd rather end up as a mad old woman living alone in a cave, surrounded by wild animals that bring me food."

His face softened as he smiled. "It sounds lonely."

"I think I'd prefer it. But not monkeys."

He laughed. "Fair enough. I doubt you'd prise Teg's meals away from him anyway." He scanned the deck. "I suggest that we go below. It's getting a little chilly out here and you need to rest."

This time she scowled at him. "You sound like old Priscilla. I could stay out here all night."

Julia lingered another few minutes to spite him, then made her way back down to her cabin, where Latonia had a hot drink warming for her on a tiny stove. She allowed the slave to undress her and pull a thicker nightdress over her head to keep out the chill. The girl did look better now after her wounding, with a little colour in her cheeks. Julia suddenly realised that she didn't know anything about her.

"Latonia, where were you born?" she asked, moved by the impulse to know more.

"I was born on one of the Graecian islands, Highness."

"Oh. Was your mother a slave too?" Latonia's back stiffened and Julia realised that she'd hit a nerve. The girl composed herself before answering. "No, Highness. I was born free, but my father..." she trailed off, eyes lowered.

Julia was appalled, but not altogether surprised. Latonia's father must have got himself into terrible trouble to sell his daughter into slavery. Perhaps he'd been a gambler? She'd heard of things like that happening.

"How awful for you. I am truly sorry." Still, there was one way she could improve her lot. "As soon as we reach Norvegia I'll free you, then you can decide what you want to do."

Latonia's face registered shock. "You will, Highness? Truly?"

"I swear by all the Gods," Julia replied. "You saved my life and this is the least I can do. I'll make sure that you have enough money to live comfortably as well. You can even go back to Graecia if you want to."

She wouldn't recommend that Latonia return to Britannia, even if it wasn't about to be ravaged by war. Latonia smiled and it was if the sun had come out. Her face was transformed by joy and relief. "Thank you, Highness!"

"Don't mention it," Julia replied, settling herself into bed. "I'll order that the required papers be drawn up tomorrow so they're ready for when we arrive, and I'll make sure that Milo and the Captain know as well. Oh, and your friend, Bodil too."

She'd seen the two of them whispering in a corridor and it was clear that they liked each other. Julia was glad for them. Anything that brought light into people's lives was to be cherished and she couldn't imagine what the woman must have suffered.

Latonia beamed. "She said she'll teach me swordplay, though I'm already good with a bow and arrow."

"Excellent!" Julia replied. She reached for a book, intending to read a little before she slept. "I'd like to join in for a bit too, if I may."

"I'll tell her," Latonia said, her voice betraying her excitement. She'd already fastened up her hammock, as the other sailors did, swinging herself into it with ease.

"You have no problem getting into that," Julia remarked, quietly glad that she'd always had a bed, even as a junior Mage.

"Oh, I'm very agile, Highness," Latonia grinned.

As she blew out the lamp and snuggled down, Julia felt that sometimes it wasn't so bad to be a Royal after all.

*

Caniculus was worried. Despite spending several hours skulking about the palace, he hadn't been able to get any other information of worth, magic helmet or no magic helmet. He'd observed Marcus carefully, but nothing seemed to be happening since the funeral. That had been a rather low-key affair, though the procession had been sombre enough, the route lined with silent crowds. Everyone was on edge, waiting for the Sword to choose the new ruler.

Caniculus had watched with the rest, fervently hoping that the shade of Artorius would return to haunt his cousin to an early grave. He doubted that the King's corpse had been buried with due rites; knowing Kite, the body had been quietly burned and shoved in a hole somewhere.

He'd spied on the official mourners for a whole day, helping himself to choice delicacies when nobody was looking and generally hanging about, but there was no official indication of Marcus's next steps. The Sword was still stuck in the front of the Basilica, the focus of everyone's attention.

It was an early morning conversation in a corridor that pointed the way.

"Yes, it's going to happen today!" one of the slaves was saying, his freckled face flushed as he relayed the news. His audience of two wide-eyed maids listened avidly as he continued.

"There's going to be a parade past the Basilica. The King will pull out Excalibur, then he's going to open the Games!"

"Can we go?" one of them asked.

"We'll be allowed to, won't we?" her companion joined in, grabbing her friend's arm in her excitement.

"We can all go," the slave announced. "The King wants everybody to see. I heard Macro telling Gwyn." Gwyn was the Steward. This lad must have been doing some skulking of his own, but it was common knowledge that slaves heard everything.

They squealed, whilst their benefactor grinned in triumph. "Get your best clothes ready, ladies. We're off to the Games!"

They scurried off, chattering happily. Being slaves, they wouldn't have the best view, being confined to the top tiers of the amphitheatre, but a holiday was a holiday. They'd probably had enough of being groped by drunken party guests, especially as currently there wasn't a lady in residence. For the time being Marcus was keeping his mother, the Princess Severina, at arm's length in her country house.

Many palace chambers were empty, a fact of which Caniculus had taken full advantage. It was sad to see the rooms, once full of life, silent and draped in dustsheets. Marcus had appropriated his cousin's suite immediately, throwing out many of Artorius's prized possessions which now lay piled in corners of the same neglected chambers. He'd probably seek to turn a profit on them or give them away as bribes, though some recipients might feel it unlucky. Still, an expensive gift was not to be sniffed at, and anybody who refused to bow down would meet the same fate as Senator Rufus. He spared a thought for the Lady Drusilla. No word had come through of her capture, so Caniculus hoped that she had escaped safely to Gaul. He'd have to see if Milo knew more when next they spoke.

His mind turned back to his current situation. These were uncertain times, he reasoned, and it was wise to see what he could put by in case he needed to make a quick getaway. Nobody would notice small items that could be easily pawned or melted down to provide him with funds. His pockets were bulging as he came to a decision. It would be better if he went into the City and reported back from there. At least he'd be able to give a blow-by-blow account of what was happening and gauge the mood of the populace.

He slipped along the seemingly endless corridors and out of the back gates that had been opened to admit a cart-load of noisy poultry. There would be further entertainments at the palace after the games had closed for the day, and produce was being shipped in from all the outlying districts. His family would make a fortune supplying arena animals in every province. He only hoped that they had enough creatures in stock to meet the demand.

Marcus was spending lavishly to curry the favour of the people, but even that wouldn't be enough if he failed to withdraw the Sword. If he couldn't, it was more likely that he would be torn limb from limb. As he dodged through the crowd on the way to the Forum, Caniculus debated with himself as to how the stunt would be managed. One thing was for sure: he'd be glad when he could take off the bloody helmet, as it was hard to avoid people who didn't know he was there. He'd already startled two people who found themselves jostled by something invisible. They'd made signs to avert evil and hurried off, muttering protective charms. By nightfall, there were sure to be rumours that unseen things were abroad in the City.

He snorted to himself and went to find a good vantage point.

*

Word spread quickly, announced by town criers and hastily printed posters slapped up on walls for those who could read. The parade would start at the palace at noon, progressing to the Londinium Amphitheatre by way of the Forum, where the King would be officially crowned. The whole city was abuzz, with many who'd come to pay their respects to Artorius staying on for the spectacle of Marcus trying for the kingship. Speculation was rife.

Caniculus took up position high on the roof of the Temple of Mercury Lugus, chewing on a handful of candied fruit that he'd pilfered on his way out of the palace. It was one of the older temples, but was going to be rebuilt very shortly to better reflect the God's importance to a major trading and commercial centre. For now, though, it was an ideal place to spy from and Caniculus hoped that he could rely on the God's protection too.

He offered up a quiet prayer as the crowds gathered beneath him, held back by barriers lined with armed legionaries and City Polis. Macro, Chief of Marcus's Guard, wasn't taking any chances with the security arrangements. The Basilica had been closed for the day and the whole of the front had been cordoned off. A specially-constructed platform had been built in front of the column that held the Sword, so that Marcus could be seen at all times. Flags bearing the Pendragon crest flew at the front two corners, though not, Caniculus noted, the Imperial Eagle. That was a statement if ever there was one, though many of the watchers would approve. After all, this was the business of Britannia and had nothing to do with the Empire.

The late morning was overcast and threatened rain, for which he was strangely grateful. The sun shouldn't shine on Marcus the

Murderer and it would serve him right if the heavens opened just as he ascended the steps. The thought of the Usurper standing there looking like a drowned rat and hauling fruitlessly on the sword, warmed Caniculus's heart. He resisted the temptation to yank off the helmet, even though it would have been more comfortable. At least the thing was waterproof.

It wasn't long before the Forum reached capacity. The route of the procession would be packed too; those owners who had rooms with a view would be charging people through the nose for the space. The balconies of the official buildings surrounding the Forum were full of nobles and senior dignitaries, watching safely away from the masses and being served dainties as they waited for the show to start. People were everywhere, climbing up fountains and statues, hanging from lampposts and even trying to scale the sides of buildings to find a perch to witness this once-in-a-millennia event. Nobody remembered the first Artorius doing it, but as many as possible wanted to see this.

Distant cheering told him that the procession had started, just as the great bells of the Basilica began their noonday ringing. Everything was on time.

He could tell where Marcus was by the noise. It wouldn't take him long to reach the Forum, even at a slow walk. He began to bet with himself what the Usurper would be in. A litter? No, too oriental. A horse? Perhaps. Most likely it would be the usual carriage. In fact, what met his gaze as the legionaries marched smartly out of the Magna Via and into the Forum, trumpets sounding, was Marcus, in full military uniform, standing in a chariot pulled by four snow-white horses. A chariot! How quaint! Unlike the Roman Emperors in their triumphs, however, there was no slave standing next to him to whisper 'Remember, you are mortal' in his ear. Marcus was standing alone behind his driver, hand upraised to acknowledge the cheers.

Caniculus spat out a hard piece of fruit and raised himself up. The noise rose to the heavens like a solid wall of sound and he found himself taking the odd glance upwards to see if there were any omens, but there wasn't a single bird in the sky. Even the hardy and cynical city pigeons had abandoned their usual perches.

"What are you planning, you scabrous weasel?" he murmured to himself as he raised a telescope to his eye, focusing in on the distant figure. He adjusted the focus, wishing that it was a musket. There was the faintest shimmer of air around Marcus, such as might be seen rising from the road on a very hot day. A magical shield.

He swung the telescope around, seeing if he could spot any of his fellow Agents. What he saw instead were many robed figures, obviously Mages, taking up positions around the edge of the Forum. His hackles rose. There was something treacherous brewing here.

Kite's words came back to him. *You will pull the sword from the stone, Sire. In public.*

The chariot had reached the foot of the steps. Marcus alighted and mounted the platform. The eager buzz of the crowd fell silent, as every eye fixed upon him. A few small children cried and were shushed, then there was nothing. Marcus paused for effect, before swaggering up to where the Sword stuck out of the column. He placed his hand upon it as the crowd held its breath, pausing for effect.

Then, with one swift movement, he pulled it out of the stone. At that exact moment, a ray of light shone down, making the weapon sparkle and flash. He looked every inch a King.

The crowd erupted, relief and joy pouring forth. Hands were raised to the heavens in thanks that the ancient magic had revealed the True King. Any rumour of perfidy and murder would now be quashed utterly. Marcus's reign was secure.

As the celebrations began, Caniculus slumped down behind the parapet, shocked beyond measure. He'd been so sure that the Usurper would fail. How could the Sword have endorsed Artorius's murderer? It hadn't seemed possible, but he'd seen it with his own eyes.

He had to break the news to his friend, and through him to Pendragon.

Now it seemed that the war would be over before it started, as he knew that the Admiral was far too honourable to dispute the will of Excalibur. Caniculus realised with a sinking heart that he might even have to pledge allegiance to Marcus himself, to save his family.

Perhaps the ancient Powers of Britannia trumped even the Gods of Olympus?

He sighed and opened a channel to Milo.

*

Morning aboard the *Wolf of the Waves* brought more grey skies and a sea fog that shrouded the Longship in a cloak of moisture. For once Julia elected to stay in her cabin and read, assured by Milo that they were making good progress up through the Hibernian Ocean. They would soon pass Mona, heading for the island of Mannin, and from there would make their way up the coast of Caledonia before rounding the topmost point and heading north-east. They still had several days journey ahead of them and she resolved to make the most of them. Probably her worst enemy would be boredom, but hopefully the weather would improve so that she could see some of the sights and the wildlife that inhabited these far-flung waters.

Latonia had performed her duties with a will, so Julia gave her permission to leave the cabin in search of Bodil.

"Don't forget to ask her if she'll train me, too," Julia reminded her. It would be useful to know one end of a sword from the other, especially as pistols contained one shot at a time and took an age to reload. After that, she'd have to use them as clubs, relying on their weighted butts. Carrying six or seven was the best option, but she only had a brace. A sharp sword, or even an axe, could be used again and again, as long as she knew how to use them effectively. She'd seen enough idiots injure themselves with their own weapons whilst showing off, or worse still, their friends.

Milo was nearby but not actually in the cabin, so she had a precious few moments to herself. She almost started to practise a spell, before abruptly stopping herself; it wouldn't do to alert the Longship that he had a Britannic Mage on board. Even though she hadn't been able to train at the Collegium, she still regarded herself as one of them.

If only she'd been born male!

The sudden realisation that she'd have been killed in her brother's place was sobering. The words before her blurred and ran as the full enormity of Artorius's death slammed into her. Yes, she knew he was dead, but somehow the thought hadn't really registered. It was only now that she understood that she'd never see him again. He was gone, just like her barely-remembered father and her mother, sent away to the far north at her Grandfather's command to strengthen ties with some tribal chieftain, and dying before ever seeing her son and daughter again.

The old King had loathed his daughter-in-law, and had had very traditional Roman views on a woman's place. If he hadn't been ailing before his death, he'd have married his only granddaughter off long before but the right match never seemed to arise until Parisius was widowed yet again. He would have approved of her marrying his old friend, but now they were both in the Realm of Shades. The old man had never really recovered from his favourite son's death and afterwards nobody had ever measured up. Her uncle had been the dutiful son, but was happier at sea.

She still remembered being summoned before her grandfather, on the odd times that he wanted to see her. He'd run an eye over her before announcing to all, "She'll make a fine alliance for us."

Every blasted time. He was like a farmer checking over his prize sow to see how well she was fattening. He'd been hard on her brother, but had had a soft spot for Marcus for some reason. Another person who'd been fooled.

Julia stared blindly across the cabin, the book forgotten, hoping that her brother, father and grandfather were cursing the Usurper from beyond the grave. Her only comfort was that he wouldn't be able to withdraw Excalibur and she didn't understand why he thought he ever could.

Maybe all this would be over soon and Britannia would be at peace again? It was a shame that she'd find out from the Norwegian Court. She wrapped her arms around herself, suddenly conscious of a chill in the cabin. Perhaps a door or hatch had been left open? Well, there was nobody about to fetch her shawl, so she heaved herself up to fetch it, resisting the temptation to call it to her using her Potentia.

Latonia hadn't reappeared, so she must have found Bodil. Julia threw the shawl around her shoulders and swayed across to the small window, in time to the rocking of the vessel. She could see the waves and the separation of sea and sky, so at least the morning fog had lifted. Surely it had to be nearly time for the midday meal? The Longship didn't have bells like Britannic Ships; the crew always seemed to know what hour it was and moved with quiet purpose, as if they could hear a voice she couldn't.

Julia moved away from the window and made her way to a small table and a dish of snacks. The sight of the sweetmeats reminded her of Teg the monkey and his taste in treats. She hoped that her uncle was deriving some comfort from the little creature.

A knock on the cabin door heralded Milo.

"The meal is ready, Highness."

She chewed and swallowed the sticky confection before answering.

"Very well. Bring it in."

He entered carrying a tray with covered dishes, and placed it deftly on the main table. She watched as he removed each one and set them down where they weren't likely to spill. All the flat surfaces had lips to stop things sliding off. She surveyed the fare with a jaundiced eye.

"I don't think I'm hungry now." Her previous craving seemed to have deserted her.

Milo cast her a reproachful look. "Well, if you will eat sweets before your meal, Highness."

"I only had one," she replied, stung, until she saw his mouth twitch, "What is it, anyway? Not more fish."

The Northmen seemed to have a never-ending appetite for fish in a myriad of permutations. Salt fish in sauce. Baked cod. Pickled herring. She suppressed a shudder.

"Actually, the King sent a couple of sheep so it's mutton today," he said cheerfully. "Don't worry. I expect there'll be fish on the menu tonight."

She groaned and rolled her eyes at him. In the evening, she was to dine with the Captain and the Ambassador. They would doubtless show her every courtesy, but she disliked the formality of it. Her uncle must have known what the usual fare would be and had taken pity on her.

"They don't seem to have a Priest or Mage aboard," she remarked, seating herself.

"The Captain fulfils both of those roles, being bound to his Longship's spirit," Milo told her. "They call him the *Gothi* and he's the one responsible for sacrifices and such. They don't have the same structure at all – it's much more personal and less hierarchical."

Julia shrugged. "Less people to interfere with government, I suppose. I should know these things. You'll have to brief me on everything you know, so I don't end up looking a fool in front of my new countrymen."

"I will. The Captain and the Ambassador should be able to help you as well."

She nodded and took a spoonful of the rich stew. It was tasty enough and the bread was still fresh, though how long that would last, she didn't know. Longships didn't have the facility for storing fresh foods the same way a Britannic Ship did, and there wasn't as much room for stores. They had to replenish them more frequently.

"Wine, Highness?" Milo was used to acting as her steward. She nodded and he poured her a glass, unfazed by the swaying vessel. She surprised herself by finishing the bowlful, then helped herself to cheese and some dried apple.

"Not bad, really," she said. "You have eaten, haven't you, Milo?"

He grinned. "Oh yes, Highness. The food on board is plentiful, if a little monotonous. The cook is worried that it's too plain for a Princess, so he's planning something interesting for later."

Julia dabbed at her mouth with a napkin. "Tell him that I appreciate his efforts and I'm happy to eat what everyone else is eating. It's more than most get."

"Why, Highness, you almost sound like a commoner," he teased, his eyes twinkling. "An apprentice, for instance."

She didn't laugh, looking down her nose at him instead and mimicking Lady Priscilla's quavering tones. "Such impudence! I should have you whipped! Apprentice, indeed!"

His mouth twitched. "I am your humble servant, Highness."

This time she couldn't hide her amusement. "It seems I was hungry after all. Tell me, how is Latonia doing? I take it she's on deck sparring with Bodil?"

Milo raised an eyebrow. "She is indeed. The crew are impressed. She's a natural."

Julia felt a pang of envy. She doubted she'd be a natural with any weapon, though she was a fairly good shot after hours of practising. It was one thing her brother had encouraged. Armed combat, however, had been a step too far for the court's delicate sensibilities.

"She's going to teach me, too," she declared, expecting resistance, but to her surprise he agreed.

"Excellent. Most Northern ladies know something of defence and can readily swing an axe at the very least. It's considered a virtue."

Julia's smile grew wider. "I'd better start being virtuous then, hadn't I?"

"And I'd better clear these away." He hesitated. "I don't like leaving you on your own."

She waved a hand. "It won't be for long. I'll come up on deck shortly and see what's going on now that the fog's cleared. Where are we, anyway?"

"Just passing Octapitarum, in the lands of the Demetae."

So, they were making good time. They would cross the wide western bay, go past the island of Mona, then continue northwards. Her lessons on geography hadn't been wasted. It was still a little chilly despite the warmth of the stew lying in her stomach, so she took off the shawl and put on a coat instead before making her way out and up to the deck. She wanted to start her lessons as soon as possible, and now was as good a time as any. The one on one politics could begin this evening.

*

Milo delivered the dirty dishes back to the galley, where the cook, a wiry, one-legged chap with a leathery skin and a bald head covered in faded blue ink seemed delighted that everything had been eaten.

"Princess, she have good appetite, yes?" he asked, in broken Latin.

"She liked it very much," Milo replied.

"Hah. I good cook!"

He returned to his pots with renewed enthusiasm that his food had the Royal Seal of Approval. Milo chuckled and was retreating out of the narrow space when his speechstone activated. It had to be Raven or Caniculus. There hadn't been one for Julia and it would have been suspicious if she'd been found with it about her person.

<Blue here,> he said automatically, before remembering that he didn't need his code name anymore. He should have arranged for a new one.

<Dog here,> came the reply. His friend sounded rattled. <I've bad news.>

Milo listened in disbelief as Caniculus reported what he'd seen.

<You're sure?> he Sent.

<The whole of Londin's sure,> his friend replied bitterly. <Everybody saw him pull the bloody thing out.>

Milo's mind reeled. This had not been part of the plan. <I thought the Gods were against him?>

<Look, I can only tell you what I witnessed with my own eyes. He put his hand on it and it came out as easily as if it had been stuck into butter. There was no resistance that I could see.>

Milo swore. <The Gods alone know how he's done it. I'll have to tell Raven.>

Caniculus' frustration seethed through the link. <How can he get away with it?>

Again, Milo knew that there was more to the story. <What aren't you telling me? Come on. I need to know.>

Reluctantly, Caniculus described how the Sword had used him <I don't remember doing it, but I must have. What I don't understand is why it got me to take it all the way to Londin, only to let that toad claim it? I assumed I was keeping it from him until Pendragon could turn up. Well, it's all over now, isn't it? The damned Fae will arrive and we'll all be neck deep in the cess pit.>

<Don't be hasty.> Even as he spoke, he knew that Dog was right. The whole of Britannia would soon hear about what had happened, plus there was the fact that Marcus was walking around wearing the blasted thing. Stupid magical artefacts! They always meant trouble of one form or another.

<I'll keep reporting in, > Caniculus said gloomily, <for all the good it'll do.>

<We'll be the happier for it. Where will you go? They'll still be looking for you.>

<I think I'll go and check on how the Games are doing,> He sounded weary. <At least there'll be some entertainment and I can gauge the mood of the mob.>

<Watch yourself. Make sure that nobody sees you.>

<Oh,> Caniculus replied, <don't you worry about that. I've got it covered. Anyway, it could be worse.>

<How's that?> Milo asked, doubting it could.

<I could be stuck on a boat with you!>

Milo blew him a mental raspberry. <Good luck!>

He rubbed his face, feeling the burden of the knowledge weighting his shoulders like a leaden cloak.

The question of the Fae still hung in the air like a foetid smell. If the good citizens of Londin knew what their new King had invited in they would have had his head, Sword or no Sword. Probably. How many people still treated the stories as more than ancient legends, or tales to frighten children?

As he reached the upper deck he took deep breaths of the fresh air, glad to be out of the confined space. The Princess was already there wrapped in a long coat, watching as Bodil was showing Latonia how to block a sword thrust. He was glad to see that they were using wooden sticks rather than the real thing.

He sidled up to Julia, wondering whether to tell her about Marcus, but decided not to. As the cousin of the King and the only marriageable royal female, her position would be assured. She wasn't a threat now that his throne was apparently secured.

As to the Fae – who knew? Maybe he intended to betray them as he'd betrayed his own flesh and blood? Or was he their puppet, to be used and discarded? The possibilities were making his head ache. It would be better to dump all this on to Raven as soon as possible. He activated the link.

<Raven?>

<Ah, Milo! I wondered when I'd be hearing from you. Is all well?>

<With the Princess, yes.> He braced himself. The old Mage would have already worked out that something was wrong. <I just heard from our friend in Londin. Marcus pulled out the Sword.>

He'd expected shock, but Raven was calm. <Really? I suppose he did it in full view of everybody?>

<Yes.>

<Naturally.> Raven's mental tone oozed disgust. <Still, the damage is done and the Fae are still on the move. I'll have to tell Cei before he hears it elsewhere. We're sailing now, though it looks like there might not be a battle after all, for which we can be thankful. This will give us time to stall.>

<For what purpose?>

<Until I can work out how Kite pulled it off. Keep me informed.>

The conversation ended, leaving Milo even more puzzled. Dog had been adamant that Marcus had pulled out Excalibur. What could be more definite than that?

"Hah!" He was jerked out of his musings by Bodil's cry as she sought to whack Latonia across the side. Her opponent slipped out of reach, her teeth bared in a fierce grin and countered with a sudden move that caught the taller woman across the arm.

"You've just lost a limb!" Latonia said triumphantly. Bodil hissed and switched the stick to her left hand, flexing the numbed fingers.

"It's a good job I have another!"

Julia laughed and applauded, along with several of the crew. Captain Ranulfson was standing to the side, brawny arms folded across his chest.

Latonia had little time to bask in her temporary triumph as Bodil forced her back with a flurry of moves before sweeping her legs out from under her. Latonia fell to the deck, twisting like a cat and leaping up once more. Bodil looked impressed, but a second later her stick was jabbed into Latonia's stomach and the bout was over.

The two women laughed and embraced. "You fight well!" the Shieldmaiden announced. "After more lessons you'll be entitled to carry a real weapon."

Latonia flushed with pleasure, her arm around the other's waist.

"You're very good, Latonia," Julia said. "I don't think I'll be fighting you any time soon."

"Thank you, Highness!"

Bodil gave Latonia a squeeze, then approached Julia. "Highness, Latonia tells me that you are going to free her," she said in the direct way she had.

"I am," Julia replied. "I was going to wait until we arrived in Norvegia, but I don't want her to be a slave for any longer than she has to. Captain Ranulfson, as the authority here, I call upon you to witness that I free this woman under the ancient law of *manumissio.*"

The Captain nodded. "I affirm your right to release this *thrall* from her bondage and that she is now a free woman."

The crew cheered as Latonia curtseyed to Julia. "I affirm that I am your freedwoman and will forever be in your debt. I owe you my gratitude, Highness."

Bodil let loose a high yodelling call that was answered from the prow as the *Wolf of the Waves* howled back.

Milo was happy for Latonia as she celebrated. She'd still be attending the Princess, but as a lady-in-waiting rather than a bound slave, or *thrall* as the Northmen called them. Slaves in Northern countries had a much worse time of it than in the Empire. She'd heard that some were even sacrificed when their owners died, to continue serving them in the afterlife. Such barbarisms were still practised on a regular basis in lands where the Gods were appeased with human blood.

The afternoon had turned cold for the time of year, and it seemed that there would be no more swordplay today. Julia would have to wait for her lesson. The dark clouds to the west were still massing, piling up one on another to form a solid wall, though the bad weather hadn't yet materialised. Away to the east, the coast of Britannia was a grey line, disappearing into the arms of the Bay of Ceredigion. A shiver ran up his back as he thought of what might be heading towards his homeland.

"I think we should go below, Highness," he said to Julia, who nodded.

"I agree, plus I think that a small celebration is in order. Here, Latonia, don't forget your cloak!"

Milo scooped it off the hatch cover where it had been thrown and offered it to her with a bow. Latonia rewarded him with a smile. As she reached out, her sleeve rode up and he saw the healed burns, shiny against the skin of her forearm. They looked for all the world like a fiery hand had gripped her. She saw him looking and threw her cloak over them, meeting his quizzical look with a twist of the mouth.

"Let's have a drink!" Bodil called across to them.

Latonia held his eyes for a second, as if daring him to make comment, then trotted off. Milo watched her go, wondering how on earth she could have come by such strange scars, then shrugged and followed. He definitely needed a drink or two.

*

Maia stood by as Raven broke the news to Pendragon. The Admiral took the news calmly enough, though a clenching of his jaw told her that it wasn't what he'd been hoping for.

"I suppose it would have been too much to expect him to fail," he said at last, "not with the whole of Britannia watching in one form or another. He was far too confident of success. The question now is, how to respond? Any hope of Alliance support is shattered."

Raven frowned. "True, but there is still the fact that the Usurper has allied himself with the Fae, and that is not to be borne."

Pendragon gave a bitter laugh. "You still call him the Usurper?"

The Master Mage raised an eyebrow. "I do not believe he withdrew the Sword legitimately. It has an intelligence of its own and would never permit Marcus to do so."

"Even despite the evidence to the contrary?"

"Just so."

"Can you tell how this thing was done, then?"

Raven grimaced. "Not yet, but remember, the Fae are known for warping the minds of mortals."

"Even if they have," Leo interjected. "How can we convince everyone that they've been fooled?"

"That's going to be a little more difficult," Raven admitted.

Pendragon ran a hand over his face. "There's one thing I can do right now. I can surrender. Ships will not fight Ships under my command if I can possibly avoid it."

Maia felt torn between relief and dismay: relief that there would be no conflict with her sisters and dismay that Pendragon would be charged with mutiny at the very least, and at the most, with treason.

"Marcus is on shaky ground," Raven pointed out. "He wasn't first in line to the throne on his cousin's death, so you acted correctly. You weren't to know that the Sword would seemingly choose him. Now that it appears to be settled you can pretend to capitulate with good grace. He'll see it as a final triumph and will want a public reconciliation. He still needs the people on his side."

"And after that, I'll make very sure to have several food tasters on constant stand-by," Pendragon replied grimly. Maia's gaze flitted to Teg, sitting on his perch and watching his new master with beady eyes. He'd taken to the Admiral immediately and liked to sit on his shoulder, a thing Julia would never have permitted. "He'll never allow me back to sea, not with what I know. I'll be quietly done away with."

"And that's why you must make all the right noises and take none of the action," Raven replied. "Let him think that you're crawling back with your tail between your legs. Say whatever you need to, but in reality you won't be going anywhere near him."

Pendragon nodded. "No time like the present. He'll be expecting to hear from me, now that he's pulled off this coup. How should we approach him?"

"I suggest that *Tempest* re-opens communications, sounding suitably chastened." Raven thought for a moment. "The *Regina* would be the best bet – she'll have a direct link to Albanus and the news will reach Marcus very quickly. After that, we'll follow the instructions we're given. The fact that we have Albanus's son and heir on board will also help our cause."

Pendragon sighed. "I'm forced to agree. We'll do as you propose, just very, very slowly in the hope that something else happens to prevent us actually having to surrender in person. Leo, inform the crew, but say nothing of our suspicions. Are we all agreed?"

Leo nodded. "Aye, sir. Danuco is hard at work, but we've nothing back as yet."

"They'll know the truth of it," Pendragon agreed. "We must sacrifice to Neptune and Jupiter immediately. In the meantime, I'll compose the message. *Tempest*, keep us on our current heading for now. The more distance we put between ourselves and the *Regina et al*, the better."

"Aye, Admiral." It seemed safer not to call him Sire any more.

"Dismissed."

He reached for tablets and stylus, his mind already on what he could say to convince his traitor son of his loyalty. Teg leapt from his perch and bounded to his master's shoulder, his tail curling around Pendragon's neck. The Admiral smiled at him and stroked the furry head.

"Well then," he said to the monkey. "I'd better get on with it, hadn't I?"

Maia gave him some privacy, turning her direct attention away to the Mage quarters. Raven was already moving to sit in his favourite chair as Polydorus poured him a generous measure of brandy. She formed out of the bulkhead, arms folded.

"What a mess," she said aloud. He toasted her with the glass.

"It could have been worse. No Ships have been lost and we can buy some time."

"There's not much we can do to disprove Marcus's claim from here," she pointed out as he sipped his brandy.

"And that's why we must work through other agents. Have faith."

He was taking this remarkably calmly. The mere thought of having to grovel to the *Regina* made Maia want to scream and throw things. She wanted to tell her sisters that it was probably all a sham, but knew that she couldn't. There were those who wouldn't return, no matter what, the *Persistence* among them. It was highly likely that she wouldn't be forgiven for her outburst in Portus. Maia didn't want to think of what might happen to the outspoken old Ship. A familiar feeling of dread had started to overtake her, as if she were still the frightened girl dreading the sound of her mistress's voice echoing down the corridor.

She forced herself to think rationally. Blandina had come to a very nasty and violent end thanks to her sister's intervention, so she could only hope that Marcus would too.

"This must be horrible for you, Maia," Raven's voice interrupted the unpleasant memory.

"I can't say that I'm looking forward to contacting the *Regina*," she admitted.

"You do what you must. You've been dealing with these sorts of people all your life and you survived. You certainly fooled Lapwing into letting his guard down, and look what happened to him!" A wolfish smile spread across his face. "We're not beaten, you know. This is just the opening salvo in a war we're going to win."

He seemed strangely confident and she found that it irritated her.

"You're up to something. What do you know that we don't?"

His smile never wavered. "Alas, my dear, some things are not for the ears of Ships, however amazing they might be. You'll find out soon enough."

He was insufferable. She withdrew into the bulkhead, fuming quietly, and went to find Leo. They had to tell her crew the news and she wasn't looking forward to it.

All in all, it wasn't a good day. Her thoughts turned to her friends, Julia and Milo, sailing on a strange sea to an alien land. She was glad that they were both well out of this situation and heading for safety far away.

Leo had summoned his officers, apprising them all of the situation. Everyone looked glum, but it would be their place to keep up morale.

"It has to be a trick," Sabrinus said, but a warning glance from his Captain sealed his mouth.

"That's as maybe, but we can't allow Marcus to have any doubts of our sincerity. As far as we're concerned he has

Excalibur, so the point is moot. We must all be good boys and take our punishment. If they catch us of course."

Amphicles and Drustan exchanged hopeful looks, but of all of them Danuco was the one who seemed most confident.

"The Gods have turned from Marcus. What mortal can succeed against their will?"

"Indeed," Leo said. "We must all have courage. Word will spread through the Ships and some may decide to break away and make directly for the nearest port. I can't say I blame them. Whatever happens, we will follow the Admiral's orders, understood?"

"Aye, Captain," they chorused.

"Good. *Tempest*, call for all hands on deck. We'll get this over with now."

Captains order, Ships obey. She obeyed.

VII

Caniculus trudged miserably through the city streets, heading for the Londin Amphitheatre. It was a place he knew well. He'd grown up hearing the roars of wild beasts and tending to their needs ever since he was old enough to pick up a shovel and, even now, he could identify each creature's dung by smell alone. A life amid the stink of animals hadn't been how he'd wanted to spend his days, so he'd been glad to apply to the Agent's School as soon as he was old enough. It wasn't as if his father didn't have his brothers to carry on the family business.

He'd got used to wearing the helmet now. It was remarkably light, unlike the things soldiers or gladiators wore, as if it was made of something other than normal metal. He supposed that Vulcan, or Hephaestus as the Greeks called him, had more knowledge of strange alloys than anybody else. He'd certainly had enough time to perfect his craft. Caniculus did his best not to think of whose hands the artefact had passed through down the centuries, keeping his mind on the job to ward off the shivers.

The streets were relatively deserted. Marcus had declared a public holiday, so everyone who was able had set off early to get the best view they could. Whole families were packed into the enormous arena, complete with picnics and cushions to ensure the maximum level of comfort. The mood of festivity was in sharp contrast to the uncertainty of the previous days, though Caniculus's gut was telling him that it was the calm before the storm. He wondered how long it would take before word came of the Fae's arrival – if it ever did. Marcus, or his advisors, had probably thought of a way to block it. In the meantime, he had to think about his own future and hope that the rest would work itself out.

The first acts had already finished as he slipped in through the stage entrance and headed down into the stuffy darkness beneath the arena. Above him, the noise of the crowd rose and fell in response to the level of excitement, muffled by the enclosing stonework. Cells on each side held everything from condemned prisoners to gladiators limbering up for the fight, all watched by guards dressed in the city colours of red and yellow and illuminated by flickering lantern light.

The animals were at the other end, nearer to the lifts that would transport their cages directly up on to the sand. The roars and snarls were audible even over the urgent voices and clanking of machinery. In the olden days, entire cargoes of beasts had been slaughtered to appease the crowds, but now with most of the animals much harder to find, sponsors tended to be more frugal with the casualties and tried to reuse the rarer species.

He hurried past the human arena fodder, hoping to catch sight of his family. Sure enough, he heard his father before he saw him. Novius was on fine form.

"Jove's teeth, Aulus! She must have woken up by now?"

His elder brother's voice boomed back, fighting to be heard over the row of dozens of frightened animals.

"I stopped giving her the herbs last night, Pa! She'll be fine in a minute!"

As Caniculus drew level with one of the larger cells, he saw that they were arguing over the chimaera. Three heads rested across her paws, eyes tight shut, breath whiffling in triplicate as she slept on.

"It's a bloody good job we've still got time," Novius bellowed, giving the creature a look of disgust. "Has Caius watered the pegasi?"

"Yes, Pa," his brother said, wearily. Their father always got like this before a job. They joked that he was harder to cope with than the animals, though to be fair he was always calm around his charges. Handling was in his blood, even if it seemed to have bypassed his second son.

"Good. Check on the elephants, will you?"

Caniculus hoped that they weren't scheduled for a grisly end. He liked elephants, despite their sometimes unpredictable behaviour.

"First act's nearly finished!" one of the stagehands yelled. Novius checked his timepiece and frowned, shoving it back inside a pocket.

"They're on time, for once."

That meant that the crowd had been treated to the preliminary round of executions reserved for criminals. Sometimes they'd be forced to fight each other, or be given a wooden sword and left to try their luck against half-starved animals. The audience would place bets on which ones would last the longest, or sit back and be entertained by their attempts to escape.

The second act would be more serious, consisting of more heinous crimes, such as treason or murder. The offender would often be cast in the role of a mythical character who came to an unpleasant end. Caniculus had seen an 'Actaeon' torn apart by dogs, a 'Hector' dragged behind a chariot and an 'Orpheus' torn to pieces by 'Thracian women', amongst others. Nor were females exempt. There were plenty of punishments for them, too: trampled by bulls, chased and run through with swords or hanged like Penelope's treacherous maids. The old histories provided plenty of examples and the crowd always delighted in new twists to the well-worn tales.

Abruptly, the chimaera's reptilian head hissed and the others began to twitch. It seemed that she was waking after all. The crowd were in for a very special show indeed, as long as she could shake off the effect of the soporific herbs. His father was watching the creature anxiously, though she couldn't leave her cage until the door was opened remotely.

Clopping hooves behind him indicated that the pegasi were on the move. Caniculus flattened himself against the wall as five winged horses trotted past, wings furled, on their way to their riders. He watched them go, hoping that his unseen presence wouldn't cause one of them to spook.

A large dark eye, framed by long lashes, rolled briefly in his direction. Then they were disappearing off down the corridor and he could breathe a sigh of relief. His family were fine and that was what he'd wanted to make sure of. Now he'd be better leaving them to it and heading up to where he could watch the show.

Nobody noticed as he slipped past handlers and stagehands to make his way out and up to the stands. Once there, he paused to get his bearings and see what he could spot across the massive expanse of tiered seating.

The Royal Box was prominent, draped in purple and snarling dragon banners. Caniculus could see Marcus, although there was no sign of Kite. The new Prime Mage was probably elsewhere, giving orders and checking that their plans weren't going awry. Caniculus sent up a quick prayer that the Gods would cause his bowels to rot. Macro, however, was very much in evidence, the light glinting off his breastplate as he guarded his Sovereign, and there were ranks of his men ranged around as well. All access to the Usurper would be heavily guarded. It was tempting to pass them all and dispose of Marcus before anyone was the wiser, but there would be other, unseen protections and Caniculus wasn't sure of the helmet's limitations. Besides which, he had a real desire to keep breathing.

He surveyed the nobles. The seats were full. Marcus's removal of the sword must have brought them all back from their country villas, eager to show their support for the new monarch. Pendragon's claim was dead in the water, he thought, pun intended, even if the news got out that he wasn't at the bottom of the ocean along with his niece. Nobody would stand against Marcus now, relieved that there'd been a smooth transition of power.

The plebeians were their usual happy selves, eager to see all the action which would preferably be served with plenty of blood and guts. Thus it had always been. What had that old Roman poet said? Oh yes, *panem et circenses*. Give the people food and entertainment and you'd have their support. Marcus wasn't daft.

Caniculus lounged against the wall and watched the spectacle. There didn't seem to be much of a second act – there couldn't have been any horrendous crimes lately, apart from the one he'd witnessed. A brief vision of Marcus and his minion meeting a grisly and public end on the sand below flashed across his mind. If only! Instead, they were lording it over decent folk. It was scant consolation that the Gods knew. There weren't any political executions either. Any dissenters, such as that poor Priest and probably Bullfinch, the previous Prime Mage, would have been discreetly murdered in a dark corner somewhere. Come to think of it, he couldn't see old Aquila anywhere. Surely Jupiter's High Priest wasn't dead too? He made a mental note to check it out later – if there was a later for him.

The smell of roast meat made his stomach rumble and he looked around for the source. It would be easy to filch a bit if he was careful, then he could find a spot with a good view and eat whilst watching the entertainment. The gladiators would be on next and they would be the best Britannia could offer.

As the sun rose higher in the sky, the temperature inside the arena increased. It was quite warm for the end of Aprilius. Caniculus felt the shadow of the awning fall across him, as it was extended by arena workers hauling on ropes and pulleys. The sight of the sailcloth reminded him of Ships and his thoughts switched to Milo, somewhere out at sea with the disgraced Admiral and the Princess, facing an uncertain fate. A shiver ran up his back despite the heat and he felt his skin prickle, as if someone had walked past his tomb in some far-off time.

A roar brought him back to the present. Lines of armed men and women were striding onto the sand and saluting their supporters in the crowd. Caniculus sucked his teeth and watched them come.

Now the real Games would start.

*

<*Tempest*.> The Admiral had finished writing.

<Sir?>

<I've drafted the message of surrender. Be ready to contact the *Regina*.>

She knew what it must have cost him.

<Aye, Sir. Do you want me to relay it?>

<No. I'll speak directly to her. She can tell Albanus.>

She marvelled at his lack of emotion. He'd had a lot of practice in concealing his true thoughts over the years, but this was a masterclass. The *Regina* would get nothing from him that he wasn't willing to give and, furthermore, be reminded of his status. He was still a Prince of the Blood, Lord High Admiral and Head of the Britannic Royal Navy.

<Opening the link now, Sir.>

She braced herself and reached out to her former classmate, forming her thoughts into an arrow winging its way over the ocean.

<Tempest to *Regina.* Acknowledge, *Regina.>*

As she did so, the memory of a red-faced Tullia pounding clothes rose into her mind. Tullia had hated every second of her enforced punishment as a servant, but it helped to remind Maia just where she'd come from.

The reply was a few seconds coming.

<This is *Regina.>*

The silence between them stretched out, though it couldn't have been more than a few seconds. Maia examined the link, using her other abilities to see if she could amplify her reach and glean more of what the other Ship was thinking. The wave of triumphant satisfaction told her all she needed to know. They thought Pendragon was beaten.

<Admiral Pendragon sends his compliments,> she answered, keeping her feelings to herself. <He will address you directly.>

<So he's heard, then?> *Regina* replied. <Marcus has pulled out the sword. He can announce that the rumours of your sinking were false and everyone will rejoice! It's a good job too, for both of us!>

<It is indeed.> Maia answered through gritted teeth.

<Can you imagine if we'd had to fight? How horrible!>

Maia had expected gloating or maybe a sneer, but *Regina* just sounded happy and not a little relieved.

<Yes, it would have been terrible.>

<And now it's all going to be wonderful! A new age of peace and plenty. I'm so glad! We can be friends again, can't we?>

What was she up to? Maia was confused. Why was she being so *nice?*

<Yes, of course.> She didn't know what else to say.

<It will all be fine. The King knows it wasn't your fault, you were just following orders in all the confusion. *You* haven't said anything treacherous.>

Maia racked her brain, as she was sure that she'd said plenty of unfavourable things. They mustn't have been reported.

<Thank you, *Regina.* I'm putting the Admiral through now.> She stepped back to allow the Admiral to connect.

He didn't take long. A short, formal declaration, exquisitely worded.

<It has been reported to me that the Sword of Kingship has made its choice. I do not intend to go against its decision. Inform your Captain that I shall be returning to Portus after I have resupplied my Ship at Malvadum. End Sending.>

He promptly closed the link.

<Well, that was interesting!> *Regina* laughed. She wasn't at all put out. <Don't worry about him. I imagine it'll all be sorted out as soon as he can meet with the King. They are father and son, after all and there have been a lot of false rumours and misunderstandings.>

So that's what they're calling Artorius's murder.

<You seem well,> Maia ventured.

<I am indeed!> The smug tone was now more like the Tullia Maia knew well. <I have a wonderful surprise for you, but I can't say anything yet. It's a secret,> she added.

<Go on. You can tell me! We're friends,> Maia wheedled. Whatever *Regina* was holding back was important, she was sure of it and she knew that the other Ship was dying to tell her.

<Oh, I mustn't!> *Regina* wailed in frustration, though Maia could tell that she was nearly bursting with what she knew. The strength of her emotion coloured the link, as if it was a secret tucked away inside a jewellery box. Maia could visualise it, sealed but not quite locked. All it would take was a little lever to gently prise it open and peep inside…

The link snapped shut before she could get to whatever *Regina* had been hiding, as if a door had been slammed in her face.

Maia mentally shook herself, blinking at the sudden ending of their conversation. A secret indeed and one that she would have to prise out of her sister Ship at the earliest opportunity.

"They believe us," Pendragon was telling Leo and Raven. "Good. They'll be preparing the population to welcome in the Old Gods next."

"The Olympians won't be pleased if their worship is supplanted," Leo pointed out.

"Oh, I daresay that they'll keep the odd temple to Neptune along the coast, but they'll combine his worship with some old equivalent, like Manannan. As long as the God gets his due he might not be too worried, despite his brother's rage," Raven said, ever practical. "It won't happen all at once. It will be a slow erosion of the Olympians' power, to the benefit of the native Gods and the Old Ones from across the sea. Foreign influences will wane as worship returns to the ancient ways. Of course, there are those that never left them, despite the years of Roman rule."

"Which has of late been in name only," Pendragon mused. He came to a decision. "Well, gentlemen. I can see only one course of action. Unless any subterfuge is proved, we must bide our time. When the Fae start to bite, then maybe we can rouse the people and gain the support of the Alliance. Until then, we are bound by circumstance and the will of the Gods."

<What a pile of *merda* this is turning out to be,> Leo Sent to Maia privately.

She could only agree, especially as the other Ships were starting to comment, some of them forcefully.

<So we're all friends again, are we?> *Leopard* growled.

<I believe that as much as I believe Marcus pulled out the damn Sword,> *Persistence* answered. <There's some trick to it!>

<We can't prove that, and after what we did I doubt he'll be in a forgiving mood,> *Blossom* cut in ominously.

<Too right, sister! Maybe we should set sail for friendlier climes?>

Maia could tell that all the Ships were worried. *Blossom* and *Persistence* had fought what amounted to a pitched battle in Portus harbour and they now knew that, in effect, they'd backed the losing side. Marcus's position seemed unassailable.

<He needs us,> *Imperatrix* announced. <Relations with the Alliance could sour and then we'd be back to keeping them out. He won't do anything.>

Maia didn't share her confidence and, from the pall of worry that threaded through the link, neither did anyone else.

<We'll be required to take an oath, I expect,> *Diadem* said. <Remember this, ladies. Kings come and go, yet we remain. This is a storm that will blow over, like any other. Give it a hundred years and we'll still be here moaning about the management, same as usual!>

Her remarks elicited a few nervous giggles. It was good to get an older Ship's perspective. She was probably right as well. Maia and her friends would be around when Marcus and his cronies were rotting in their tombs – or buried in unmarked graves. She hoped it would be the latter. Perhaps, in a couple of centuries, she and Raven would sit chatting about it all. To a Ship, a hundred years was like ten years to anyone else and she'd only just completed two of the latter. She couldn't imagine what the world would be like in several hundred years. Maybe they'd all be powered by steam engines instead of sails, or fly through the air like birds? New inventions seemed to be cropping up constantly. She and *Patience* could tell the new Ships how she used to have sails, just like the ancient ones remembered their oarsmen from when they were galleys.

Leo's voice dragged her back to the present.

<*Tempest*, adjust course for Malvadum. We'll take on supplies, then crawl back to Portus.>

The other Ships had their orders too.

<Pity it's not Abona,> *Imperatrix* grumbled. <I like Abona.>

<We're nearly there, anyway,> Maia pointed out. <At least we can take our time in getting back to Portus.>

Maybe by then they'd have better news as well.

*

It was mid-morning when Milo saw the dark clouds almost upon them on the westward horizon. He'd just popped up on deck for some fresh air, leaving Latonia and Julia playing a game of *tabula*. A few of the crew had noticed as well and were peering into the distance with scowling faces.

"A storm?" he asked one fellow.

"It's been threatening for a while," the man answered. His eyes glazed over momentarily. "*Wolf* isn't happy about it."

So, they could communicate with their Longship in a limited fashion. They must have undergone some rite or other, binding them to the spirit like their Captain had. Maybe he'd have time to ask someone about it at some point, unless it was a sacred mystery and not for outsiders.

"It's fast moving," he observed and the man grunted.

"Too fast." His head jerked, as if he was receiving orders. "You should go below," he told Milo. A subtle tension had crept over the vessel, as if its spirit's anxiety was permeating the atmosphere.

Milo rubbed the back of his neck. All his Agent's senses were warning him that something unpleasant was near. He'd always known that he had a nose for danger ever since he was small, and he pushed the feeling to its limit to try and get a sense of what might be approaching.

A bitter taste flooded into his mouth, as if it were filled with chewed grass. He hawked and spat over the side to try and clear it, but the sourness remained. Whatever it was, he hadn't experienced it before. It didn't have the feel of Divine Potentia, the heaviness that preceded the arrival of the Gods. That hit like a lump of lead, together with a deep vibration that throbbed in the earth like some hidden engine powering up. This felt more…green.

Now why had that colour come into his mind?

Green, like the magic that had summoned the bone construct in Londin. The green that told him it was Fae. He headed below decks and aft, towards Ranulfson's quarters. Two burly crewmen blocked his way as he left his accustomed path.

"I need to see the Captain, now! We're in great danger!"

They exchanged glances, then one nodded. "Wait."

Milo forced himself to remain calm as the man lumbered off along the corridor. If he was right, every second could make a difference. Almost as an afterthought, he activated his speechstone and opened a link to Raven.

<A line of storm clouds, you say?> the ancient Mage replied, once Milo had explained. <Interesting. Sillina warned us of nine Fae vessels making the crossing, but didn't say where. It seems appropriate that they should choose a narrow point and seek to conceal their approach, though I thought they'd head for Mona first.>

<Do you think they will attack?>

He could visualise the old man setting his jaw as he deliberated.

<Unknown. Will they be able to distinguish one type of Ship from another? Hopefully they will, but you should be prepared.>

<I'm waiting to see the Captain.>

<Good. Follow his advice and keep me apprised. Protect the Princess at all costs. Believe me, the Northmen will. One more thing. Be wary of using your speechstone when they're near. They might be able to intercept communication.>

<Understood.> It stood to reason that the link might not be secure, but it would be a blasted nuisance.

Their conversation ended and he was just mulling over Raven's warning when the guard reappeared, beckoning him forward. The cabin was partitioned off, with the side he was entering being the business end. The other area had been set up as temporary sleeping quarters. It was bigger than he'd imagined, but small compared to the larger Britannic Ships. Ranulfson was sitting at his desk, which looked to be of Italian make. So, they did allow themselves some luxuries.

"You wished to see me?" The Captain regarded him curiously but respectfully, and in that instant Milo knew that his supposed status as a servant had been doubted all along.

"Thank you, sir," he began. "It is my belief that we are about to cross paths with Major Fae."

Ranulfson became very still, his eyes fixed on Milo's face, yet slightly out of focus as he consulted with his Longship.

"You have proof of this?" he asked mildly.

"I know the signs. I've come across them before, plus we know that they're on the move. According to the Goddess Sillina, nine vessels sailed from Hibernia some hours ago."

He plunged on, knowing that the time for secrecy was over. "It's known that Marcus has allied himself with them and intends to rule with their aid, or more likely as their puppet. Our Gods have spoken against him, which makes his removal of the Sword even more unlikely."

The Captain's face grew grimmer. "If Sillina says it is so, I have no reason to doubt her. Well, Master Government Agent, what do your superiors think?"

"I answer to Master Mage Raven, not Marcus," Milo replied, ruefully. Of course the Northman hadn't been fooled. "My priority is the safety of the Princess."

Ranulfson nodded. "Good. It is my priority also. We will offer no resistance, unless they show hostile intent." He held up a hand as Milo opened his mouth to protest. "But I think it best that we increase our speed and petition our Gods, just in case."

"And ready your weapons."

Ranulfson's teeth flashed white in his beard. "Just so. We have had dealings with these creatures too, a couple of hundred years ago when we sought to colonise Hibernia."

Milo twitched. "What happened there?"

Ranulfson shrugged. "We don't know exactly. We never heard from our people again and the project was abandoned after the Gods sent unfavourable omens."

Milo raised his eyebrows.

"Ours don't like the Fae either," he admitted.

Ranulfson regarded him evenly. "I will make sacrifice and ask Tyr to aid us."

Milo knew that he was speaking of their Battle God.

"I'll stay with the Princess."

Ranulfson rose. "Good. You know what to do if things look hopeless."

Both men knew that capture by the Fae wouldn't be an option. Milo met the Captain's eyes.

"I understand."

"I will kill the remaining sheep," Ranulfson said, as they left. "It's a pity that we can't eat them over and over, like Thor's magic goats, eh?"

He clapped the Agent on the shoulder and swung himself up the ladder.

As he returned to Julia's cabin, Milo fingered his concealed dagger and prayed that he wouldn't have to use it. With any luck they would slip by, out of sight of whatever was riding in the Hibernian vessels.

"Ah, Milo. You've come in the nick of time," Julia told him as he entered. "I'm not doing well at all."

Across from her, Latonia was grinning like a well-fed cat.

"I take it you're losing, Highness?" Milo asked. Julia smiled ruefully.

"I'm getting my backside well and truly kicked."

Latonia smothered a giggle as she made the final move that proclaimed her the winner. Milo surveyed her strategy.

"Masterful," he said, with a bow. The former slave's eyes sparkled. She really was very pretty, but Milo knew that she only had eyes for her fierce Shieldmaiden. Unfortunately, his next words would spoil the celebratory mood.

"Highness, you should know there are Fae vessels on the horizon. We're hoping that they pass by, but the Captain has ordered his Ship to increase course in the hope of avoiding them."

Latonia's eyes widened.

"They won't attack us, surely?" Julia asked. "They'll want to make landfall as soon as they can. I was always told that they aren't creatures of open water."

"We only know what the old stories tell us, Highness," Milo replied. It's possible that they have human servants who know something of the sea. Several hundred years is enough time for them to have adapted."

"There's one thing in our favour," Julia said. "There's a lot more iron around now. In some places, I swear the very air will poison them, it's so full of fumes."

"Is it true that iron poisons them?" Latonia asked.

"We think that it gives off some form of miasma that weakens their abilities," Milo told her, "but it's never been studied. Some of the Fae don't like it, but others seem less affected."

"They must have found a way around it, or they wouldn't even be trying to invade," Julia frowned. Then her face changed as a thought struck her. "But what of Excalibur? Its proximity is fatal to them, or so they say."

He couldn't put the moment off any longer.

"Highness, the report is that Marcus has withdrawn the Sword. It was witnessed by the whole of Londin, though Raven suspects that it was a falsehood engineered by Fae glamour."

The colour slowly drained from Julia's face.

"Oh Gods! He might try to destroy it, or certainly put it out of sight. Maybe even bury it."

A knock at the door was immediately followed by Bodil's face.

"Please come on deck. The Captain is speaking to the Gods."

She hesitated for a second, aware of the tenseness in the cabin, before withdrawing.

162

"You'll need your coat, Highness." Latonia bustled over to where it hung on the bulkhead and helped her mistress into it. Julia pulled the thick folds around her though the air wasn't cold. She seemed instead to be assailed by a chill that was nothing to do with the sea but exited with her head held high, Latonia at the fore. Milo brought up the rear.

On deck, the solemn beat of a drum rang out across the water, together with a low chant from the crew. The sheep's throat was already cut and the spilled blood gathered into a bowl. Ranulfson's second-in-command, a tall blond man who answered to Snorri Fairhair, was marking each man with a dab on the face. Julia walked up to where the Ambassador was standing, her eyes fixed on the horizon. Milo followed her gaze to see that the storm clouds seemed to have dissipated into a bank of fog that obscured the water in a silvery curtain.

Julia submitted to Snorri's bloody finger, though Milo could tell that she wasn't enamoured of the ritual. It was something she would have to get used to. Ranulfson's face was plastered with the stuff, as was Gudrun's. Standing next to the Princess, Latonia was similarly marked. Bodil's features soon bore several dripping lines, and then it was his turn.

The coppery smell hit his nose first, then a line of warmth was smeared across his forehead. He blinked as a drop bypassed his brows and ran down the side of his nose. Snorri's pale eyes were fixed in concentration as he consecrated the crew and passengers to the Aesir. Milo hoped that it would all come to something. He'd have preferred to petition Neptune directly, but he supposed that the Northmen would also sacrifice to Njord, as their God of Sailors. Or one of them, anyway. They seemed to have a couple of pantheons or families and he wasn't always sure who belonged where.

Mighty Neptune, raise your trident to stir the sea and sink our foes, he prayed. In this situation, one friendly deity was as good as another. It would certainly solve a lot of problems if the enemy vessels foundered before they even reached Britannia.

Wolf of the Waves was working hard now and he could see the strain in the faces around him as the Longship drew energy from his human crew. This was where a Mage would come in handy, he thought, but Longships operated on quite a different system. They were skimming the water at top speed but, bit by bit, the creeping line of fog was encroaching on their position. Another few minutes and they would be engulfed.

The chanting stopped abruptly, as Ranulfson raised a hand for silence. Sound carried across the water and the drum alone would be enough to give away their position. The only sounds now were the creaking of the vessel and the splashing of the waves breaking over the bow.

The Ambassador caught Milo's eye and signalled him over.

"Excellency?"

"Get the Princess below. Pack essentials in case you have to leave in a hurry."

He nodded and went to mutter in Julia's ear, conscious all the while of the increasing tension. All of a sudden, the crew broke formation and began to arm themselves, many hurrying to take up position on the guns. He hustled a compliant Julia back to her cabin as quickly as he could, then told her to dress warmly.

"Put on as much as you can manage. You too, Latonia. It can be cold in an open boat."

Latonia paused for a moment as she rummaged through a chest, then resumed, her thought left unsaid. Presumably she objected to leaving Bodil, but the Princess would need her.

"You think they'll attack," she said, glancing over her shoulder at him.

"I know it." He couldn't say how he knew, but he did. The Fae weren't sophisticated enough to distinguish between nations; all they would see was a lone vessel full of humans for them to hunt and take and he didn't intend to be around when they did. Maybe a small boat would have more chance of getting to shore whilst their attackers were distracted. At the very least, out on the water both he and Julia could use their Potentia freely and provide some sort of cover for themselves. On the *Wolf of the Waves*, they were easy targets.

Both women worked quickly, bagging clothes, food and weapons into bundles that were light enough to carry.

"What now?" Julia asked him when they were ready. "Do we just abandon ship?"

"We have to. Now."

"And if the Captain objects?"

Milo raised an eyebrow at her. "I doubt he will. Besides, if he manages to stay afloat, he can swing by and pick us up later."

"But they're heading for land. We won't be any safer."

"We can conceal ourselves until they pass by," he pointed out. "They'll be too busy fighting angry Northmen. Let's hope that their Gods show up, eh?"

"They're too far away," Latonia spoke up. Milo shot her a puzzled glance, but realised that she could be right. If they hadn't been able to protect the settlers, maybe there was a range limit?

"We'll have to rely on Neptune, then."

From the wry look on Latonia's face, he didn't think that was a viable option either. The Gods were notorious for not coming when called, instead appearing when they were least expected. He could attest to that fact himself.

Swift One, if you're listening in, we could really do with some help right now!

Mercury had shown him favour before, in person no less, so it was worth a try. Latonia was watching him with barely concealed amusement and he was struck at how much she'd changed since gaining her freedom. She didn't seem to be afraid of anything anymore; in that respect, she was a lot braver than he was and he envied her sanguine attitude.

Personally, he thought they'd be lucky to see the sun set.

"Come on." He urged the two women out and up on deck. The daylight had already changed, taking on a misty, translucent quality more akin to dawn than early afternoon. Sounds were muffled and faces appeared and disappeared like wraiths. One of them belonged to Bodil.

"What are you doing?" she demanded.

"Leaving," Milo answered, tersely. "Help me with the boat."

"You'll need *Wolf* to do that for you," she said.

"Then I'll ask him." He turned towards the prow and spoke.

"*Wolf of the Waves*! We need you to lower your boat. I can protect the Princess at sea, but not here!"

A nearby crewman lurched out of the thickening mist.

"Ja! Komm!"

Milo knew enough to understand that the Longship would aid their departure. Having no voice of his own, he could use his crew when necessary. It was as if the Longship was some

165

intertwined organism with many brains and hands. The three of them hurried across the deck after the sailor to where a boat was already waiting to be lowered. It hung without movement from its winch and, looking over the side, Milo could see that the sea had turned to glass. Whatever magic the Fae were using had rendered the waves as calm as an atrium pool.

Hands helped them aboard, but at the last minute, Latonia refused.

"I'm staying to fight," she insisted.

"What? You can't! It's not safe!" Julia was horrified.

"I'll be fine." Latonia smiled and vanished into the swirling tendrils of fog. Julia cast an imploring glance at Milo, but he was already aboard. The boat began to drop and the flanks of the Longship moved upwards, as if it were ascending and they were hanging, suspended and motionless.

"It's her choice!" Milo hissed, clutching at the gunwales. Just then, a head appeared at the rail.

"You'll need this!"

A bundle fell at Milo's feet, as Latonia's head disappeared into the fog. It was his, he realised. In his haste, he'd not thought to bring it, throwing on an extra cloak and shoving bits into his coat pockets instead. He didn't know whether to thank her or curse her for her stubbornness.

The boat hit the water and rocked, steadying itself. Working quickly, they released it from its ropes and Milo unshipped the oars. Across from him, Julia's face was a white blob against the greyness of their surroundings.

"Tell me you can row," he said.

"I was never allowed to learn."

"Blast it!"

Hopefully he'd manage alone. "At least you can help to push us away."

She followed his lead and soon they were bobbing in the Longship's wake, the sounds of his passing fading into the thickened air.

"What do we do now?" she whispered.

"We hide." He shipped the oars and crouched down, signalling for her to do the same. "Can you cast a spell of concealment?"

She grimaced. "Only a little one. I can do small items, like cups and bowls."

"Well, we're going to need something bigger. Which form do you use?"

She whispered the words. It was a beginner's spell. Raven had been cautious with his pupil, not wishing to overload her – or perhaps give her too much power.

"Try this one instead. Focus your Potentia and repeat after me, concentrating on creating a sphere around our boat."

He brought the words to mind, feeling the ripples of the magic spreading outwards on the wave of his intent. He heard Julia begin to repeat them, then the force of her Potentia took over from his, as if little trickle was swamped by a flash flood. Her power burst outwards, enclosing them in a silent explosion of raw energy that did all he could have wished for and more.

"Good!" he managed to whisper, once he'd recovered from the shock. "Now you must maintain it."

"I can do that," she replied confidently. "This spell is so much better than the one Raven taught me!"

Milo choked back a laugh. The old Mage hadn't been exaggerating; if anything, he'd played down his apprentice's Potentia to a significant degree. Milo just hoped that it was enough to save the pair of them.

A second later, the fog parted and the first vessel appeared. The amulet reacted immediately, chiming a warning before he shut it off. It only confirmed what he'd been dreading.

He hadn't known what to expect, but it wasn't this. The vessel looked like something from an old storybook, its single mast reaching for the sky and the top hidden by the encompassing mist. A lone square sail billowed out, propelling the boat onwards as it glided over the uncanny calmness of the water. The sudden chill that gripped his body spun its own warning that something dangerous was approaching, and he realised that he was holding his breath. Shadowy figures draped in cloaks stood in the bow, pale faces set to the east and he wondered whether these were human or Fae. He couldn't tell and it was too risky to try to get a better look. There was something uncanny the way that the vessel moved, silently without the creaking of rigging; it seemed to cut the still water like a blade parting flesh, leaving barely a ripple behind. Beside him, Julia clutched the bench seat, her face rigid in concentration as she held the spell of concealment.

The first was only just past when another appeared, then another. Other shapes were barely visible in the mist, but Milo knew they were there. The sour taste in his mouth made him swallow convulsively, but he didn't dare spit and break Julia's hold on her Potentia. She was already doing more than any Mage of his acquaintance was capable of save Raven, and he was a man apart.

He was just beginning to think that they'd be noticed, when an eerie call split the fog, sounding more bird-like than anything. Julia shot him a frantic look, but he shook his head. If they'd been spotted there would be no chance of escape. He gripped his dagger, knowing that he might only have seconds to use it, first on her and then on himself.

Another sound drifted over the water, a roar that could only have come from human throats, together with the noise of metal clashing on metal.

Wolf of the Waves had returned.

"What are they doing?" Julia whispered.

He thought quickly. There could only be one reason why the Longship had turned back.

"Providing a diversion."

The yelling intensified, together with the high calls from the Fae vessels. Both sides had clearly sighted each other.

"They must be mad!" Julia was horrified.

"Their first duty is to you," he replied, straining his eyes to see through the mist. "They won't have time to stop for us now."

"I can help them!" she insisted.

"No, you can't. Come on."

The crack of musket fire and the boom of cannon drowned out any protest she might have made, filling the misty air with the sulphurous stink of black powder.

An answering flare of green lit the water with a sickly glow.

"Is that how they fight, with magic?" Julia whispered. Milo bent his back and cursed the fact that she couldn't use the other set of oars.

"Yes and with stone arrows and slingshots. They can be just as deadly as musket balls."

He began to row away from the battle as fast and as quietly as he could. Behind him, Julia maintained the concealing sphere, listening helplessly as the yells turned to screams. The ordnance spoke again and again, though the Fae weapons were silent. Many a man would fall without seeing the dart that struck him, and swords would be useless unless they could snag the vessels with grappling hooks and then board. The Fae would want to avoid that at all costs. The reduced visibility was in their favour as well.

Julia grabbed his arm. He turned to look over his shoulder as another vessel appeared, heading into the fray. He froze in place, trusting that his companion would do the same and praying frantically that the vessel would miss them. It passed by their position with barely an arm's length to spare, a grey wall of smooth-grained pale wood almost close enough to touch.

He was relieved to see that the Princess had not faltered in her spell, her lips moving silently and her forehead creased as she maintained their illusion, but his relief turned to alarm as he realised that they were being dragged along in the vessel's wake. Even when he resumed rowing, the pull of the magic propulsion was too much and they were carried along behind it, helpless to affect their course or turn aside.

He cursed soundlessly. Concealment was all; he couldn't afford to ask Julia to stop to try and break free. They would just have to follow and hope that there would be an opportunity later.

"Keep going!" he muttered and she obliged, though her face showed him that she was as anxious as he was. All they could do was hang on as they were towed ever deeper towards the sounds of battle. The shield was an excellent defence, but he doubted that it would survive a direct cannon hit.

Ahead of them, the high stern of the Fae vessel glowed silvery-green as its crew mustered their weapons to attack the *Wolf of the Waves*. The noise grew louder, reverberating over the water as the Longship's guns fired again and again, until they drew close enough to spot the muzzle flashes. The taint in the air grew worse and he pulled his tunic up over his nose and mouth to block off the worst of it, motioning to Julia to follow his example.

Then they were through. Ahead of them, a clearer space opened up to reveal the truth of the Longship's desperate situation. *Wolf of the Waves* was being harried by four Fae vessels, like a bull being baited for sport. Her crew were working frantically to fire at the enemy, but strong magical shields were deflecting most of the iron shot. Milo reflected grimly that the Fae must have learned a few tricks since their last battle with mortals. The projectiles couldn't hurt them if they had no way of reaching their intended targets. Phalanxes of Fae archers were sending wave after wave of arrows on to the deck of the Longship, where bodies were toppling like scythed wheat. Milo could hear the howling as *Wolf* urged on his warriors. There was no hope for them now and he could do nothing to aid them.

Then the guns stopped. All the figures on board the Longship suddenly disappeared, as if they'd taken cover and Milo grinned mirthlessly. The Northmen were trying a new strategy. The Fae seemed confused. They cried to each other, their voices skimming over the water, before coming to a decision. Two of the vessels turned and headed directly for the Longship, anticipating the kill, whilst the others, including the one that had them in its grasp, hung back. It slowed and took up position, presumably to watch the fun as the humans were dealt with once and for all. This gave Milo and Julia their chance. He manoeuvred the oars back into the water and moved off as stealthily as he could manage.

He watched as he rowed. The Fae vessels had got close enough to allow their sailors to jump across to the Longship's deck, which they did with graceful leaps. They reminded him of a tumbling act he'd seen once; the Fae seeming to hover mid-air, as if defying natural laws of motion before landing lightly on their toes, weapons drawn. The metallic blades shone with a bronze sheen, not the cold silver of steel or iron, but just as deadly. They began to look about them, as if wondering where everybody had gone.

It was then that the hatches opened and the Northmen struck. Several Fae fell to their swords before they realised what was happening, but the others soon re-grouped. Even at this distance,

Milo could see the figure of Captain Ranulfson laying about him with a war axe, cleaving flesh and bone, whilst beside him smaller, slighter figures held their own, their battle screams cutting through the yells. As they passed once more, he glimpsed Ambassador Gudrun fighting alongside her comrades, grey hair flying as she slashed at her attackers before disappearing beneath a flurry of arrows. A taller figure could only be the faithful Bodil, with Latonia at her side.

It was all he could make out before the mists closed up again and they were in a sea of swirling vapour, the noise turning to muffled sounds that seemed to be happening miles away. He had no idea of direction. Opposite him Julia sat rigid, still casting Potentia. Tears streamed down her cheeks to dampen the cloak she had wrapped around her face, her eyes wide with horror.

Was it Milo's imagination, or was the air becoming sweeter now? He strained and heaved at the oars, knowing that every stroke took them further away from the immediate danger, though what would await them after that he had no way of knowing. His duty was clear – to protect the Princess and, for him, nothing else mattered.

*

Crouching beneath the latticework of the hatch, Bodil also knew her duty. The Captain, in consultation with his Ship, had given the order to hide. Truth be told, they'd all expected to make short work of the Fae's more primitive vessels; iron cannonballs and musket shot were supposed to smash their magic to pieces and render them vulnerable, but that plan had failed.

"They have shields, like those of the Britannic Ships but stronger," the Ambassador had hissed at her as they armed themselves, ready for battle.

"I thought they used glamour," Bodil frowned.

"Ha!" Gudrun tapped her mail shirt and helmet. "We're protected by these, though unarmed folk won't be as lucky. When they make land the peasants won't be able to stand against them."

Bodil grabbed another pair of knives "Then let's make this count, shall we?"

Gudrun grinned back. "I shall see you in Valhalla this day. If you get there before me, save me a seat!"

"Do you think your Gods will welcome me?" Latonia looked very different in her borrowed mail. Bodil approved of the eagerness in her eyes.

"I'm sure they will, if you die fighting," Gudrun answered. "We shall live forever in the Hall of Odin, with fighting every day and feasting every night!"

"It will be magnificent," Bodil assured her, "and we will be together always, Shieldmaidens forever!"

They'd remained below whilst the first wave of warriors fought and died, but now it was time to make their stand. As soon as the Fae got close enough, they would burst out from the hatches and cut them down before they could react. It was a last, desperate chance to make their deaths count for something and win the approval of the Gods. Better that than dying in years to come, enfeebled by old age and prey to the claws of time. She'd had a good life.

Now she stood on the ladder, Latonia and Gudrun below her, waiting for the order. Even though she couldn't tell what was happening on deck, she knew that it wouldn't be long coming. The Fae moved like cats, but the *Wolf* saw all and he would give the signal.

Now.

The voice was in her head and she sprang up, pushing open the wooden covers and jumping on to the deck. There were three Fae, bows raised as they scanned for signs of movement. She dispatched the first cleanly, running it through with minimum effort. It died silently, pale blood staining her blade and owl eyes wide in shock. She caught the next with a knife thrown left-handed into its brain and it collapsed like an emptied sack. A screech beside her told that Latonia had dispatched the other, then there was no time to think as more of the creatures poured over the rail and attacked. Her trained instincts took over and she slashed, parried and stepped with unconscious grace.

To her left, she was dimly aware that the great wolf spirit had detached from the prow and was attacking several enemies at a time. Captain Ranulfson's axe cleaved Fae flesh over and over, until a howling from his Longship told her that he'd fallen. *Wolf of the Waves* mourned, but she had no time to. Bodil blocked blow after blow until her arm ached and her breath came in short gasps, but still they came, over and over, their thin mouths stretched in feral smiles as she cut them down.

A sharp pain in her side told her that a blade had darted through her defences and caught her. She hissed through her teeth and removed the Fae's head, but she could feel the trickle of warmth as she bled.

"Bodil!"

She turned, to see Latonia dispatch another. Gudrun lay sprawled on the planks, several arrows piercing her breast. The Ambassador had beaten her to Valhalla after all.

"Latonia!" She staggered over, one hand pressing her side. They were the only two humans left standing, surrounded by smiling Fae.

"I think we've had enough of this, don't you?"

She must be exhausted, or why would she think that her friend's eyes were glowing gold? The Fae must be affecting her mind somehow. Then light was spreading outwards in a great wave from Latonia's outstretched hand, and where it touched, Fae flesh was crumbling like blown ash. Bodil felt her jaw drop as the Potentia spread outwards like spilled milk, obliterating everything before it, until the decks were clear of all but the two of them and *Wolf of the Waves*.

"Come, Bodil," Latonia instructed, taking her arm. "It's time to leave."

The spirit of the Longship approached slowly, as if uncertain, his wooden claws clicking on the deck.

"*Wolf of the Waves*, your place is with the Princess. Go and find her. Take her to shore and tell her to go to Luguvallium. She is under my father's protection."

The wooden beast cocked his head as if to argue, but the Goddess's eyes glowed brighter and he clearly thought better of it. He dipped his head in homage, then one swift movement took him over the side. Now that the link with his vessel was broken, it began to list and Bodil braced herself.

Hoof beats above her made her look up. An armed woman on a magnificent horse was descending from the clouds. A voice like a brass trumpet followed it.

"Hail to you, daughter of Jupiter!"

"And to you, handmaid of Odin," Latonia replied. "You have many to carry this day!"

"Indeed I do." The Valkyrie reined in and regarded Bodil thoughtfully. "What about this one?"

Latonia's silvery laugh echoed in the silence. "Oh, she's mine! For now, at least."

The rider didn't look happy, but nodded brusquely. "Very well. I haven't come for her anyway."

She leaned over and scooped up another instead. Gudrun settled herself firmly on the horse and raised a hand in farewell. Bodil could only watch as the Valkyrie wheeled the horse about and galloped away into the sky, before disappearing in a flash of rainbow colours.

"You do want to stay with me, don't you?" Latonia whispered softly in her ear. Bodil turned and met the gleaming eyes of the Huntress.

"Yes," she smiled. "For now."

VIII

Malvadum was deceptively peaceful-looking, silhouetted against the rising sun. The fleet arrived without incident, anchoring off the pretty harbour with its backdrop of hills. Maia admired the morning view, wishing mightily that this was just a routine voyage. Even though Pendragon and Raven had talked deep into the night, neither had been able to come up with any counter to the fact that Marcus possessed – or seemed to possess – Excalibur. Maia had watched silently, feeling the Admiral's despair.

"We'll just have to play along, for now," Pendragon had said, stifling a yawn. "Unless you can suggest something else?"

"Not at the moment," Raven admitted. "But don't give up hope."

Nobody was satisfied, but there was little anybody could do. The message had been sent and all they could do was await developments.

<He's really going to give himself up, then?> *Patience* asked Maia, who was keeping her sisters, and through them their Captains, informed of developments.

<What choice does he have? Excalibur has the last word.>

<Hah! From years and years ago,> the *Leopard* chimed in. <It could have lost its magic.>

<Marcus pulled it out and that's that,> *Blossom* said wearily. *Leopard* growled down the link. <It's a trick. Excalibur wouldn't pick a murderer!>

<We have no way of proving it, do we?>

The other Ship subsided, but her rage rumbled through the link like distant thunder.

<If Pendragon sets foot on land, 'e's a dead man!>

Persistence had been quiet for hours and her outburst startled Maia. She checked on the Admiral, only to find that he was indeed readying himself to leave her. Raven and Leo were trying to talk him out of it, but Pendragon was adamant.

"I can do nothing from here," he insisted. "I must at least make a show of submission and I doubt that he'll execute me out of hand."

"No, he'll kill you by stealth, as he did your nephew." Raven's dry tones made Pendragon pause for a moment, before sighing.

"Nonetheless, I have to go. My only consolation is that we sent Julia north. Marcus will be disappointed to get only one Pendragon." He signalled to his servants, allowing them to finish dressing him in his full, princely finery. A final adjustment to his hat, and Cei, Prince of the Realm and Lord High Admiral stood ready to meet his fate.

"I'm not asking you to come with me," he continued. "In fact, I'd rather you remained here. The Gods alone know what will happen, and I'll have the knowledge that you stand ready to move against our ancient foe should the occasion arise."

"But, sir, you can't be without protection!" Leo's face was flushed and he was clearly in distress. The death of one friend and the treachery of another was hard for him to bear and Maia's heart bled for him. His eyes widened in shock when Pendragon actually laughed.

"Forgive me," he said, quickly seeing the expression on the young Captain's face. "I don't take this lightly and I'm not mocking your concern for my well-being." He glanced over at Raven. "Take my word for it, if anyone threatens me, they'll have more to deal with than they bargained for."

Leo's gaze followed the Admiral's to the wizened features of the Master Mage. Comprehension dawned.

"Ah, I see. But will it stop a musket ball?"

"It will," Raven confirmed, "plus poison. The spell is a subtle and complicated one, but I had plenty of time to prepare it on the voyage."

Leo forced a grin. "So, you are like Achilles? No vulnerable bits, I hope?"

All three laughed and the mood lightened. "Not for a couple of days, at least," Raven said, "and by then we should know the lie of the land."

"Literally," Pendragon said. He straightened and placed his hand on his sword hilt. "*Tempest*, ready the boat. Is my escort ready?"

"Aye, Admiral."

She debated whether to tell him that the other Ships weren't happy, but thought that he probably knew. She was truly feeling out of her depth now and wished that she could have dissuaded him, but her first duty was to her crew, even if he had been her Captain in all but name. She would have to rely on Leo now. It was time for the young man to step out of his mentor's shadow and make a name for himself, unless the trip was short-lived and Pendragon was forced to retreat back to relative safety.

It wasn't long before he and his escort of marines were making their way over to the harbour entrance, his gold braid sparkling in the morning sun. Maia had to fight the overwhelming urge to turn her boat around and bring him back.

"His fate is in the hands of the Gods now," Leo said, standing beside her, telescope raised. "It seems that the welcoming committee's already arrived."

Maia magnified her sight and immediately spotted the group of men on the quayside. Some were local worthies, but there was a troop of legionaries discreetly formed up behind them. She felt a surge of apprehension.

"Are they going to arrest him?"

"I expect they're going to take him into custody, under the pretence of being an 'escort party'," Leo replied in disgust.

Maia concentrated on the link to her boat, guiding it smoothly alongside the harbour wall. The tide was in, so there wouldn't be many steps for the men to mount, but she hoped that Pendragon would wait for the marines to precede him. Her fears were justified when he disembarked and marched up the steps to the quay, regardless of Osric and his marines scrambling to keep up. The leader of the group came forwards and bowed. Maia strained her senses to make out what he was saying, but the distance was too great. From the man's stance, it seemed that he was at least being respectful. She supposed that he would be the leader of the local council.

The man gestured towards the soldiers and one stepped forward. Maia ran through the ranks in her head, as she had been taught them. This man was a very senior officer.

"It's a Legatus," Leo hissed. She shot him a look. Her Captain was definitely unhappy.

"Marcus will have ordered him in by portal," Raven remarked, appearing beside them. "It wouldn't do to have a Prince greeted by a mere Praefectus."

There was some gesturing going on as the Legatus was introduced.

"What's happening?" Raven demanded.

"They want to escort the Admiral," Leo said, his eye still glued to the telescope. "Osric is glaring daggers."

It was true. Her Captain of Marines had moved up to flank the Admiral, his men behind him, ready to face off against the superior force of legionaries. Pendragon waved a hand, seeming to conclude the matter and moved off, the Legatus by his side and the marines following behind him like so many shadows. The soldiers fell into step after them and so, with two sets of military escorts, Pendragon strode off to disappear from view into the largest building, which she guessed was a temple.

"What happens now?"

"He'll have to swear an oath of allegiance," Leo sighed.

Maia was dismayed. "But won't that mean that the Gods will hold him to it, no matter what?"

Raven smiled mirthlessly. "We've already discussed that. He'll swear fealty to the bearer of Excalibur, then if it turns out that it's all mist and magic, he won't have to break his oath."

Leo grunted. "Clever."

"Indeed. Let us hope that it will buy us the time we need to uncover the ruse."

The other Ships were clearly as disconcerted as Maia was and she tuned into their complaints and observations with half an ear, her eyes still fixed on the shore. She was dismayed to see a cohort of soldiers reappear and take to boats, under the command of a centurion.

"Where are they going?" she asked Leo. Her Captain frowned.

"Not sure, but they're coming out to the fleet."

Blossom's voice burst into the link, her tone edged with alarm.

<I've orders to prepare for a boarding party!>

<Jupiter's teeth!> It was *Persistence*, <We'd better run, girl. Come on!>

The sound of her chains rattling as she began to haul up the heavy anchor punctuated her warning.

<I can't!> *Blossom* answered in despair. <They have my Captain's family hostage!>

A spark of rage ignited in Maia's core. How dare they? The next voice confirmed her friend's fears.

<All Ships! All Ships! This is Admiral Albanus. Those in Malvadum harbour are ordered to hold their positions. The *Blossom* and the *Persistence* are charged with mutiny and will be dealt with according to naval law. By order of King Marcus.>

Her sisters' cries of dismay were immediately drowned out by the *Persistence*'s reply.

<That scum-suckin' traitor's no king o' mine! My Captain 'as no family to threaten, so 'e can shove 'is order up 'is feculent arse! Good luck, *Blossom*. If I can't save you, I'll be sure to avenge you!>

The old Ship, her vessel released from the seabed, unfurled her sails and swung away towards the open ocean. The tide had ceased its flow, so there was no resistance as she fled. Maia could hear the jeers and shouts of her crew as *Persistence* thrust every ounce of her Potentia into her forward motion. Maia didn't blame her; if found guilty, it meant death for her crew and, at the very least destruction of her vessel and a long period of imprisonment ashore. Maia's memory conjured the dying shrieks of another and her timbers creaked in sympathy with her fears. Surely they wouldn't dare harm *Blossom*, one of the most beloved Ships in the Fleet?

<Where will you go?> she Sent after the rapidly dwindling Ship.

<Where that swine can't find me!> was the grim reply. <Better yer don't know.> Her tone softened. <I'm so sorry, *Tempest*. Good luck!>

<All Ships! Ready cannon and pursue! A bounty will be paid for the *Persistence*'s re-capture!>

She could picture Albanus now, his jaw set as he spat out the order. He'd have taken great delight in supplanting Pendragon. Leo and Raven listened as she relayed the orders.

"Impossible. We'll never catch her now. She was always one of the fastest Ships in the Navy and she's had a head start. Poor Plinius! He can't risk his family, not even at the cost of his Ship and crew."

"*Blossom* wouldn't abandon them anyway," Maia agreed, watching as the boats approached her friend's flanks. "What will they do?"

"He's complied so they'll probably spare his crew, but as for himself..." Raven trailed off, his brow furrowed. "This is monstrous!"

"*Tempest*, relay my compliments to the Admiral and say that, with regret, there is no way we can catch the *Persistence* now," Leo commanded. It was clear to all of them that whatever power Pendragon had was now gone and Albanus was in command, for all the show of deference.

The boats had reached the *Blossom* and the legionaries began to ascend the ladders, swarming up and on to the deck like so many red-coated cockroaches.

<I've been ordered to detach and to cease all communications,> *Blossom* Sent, resignation in her voice. <May the Gods bless and preserve you all, my dear sisters.>

The shock raced through the link as she fell silent. The commotion on board her vessel increased, then abruptly stilled; if there had been resistance, it had been quashed. A few moments later, the familiar figure of Captain Plinius began to climb over the side, then there was a longer pause as his Ship detached from her vessel. Maia could tell when it happened; as the vessel suddenly grew inert and became simply a mass of floating wood, metal and limp ropes.

They hoisted *Blossom*'s Shipbody down into a boat, bound like a condemned felon on the way to the arena.

<What can we do?> she whispered to Raven.

<Nothing, at present.>

<Will they...> she trailed off. The *Livia*'s fate was still a raw scar in her memory and she could almost smell the charred stench of burnt wood floating in the air.

<I doubt it, but I'm sure Marcus will want to make an example of her. She trained most of the Navy, and punishing her will be a lesson designed to warn everyone, especially his father. The Usurper has no bond with her, so he won't care.>

Marcus had refused to join the Navy, opting to parade around in a splendid legionary officer's uniform instead. He hadn't earned any of it. What did one Ship matter, however beloved, when he could use her to cow the others into submission?

<They haven't even put them into the same boat.>

It was true. *Blossom* and her Captain were already separated as they were dragged toward the horrors that awaited them on land. Maia concentrated. She'd managed to contact Raven with an effort of will. Surely she could reach Plinius now?

She reached out, his warm brown eyes uppermost in her mind, finding the thread that connected them both, forged of love and loyalty.

<Captain! Captain Plinius! It's Maia.>

She felt his surprise. <Maia? How? They've taken my earring.>

She almost smiled. <I have my ways. I can talk outside the link sometimes and, before you ask, only my officers know this.>

<Remarkable!> He was trying to sound like his usual calm self, but she sensed his emotion churning beneath the surface.

<Is your family safe?>

<As long as I co-operate, Marcus has sworn to spare both them and my crew and I have to believe him. I fear that *Blossom* and I are to be sacrificed for our defiance. You must survive if you're to salvage anything from this, my dear. Do what you can and may the Gods protect you all.>

She gently broke the link, gathering her thoughts whilst retaining the calm green thread that linked her to her former Captain. It was some small consolation that she could still reach both him and *Blossom* as necessary.

She reported his words to Leo, feeling his frustration mirror her own. Plinius and his Ship seemed doomed.

And there was nothing any of them could do to stop it.

*

181

Milo felt like his arms were about to fall off. He could only guess how long it had been since they had escaped the Fae vessel. The constant stretch and pull as he rowed marked some sort of time, but his brain refused to make any sense of it. It was only when they finally cleared the mist that he realised that there was perhaps an hour to go until sunset.

Julia had dropped the spell of concealment a while back and was sitting slumped on her bench, dozing. Milo had made her eat a few bites and had grabbed a little for himself. It was important for them both to keep up their strength, but he hadn't dared stop until it was clear that the Fae had moved on. He mourned the loss of *Wolf of the Waves* and his brave crew, but duty was duty. He could only hope that they had all been welcomed by their Gods and were having a better time of it in the afterlife. As it was, he was stuck in the middle of the open sea with only the setting sun to guide his path. Its rays lit up his face as he pulled to the east, praying that they would sight land soon.

Across from him Julia jerked once, then opened bleary eyes.

"Hello again. You'd be better lying down on the bench," he told her. She sniffed and rubbed her eyes.

"Where are we?"

"Heading eastwards. With any luck, we'll sight land, or a friendly vessel."

She regarded him doubtfully. "And if we do? I can hardly say who I am, can I?"

"No," he admitted, "but we can tell the truth when we say that we're the survivors of an attack."

Her face creased in misery. "Poor Latonia! I wanted her to live a happy life and enjoy her freedom with Bodil."

"I know, but that wasn't her fate. She might not be dead," he added.

"I think death beats being enslaved by the Fae." He regarded her bleak expression and silently agreed.

"Well, we can't help her now. We have to get to shore."

He stopped rowing and pulled in the oars, before examining his palms. Blisters were already starting to form and he murmured a healing spell over the puffy, raised skin.

"You need to eat some more," Julia told him, bringing out one of their packages of provisions. He couldn't argue with that and

182

unwrapped the meat, bread and cheese before tucking in with a will. A few swallows of wine helped too and that, as well as the magic, helped him feel a little more refreshed.

"How far do you think we are from land?" Julia was watching him eat, her dark eyes intense. He shrugged.

"Not too far. A few miles."

He hoped that they hadn't been swept south. Maybe they would be far enough away from the Fae to risk using his speechstone? He was just debating the subject when the sea behind them rippled and a dark head breasted the waves.

Julia cried in alarm and drew her pistols from her belt, cocking and aiming them in one smooth movement. Milo wrenched at an oar, hoping to fend off whatever it was. At least it didn't appear to be very big, but who knew what lay hidden beneath the water? The ocean was full of perils.

The head stopped, rising from the water. The black oak of the Longship's spirit body pawed the air for a second, before falling back with a splash.

"*Wolf of the Waves!*" Julia called out in relief. "We thought you'd been destroyed!"

She lowered her pistols as the great oaken wolf paddled alongside them. This close, she could see the sinuous spirals and curls carved into his entire Shipbody, speaking of beliefs and customs she could barely comprehend. His jaws opened as he grinned up at them.

"My vessel is gone," he rasped, "but I still have my duty to you, Princess."

His voice was harsh, just as she imagined how a wolf would sound if given the power of human speech. So he could talk, then.

"It's good to see you," she said, thinking how feeble it sounded, but it didn't seem to bother him.

"I will come aboard now," he replied.

Julia had a moment of fear that he would capsize the little boat, but he was up and over the side, taking up position at the prow before she could open her mouth again. She feared that there wouldn't be any room, but most of his body sank into the wood of the boat, until only his head and forequarters were left, positioned as he was on the Longship. Milo had remained silent, watching in fascination as the spirit settled himself.

"We go now," the Longship said. "Put your oars away."

"Where to?" she asked.

"I have been ordered to take you to shore. Then you must go to Luguvallium."

Julia exchanged a look of surprise with Milo, then grabbed at the gunwales as the boat abruptly picked up speed. Luguvallium was the westernmost town on the Wall that split Britannia from coast to coast. They must be farther north than she'd supposed.

"Ordered? By whom?" Milo asked the spirit.

Wolf of the Waves twisted his head around to grin at them both.

"Your Gods."

Julia swallowed. This was getting complicated, but it was good to know that the Olympians were doing something at last.

"How far away are we?" Milo asked, ever practical.

"We have passed Mannin, so will head east until we reach land. From there it is about sixteen miles to the city."

Milo sucked his lip. "The roads are good. It should be easy enough to hide in the traffic." He sounded more confident than she felt, that was for sure.

"Do you think Marcus knows that I left the *Tempest*?"

"If he does, he'll think you dead," the Agent replied bluntly. "Someone aboard the Fae vessels will have reported the battle."

"Can you contact Raven?"

"Too risky. Our best bet is to lay low and concentrate on getting to Luguvallium."

She knew he was right, though their lack of information gnawed at her constantly.

"Your life is more important," Milo insisted, giving her a knowing look. "We'd better think of a name for you and a cover story for us both."

"Unless the Fae have got there first, then nobody will care who we are," she said, feeling her stomach churn uneasily.

Milo sighed. "True."

The wolf's head swivelled to regard them.

"Do you want me to contact the *Tempest*?"

Milo blinked in astonishment. "You can do that?"

"I can try."

Julia's spirits rose. "This solves a lot of problems!"

184

Milo's face darkened. "No! The fewer people who know we survived, the better. I said it was too risky to contact Raven, and I meant it. We're better off in the wind for now. Maybe when we reach land, but not now. Thank you, anyway," he added.

Wolf of the Waves turned back to his task without another word. Milo left him to it and began to quietly mull over their options.

They were forging ahead at greater speed now. *Wolf of the Waves*' magic extended through his boat, the subtle thrum as comforting as a heartbeat. Ahead, the dark had swallowed up the waters, leaving them alone in the night and heading for an uncertain future.

The Agent huddled further into his coat and tried to doze, hoping that the morning would come soon.

*

Maia spent the rest of the morning quietly fretting, whilst trying to comfort her unhappy crew. Her officers were relying on routine to keep everybody busy in the hope that it would relieve some of the tension. Everywhere she looked, men were occupied in cleaning, checking and maintaining her vessel, though she'd hardly had the chance to wear anything out. Still, seawater rotted everything it touched given half a chance, so scrubbing and polishing was a constant fact of life afloat. Around her, she sensed that the other Ships were going through the same motions, though the hulk that had lately been the *Blossom* floated lifelessly. Her crew were still aboard under guard. It was easier to control them there than to ferry them to land and the local jail probably didn't have space to hold them all anyway.

As she'd anticipated, the link with Pendragon had snapped soon after he'd entered the temple. Nobody was surprised. The Legatus would have had his orders firmly impressed on him and that meant that Pendragon was to be immediately isolated from his allies. It was possible that Marcus didn't trust his father's apparent capitulation. Having no honour himself, he couldn't imagine it in others.

Maia was gazing shoreward as Raven joined her. They stared at the land together, watching as the port was lit by the lingering sun.

<What do we do now?> she asked him privately.

<Watch and wait,> he replied. <We have no other choice.>

She glanced over at him. <Will they come for you?>

He snorted audibly. <I'd like to see them try. They've probably decided that it's safer to leave me where I am.>

<I keep trying to reach *Blossom*,> she told him, <but she's not answering.>

<She might not want to worry you.>

She turned to him, eyebrows raised. <Worry? Are you serious? I swear, if they hurt her I'll fire on them myself!>

She felt her *tutela* grow in response to her burst of emotion, the storm cloud darkening and the flashes of lightning increasing along with her anger.

<Be calm,> Raven ordered, his milky eyes still seeming to search the distance. <We still have hope.>

<You're keeping things from me!> she accused him.

He grinned, his skin disappearing into a mass of wrinkles.

<Of course I am. The game isn't finished and I know how to throw a Venus to win when necessary.>

A winning score was what they needed now. Maia cast about for any possible advantage they might have.

<I can try to contact the Admiral. It worked for Plinius, but he doesn't want to talk now either. I feel like he and *Blossom* are ready for death...>

She fell silent, unwilling to elaborate.

<I'm sure they are. Plinius is a stoical sort and is doubtless ready to accept his fate for the sake of his family, in the old Roman tradition.>

Maia felt her annoyance rising and didn't answer. What wasn't he telling her? She itched to do something, anything. She was getting to the point where she was tempted to try to draw on her Divine family connections and damn the risk, but the vision of her aunt unleashing her fury on Malvadum gave her pause. It wouldn't do to put her sisters in danger, or the innocent townsfolk for that matter. Cymopoleia delighted in destruction and there was no telling who would get hurt. Maybe she should have a word with Danuco and see what advice he could give her? There hadn't been a repeat of the time when she was sure that he was channelling a higher Power, but she was aware that she was still very much under probation.

It was some consolation that Neptune had looked upon her with favour. Now she was sure that his warning had meant this. Not all dangers came from the sea and they certainly had as much as they could cope with at the moment. Just because Jupiter and the others weren't in evidence didn't mean that they weren't acting behind the scenes.

At least she'd heard nothing of the Huntress since the confrontation in the forest, for which Maia was immensely thankful. It seemed that Diana was off somewhere, enduring her own form of punishment for defying her father. Maia spent a few minutes wondering what it was and whether Marcus would suffer similarly. Surely patricide would earn him a very special place in Tartarus, to be tormented for eternity? It was the least he deserved. She hoped that Blandina and the Cyclops were there too, being beaten daily and scrubbing floors that never got clean, or until Pluto reckoned that they'd suffered enough. After that, who knew? The Priests were silent on the matter and the Gods said less.

Maia was jolted out of her vengeful thoughts by her Captain.

<Tempest, report to me in my cabin.>

<Aye, sir.>

Even as she replied, she dissolved her Shipbody and melted through the wood to re-form below decks. The space felt dark and enclosed after the openness up top, and she hoped that she wouldn't be here for long. Still, it had got her away from her ever-irritating Mage.

Leo was sitting at his desk, logbook open, having just finished the day's entry. She resisted the urge to take a peek; he wouldn't have written anything incriminating, just a bald recounting of the day's events. The drama of the morning had given way to boredom and inaction. Her gaze drifted to the miniature picture propped up on his desk. The reminder of her father comforted her, as if he were able to listen to their conversation.

"Raven tells me that you might be able to reach the Admiral, despite the loss of his earring?"

187

"I might," she said, adding, "but it isn't certain."

He sighed. "We need information, and I'm counting on your abilities to be one of our secret weapons."

"Only one?" she shot back, her hopes rising again, tinged with frustration that she didn't have the full picture.

"Even I don't know what Raven's up to," Leo admitted ruefully. "I feel like giving him a good shake and demanding he spill his secrets, but that wouldn't be wise."

"No," Maia agreed. "Definitely not. But if he has a plan, I wish he'd produce it."

"We need a *deus ex machina*, before everything goes to the dogs."

"Yes. Let's hope that the clouds part and the Olympians come charging to the rescue, like in all the plays. We need a happy ending."

"Or Artorius Magnus returns as legend promises."

Maia rolled her eyes. "If so, he's taking his time about it. I don't think that even his fabled Company would be much use against guns."

"What are the other Ships saying?"

"Nothing much. Everyone's gone quiet waiting for news, plus they don't want to compromise themselves. You never know who's listening in."

Leo grimaced. "True. Marcus's spies are everywhere and there's a lot at stake. Still, I want you to try and contact the Admiral. If you can establish a link, we'll have our own network and, if the worst comes to the worst, we can do something. He should be safe for a while, but that won't last."

"You think his son will kill him?"

Leo's handsome features turned bleak. "I never would have thought he'd kill Artorius. Right now, I think him capable of anything. Go ahead. That's an order."

She nodded, already running visualising the threads in her mind. The pink one for *Blossom*, blue for *Patience*, green for Plinius and red for Raven. They made a pretty braid in her mind's eye as she ran her awareness over and through them. It was time to weave another, one that would connect to her beloved Admiral. If it worked.

She forced her doubt aside. She'd been successful so far and they'd already been connected through a link, which seemed to make it easier. She gathered her strength and *reached*, concentrating on the sense of the man, his dark eyes and commanding voice, the authority and experience he carried with him like a wand of office.

Maia felt the connection writhing outwards before latching on to an anchor.

<*Tempest!*> He knew her immediately. His thread was a vibrant purple in her mind, as rich as any emperor's robe. Relief flooded through her.

<Admiral! Are you all right?>

<Yes. So, your gift works with me as well! I can't say I'm sorry. I'm still being treated with the deference due to my rank. No dungeons as yet. I take it that this ability is part of your special legacy?>

She'd been told that he knew about her Divine parentage.

<I think so. Either that or something bequeathed from the *Livia*.>

The shudder that ran though him at the mention of the doomed Ship rippled along the thread. <Whatever it is, I thank the Gods for it. Report!>

<All is well here and with the rest of your fleet, but everyone wishes we could help.>

<I heard that the *Persistence* escaped.>

<She did,> Maia confirmed, <throwing curses as she went.>

<Hah! Good for her. I only wish that the same could be said for *Blossom*. I fear that something dreadful is planned for her.>

<Do you know where she is?>

<Nobody will tell me, but I believe she's unharmed for the moment, as is Plinius. I asked for him to be brought to me, but my request was refused.>

Maia knew he'd tried his best. <Have you sworn the oath?>

<To the bearer of Excalibur,> he answered grimly. <They didn't push me further, thank Neptune. Have you any news on that front?>

It pained her to admit that she hadn't. <No, nothing.>

<It seems that information is in short supply. I did have to tell them that Julia is not here.>

189

So that was why she hadn't been boarded.

<Do they know where she is?>

<I told them that she's been sent away to parts unknown. I could tell that the Legatus wanted more. He's hanging back for now, but I expect that will change. With any luck, Julia's halfway to Norvegia by now. By the way, tell Raven that our friend stands ready.>

<Friend?>

<Yes. Repeat my words exactly. As we can now communicate directly I'll need you as a go-between, but I can't explain further at this time.>

Maia suppressed a burst of excitement. This had to be one of Raven's Venus throws. She'd try to worm more information out of him when she could.

<I'll tell him, Admiral,> she promised.

<Good. In the meantime, is this one way, or can I reach you?>

<It's only ever been one way,> she admitted.

He was silent for a moment. <Keep checking in. Hourly in the day and every two hours at night. I'm used to being woken and I've needed less sleep as I've got older.>

Pendragon wasn't saying it, but she knew that he was glad of her company.

<Understood, Admiral.>

<There's one more thing you can do for me. There will be a delivery you must make tonight. Choose someone you trust to aid Raven and yourself, but don't tell Leo, for his own safety.>

She couldn't tell her Captain? It wasn't what she would have chosen, but orders were orders. <Acknowledged. What do you want me to do?>

<Give Raven the message I told you earlier. He'll explain.>

His attention shifted for a second and she knew that he was no longer alone.

<The Legatus has appeared,> he informed her. <There'll be more polite questioning in the guise of conversation. It's obvious that Marcus wants Julia under his control as soon as possible. You have your orders, *Tempest*. End Sending.>

Maia automatically closed the private link at his command, before selecting the red thread that connected her to Raven.

<Raven, I got through to the Admiral. He ordered me to tell you that 'our friend stands ready.'>

<Excellent. Did he mention anything else?>

<He's being treated well for now and said there's to be a delivery tonight. We're to choose someone who can be trusted.>

<I understand. I'll explain later.>

Maia bit back her impatience and focused on her Captain, who was waiting patiently for her to report.

"I got through, sir. The Admiral is unharmed and sends you his compliments."

Leo relaxed visibly. "Thank the Gods. I take it that he's under guard?"

"He is. Marcus is desperate to know where we sent Julia, but Pendragon's refusing to tell the Legatus anything."

A wolfish smile crept over Leo's face. "Good. Julia should be well out of reach now." <And I can't see King Harald sending her back,> he added mentally, aware that they had to be careful, even here.

It wasn't what the Princess had wanted, but Maia was glad that Julia would be safe and far from her cousin's grasp. Now all she had to do was wait to see what Raven had planned. What on earth was this special delivery and how could it help? She told herself to be patient and settled down to wait.

*

Stolen meat always tasted sweeter, Caniculus decided. It hadn't been as easy as he'd hoped to sneak up and snaffle a few skewers of grilled mutton, but now he was leaning on a wall near the best seats, chewing surreptitiously. Around him, nobles and senators were chatting and observing the action, unaware of his presence. It had been far easier to help himself to some drinks whilst the attending slaves weren't looking. Fortunately, everything he touched also became invisible; he'd have frightened people to death if they'd seen a wine glass hovering mid-air.

It was good stuff, but he restrained himself, switching to fruit cordial after a few swallows. He was on duty, after all. His job now was to report everything he could to Milo, who would presumably tell Pendragon, the 'True King'. It comforted him that the Gods obviously didn't mean Marcus, Sword or no Sword. He'd have to trust they knew what they were doing, even if he didn't.

He wiped grease off his mouth, careful not to dislodge the helmet, and leaned forward for a better view of the current fight. The crowd howled as the retiarius snagged his opponent with his net and brought the more heavily built murmillo crashing down. Caniculus waited for the crippling blow, as the former raised his trident to strike.

"Hah, the fish is caught!" bellowed a corpulent senator, his face flushed with wine and excitement. His friends joined in, craning their necks avidly so as not to miss anything.

"I've got ten denarii on this lad, Papirius!" his friend shouted over, before encouraging his favourite. "Get him, Kalendio!"

It wasn't Kalendio's day. The murmillo, despite his armour, rolled at the last minute and three prongs bit into sand instead.

"Not quick enough," the gambler scowled. "Blast it!"

"You should have bet on the fish!" Papirius laughed, his chins wobbling.

He was answered with a curse.

It was then that Caniculus felt the hairs on the back of his neck rise up. Somebody was watching him.

He straightened up, checking that his head was still fully covered before glancing around. A man had appeared next to him, arms casually folded across his broad chest and one shoulder against a pillar. He looked like an ex-gladiator, Caniculus thought instantly, noting the square face and muscular frame. The man's eyes were definitely fixed on him.

The Agent could only stare as the man's grin widened, showing white, even teeth. Some would have called him handsome, but Caniculus' insides turned cold. No mortal man could see through the Helmet's disguise.

"Greetings, Little Dog," the stranger rumbled. His voice was more penetrating than it should be, cutting easily through the surrounding clamour.

Caniculus swallowed past a suddenly dry throat.

"Lord."

"Yes, being able to see you is a bit of a giveaway, isn't it?" Deep set eyes glittered. "I'm just here for the fun."

He gestured to the fight, where Kalendio was backing away from his opponent's powerful swings.

"It's a good match."

"It is, though I fear Kalendio has bitten off more than he can chew. He'll have to be at the top of his game to beat Flamma."

Caniculus had never imagined that the Gods would indulge in so much small talk, having now met three. Before him, the man threw back his head and laughed.

"I was told that you were amusing and I see I heard aright! Still, you're probably wondering why I'm here."

Caniculus frantically ran through the list of Gods in his head. Which one was this? He must be senior to have spoken with Mercury and Athena. Then, his stomach plummeted to his boots. Ex-soldier type, loving the fighting, looking like someone you wouldn't want to take on in a bar fight. It had to be...

"*Ex*-soldier? Really? I'm always ready for battle. But you're right about the bar fight. You really wouldn't want to annoy me."

It was the edge of cruelty in the smile that tipped his hand and the slightly mad look of someone who'd been punched too many times – or who loved dishing it out. Caniculus clamped down on his thoughts instantly, trying to project awe and obedience instead. The stranger nodded.

"Very wise, my friend. Have no fear, though. *You* are protected, for now. How goes it, O servant of the state?"

"I'm to report on what I see," he croaked.

"Good. And what did you see?"

Caniculus thought quickly. "Marcus pulling out Excalibur."

Amusement flashed across the God's face. "It was a good show, wasn't it? Very convincing."

The warmth of sudden hope filled Caniculus, like good *aqua vita* on a cold night.

"It was a show, then?"

"You're damn right it was." The God's mouth twisted. "Marcus thinks he's clever, but there's more to magic than he knows, even here at the edge of Empire. I definitely don't approve of the new friends he's made, either. And neither do my parents."

The God pushed off the wall and faced him, legs firmly planted. Behind him, the crowd howled as Kalendio was brought to his knees.

"Looks like it's time for someone to go down fighting," the Immortal said with relish.

Caniculus didn't dare take his eyes off him, though the crowd was baying like an eager hound desperate for the kill.

"What do you want me to do, O mighty one?"

Gold-flecked eyes darted to the arena and back to meet his gaze.

"Go to the Forum and check, of course. So much can be hidden, if you know how. Look, the match is over."

Caniculus followed the pointing finger towards the Royal Box.

Marcus gave the signal. Flamma's sword plunged down. The crowd sighed as a man's life ended.

When the Agent looked back, the God was gone. It was only then that his muscles relaxed a little and he realised he'd been holding his breath. It had to have been Mars. Nobody else could project that aura of violence and love of bloodshed. His very presence had made Caniculus's sphincter want to loosen, even though he'd had the feeling the God was trying not to scare the living daylights out of him. How he'd be otherwise wasn't something Caniculus wanted to dwell on. Nor could he ignore the God's advice. There would be no more games for him, he decided. It was disappointing as he'd wanted to watch the pegasi battling the chimaera, but now was the time to act, whilst most of Londin was otherwise occupied.

"*Merda*," he muttered to himself. One of the nearby slaves twitched a little, a momentary frown crossing his face as he heard the disembodied voice. Fortunately, he was called over to replenish glasses as Papirius toasted his success and consoled his friend on the loss of his wager.

Caniculus slipped away from the action, down the marble stairs and out through one of the many exits. If he got a move on, he could be in the Forum within the hour. Behind him, the entrance of the animal acts was greeted with a wall of noise that could be heard across the city. Cursing his luck, he set off at a jog through the quiet streets, hoping that he could get to hear what had happened later, if he ever made it back to his family. It was all very well talking to Gods, but right now he'd have settled for a cheap seat and an afternoon's entertainment. For a moment he contemplated trying to reach Milo, but then thought better of it. He hadn't exactly got any definite news yet, and he needed more information.

How had Marcus done it? *"It was a good show,"* the God had told him. It had to be some sort of glamour, and a strong one to fool so many people.

A few shortcuts later, he reached the edge of the Forum. The usual traffic and noise were largely absent, with just a few people in evidence. He wondered that they weren't bothered about the Games; if so, they were in the minority. The entertainment was a national obsession, that and discussing the weather. It made his job easier to have fewer people around, but he'd have to be careful not to make any noise.

The steps of the Basilica were empty, all business shut down for the public holiday. The staging and cordon that had been erected for Marcus's triumphant withdrawal of Excalibur had been dismantled, leaving the building looking much as usual. There didn't even seem to be any guards, though Caniculus knew that there'd be some form of security, even if it wasn't in evidence. Just to be sure, he took up position next to one of the pitted columns that fronted one of the Twelve's older temples to take in the lay of the land.

Nothing. No guards, no watchmen. The place seemed deserted: its great bronze doors firmly sealed for the duration. His eye travelled over the column that had held the Sword. It looked just like the others, its base painted red and the rest of the stone softened by centuries of propping up the portico of the Londin administration building. There was talk of demolishing it and constructing something bigger and better, as the Basilica was getting on for five hundred years old and the oldest parts were starting to look shabby. Despite some Senators' objections, Jupiter's temple had been given priority instead. The rise in industrial pollution was taking its toll on the marble, leaving little pits and smoke stains which didn't help its overall appearance.

Caniculus took a deep breath and headed out across the large flagstones. The sun was shining now, but a quick check told him that no shadow gave away his passage. Vulcan's work was truly magical, an Agent's dream accessory.

He arrived at the Basilica unchallenged and stared up at the column, estimating just where the Sword had been. There wasn't any mark. His forehead creased as he surveyed the marble. Surely there should have been a hole, or even a line? He reached a tentative hand upwards. Damn it, he must have either levitated or jumped to thrust it into the stone. No wonder Marcus had needed steps. There wasn't any way he could have climbed it either. How did Mars expect him to find anything?

Caniculus cursed to himself silently and jumped, hand outstretched but well away from the column. The sacred weapon was sharp and he didn't fancy losing a hand. It was best to err on the side of caution. After three jumps, he still hadn't hit anything. He glanced up at the sky. Perhaps Mars and the other Gods were up there now, laughing themselves stupid at his attempts?

Twice more and nothing. Then his hand bashed against something hard. A hilt.

Jupiter's beard! It was still there. Where better to hide something than in the place everyone least expected? It wasn't really in the way, unless a giant or a very tall centaur happened by. Most people would just walk right by, completely unaware. He wasn't able to detect any residual or active magic, unlike Milo who perhaps could have felt it. Caniculus' skillset was purely mundane. Just to make sure, he tried again, estimating where his hand had touched the metal.

This time, his fingers closed briefly on the pommel and his doubt evaporated. It was the Sword all right. He even fancied that there was a faint thrill of recognition as he touched it.

"Yes," he muttered. "Me again. What do you want me to do now?"

If he'd expected a reply, he was disappointed. The only thing he could do now was to make his report, as he very much doubted that it would yield itself to his attempts to dislodge it.

Trusting that the helmet's protection would hold, he activated his speechstone.

<Dog to Ferret! Dog to Ferret!>

Caniculus could feel the excitement bubbling up inside him. This was probably one of the most important messages ever Sent in the history of Britannia.

The reply came after a short while.

<Ferret here. What's happening?>

Caniculus couldn't contain himself. <Marcus doesn't have Excalibur! I repeat, Marcus doesn't have Excalibur!>

The silence that greeted him made him wonder if the link was still active. It was a few seconds before Milo responded.

<Are you sure?>

<Absolutely! It's still stuck in the column. The whole thing was a glamour or some sort of mass influencing spell. No wonder the place was crawling with Mages.>

<Thank the Gods!> Relief washed down the link. <How did you find out?>

<I had a tip off,> Caniculus hedged. He'd already decided to keep Olympus's involvement to himself for now. If the Gods wanted everyone to know, Mars would have proclaimed it in the middle of the Forum instead of having a word on the quiet.

<I'll let Raven know as soon as I can. Have you heard anything about Pendragon?>

Caniculus was puzzled. <Aren't you with him and the Princess?>

<No, we had to part company. You'd hate to be where I am right now, believe me.>

Caniculus thought for a moment. Mercury had given him his speechstone personally. Presumably, it was safer to use than the standard issue, but he'd never spoken to Raven and there was no guarantee that the Mage would be reachable or believe him if he managed to get through.

<You'll have to risk it,> he told Milo.

<For this, I will,> his friend agreed. <Are you all right?>

Caniculus reached up automatically, touching the smooth metal of the encasing helmet.

<Don't worry about me, lad. I've got protection.>

<Really?> Curiosity filled the link, but Caniculus refused to be drawn. Heaven knew who, or what, was listening in.

He sighed. <As I said before, you wouldn't believe me if I told you. Look, are you safe?>

197

He knew that his friend was weighing up how much to say. It seemed neither of them could be completely honest with each other.

<I'm all right,> Milo allowed, though his words were tinged with apprehension. <Look, I have to get the message out. Pendragon needs to know now. Oh, and take care of yourself, right?>

Caniculus snorted. <Always!>

The sense of the other vanished as the link was severed. Caniculus tried to sort his impressions, the implicit sensations that came with this form of communication, but all he got was a feeling of wide open space and movement.

Poor old Milo must still be at sea. Caniculus shuddered and turned his mind to his task, whilst part of him wondered if he could sneak a bread roll and some cheese from a nearby shop. It seemed a long time since lunch, and the sun would be setting soon enough. Then it would be time to make himself scarce in one of his bolt-holes and await developments. He closed his eyes, took a deep breath and scuttled off into the lengthening shadows.

IX

It was just past noon when Maia spotted the party of soldiers by the harbour. She alerted Leo immediately, increasing magnification to try and work out what they were erecting. The sound of hammering rang around the town, echoes bouncing off the stone buildings.

Slowly, a tall pole began to rise above their heads with something colourful and vaguely human-shaped fastened near the top. A sacred image? Was Marcus erecting something to honour his evil allies already?

A chill struck through her like an icy dagger. This was no Goddess. Simultaneously, she felt the link open as her sisters reacted.

<*Tempest*, can you see?>

Patience sounded stricken.

<Yes,> she replied, riding the waves of shock and anger that were rippling through her.

Leopard was cursing in a steady growl.

<What can we do?> *Unicorn* demanded.

<Nothing,> *Imperatrix* cut in, <unless you want to join her.>

<She's right,> *Diadem* added, pain in her voice. <Stand down and inform your Captains.>

Maia could only watch as *Blossom*'s Shipbody was hauled ever higher. Before she could try to contact her friend, an alert told her that a message was coming through from the Admiralty. She braced herself for the hated voice of Admiral Albanus.

<All Ships! This is Admiral Albanus. As you can see, the *Blossom* has been condemned as a traitor and mutineer. For her failure to obey, she will remain in Malvadum shorn of her vessel. All communication is forbidden and, be warned, the link is monitored. Any Ship breaking this command will join her in her punishment. Her Captain, Gaius Plinius Tertius, has been found equally complicit and will be executed by hanging at dawn. By order, His Royal Majesty Marcus the Third, King of the Britons. Gods save the King!>

The link fell silent. Maia could make out *Blossom* more clearly now. She seemed unharmed but smaller somehow, as if being ripped from her vessel had weakened her. She still clutched her *tutela*, though it was a simple bouquet instead of the weapon that she could have created. Thick chains bound her to the stake, pinning her arms, so that she held the flowers awkwardly against her breast. Her head was raised in defiance, lips firmly compressed as she gazed out to sea.

In the seconds that followed, Maia slowly became aware of the sound of more hammering. The soldiers hadn't finished their task and another structure was being built in full view of them all and slightly in front of where *Blossom* was chained.

It was only then she became aware of Leo speaking urgently to her. He and Raven had come up on deck to witness the *Blossom*'s humiliation and preparations for Plinius's execution. She relayed Albanus's message. Leo's normally ruddy complexion turned ashen.

"*Tempest*, what else can you see?"

He was holding a telescope; but he wanted her confirmation.

"They're building a gallows," she said, dully. It all seemed so unreal. How could her friends be condemned thus?

"Don't give up hope yet," Raven said. "Can you reach her?"

He raised an eyebrow in her direction. Of course, Sending to her through the link was forbidden. Albanus had told them it was being monitored, and Maia knew just who was standing by ready to report anything that was said. Ships didn't usually bother to broadcast to everyone, but they could listen in to directed messages if they made the effort. It seemed that, in Marcus's Britannia, courtesy and privacy were now a thing of the past.

It was fortunate that the *Regina* didn't know about Maia's special abilities.

"It's forbidden," she said aloud, adding privately, <I'll try.>

<Do it.>

She reached for the vibrant pink thread, separating it from the mental braid and running her thoughts out along it, as if a cable connected the two of them across the water.

<*Blossom*.>

The answer returned, strong and unwavering.

<Maia.>

200

She hesitated. What could she say that didn't sound totally stupid? The silence stretched out. <I'm so sorry, > she said eventually, wincing inside at the inadequacy of the phrase.

<I know,> came the reply. <I also know you can't do anything to help. Marcus and that swine Albanus are determined to make an example of me. At the moment, this is the worst they can come up with. To tell the truth, I thought I would be burned.> Maia was shocked. <Surely not?>

<Oh yes. As you know all too well there's a precedent, though I haven't actually murdered anybody. Yet,> she added grimly.

<Will they just leave you there?>

She felt her friend's mental shrug. <Who knows what's going on in their warped little minds? I could be left like this for decades, or paraded around for all to see. The disgraced Ship that dared to disobey.>

<But Marcus wasn't officially King! The crown should have gone to his father, not him!>

Unexpectedly, *Blossom* laughed. <That doesn't count. They always backdate their reigns when it suits them. You can make a whole lot of traitors that way.>

It was true. Emperors had done it more than once.

<There has to be something we can do,> Maia blurted out, before groaning at her predictable response. <If only to save Captain Plinius. I got through to him, you know, but it was as if he was saying goodbye.>

Her grief darkened the link as she remembered Plinius's words to her.

<He wouldn't want you to grieve,> *Blossom* said softly. <He has a stoical attitude, as you know all too well. He's prepared to die as bravely as he's lived to protect his family, and I shall always mourn his loss. Now, you must think of your Captain and crew. Is it true that you still have Raven aboard?>

Maia pulled herself together. It wouldn't do to lose control of her vessel because of her turbulent emotions.

<Yes. I think he's planning something, but I don't know what.>

<There you are!> *Blossom* consoled her. <If anyone can do something, he can. Don't give up hope, girl! Even if Marcus did

pull a bit of metal out of a stone, he's not got the Olympians on his side. Who knows what will happen next?>

Maia tried to feel a little better, but the dread of what next day's dawn would bring rose up before her like a vision of doom. It touched her that her friend was trying to cheer her up, despite her own terrible situation.

<I'll pray for you both,> she offered.

<Thank you. I hope the Gods are listening. At least I can talk to you. I know the rest of our sisters can't. I take it that the *Regina* and her friends will be spying on us at every opportunity?>

<I suppose so. How can they monitor everyone all at once?>

<They'll have help. All those rogue Mages will have been put to work – and knowing Marcus he's enlisted other, worse things as allies. Fae magic is powerful enough to augment any existing systems he has in place. Mind what you say through the link. My advice is to keep your head down and your ears open. Give my regards to Leo and Raven. I don't suppose you've heard anything about Pendragon?>

<Only that he's being treated well, though under guard. He doesn't hold out much hope of a long-term future, even though he's sworn to obey the holder of Excalibur.>

<Has he now? Not mentioning Marcus by name. Interesting. Now, you must sign off. Tend to your crew and your vessel. Things will be as the Gods wish it, not Marcus or his poxy followers. Stay strong!>

<We all send you our love,> Maia told her. <Ships and sailors alike. Marcus will pay for this.>

<I hope so. Until we speak again.>

Reluctantly, Maia withdrew, weaving the thread back into its braid, safely stored until the next time she could draw on it. The mere mention of the *Livia* and her dreadful end made her more determined than ever to act in whatever way she could. Maybe it was time to use her Divine connections after all?

She'd have to talk to Danuco. Maybe her aunt, Cymopoleia could be persuaded to strike Marcus dead with a well-aimed bolt of lightning? It was a more cheerful thought and she felt slightly better. In the meantime, she could contact *Patience* too without anyone else listening in. It seemed that her strange ability was needed now more than ever.

She reached inside, selected the shimmering blue thread and opened the secret link to her friend.

*

The waiting was interminable. Maia found herself scanning and re-scanning the harbour constantly, searching for any sign of movement or indication as to what was happening on shore. Even the usual chatter from the other Ships had stilled as the day wore on, each minute seemingly longer than the last until she felt that she could scream with boredom and frustration.

She had to admit to herself that she'd been shocked by *Blossom*'s pragmatic attitude to the imminent execution of her Captain. It was as if some of Plinius's stoicism had rubbed off on to his Ship. Was it just because she was older and had seen so many lives snuffed out? It was if her mentor had shut down her emotions for a time. Maia wished she could do the same, though the physical sensations she used to feel were transmuted into something less definable. She had no stomach to sink, no heart to pound, only timbers, ropes and sailcloth that felt no fear or pain. Her anguish was purely mental, a thing apart, unable to sink its claws too deeply into the solid oak of her Shipbody.

Aboard her vessel, the naval routine carried on as usual, though the tension showed in the line of men's jaws and the subdued talk. Leo paced the quarterdeck for the good part of an hour, reassuring the crew and conferring quietly with Sabrinus and Amphicles, before closeting himself in his cabin for the remainder of the afternoon. Raven was in the Mage quarters, mixing up some potion or other which he poured carefully into hollow clay spheres. If she didn't know better, she'd have thought they were some form of grenado, but there was no fuse or powder. Still, Maia sensed a deadly purpose to his toil. She didn't want to disturb him by asking about it, so watched quietly from her position on deck.

Now would be a good time to have that conversation with her Priest. He was standing in his accustomed place at her altar, head covered as he prayed. She already knew he had a particular tie to Jupiter, unlike most Ships' Priests who owed allegiance primarily to Neptune.

She swept over in her Shipbody, taking up position next to him and waiting politely for him to become aware of her presence. It was only a few seconds before he turned to face her, pulling back the hood of his robe.

"What can I do for you, Lady?"

He had started calling her that in private, aware of her Divine origins. She wasn't sure exactly what he knew about her situation, though she suspected that there was a lot more to him than he was telling her. In that respect, he was like her Mage, full of secrets.

"I was wondering if –." How could she put this? "Can we count on any help from –?"

She raised her eyes heavenwards, before returning her gaze to his face, alert for any tell-tale glitter in his pupils that spoke of something more than mortal.

"The Gods are keeping their own counsel for now," he said. "Though I sense their interest. We are but a tiny part of their plans." His face was solemn.

"I don't suppose I could make a petition of my own?" she asked, trying to sound as innocent as she could.

"Anyone can petition the Gods," he agreed, "but sometimes it's best to let things run their course. Be assured they haven't forgotten you."

Now that could be read both ways, she decided. It was best to play it safe.

"I know my duty to the Gods and the King."

He nodded. "Good. You're doing well in trying circumstances. Don't forget, the power of Olympus is formidable!"

As if she didn't know it! Well, she'd tried. In his own way, her Priest was as annoying as her Mage.

"Indeed. Thank you."

She withdrew as gracefully as she could, trying not to let her annoyance show. Naturally, anyone could petition the Gods. It was whether or not they got an answer that troubled her.

Across the water the other Ships were riding at anchor, sails furled, though she could spy tiny figures doing much the same as her crew were doing. Cleaning, polishing, checking machinery, changing watch: all the minutiae of life in the Britannic Royal

Navy. Normally, there would be happy parties on shore leave, small boats whizzing merrily about conveying goods and passengers to the various taverns and bath houses, but for once the waves were empty save for the great vessels and several inanimates. Even the sea was flat and lifeless, more like a sheet of metal than a moving body of water and without the slightest hint of a breeze. The air felt stale and heavy.

Maia forced her attention to her crew, checking on the youngsters who were getting ready for bed and whispering words of encouragement to the smallest. Sprout was already asleep in his hammock, snoring softly, his tufty hair sticking out of his blanket. He had an early start in the morning. Hyacinthus and Big Ajax were sitting together, the former patching a shirt and the latter whittling away at a piece of wood.

Maia remembered her little dog, a present from the large, gentle sailor and instinctively touched her breastplate. She had kept it in defiance of the Navy, which didn't want their Ships to have many possessions that tied them to their past. It would stay with her until the end. She may have lost the necklace that her friend Briseis, now *Patience*, had given her, but she'd not be parted from this precious gift.

She was doing her rounds as usual, checking on both crew and vessel, conscious of the fading light as the evening drew nearer, when a startled exclamation from Raven caught her attention. For a second she thought that he'd had an accident, but then realised that it had been a cry of triumph.

Maia formed in the Mage quarters, then stopped in astonishment. The ancient man was waving his arms wildly.

"I knew it! I bloody knew it!" Other words followed, unintelligible to her.

"What is it?" she asked, when he paused for breath.

"As many Ancient Egyptian swearwords as I can remember," he answered, his face splitting into a grin. "Heron taught me a load of them."

She pulled an exasperated face at him. "Not that!"

"Oh," he replied, archly. "You want the news? Well, guess what? The whole sword-from-the-stone thing was a fake. It's still stuck in the Basilica, invisible to all."

Maia felt her jaw drop.

"Who knows?" she demanded, as soon as she recovered herself.

"Currently? Four of us, you, me, Milo and his informant, though I intend to make sure that everyone else does before too long."

"Do you want me to broadcast it?"

He raised a hand. "Gods, no! What would Marcus do first if he knew the game was up?"

The answer was obvious.

"Remove the remaining claimants to the throne."

He nodded. "Exactly. Now listen. You know I told you that there was to be a special delivery? It's going to happen tonight…"

*

The lights of Malvadum twinkled in the darkness like glints in the dark eyes of Pluto, God of the Underworld. The night had turned chilly and Drustan, who was on watch, had wrapped himself in his warmest coat. Other crewmen were mere dim shapes in the gloom, gazing into the night and alert for whatever might come their way.

One thing at least was expected, though Raven had been his usual enigmatic self.

"Ready a boat when I tell you," he told her. "The delivery will manifest itself aboard, then you can send it to shore."

"Are you going to tell me what it is?" she'd demanded, scowling.

He grinned at her. "No."

Now Maia was listening with one ear and checking everything else with the other. Raven loved to play his little games sometimes. Questions buzzed in her head like swarming bees, or maybe wasps as they were busy doing little more than tormenting her.

It was three o'clock before the order came through. She readied and launched her boat as quietly as she could, ropes slipping easily through greased pulleys. Drustan oversaw the operation on her order, only speaking when necessary. Only trusted men had been chosen for this night's work.

But what was the point of launching an empty boat? Her Ship vision gave her a clear view of it, bobbing gently on the still water, nestled against her hull as if it didn't want to leave her protective flank. Then, abruptly, it wasn't empty.

Raven appeared, sitting in the bow. Next to him was a domed object, covered by a cloth. Maia peered closer, puzzled.

<Raven, what are you doing with Teg's cage? And why are you going ashore? You know they'll arrest you!>

<Never you mind,> came the tart reply. <I'll be fine.>

<All to take Pendragon his monkey?>

A smug feeling that wasn't her own danced into her head. <And the rest.>

A little light began to dawn and she doubled her vision to check the Mage quarters. The rows of strange spheres were gone. He must have packed the cage with them.

<Very clever, Master Mage,> she retorted, even as she extended her Potentia to power the boat away across the water.

<Ha! Even more so than you think.>

<Just take care,> she said to his retreating back. <I know you probably won't die, but it's still dangerous!>

<Stand ready for further orders,> he commanded.

Movement in her Captain's cabin showed that Leo was awake and dressing. Maia promptly whispered in his ear, secrecy be damned.

"Is there something I should know, sir?"

Blast it, the man was grinning too. She was surrounded by grinning men without the faintest idea why. Raven must have had words with him, despite the King's orders. Did everyone know the plan but her? So much for all-knowing Ships. They must have passed secret notes between themselves.

"Stand by, *Tempest.*" His voice was low, but full of excitement. He looked like a small boy about to put a frog in his sister's bed. She switched to their link.

<What are you and Raven up to?>

<You'll know soon enough.>

Suddenly, he was all business again, his face composed as Victor finished dressing him and brought his coat and hat.

Frustrated, Maia checked her vessel, to find that Leo wasn't the only one up. Amphicles was rousing himself too.

<*Tempest*, alert the next watch, then make ready to sail.>

Leo's order made sense in the context of everything else that was happening tonight, though she would have to be quick if she wanted to make the tide. Maia reckoned she only had an hour and a half before it would be an uphill struggle, even with her Potentia and the wind in her favour.

<Has Raven told you about Excalibur?> she asked him.

<Oh yes.> Her Captain's disgust at his former friend was plain. <May the Gods rot Marcus! I thank them that we owe him no loyalty.>

She switched direct attention to her boat. It was almost at the quayside now, its sole occupant bringing to mind Charon, Ferryman to the Underworld. She hoped that it wasn't a presentiment. Just then, something flitted across the waves, making directly for it. It moved so quickly that she couldn't be sure what it was. A seabird? A bat? It had wings, whatever it was. She could have sworn that it crashed into the boat and disappeared from view. Alarmed, she contacted Raven.

<What in Hades was that?>

<Someone I was expecting.> He didn't sound worried at all.

Someone? Maia was getting tired of cryptic clues without any answers. Almost absently, she checked through her vessel once more to prevent her snapping at her Mage and saying something she'd possibly regret later.

And stopped, bewildered, to see Hyacinthus with a sleepy Teg on his shoulder. There were no other monkeys on board.

All she could do was stare. If Teg was here, then what, besides the grenadoes, was Raven taking ashore?

*

The shout came just when Raven expected it. The guards on the quayside would be extra vigilant tonight.

"Ahoy the boat! State name and purpose!"

In answer, Raven muttered a word. A bright light sprang from his fingertips, illuminating half the quay.

"I am Master Mage Raven," he replied calmly, projecting his voice so that all would hear. "I have come ashore to see Admiral Pendragon."

There was a brief silence, then a flurry of anxious voices. He smiled to himself. Dealing with the one and only Master Mage was definitely not what any ordinary soldier was equipped for. They would be forced to get the Legatus. He'd spent the last several hundred years building up a fearsome reputation, so now every legionary ashore would be quaking in his *caligae*.

"Approach," came the cautious reply, "but know that we are armed!"

"I expected nothing else."

As if that would help them. Under the cloth, something stirred.

"Not long now," Raven muttered. "Sorry you haven't got much room in there, but I need the grenadoes as well. Remember to hold your breath."

A soft mumble answered him.

"No, they won't be able to see the grenadoes, just you. Pretend you aren't sitting on them."

The raspberry he got in reply spoke volumes. Raven composed himself – laughing in the faces of the guards wouldn't do anybody any good. They were probably getting chains ready for when he disembarked. It was time to play the second card in his arsenal.

The boat drew up to the steps, where a brawny legionary grabbed the gunwale and its rope, securing it to an iron ring. Fortunately, there wasn't too far to climb up.

"Ah, young man. Could you take the cage please?" Raven quavered, acting for the world like the ancient man he appeared. "I swear this monkey's been overfed. He weighs a ton."

"Monkey?" Another voice snapped. A face peered down over the harbour wall, surmounted by a crested helmet.

"Yes, Centurion. It's Prince Cei's pet monkey. He's been pining and I know that his master's very fond of him. I thought I'd bring him along, as I was coming anyway."

The first legionary took the cage with one hand and helped Raven out with the other.

"Thank you for helping an old blind Mage," Raven said to him. He presumed that everybody knew, but it didn't do any harm to give them a reminder. The more helpless he seemed, the better his plan would work. He regretted not telling Maia all of it, but if something went wrong he didn't want her condemned as well. He knew she was furious with him, but better that than in more trouble. If he succeeded, she'd forgive him readily enough. Probably.

At the top of the steps, he found himself surrounded by a ring of guards bearing lanterns. The soft light cast sinister shadows on their faces, so heaven alone knew what it did to his. The cage was lifted and the cover drawn back to reveal the jauntily dressed little creature. It regarded them all solemnly, before peeling its lip back and chattering at being disturbed.

"Well, it's a monkey all right," the Centurion said. "I'd heard he favours them."

"I'd like to make sure that he gets it personally," Raven interjected. "It was a present from the Princess Julia and has great sentimental value."

The Centurion hesitated. "That's not up to me," he said. "You'll be taken before the Legatus. What he says goes around here. There's a Mage, too."

"Really?" Raven didn't have to feign interest. "Which one?"

"Yellowhammer."

One of Bullfinch's cronies. Raven remembered him of old and knew that the man had the morals of the lowest street thief. He'd have been quick to join with the new regime to save his own skin, though Raven suspected he'd already been part of the cabal plotting to take down Bullfinch. Raven hadn't been able to stand the former Prime Mage, but he never would have agreed to Marcus's blatant misuse of power. Maybe one day he'd find out what happened to his old adversary. Until then, he'd better not underestimate Yellowhammer. The man was a vile creature, but he had Potentia and no scruples about using it in whatever form he thought would benefit himself.

"We are acquainted," Raven said, cheerfully. "Now, if one of you kind gentlemen would give me his arm, we can get going."

He held out an arm, waving it around a little to reassure them of his total inability to see and, as he'd hoped, the Centurion fell for it.

"Come along, sir, and I'll take you inside."

The note of relief in the officer's voice told Raven that they all thought his reputation had been greatly exaggerated. This poor old man was clearly a shadow of his former self and so old that he was like to expire on the spot unless they got him somewhere warm as quickly as possible. He suffered himself to be led across the cobbles and towards the looming pillars of the harbour administration building.

"The Legatus won't be long, sir. He's staying in the Mayor's house."

"Is that where Prince Cei is as well?" Raven asked, ingenuously.

"Yes, sir."

So, the Mayor had a houseful of guests. Raven doubted that he would be one of them once Yellowhammer knew of his arrival. A cell in the local Polis Offices would be more like it. He had to get to the Mayor's residence now. The soldier carrying the monkey cage was following on, much to Raven's relief.

"I *really* need to see His Royal Highness and the Legatus," Raven insisted. "I have valuable information about the Princess Julia's whereabouts."

He hadn't wanted to play this card, but it made more sense that he would have something to bargain with rather than turning up with empty hands. Marcus would expect him to grovel for his life, much as he would do if their positions were reversed.

His escort was halted as the Centurion mulled over his words.

"Fine. It'll save everyone a trip. We'll take you to the Legatus, then he can decide."

The fact that it had begun to rain helped. No important personage liked to have to cope with a dark, wet night and every soldier liked to pass tricky decisions up the chain of command as soon as possible. The Centurion was in way over his head and he knew it. The sooner he could offload his problem on to someone else, the happier he would be.

The Mayor's residence was a reasonably-sized villa set back from the main street, fronted by a high wall in the old style. The gateway was guarded and two legionaries snapped to attention as they approached.

"Centurion Lucius Venidius Dama to see the Legatus."

"He said he wasn't to be disturbed, sir," one answered.

"Just tell him I have an important person to see him." Dama snapped, his patience finally wearing thin. He outranked these

211

soldiers and they knew it. Fortunately for them, they weren't in the mood to argue and the party was waved through into an inner courtyard. Before them stood the house, pillars framing the main entrance. Lights were burning inside, so not all of its occupants were asleep, even at this late hour.

More guards appeared from around the corner of the house and a hurried conversation ensued.

"It's his pet monkey," the Centurion hissed. "Just take it in, for Mithras' sake! And tell the Legatus!"

Raven was aware of the worried glances cast in his direction.

"Have you searched him?" another officer asked. He gestured for one of the others to take the message.

"What do you think? We checked the monkey. If you want to search him, you can do it."

More muttering followed, but eventually Raven was escorted up the steps and into the atrium. It had all the hallmarks of an official residence, he thought, imposing enough from the outside, but inside things were a little shabby around the edges. Malvadum wasn't a big town, mostly relying on the fishing trade. A large statue of Neptune, trident in hand, dominated the space. Naturally, this place's loyalties looked to the sea. Raven reckoned that there hadn't been this much excitement in the area since the first Artorius was alive and kicking.

Hurried footsteps announced the arrival of a flustered servant. He didn't look local and his next words confirmed Raven's impression. He was probably one of the Legatus's personal secretaries.

"Centurion Dama, thank you. The Legatus will see the Master Mage in the reception hall. Bring him through."

Relief boiled off Dama like steam. Raven was gently but firmly escorted to the left, through a set of double doors and into what was the main receiving room. Someone had tried to make the place look impressive in the past, but now the mosaic floor was a little worn and the murals starting to flake. There were no chairs, so Raven stood and waited, whilst the legionaries stood to attention flanking him. The cage was placed carefully to one side.

They didn't have long to wait. Another door at the end was flung open, just in time for the Legatus to enter, several lackeys orbiting him like moons around a planet.

Raven didn't recognise him, but then again, he'd hardly been at the centre of politics lately. He'd probably know his family, and possibly a distant ancestor or two.

"Master Mage Raven." The Legatus's voice was cultured, without a trace of provincial accent. Carefully-oiled hair hid a receding forehead over a snub nose and eyes just a shade too close together. "Permit me to introduce myself. I am Gnaeus Salviarus Sulio, Legatus to His Majesty King Marcus, and I bid you welcome."

Raven inclined his head. The name Sulio was a giveaway.

"Delighted to meet you, sir. You're one of the West Country Salviarii, are you not?"

Sulio preened a little. "I am indeed. My father was one of the old King's counsellors. You may remember him?"

Raven did. Salviarus the Elder had not been a bad advisor but had died suddenly a few months before.

"My condolences on your recent loss," he offered.

Sulio nodded gravely. "Alas, the Gods decreed that he must leave us at last. Still, eighty-five is a decent age, you must agree."

"It is."

Compared to him, the man had been a mere stripling. Another generation dead and gone. Sulio interpreted his sigh as fatigue.

"Please, come this way to more congenial surroundings, Master Mage. I'd heard that you were aboard the *Tempest*." Sulio gestured to his aides. "There's a warmer room here where we can sit and discuss matters in private."

Ah, so it wasn't going to be a damp cell after all. They must really need this information. Raven was surprised that Yellowhammer hadn't joined them, but he wasn't sorry for it. If the man wasn't in the building, so much the better.

"Before we do, might I trouble you to see that this monkey is delivered to His Royal Highness?" he asked. The Legatus looked a little startled before catching sight of the cage, still securely covered with its cloth.

"A pet?"

He glanced at Dama, who looked straight ahead with the stolid expression of a soldier who'd seen it all.

"That's right," Raven agreed.

"Well, I suppose that won't be a problem."

"And the Prince is well?"

"Of course," Sulio said smoothly. "He is being entertained as an honoured guest by the people of the town."

"I look forward to being in his presence again," Raven said. "I can make my report to him, as doubtless he has been worried about his beloved niece."

Sulio did his best not to twitch. "I have been appointed the representative –"

"Excellent!" Raven interrupted. "I can tell you both, then I won't have to repeat myself. At my age it can get a little tiresome. Do lead the way, young man."

Sulio caved in with as much grace as he could. "Centurion, you and your men may return to your post. This way please, Master Mage."

The first servant took over guiding duties as they made their way from the draughty hall to an adjoining room. A good fire crackled in a large hearth and the rest of the light came from several large lamps ranged about the walls. Raven permitted himself to be led to a couch. Sulio seated himself in a chair opposite.

"Some wine?"

"I won't say no."

The Legatus beckoned over an aide and whispered in his ear. The man left, presumably to tell Pendragon. Another filled two glasses and brought them over.

"Your good health, sir," Raven toasted him and the Legatus followed suit. The wine was a fruity white, probably from Gaul and Raven smacked his lips in appreciation.

""Very nice."

"And how are the *Tempest* and her crew?" Sulio asked.

"All are well," Raven said, "though understandably discomfited by recent events."

Sulio grimaced briefly. "It is most unfortunate that there were, shall we say, misunderstandings. I trust that everything is now clear?"

"Very."

"And there is no doubt as to their loyalty?"

"None whatsoever." *But not to your Gods-damned murderous excuse for a monarch.*

Sulio was mollified.

"That's good to hear! I'm sure that His Majesty will be pleased."

And you'll be the one to tell him the good news.

Raven could almost smell the Legatus's ambition.

The aide returned and made his announcement.

"His Royal Highness, the Prince Cei."

Raven felt himself relax just a little. They'd be in the same room and that was all he needed. Getting Plinius out as well would be more problematic.

Pendragon strode into the room and made a beeline for Raven, completely ignoring Sulio.

"Greetings, my old friend! What news have you for me?"

The two men embraced, whilst Sulio hovered, eyes darting from one to the other.

"Plenty, Highness." Raven knew that Cei hated to stand on ceremony, but for now it had its uses, to remind his captors who they were dealing with. "But first, I've brought an old friend to see you."

The cage was resting on the floor beside him. Pendragon cast it a look.

"Your pet monkey, Sire. *Tempest* thought you might like to have him with you. He's been pining, haven't you, Marinus?"

Pendragon's eyes crinkled as he smiled.

"Ah, poor Marinus. I have missed him. It will be good to see him again!" He gestured, and a servant removed the cloth. Raven gestured and the door to the cage flew open, allowing its occupant to make a leap out and on to the Admiral's shoulder. Pendragon gave the furry head a stroke as the monkey chittered quietly.

"Would you care for some wine, Highness?" Sulio asked, eager to turn the conversation back to himself.

"No, thank you," Pendragon said, seating himself in the other vacant chair.

"The Master Mage has news of the Princess Julia," the Legatus continued. "Do pray tell us of her whereabouts, sir. King Marcus has been greatly concerned about her safety."

"As am I," Pendragon's deep voice cut in. "But I think there is something that we need to know first. In private please, Sulio." The Legatus's brows drew together, but he dismissed his servants with a wave. "Wait outside."

It was only when they were gone that Pendragon turned to Raven.

"What happens now?"

"Firstly, I need assurances as to Captain Plinius. I take it that he is confined in one of the cells?"

Sulio nodded. "He is. The King has decreed that he be hanged in the morning."

"What is the charge?"

"Mutiny." Sulio's face cleared. "Ah, you wish to strike a bargain," His confidence returned and his posture relaxed. "I don't have the authority to release him on parole, but I could make arrangements – if the information you give me leads to the retrieval of the Princess."

"And his family?"

Sulio inclined his head. "As I said, it can all be arranged to everybody's satisfaction. He wouldn't be returned to his former station, but he needn't end up kicking on the end of a rope like a common criminal. He's lucky he wasn't dragged off to the arena."

"But if the charge turned out to be false, what then?"

The Legatus chuckled. "Hardly! He ordered his Ship to evade a legitimate order, firing upon the authorities as he did so –"

"But Marcus wasn't legitimised then," Pendragon interrupted. "Plinius still believed that I was the rightful sovereign. Would you damn a man for loyalty?"

Sulio sighed theatrically. Truly, the man had missed his calling. He'd have been a sensation on the Londin stage. "It is what it is, Your Highness. I understand that there have been appeals on the Captain's behalf, but Marcus pulled Excalibur from the stone and his word is now law. Believe me, I am not unsympathetic. Plinius will have the opportunity to end his life by his own hand, in the time-honoured way. Thus honour, and the King, will be appeased."

"There's nothing of honour in this," Pendragon stated evenly.

"No, nor truth either," Raven agreed. "It was a glamour, Your Majesty. Marcus faked it all. Marinus! Now!"

There was a moment of silence, just long enough for Raven to see the Legatus's jaw drop. A sudden blur of movement, then Sulio's head vanished, engulfed in the jaws of the largest bear Raven had ever seen. The dull crunch of bone was loud in the silence. The bear let the body fall gently to the floor and licked the blood from its muzzle, turning its beady eyes to fix on Raven. The Master Mage hastily grabbed the monkey cage and emptied its contents into the pockets of his robe.

The three of them waited, but there were no cries of alarm.

"That should do it," Raven remarked, "Well done, Marinus!"

"What about Plinius?" Pendragon asked.

"He won't leave whilst his family are under threat," the ancient Mage replied. "Leave him to me. Marinus, get the King out of here. With your permission, Sire?"

Raven sensed the mantle of responsibility settle on Pendragon like the rock of Sisyphus.

"I agree. Do what you can for the Captain." He turned to the shapeshifter. "How are we going to do this?"

Marinus raised a paw and pointed to the window wall, then gestured for them both to stand back. His fur was starting to ripple, the coarse hair metamorphosing and smoothing out into tough scales that shone with a metallic gleam in the lamplight as his body elongated, muzzle stretching into huge, fanged jaws. Swellings on his flank began to stretch into wings, bony struts sheathed in leathery skin. Larger and larger he grew, forcing the two men back against the walls. His throat was already glowing red where the fire was igniting and the stink of hot metal filled the air. Raven took that as his cue to leave.

"I'll distract the servants. Go!"

Pendragon knew better than to argue. He was running to scramble aboard the creature's back even as Raven slipped through the door and bellowed at the waiting men.

"A dragon's eaten Sulio! Run!"

A splintering crash emphasised his words as the outer wall was breached, followed by a roar that shook the building to its foundations.

The servants needed no further urging. They shot off in the opposite direction, too terrified even to yell. Raven opened the door he'd just left through and peered into the room. There was little left of the furnishings, and a huge, jagged hole in the brickwork spoke of Marinus's hasty exit. There was another ear-splitting roar as the dragon landed in the courtyard and spat a blast of fire, igniting everything in its path. A couple of answering shots bounced off its scales, but no more. Any sensible soldier was running for shelter from the deadly flame.

The great beast crouched on its haunches, its vast wings outlined against the burning building before it leapt into the night sky. A sound like Jupiter's bedclothes flapping on the line filled the courtyard as it gained height. Raven had just been able to make out the tiny shape clinging to its back. As he headed off in the direction of the cells, grenadoes at the ready, he only hoped that Maia and the others were ready to sail as fast as they could.

This time they'd literally burned their bridges.

*

The sudden blaze on shore had all the anchored Ships instantly speculating. Leo pelted up to the quarterdeck to take up position next to his Ship.

"It looks like it's a big one. The Basilica?"

Maia increased magnification. "Seems so." A stab of panic made her ribs creak and there were shouts of warning from her crew.

<Calm yourself!> Leo's voice sounded in her head and she forced the emotion down. Simultaneously, she was aware of something large heading in her direction, skimming the waves. Leo saw it too, a glowing shape reflected in the dark waters.

"What in the Gods' name is that?"

It was too big to be a seabird, or any other flying creature she'd ever come across. Before she could raise another alarm, the thing dipped into the sea with a splash that was clearly audible across the water. It seemed to fold its wings and alter shape as she peered at it through the darkness. Then a long neck rose from the waves, surmounted by what looked like a horse's head.

"Sea monster!" she managed to say, before a cry cut across the distance between them.

"*Tempest*, ahoy! This is Pendragon!"

Her crew were at the rail now, led by her Captain.

"Get a ladder down!" he ordered. "Steady now!"

The great beast's rolling eyes appeared above the deck as it reached her flanks. She could see the small figure balancing on its broad back, then running lightly to the waiting ladder. Pendragon climbed up nimbly enough, to be greeted with a flurry of helping hands to hoist him aboard. His normally stern face was split with a huge grin as he climbed aboard, clasping Leo's arm as he tried to salute.

"Enough of that! I'm safe, thanks to some very good friends. *Tempest*, order all Ships to weigh anchor and make sail. We're heading north as fast as we can. I take it that you know what Marcus has engineered?"

"I do, Sire."

For a second, a rueful grimace replaced the smile. "It seems that my duty is not yet done. We must get to the Princess before the Usurper does. She is the future of the Pendragon dynasty now."

"Please come below, sir," Leo urged, adding privately to Maia, <get Hawthorn on stand-by to check him over.>

<Will do,> she Sent back.

"Have you seen Raven, Sire?" she asked aloud.

A look of satisfaction crossed Pendragon's face as he strode across the deck. "He's sorting something out. I hope he'll be joining us when he's finished, but we can't afford to wait."

Maia set about her tasks with a will, answering the queries from the other Ships whilst operating her capstans, pulleys and ropes. Clanking and rattling soon echoed across the water as the other Ships followed suit.

<But what about *Blossom* and Plinius?> *Patience* asked her, across the background chatter.

<I don't know, but I think Raven's doing something.> Shouts and running figures on the waterfront told of frantic attempts to stop the spread of the fire. Many of the buildings in Malvadum

were old, and the hungry flames would be more than happy to devour them if they could.

<It seems like he's done enough. What on earth was that creature? It seemed to be flying, then swimming?>

The mysterious beast had dived beneath the waves as soon as Pendragon had left its back, with nary a ripple to show its passing.

<I have no idea,> she replied, scanning the growing devastation on shore. The *vigiles* of Malvadum had started the fire appliances, and steady streams of water were pouring on roofs and through windows, shining like molten metal in the light of the flames. Maia hoped they would get it under control soon. It wasn't the townspeople's fault that they'd had to obey Marcus and his gang of thugs.

"*Tempest.*" The Admiral was speaking to her from the Great Cabin, where he was changing into dry clothes, fussed over by Victor and several other servants. "Please send my compliments to Captain Boduogenus and the *Leopard*, will you?"

<Aye, sir,> she replied, puzzled.

The *Leopard*'s mental voice had a distinct note of satisfaction to it.

<So, the Old Man's fine then?>

<He is. Have you seen anything like that beast? Where did it go?> Maia was all too aware of her inexperience, though she'd faced monsters that would give anyone nightmares. To her surprise, *Leopard* laughed.

<Remarkable, wasn't it? Don't you worry, the King has friends in high places and that's all I can say. A good job, too!>

<Couldn't it have helped Captain Plinius and *Blossom*, too?> she asked, plaintively.

<Pendragon was the priority,> her sister Ship answered. <I hear that the Master Mage is still there, so don't give up hope. We'll have to wait and see. Meanwhile, you have your course.>

<I do.>

<Then do your duty. Gods save the King and damn the Usurper to Hades, eh? North it is.>

Maia withdrew, hearing the speculation and muted conversations among her fellow Ships as their crews readied themselves for the journey. Pendragon was feeding Teg pieces of fruit and discussing strategy with Leo and her officers.

The little monkey looked happy to see his master returned, but Maia couldn't help but wonder. What had been in that cage? *Leopard* knew, but wasn't telling. Yet another mystery to ponder on her new voyage.

She hoped that they would find Julia soon, then both Pendragons would be re-united against the enemy and his terrifying allies. And where was Raven?

Sails billowing in the wind, she was gliding away from land when the noise of the explosion reached her, a dull thud like a muffled cannon firing. Thicker smoke was rising from the rear of the Basilica; the flames from the other buildings were almost extinguished. This was something new.

<*Blossom*!> she Sent through their private channel, hoping that the old Ship would respond. <Pendragon is safe aboard my vessel. Are you all right?>

<My Captain! The whole rear of the Basilica's gone and that's where the cells were!>

<He'll have escaped.> Surely Raven wouldn't have let his old friend die? *Blossom*'s voice was choked with grief.

<They're carrying out bodies and... oh Maia! He's dead! Plinius is dead!>

The Ship's wail of anguish was cut short. Maia was left, fumbling at the frayed edges of the once-vibrant braid. Its colours were dimmed now, entwined with suffering and grief.

She relayed the information to Leo, whose face crumpled as he listened, then told Pendragon.

"*Blossom* has told me that Captain Plinius has been killed in a blast onshore, sir," she said, quietly. "They must have stored powder near the cells."

"Is she sure?"

"She saw them carrying out his body."

Pendragon's shoulders sagged. "Then I pray that the Gods avenge him. Any news of Raven?"

"Not yet, sir."

Even as she spoke, she selected his red thread and opened the link. For a few seconds there was no answer and she feared that he too had been lost. Then his voice was in her head.

<How is Pendragon?>

She bit back an acerbic reply. <Quite safe. *Blossom* says that Plinius is dead in an explosion. She saw them carry out his body,> she added quickly, before he could question her.

<Have you told her that Marcus faked the retrieval of the sword?>

It seemed an odd question to ask, seeing as she'd just told him that a dear friend was dead.

<No. She was overcome –,>

<Then tell her. Now. Force the information through if you have to. She must save herself.>

<Raven –,>

He cut her off. <Can't talk now. I have to find out where Milo and Julia are. I've a bad feeling about them.> He was definitely preoccupied and she knew better than to quiz him when he was in this state, but she was determined to try.

<Surely –,>

<Do as I've told you!> She recoiled from his brusque tone, but felt him relent. <All is well, believe me. We can grieve for Plinius later. Now, do your job and I hope to see you in a few days.>

Again, she found herself grasping at empty air, the thread withdrawn before she could clutch at it. What *Blossom* had done unconsciously, Raven did deliberately. The old Mage had shut her out. It hurt more than she thought it would and she relieved her feelings by cursing quietly to herself. Why was he keeping so many secrets from her, now of all times? She'd already proved that she could keep her mouth, and her thoughts, sealed. Her continued existence depended on it. Why wouldn't he trust her, the stubborn, annoying old man? She consoled herself by thinking of all the things she would say to him once he reappeared, as he surely would, turning up as if nothing had happened. Now she had to reach *Blossom*.

<*Blossom*. It's Maia. Please talk to me. I have news!>

It took several tries before the thread twitched and a dull voice whispered.

<*Blossom* here.>

<I'm so sorry. Everyone will grieve. We all loved him.>

<At least they won't move against his family now.>

Maia took a deep mental breath. <Raven found out that Marcus used magic to make everyone think he pulled out the sword. It's still there, hidden. He isn't King.>

<He isn't?> Shocked and distraught though she was, *Blossom* couldn't hide the spark of hope.

<No. After…after what's happened to you, more Ships must surely come out against him. Raven said that you must save yourself.>

Maia felt the link grow stronger, as if some of the colour was returning to the pink.

<Oh I will, girl. Plinius would want me to, and there's no hold over me now. These chains don't stand a chance. Where are you headed?>

<North, after Julia.>

<Then I'll catch you up, somehow. I can still see my vessel.> Her voice grew stronger. <They forget I'm made of old oak, and not much can withstand that. The soldiers have gone to help put out the fires, so I'm getting out of here. Hah! There go the chains. I can climb and walk when I have to!>

This was more the *Blossom* she was used to. A few oaths followed.

<Can you manage?> Maia Sent, anxiously.

<Oh yes. I'm facing the harbour. Sliding down the pole now. I haven't walked for a while. The exercise will do me good.>

Maia encouraged the Ship as she made her way across the few feet of cobbles. It was true that they didn't often walk. Maia's first sight of one had been when the *Diadem* was re-installed and she remembered the slow, stately glide that was their form of locomotion.

<How will you get to your vessel?>

<I can see your boat tied up. I don't suppose you can still control it?>

Maia concentrated. She was further away now, but there was still a faint thread linking her to the wood.

<I'm going to try.>

It was almost at the edge of range, but she knew when the Shipbody climbed aboard.

<I managed the steps!> *Blossom* announced. <Not many can do that. Right, my girl, off we go!>

The best part, Maia reflected, was that nobody had noticed. Or, if they had, nobody was saying. She stretched out her Potentia to its fullest, latching on to her boat and feeling the familiarity as she guided it through the waves. The water was only a little unsettled, making the going easier than it would have been.

<That's it. I can see my vessel!> *Blossom*'s excitement was tempered by the thought of what she would find there. There would be no Captain to greet her with a cheery wave, just a young First Officer, who would be feeling a little out of his depth. It was a pity that Durus had transferred to the *Farsight*. Still, Manius would benefit from an experienced Ship and crew, despite not having an earring.

Maia composed her thoughts before informing Leo and Pendragon of developments, just as *Blossom* reached her vessel

"*Blossom*'s escaped to her vessel? Thank the Gods!" Pendragon said. "As for Raven, did he say where to rendezvous?"

"No, sir."

Pendragon raised his eyes heavenwards. "That's Mages for you."

"And meanwhile, we don't have one. It will put us at a serious disadvantage should we meet the Fae," Leo said.

"True. We can't rely on our ladies for everything. We'll have to make do with powder and iron. There are other avenues of support we can look into as well. In the meantime, Captain, I'd be obliged if you brought the crew up to date. *Tempest*, a word here, please."

Leo saluted smartly and left for the quarterdeck.

<What's this about, then?> he Sent to his Ship.

<No idea,> Maia answered, though the *other avenues* remark provided a clue and she dreaded having to answer to her King.

She emerged on to her accustomed place, feeling more like a wall decoration than ever.

Pendragon turned to greet her, his dark eyes boring into hers. It was all she could do not to squirm.

"I wanted to discuss certain advantages we may possess," he began, his voice lowered. "Do you think that you might be able to call upon Divine aid?"

Maia thought about it. "It's not a sure thing," she said, hesitantly. "I often have favourable winds and sometimes information, but it seems random, as though there are other things that are more important. I could call on my Aunt," she whispered, "but only as a last resort. I feel that she could do more harm than good."

Pendragon shuddered slightly. "Yes. I know that one of old. Unpredictable is the word. Still, I hear that Neptune favours you?"

"He was most gracious," she said, remembering the Sea-God's words. "But I can't promise anything. I swore to Jupiter that I would keep everything secret and I'm being watched."

She didn't want to endure the gaze of those pitiless golden eyes again.

"Quite. Still, if ordered to, and in extreme circumstances, would you try?"

She made up her mind on the instant. "I would. *Captains order, Ships obey.*"

A strange look suddenly flitted across his face, as if he were seeing someone else. The Admiral had his own ghosts to contend with. Had it been the *Augusta*'s standard response? Maia had no doubt that he'd loved her, even if her heart had belonged to another Admiral, long dead.

It was only an instant, then he was back to his usual business-like self. "Good. I know I can rely on you. Be assured that you are not the only port of call in this particular storm. In the meantime, we must follow my niece and hope that we can find news. Nothing has come from Norvegia, as yet and I know that *Wolf of the Waves* is as swift on sea as his namesake is on land. Keep an ear open for news from other Ships. Someone must have seen them."

"Aye sir."

He nodded, his mind already turning to other things. "Dismissed."

Maia returned to the quarterdeck and her Captain, determined to find out what she could, the feel of the Longship's braid in her mind. The waters they were sailing were treacherous, full of submerged rocks and reefs. Many a vessel, even Ships, had fallen foul of the western coasts and she was determined not to be one

225

of them. She would need all her skill, and that of her crew, to navigate the dangers ahead.

Blast Raven and his schemes! Her crew were formed up, listening to their Captain tell them of Plinius's death, dismay on every face. There would be many a muttered prayer for the soul of one of their own in the coming days. Hawthorn and Rowan were busy too, treating minor ailments. She would be relying on them more now that she was Mageless, and they knew it. Danuco, too, would be kept busy.

A chorus of voices over the link told her that *Blossom* was back and once more joined to her vessel. Joy and sympathies poured forth in equal measure as the Ships exchanged news and greetings.

After all, who could truly understand what it meant to be a Ship, save themselves?

X

A raucous shrieking startled Julia from an uneasy doze. She opened bleary eyes to see the culprit overhead, wings white against the grey sky.

"Bloody gull," she muttered, all too aware of her stiff, cramped limbs and damp cloak. She looked around to see Milo scanning the dawn horizon, where heavy clouds were threatening rain.

"Good morning!" Milo said. He turned to face her, swinging his legs back over the bench.

"So it's morning," Julia said, without enthusiasm. "Where are we?" It felt as if they'd been on the sea for days instead of hours.

"*Wolf of the Waves* says we're approaching the coast now," Milo told her. "It shouldn't be long."

"Good. I'm starving." She was also aware that other pressing needs were making themselves apparent. It was at times like these that she wished once more that she'd been born male. There were certain advantages in the ablutions department.

"I'm sorry, but I haven't any food. Here, have a drink." He offered her a leather flask.

"In a minute," she replied. "Would you mind looking the other way?"

He nodded and returned to his former position. Julia managed to hang on to a rowlock and felt much better afterwards. Fortunately, the sea was still relatively calm; she had no desire to fall overboard whilst relieving herself. Yet another hazard that was never mentioned in the annals of history.

"I'll have that drink now, thank you," she said, once she was safely back in her seat. The watered wine refreshed her, though did little to ease the hollowness in her stomach. "Good morning, *Wolf of the Waves*."

The black shape at the bow twisted its head in her direction.

"Hail, Princess! Do not fear, we are almost at the coast."

She peered into the east, seeing the long, low shape of the land, with mountains to the south of the estuary. That would be the lake region; a remote, but pretty place. She'd always wanted to go there. They were making good time then.

"Any sign of Fae?" she asked.

"No, thank the Gods," Milo answered. "*Wolf* thinks they will have landed somewhere further from a fort. There are quieter stretches on the coast."

"And what do you think they'll do first?"

Milo spread his hands. "Who knows? If I was in their position, I'd scout out the land, take what resources I could and wait for reinforcements."

"Yes, they'll probably establish a beachhead," Julia agreed. She felt sick at the thought of what they would do to anyone they found. A small village would have few defences and be easy pickings for marauders. Many had taken steps to guard against Alliance raids in the past, but Fae were another matter. She dismissed the thought. Their priority was getting to land, then finding food and shelter without coming to Marcus's attention. As to Luguvallium, she'd never been there and had no idea what awaited them. It would be easier to hide in a city and she knew that Milo had experience of that. She would just have to put her faith in him, and the Gods, of course. She wondered which ones were watching over them.

It was lighter now and their destination was becoming clearer.

"I'm going to contact Raven," Milo said suddenly.

She gave him a sharp glance. "I thought you said it was too dangerous?"

"I feel I need to. I won't give too much away, but my gut's telling me it's important."

"And you never argue with your gut?"

"Not if I'm sensible," he grinned.

His eyes unfocused and she knew that he was accessing his speechstone. A brief nod told her that he'd got through. She watched, impatiently, as a slew of emotions crossed his face, relief, acceptance, then finally sorrow. He ended the communication with a sigh.

"Tell me!" she demanded. "What's happened?"

Milo blinked. "Seems we've missed even more excitement." He ticked off points on his fingers as he spoke. "Firstly, your uncle is safe. He was arrested at Malvadum, but has been rescued. Secondly, his Fleet is out at sea, heading north. Thirdly." He sighed again. "They arrested Captain Plinius and his Ship, *Blossom*, was forced to detach. He was killed in an explosion during your uncle's rescue, though his Ship saved herself and is back with her vessel."

Bitter-sweet news indeed. "I didn't know Captain Plinius," Julia said, "but I've heard of *Blossom*. Didn't she train *Tempest*?"

Milo nodded. "She's been training Ships for a good few years now. This will hit the Fleet hard. Captain Plinius was an honourable man and a fine Captain."

"Another crime!" Julia spat. "May Marcus rot! First Excalibur, and now this!"

"Either he was evil all along, or greed and ambition have corrupted his soul," Milo replied.

"Poor *Blossom*. We have to show the people the truth. Can't anyone break the glamour on Excalibur? Marcus must have powerful Mages at his disposal to pull off a spell like that."

"Fae magic is very strong and it's the sort of thing they're supposed to specialise in."

He sounded like he knew what he was talking about.

"Fae? Have you come across it before?"

"Yes." From the look on Milo's face, it hadn't been a pleasant experience. "We must be on our guard against it."

"But you have that amulet. The one that made you nearly floor me."

That made him laugh. "I do. It's an excellent defence – when it knows what it's up against. Funny how it sounded off at Raven's glamour of you."

Julia saw what he was getting at immediately.

"Do you think there's a link between certain sorts of Mage spells and Fae ones? I thought all Potentia comes from the Gods?"

Milo raised an eyebrow. "I don't doubt it. But which ones? Anyway, that's something to think about another time. Raven also passes on his best wishes to you, after being horrified at our predicament. He hoped you'd be well on your way to Norvegia by now, not stuck in a small boat."

"Did you tell him where we're going?"

"I did, in a coded way. I also told him what *Wolf* said about the Gods. Raven said that we must go to the Forum in Luguvallium and wait for someone called Emrys. He's an old friend, apparently, and can be trusted."

Julia raised an eyebrow. "How will this Emrys know who we are?"

"Raven seemed sure that he would. Perhaps he has magic too? Anyway, I wasn't going to argue."

"As if that would get us anywhere," She agreed.

They were bearing down on the coast now. Julia huddled into her cloak, wondering whether she'd ever feel warm again. If only Raven had taught her a heating spell! Princesses didn't usually have to cope with cold and hunger. Her thoughts drifted back to her friend, the *Tempest*. She must have been shocked to find out about Captain Plinius. It was a shame she couldn't talk to her and tell her how sorry she was.

As the land rose up before them, Julia saw that *Wolf of the Waves* was guiding his makeshift vessel on to a beach, composed in equal parts of sand and pebbles. Dune grasses waved above the shoreline and it seemed deserted enough. She was glad when the boat grounded itself, allowing her to get ashore without getting her feet soaked. Milo had already leapt off and stood, surveying the prospect. The wind was fresh off the sea and seemed to be rising a little now that they had left the boat. Julia felt only relief as she stamped her feet and massaged her legs to get the blood flowing again. She hoped that the land would stop moving soon as well. Few of her family were good sailors for some reason, and she was no exception. Thank the Gods for Raven and his Magic Drops, even if he could be a stubborn old prune.

"It's a pity we have nothing to sacrifice," she said, thinking of the Gods. Neptune had been kind to them.

"Do you have any jewellery?" Milo asked, ever practical.

Julia rummaged in her pouch. She'd grabbed some items of value on the way out. Gold was always useful. She withdrew a dainty chain. "What about this."

Milo looked it over and nodded in approval. "That will do."

She returned to the shoreline and raised her hands in supplication. "O great Neptune, we thank you for our safe passage and offer this gift in return."

Balling it up in her hand, she hurled it as far as she could into the waves. The lap of the surf was her only answer, though she stared into the water for a while.

"Did you expect someone to catch it?" Milo laughed, coming to join her.

"Maybe," she said, giving him a look. "Stranger things have happened."

"True. Anyway, the offering has been made and he must know about it. We certainly had decent weather on our trip here. Now we need help on land."

"And something to eat and somewhere to get warm. Do you think there's a tavern over that hill?"

Milo threw his arms wide. "Who knows? Come on. We'll say farewell to *Wolf* and get going."

Wolf of the Waves was waiting for them by the boat, as if unwilling to leave it.

"Can you come with us?" Julia asked.

The Longship's jaws stretched, his wooden tongue lolling. "No, my Princess. I am a creature of the sea, and to the sea I must return. I will find one of my fellows and take passage with him." He cocked his head, regarding her. "I believe that your path does not lie in the lands to the north. King Harald will have to look elsewhere for a bride for his son."

"Really?"

"Yes. I am old and I know things beyond the ken of mortals."

"So you're not mortal, like our Ships."

Wolf's jaws gaped wider, as if laughing. "We are not like your Ships at all. Give my regards to that Hel-cat *Leopard*, when you see her!"

"I will," Julia promised. *Leopard*, eh? What was all that about? "Many thanks for your courage and faithfulness."

"Marcus is a false ruler. My King will be very interested to hear this and also about the Fae, as we are old enemies. I must go now. May your Gods watch over you!"

Milo and Julia helped the ancient creature back off the beach and into the waves, where he swung his little vessel about and headed off out to sea.

"I did get my feet wet, after all," she said ruefully.

"That's how it goes," Milo replied. She rolled her eyes at him and squelched up the beach, wishing she'd put on boots instead like him. Wet stockings had no appeal, but lighting a fire would be risky. Perhaps they could find a grove or somewhere more concealed and dry off a little? She was about to suggest it when he grabbed her arm and pulled her away, heading for a low dune. She ran without complaint, though his grip was bruising. A few seconds later, she heard the voices. Sudden fear rose in her throat, until she realised that they were high-pitched. Children. Sure enough, three little ones were running along the beach, chasing each other and shrieking against the freshening wind.

"It's all right," she hissed to Milo. "Surely we have nothing to fear from these?"

"Children prattle," Milo replied. "Then word spreads. It's best if they don't see us."

Julia watched them at their games, envying them their freedom. She'd never been permitted to run anywhere in such an undignified fashion, let alone surrounded by air and sky. It had always been 'Highness, you will sully your slippers!', or 'that is not the way a princess behaves!'

She sighed quietly and Milo shot her a sideways glance.

"I don't suppose it's always been easy, being a princess?" he whispered, divining her thought.

She shook her head. "Did you ever get to run along a beach?"

"Only when I was being chased by smugglers."

She stifled a laugh. "I don't suppose it's always easy being an Agent, either?"

He snorted quietly, watching as the children disappeared into the distance.

"No, but it's not boring. Even so, I admit that I'd like a little more relaxation sometimes."

Julia was struck again by a feeling of familiarity with the man. If only she could place where she'd met him before! She was torn from her mental effort when he stood up and brushed the sand from his breeches.

"Time to go. If we head inland, we might be able to find some shelter. A farmer's barn would be best."

"Do you know the way to Luguvallium?" she queried.

"It's mostly due west and there are roads. We'll be ordinary travellers on the way into the city. If we mingle with the crowds, we'll be fine. Follow my lead."

It wasn't long before they left the coast behind and came to a minor road. Milo had found a farmhouse and managed to procure half a loaf of bread, some cheese and a handful of dried meat, by what means Julia didn't dare ask.

"Picking locks is a skill every Agent has," he informed her, grinning. She was too tired and hungry to argue. Also, her feet were getting sore and she told him so.

"It's the wet stockings," he said. "Look, there's a thicket. Let's rest up and I'll find some firewood. It's no good if we get you to Luguvallium, only to find you've caught a chill."

That sounded like a wonderful idea, so she helped him to gather dry sticks and old pine cones for tinder. Fortunately, there hadn't been any rain for the past few days, so sitting on the ground wasn't as uncomfortable as it might have been. They sat either side of the small fire, eating their rations and watching steam rise from her sodden stockings that were hanging from sticks.

"Not what you're used to, eh?" Milo teased her.

"No. Next time, I want roasted boar with *garum* and a selection of sweetmeats."

He chuckled. "Absolutely. No problem! I'll have to rob a rich man's villa next time. Tell me if you see one."

Her stomach full and her feet finally dry, Julia lay back for a moment, resting her head on her bag and yawning.

"Give me a minute."

When she opened her eyes, it was dusk and a blackbird was singing its song to the gathering dark. She sat up, alarmed.

"How long have I been asleep?"

"You needed it." Milo was sitting opposite her, chewing on a piece of leathery meat. "Don't worry. We're only a few miles from the city. We can set off before dawn and get to the Forum just as everything's opening."

"You need to rest."

"And I intend to. You can take the watch now."

She dug around in her bag for the last pieces of food as Milo stretched himself on the ground and pulled his hat over his eyes. "One more thing," he added. "Don't let the fire go out. If you see or hear anything suspicious, wake me at once. Got that?"

"Yes, Milo." He'd dropped the Highness part and she supposed that was just as well. What could she call herself now? She wasn't wearing apprentice Mage robes, so she couldn't get away with being Little Owl again. She began to consider names, before standing and giving her legs a shake. She'd have to find some more wood if they wanted to keep the fire going for the next few hours. She'd never appreciated before how much fuel the blasted things needed. Palace hypocausts had slaves shovelling in wood and coal to power them, and she'd never given it a second thought.

Eyes open and ears alert, she picked her way through the gloom to add to the pile Milo had already found. There was smoke, but that couldn't be helped and plenty of impecunious travellers camped out on their trips if they couldn't afford the night in an inn. They were simply two more. A few armfuls later, she settled down by the fire to wait and get as comfortable as she could.

It was going to be a long night.

*

Milo awoke a couple of hours later and insisted that she get some more rest. Julia promptly fell asleep, listening to the owls and the distant bark of foxes. She woke abruptly to the sounds of grunting and snuffling. Had a monster tracked them down already?

"Don't worry, it's only a hedgehog. Noisy little creatures, aren't they?"

Milo's voice reassured her. He was sitting, unmoving, his features outlined by the dwindling flames. Julia shivered.

"The fire's going out."

"I let it die on purpose. We need to head off so we can get to Luguvallium by daylight."

There was little for breakfast, though Milo had replenished the wine flask with beer during his larcenous foray. She pulled on her dry stockings, relishing the warmth on her aching feet. Her shoes were still a little damp, but much better than they had been.

"Ready?" Milo asked, wrapping himself in his cloak.

"Yes," she replied, doing likewise. "What about the fire?"

"Leave that to me. Head off in that direction and I'll catch you up in a minute."

Julia was puzzled, but did as he asked, taking care not to trip over roots or fallen branches, though she reckoned that they'd burned most of those. A hissing behind her spoke of the fire being doused and she hoped that he'd not used any of the beer.

"That's done." His voice sounded from just behind her. "Quite a relief, really."

So he hadn't used the beer after all. She'd had to go in the bushes, which was definitely not what she was used to. There were no servants to offer scented water and hand towels afterwards, either. She decided that she would appreciate the little luxuries in future.

They trudged along in silence for a while. Julia had no idea where they were going. She'd offered to conjure a light, but Milo had refused.

"Too easily seen in the dark. Your eyes should be accustomed to it by now anyway."

It was true. She could see better than she thought, aided by a growing light that heralded the dawn. Shapes began to take on more definition around her and up ahead she could see an open space.

"Is that a road?" Her voice sounded loud in the stillness.

"Yes. Let me go first and see what's what."

He slipped away, lithe as a weasel through a wall. She didn't have to twiddle her thumbs for long before he was back.

"All's clear. Come on. I hope to get some breakfast before we meet up with this Emrys."

That sounded like a good idea to Julia. She tried not to think about what she'd like to eat, concentrating on putting one foot in front of the other. It wasn't that she was unaccustomed to exercise, but it had always been under supervision, and never for long. When she'd been aboard the *Tempest*, there hadn't been much walking done either. She'd have preferred to ride.

"I don't suppose that you could find us a couple of horses?" she asked her companion.

"You can forget that for a start," he replied shortly.

"It was just a thought," she grumbled.

"Sore feet?"

"I'm just not used to this."

"No, I suppose you aren't. Welcome to the real world, where people don't ride around in carriages all the time."

She pulled a face at him in the concealing darkness, but held her tongue. It wouldn't do to fall out with him now and he was probably as sick of all this as she was, plus there was the fact that he'd had less sleep. They trudged on in silence as the world awoke around them, their only observers the birds and a few startled rabbits. The packed gravel surface had a few weeds but it seemed fairly well used and at least she wouldn't have to worry about falling flat on her face over a tree root.

After a couple of hours, they heard the sound of hooves and a rumble of wheels. They moved over to the side of the road to allow the farm cart to pass. It seemed to be piled with a variety of produce, heading for the city to be there at first light, as was the custom.

"It must be market day," Milo observed. Julia watched the driver and his mate enviously as they passed them.

"So there'll be others?" She couldn't keep the note of hope from her voice.

"I expect so. We're coming up on the main road from the west, so it will be busier."

"And we can blend in with the crowd?"

"That's the plan."

"And get a lift?"

It was definitely getting lighter now, because she could see him roll his eyes at her.

"Perhaps. If the Gods favour us."

Julia was just wondering which one to petition when they reached the junction. Groups of people could be seen ahead of them, many carrying baskets and bundles. One man was leading a string of laden packhorses and there were a few carts as well.

Milo was right: it would be far easier to merge into the background here, as just two anonymous travellers heading to market.

Despite the fact that there were several modes of transport, none seemed to have room for a weary princess. Julia eyed their fellow pedestrians and reflected that she should be glad that she wasn't having to carry their loads. Many had baskets on their heads as well as packs on their backs.

"Isn't there any public transport?" she asked Milo.

"Not sure," he said. "There might be. Keep your eyes open, but don't get your hopes up."

"I suppose this lot would take it if there were."

Milo shrugged. "Maybe, maybe not. They might want to save a few coins, or the public transport won't take their loads as well. It's only once a week and they'll be used to it. Either that, or these are slaves doing the donkey work whilst their masters take the omnibus."

That sounded more plausible. Julia glanced around, hoping for one of the brightly-painted public carriages to appear. She'd seen them on the streets of Londinium, though naturally had never ridden in one. She was just about to ask how far it was, when a milestone proclaimed Luguvallium to be eight miles ahead. A few people were standing by it, chatting amongst themselves. Milo hailed one, a woman with a blue hood pulled up over her greying curls.

"Good morning, madam. Are you waiting for the omnibus?"

"Aye, we are. It should be along shortly." Her accent was strange to Julia's ears; another reminder that she was far to the north. She noticed that Milo had spoken in the same fashion. Another skill of an Agent, she supposed, to blend in whenever necessary.

Milo nodded his thanks and gestured to Julia to get in line.

"Have you enough money?" she muttered.

"We'll be fine. It'll only be a few coppers."

Julia could have wept with gratitude. She sat down at the edge of the road and stared into the ditch and the fields beyond. Her father and grandfather had visited here to see their people, but she'd never been further north than Letocetum, and then she hadn't seen much of the land. It had all been civic receptions and speeches, with lots of gracious smiling and waving. This was far more interesting, if painful. She took off a shoe to empty out a small stone and massage her toes.

"Sore feet?" The woman Milo had questioned smiled down at her. Julia nodded. "You look tired, lad. Never mind, the bus will be here soon."

Julia did her best to look grateful, not daring to open her mouth and be marked as a stranger.

"We had an early start," Milo said.

"Aye, I could tell. You'll have to give him a good breakfast when we arrive. You his father, then?"

"Uncle."

"He looks like you, so he does. I've got three, but they're all grown now and working the farm."

Any reply Milo might have made was forestalled by the noise of horses approaching at a brisk trot. The queue of people began to pick up their belongings and the person at the front stuck out an arm to alert the driver. Julia heaved herself off the verge and moved behind Milo, who was counting coppers from a worn leather purse, ready to pay the driver.

"Two for the Forum, please. One way."

The driver raised his eyebrows, but made no other comment. Julia followed Milo down the length of the carriage, which was arranged with benches running down either side. Rolled-up oilcloths stood in for window glass. The Agent led her almost to the back, well away from the chatty woman, and she managed to squeeze in between him and a red-faced man who smelt faintly of animals. Julia didn't have the experience to guess which ones, but as he turned to his neighbour and started discussing cows, she guessed that that was what it was. Apart from meat, cheese and milk, she didn't know anything about them, so listened with interest as they talked of yields, the price of feed and, naturally, the weather.

She was still tired and not exactly comfortable, but it beat having to walk the rest of the way. Everyone seemed to be excited to be going to the city and conversations passed over and around her. Milo appeared to be dozing, but she knew it was an act. He would be listening out for any threats, or even gossip that he could use, but it all seemed banal; surely nothing of import

238

would be discussed here? She decided to follow his example and closed her eyes.

A hand gripped her shoulder and her eyes flew open.

"We're just coming to the city now." Milo grinned at her. "I thought you'd like to get your bearings."

Julia resisted the urge to snap at him and rubbed her face instead. She must have slept for a while, soothed by the voices and the warmth. She yawned and looked out of the window. The lines of tombs told her that they didn't have long to go and, sure enough, by twisting around and sticking her head out as far as it would go, she could see the bulk of a triple-arched gatehouse ahead, built of red sandstone. It was by no means the biggest she'd ever seen, but it was imposing enough. Leading up to it was a high wall with a ditch before it. They must have been following its line when she was asleep and she regretted not having had sight of it before now. The ancient structure was a marvel, built a thousand years before by the great Emperor Hadrianus and stretching coast-to-coast right across the neck of Britannia. These days it was less for defence and more about taxes. Beyond it, smoke rose over the town and the wind carried the smell she always associated with Londin: a stink that told of lots of people living in a confined space.

The omnibus let some people off at the gate, but most stayed aboard until they'd entered the town proper. The way in was broader than she'd supposed and very busy. Milo had been right – a town was the best place for them to hide. Nobody would pick them out in this, even if anyone was looking for them. Julia had been worried that someone would recognise her, but had to laugh at herself. No-one would guess that this scruffy, exhausted boy was the exalted Princess Julia Victoria. She'd always hated the hours of preparation, the make-up and the fancy hairstyles. Now she was glad that they had been just as much of a disguise as her current state.

The omnibus finally came to an intersection and turned into an open space that was filled with stalls and noise. Temples and civic buildings towered overhead, all made of the same red stone with some marble frontages and columns. They were at the Forum.

The carriage emptied quickly, everyone scurrying off about their business. A few were met with cries of greeting and Julia felt a momentary pang of loss. The only ones who had ever shown her such a heartfelt welcome were Senator Rufus and Lady Drusilla, but those days were now gone forever.

"Cheer up," Milo whispered in her ear. "Keep your eyes open for someone who might be this Emrys."

"Raven said that he'd find us," Julia hissed back, scanning the crowds. "Don't you even know what he looks like?"

"Course not. That would make things too easy. Come on. Let's get something to eat. I intend to wait in comfort."

Julia had to agree. Her stomach was busy reminding her that it was empty and it was an unaccustomed and unpleasant sensation. There were no sugared almonds and honeyed dates to nibble on here.

Milo led the way to a cook shop and stood for a moment perusing the menu.

"This will do. What do you fancy?"

"Something that won't give me food poisoning," she grumbled. To her annoyance, Milo thought that was funny.

"You wouldn't like some of the places I've eaten in, then."

In the end, she settled on a cheese roll, reckoning that it would be filling without containing dubious meat products. Milo cheerfully munched his way through a pork pie and liberal amounts of pickles as they perched on stools under the awning. Julia watched the passers-by with interest. Despite the hunger, fatigue and sore feet, she had to admit that it beat being carted off to be delivered to a Northern princeling. Even the knowledge that her cousin was hunting her didn't dull the feeling that this adventure would mean more than any amount of titles and fancy jewellery.

The memory of her brother's face rose up before she could stop it. He'd seemed to think that a good marriage was all she could hope for, along with presents and high status. Her eyes misted up before she could stop herself. Poor Arty, slain before he could do barely anything at all.

"Are you all right?"

Milo's dark eyes were filled with concern. Julia blinked furiously.

"Something in my eye."

"Want me to look?"

"It's gone now."

She sniffed and carefully wrapped up the remainder of the roll, her appetite gone. The sense of a new adventure had gone, too. All she wanted was to meet this mysterious Emrys and get somewhere safe.

Beside her, Milo tensed. A tall man wrapped in a *birrus*, the old Britannic cloak, had sidled up. Piercing grey eyes fixed the pair of them, then he nodded as if satisfied.

"You'll be the two I was told to meet. I'm Emrys."

His voice was resonant, with traces of a western Britannic accent, not unlike Raven's. Julia couldn't help but stare. There was something about him, as if like spoke to like and part of her recognised him, but she couldn't explain why.

He threw back his hood, revealing beaky features and snow-white hair twisted into a long braid. She guessed that he was in his sixties, or thereabouts. He looked like a friend of Raven's; he had that same air about him. Was he some sort of magic-worker too?

"I'm Milo and this is Julius."

They were common enough names and fitted with their disguises.

"Pleased to meet you. Have you eaten?"

Milo nodded.

"Good. It's not far. Come on."

Without further ado, he led the way across the cobbles and through the orderly rows of market stalls packed with produce of all kinds. Julia kept a lookout for legionaries, but only spotted a couple of City polis leaning on a column and surveying the crowds in a desultory fashion. She resisted the temptation to ask where they were going, walking steadily with Milo behind their guide. Emrys led them down a street off the Forum lined with artisan's workshops, then ducked into an alley. They skirted some dubious-looking piles of refuse, before coming to a halt before what was obviously a side door to one of the businesses. Emrys muttered a word under his breath and a patch on the faded blue paint glowed briefly before the door swung open to admit them. Julia's fingertips prickled as the spell did its work. So, the old man was a magic-worker and, she suspected, a Mage though his name denied it. Perhaps he was hiding as well? It would explain his friendship with her mentor.

Beyond lay a flagged yard. Crates were stacked in a corner, stuffed with straw and she saw that they contained pottery. There was no sign of a kiln, so either it was somewhere inside or this was a retail enterprise, selling imported wares. She only managed the briefest glimpse before she was hustled up some stairs to the upper story of the building. Another spell opened yet another door, then they were inside.

She'd expected some sort of office, but it was an apartment. There were no luxuries, but it seemed comfortable enough, with a couch, chairs, a table and two other doors, which she presumed led to a bedroom and maybe a kitchen. The walls had old-fashioned red and yellow painted plaster in panels, but there were no personal effects. It could have been one of the better rooms in an inn, she thought. The word 'bolt-hole' sprang to mind. She jumped as the wood in the hearth burst into flames. Their host must have made a sign, but she hadn't seen it.

"Make yourselves at home," Emrys said. "You'll be here for the night, maybe longer."

Milo had already checked the rest of the rooms. "And then what?"

"Then I'll be taking you somewhere else."

"Where?" she asked, trying not to sound too demanding.

"The place you need to be."

He was definitely a Mage, she decided. Everything was riddles.

"You can do magic," she stated.

It wasn't quite the same as saying, 'so why don't you have a bird's name?', but the implication was there.

"So can you, *Julius*."

She tried to stare him down, but turned away after a second. Much to her surprise, he sighed.

"We're all in hiding here. I can't tell you any more at the moment, but Raven was right to entrust you to my care. We have a journey to make, all three of us. Rest while you can. I'll get the provisions."

He moved to go. "Oh, and the door won't open for anyone but me."

Milo nodded curtly. "We understand."

Julia waited until his departing footsteps faded.

"By the Gods! Are we trapped?"

Milo shook his head and made himself comfortable in the nearest chair.

"There's always the windows. Get some rest. I've a feeling that Emrys is going to take us on a long haul, probably to the back of beyond."

Julia groaned and threw herself down on the couch.

"So we just wait here?"

"There's a bed in the other room. Why don't you have a lie down?"

Julia glared at him, but had to admit that it was a good idea. The heat was beginning to penetrate the space, making her sleepy, so she heaved herself up and went into the next room. There was a wooden-framed bed with blankets and a pillow, which would do. A small table had a bowl, a ewer of water, soap and a linen towel, so she shucked off her damp outer clothes and had a quick wash. It felt good to be cleaner, even if the water was only lukewarm. She regarded the dirty dregs with distaste. What a grubby urchin she'd become!

The bed beckoned. The blankets weren't the softest, but they were a comfort. She pulled them up to her chin and stared at a line of flowers painted on the wall.

Milo was right. Sleep was the best thing for them both now.

*

It seemed to be one set of rocks after another, Maia thought. The way up the western edge of Britannia was wild and rocky, despite the guiding light of the various pharos lighthouses that were a boon to sailors. Every second was spent scanning the way ahead and consulting her mental store of maps and charts. It didn't help that she'd never sailed this way before. The east coast was more familiar to her, though it had its share of treacherous sandbanks. The other Ships helped as best they could, calling out instructions when needed whilst shepherding the crews of several inanimates who were mostly managing to keep up.

<Why are we going north? Is it solely to catch up with the Princess?> she asked Leo.

<The King thinks we'll be able to regroup and find allies. I think it's too late to get to Julia now but it's hard not being able to find out what's going on.>

Maia could only agree and knew that losing Raven was a blow, even if only temporarily. She hadn't heard from him for several hours and was loathe to try to re-open the link after his abruptness earlier. She told herself not to be petty, that there were other, more important things for him to think about, but she couldn't help feeling rejected. That, combined with Plinius's death, left her feeling sad and strangely abandoned. She was very tempted to see if she could contact *Wolf of the Waves* to get some good news for once.

She glanced over to where Leo was standing, his profile outlined by the rising sun. There was closeness there, but not the intimacy she'd had with the old Mage, or Plinius for that matter. Though she'd never been inside Plinius's head, he'd stood by her through uncertainty and trauma and she'd come to rely on his presence. No wonder some of the older Ships seemed callous about losing crew. They had to constantly think of the future and store their true feelings deep in the hidden parts of themselves. Only when they began to fail did the chains of memory loosen to let everything rise again, like ancient wreckage drifting up from the dark depths of the past.

She repressed a shudder. This was her fate now, constantly replenishing the old with the new and learning to let people go when it was their time.

<All right there, old girl?>

Her Captain had turned to her, sensing her pain.

<No, not really,> she admitted. <Losing Captain Plinius is hard.>

He moved to her side, stretching an arm to encircle her waist.

<Are you supposed to hug your Ship?>

He smiled, though his eyes were sad. <There's probably a regulation against it, but I don't care. We're both new to this. And I can hug my cousin.>

She returned his smile. It was true that she sometimes forgot that he was family as well. Pearl's appearances were too sporadic to rely on and she would as soon not have her terrifying aunt appear. If only she could speak to her mother, but that was never to be.

<It's nice to have family at last.>

<I agree.>

She wished she could tell him about her sister. Maybe one day.

Maia checked her position automatically. They were rounding the headland, near Octapitarum. She could see the small islands that were a trap for the unwary, and the larger island beyond. Once past these, she would head across the great bay of Ceredigion. She was mulling over her course, when the Sending slipped into her mind in a flash of red.

<Maia, can you hear me?>

Relief that he was safe warred with indignation.

<Oh, so you want to talk to me now?>

She heard him sigh at her immaturity.

<Slow down and prepare for us to come aboard. You'll need your hoist as well. I've brought you some presents.>

She was intrigued despite herself.

<Presents?>

<Yes. Alert the King.>

Maia immediately dropped speed and relayed the information to Pendragon and Leo, both of whom were as puzzled as she was.

<He will have found us an advantage,> the Admiral Sent decisively.

She spotted the boat immediately, a sturdy little fishing boat heading determinedly in her direction.

<I can't get in much closer,> she warned Leo. <Those rocks are nasty.>

<They'll come to us,> he replied. <That's a local boat and the crew know the waters around here.>

Sure enough, she spotted the familiar figure of the Master Mage on the deck, even as the shadows fell across the ocean. Nor was he alone. Two others stood beside him, with the billowing sail in the background. Maia wished that she could help them, but she had no control over their craft. As they drew closer, she saw that they were both male, but more than that she couldn't quite make out, as both were hooded. Only Raven was recognisable with his wispy halo. He raised a hand in greeting.

Her crew were already preparing to lower rope ladders.

<Tell them there's no need,> Raven Sent. His mental tone sounded gleeful and Maia wondered what he was hiding this time. There were several crates on the deck of the boat, so they had to be why she would need her hoist.

There was some shouting from both crews as the little vessel pulled up alongside her protective flank and the sail was furled. Thrown ropes helped to keep them together, rising and falling with the waves.

"What has he brought us?" Leo muttered, saluting as Pendragon came on deck to see what all the fuss was about. The two hooded figures began securing the crates in nets she lowered for the purpose, but Raven rose from the deck, floating gracefully upwards and over the rail, to land gently before the astonished crew.

"Greetings, Sire, *Tempest*," he said calmly. Please permit me to add two more crew to your list – plus certain new inventions that I think will come in very handy."

He sounded far too pleased with himself.

"Welcome aboard, Master Mage," Pendragon answered, with a rare smile. "We've missed you! Come below and we can discuss these new developments."

"One minute more, if you please, Sire," Raven replied. He signalled to Maia to lift the crates. "Gently now, *Tempest*."

She raised an eyebrow at her Captain, but proceeded to raise the cargo smoothly upwards, until her crew took over, guiding the crates to the deck.

"These need to be stowed below," Raven explained. "They're weapons."

"What weapons?" Pendragon asked, but Raven shook his head.

"You need to ask their inventors, Sire. Look, here they come."

The passengers spoke briefly to the crew, who doffed their caps and bowed respectfully, then both took to the air. They were Mages! A knot of excitement welled up in Maia's wooden breast. Mages and inventors? She knew two of those!

Their hoods were blown back by the speed of their elevation and Maia could have cried with relief. One old, one young, the familiar profile and the port-wine birthmark were unmistakeable.

"Heron, Robin! Welcome aboard!"

The crew, some of whom knew the Mages of old, cheered lustily, quickly informing their fellows just who had appeared.

"First we 'ad none, now we've got three of 'em!" Hyacinthus whispered to Sprout. "That'll even the odds!"

The Mages bowed solemnly to the King.

"It's good to see you, Heron," he said. "And this is?"

"May I present Robin, a Mage-Artificer of uncommon skill," Heron answered, bowing. Robin flushed, then followed suit.

"Excellent! I'd heard that you escaped the Usurper's purge. You'll have heard that his claim is false, an illusion achieved through Fae glamour?"

Heron's face darkened. "I have, Sire. It is an evil work indeed, and one that must be countered with pure intent and the application of *Scientia*." His eyes turned to the crates. "We are here to assist you in any way we can."

Pendragon nodded and Maia thought he relaxed just a little.

"Then come below, gentlemen – unless you have more surprises for us, Raven?"

The ancient smiled, his face creasing into a map of wrinkles. "Not at the moment, Sire. And I am rather thirsty."

"Nothing that a good amphora of wine won't satisfy."

Robin smiled at Maia as he passed and she knew that they would talk later. The Mages looked strange dressed in ordinary clothes, but it would have been foolish to have kept their robes. She would tease the story of their travels out of him when he'd had a chance to get settled in. Olympus knew how many days they'd been on the road, hiding from Marcus's legions. In the meantime, she'd have to see to the safe storage of the mysterious crates.

She could only hope that this would be the advantage they sorely needed.

XI

It was full dark when Julia awoke.

The low voices in the next room were just on the edge of hearing and, whilst she couldn't make out individual words, there was something in their tone that put her on immediate alert. She threw off her blankets and grabbed her clothes, drier now, though still with a faint musty smell that she did her best to ignore.

In the main room, Emrys turned as she entered.

"You're up. Good. We have to move and now's the best time. Get your things."

Milo was already stuffing a bag with provisions.

"Where are we going?" she asked.

"Away from here as fast as we can to a place I know. The Fae are on the move, heading inwards from the coast."

"They won't attack here, surely?" she questioned him, determined to glean as much information as possible.

"There's no need. The Sixth Legion is on its way to garrison and lock down this area because of supposed insurrectionists. Marcus has them working in concert, though I doubt the army know what's actually happening. Very clever."

His mouth twisted in distaste.

Julia understood. They had to get away before the military arrived and started asking questions. Stopping travellers would be a priority. She only hoped that Emrys knew what he was doing.

She hurried back to the bedroom and snatched up her meagre possessions. This had to be the fastest packing any Royal had ever done, as it usually took a dozen servants days of preparation for her to go anywhere. One last check and it was finished so she slung the bag over her shoulder and joined the others. Milo thrust a flask into her hand.

"Here, drink this. We can eat on the way."

She nodded her thanks. He had three bags, including the one he'd brought with him. She didn't have much.

"I can take one of those," she offered. He smiled at her, his face outlined by the lamplight.

"Thank you, but I can manage. Now, we're off. We'll make a brief stop at the latrines, then we have to make tracks."

"Do you know where we're going?" she whispered, glancing over at Emrys, who was standing at the doorway as if listening. He shook his head. "Not yet. I might when I see which way we're headed. I've been in these parts before."

Julia resigned herself to the fact that there wasn't anything to be gained by asking more questions.

"I've been in communication with Raven," Emrys announced. "He approves of my plan. Milo, he has a message for you. If anything comes through from your mother, you're not to answer. Do you understand?"

Milo stiffened. "My mother?" he sounded disbelieving. "Why would she contact me after all this time?"

"Raven fears that she's working with the Fae now."

The Agent was silent for a few moments. He looked shocked. "I understand," he said at last.

It was on the tip of Julia's tongue to demand to know more, but something in his face warned her not to. He'd tell her in his own good time, or Emrys would, she supposed. Who was Milo's mother and what did she have to do with all this? Milo pulled up his hood to hide his face and she did the same, following the two men down the stairs. Soon, they were off into the quiet streets, slipping through shadows.

She felt the sudden presence of Potentia surround them and wondered at Emrys's ability to cast this most subtle of spells. Perhaps he could teach her on the road? She wasn't yet confident of her own powers, though she'd become better at illusion. Spending time as a spotty-faced youth had given her a feel for the casting, and she itched to put it into practice.

The street plan of Luguvallium was familiar to her from virtually every other town in the Empire. The buildings were divided up into blocks, or *insulae,* some four or even five storeys high. There were few lights and she concentrated on not tripping in the dark, watching Emrys's back in front of her. Milo was bringing up the rear, his steps almost silent on the paving stones. They were heading for the edge of town and she realised that they would have to exit through one of the four gatehouses. Locked gatehouses. She chewed her lip, deciding to leave that part of it to their guide. Maybe he'd bribed the guards?

To her surprise, they halted at a section of the outer wall. Emrys pressed his hands against the stone and concentrated. The air thickened and abruptly the stones to the side of him seemed to ripple and fade to nothingness.

"Quick now," Emrys grunted. "Pass through."

Milo stepped past her and vanished into the gloom. Julia had no option but to follow. It felt as though she was passing through a furry curtain, the strands tickling her face. Then she was on the other side of the wall and remembering to breathe again. After a couple of seconds, Emrys emerged. He made a pass with his hands, as if smoothing over the rent and the stones settled back into their accustomed places. Julia tried not to gape. She'd never seen magic like this before that wasn't pure illusion. Part of her felt safer immediately, knowing that he had that sort of power to draw on; the other part of her wanted it for herself.

She didn't dare break the silence, but hurried after the tall figure as he slid down into the town ditch and up the other side. In past times, it would have been fortified with stakes and other deterrents, but now it seemed to be half-filled with assorted rubbish, some of which squelched unpleasantly under her feet, releasing a strong smell, and she prayed that she wouldn't sink into it too far. Hands helped her up the bank and on to the roadway running around the old walls. They'd been extended over the years, but a straggle of less organised houses and huts spilled around the edges of the town, where various people had set up homes on the margins. The roads weren't paved here, but Emrys led them both unerringly through stinking alleyways, past middens and pens where livestock moved restlessly, squeezing through gaps in fences and past shuttered windows, until she could see the main road with its lining of tombs. The night was still unrelieved by moon or stars, heavy cloud overhead blocking out any light but Julia realised with a shock that she was suddenly able to distinguish things in the pitch-black. Some Mage sense had taken over from her normal eyes. The world around her seemed strangely monochrome, outlined in a silvery-purple that was not of the mortal realm. Was this how Raven saw his surroundings?

She must have gasped, as Milo was by her side in an instant.

"What is it?"

"I can see in the dark."

"That's a help. I can too. We're born to it. Has it only just happened to you?"

"Yes."

"It's come when needed."

"Quiet!" Emrys muttered. She looked ahead to find him frowning at them. Satisfied that he'd been obeyed, he waved them onwards, crossing through the tombs and over the road in a swift glide that made him seem more shadow than solid being. Julia did her best to copy and soon they were under the cover of a hedgerow. To their left, the bulk of the city loomed, the great Wall stretching away to either side. Only then did the old man seem to relax a little. Julia decided to risk a question.

"Where to now?"

"We go south, but cautiously. There is a place, deep in the lake country, where we have friends. I was hoping to get you to the Heart of Albion directly, but it has been compromised."

"How can that be?" she demanded. Everyone knew of the most sacred place in the land. It was an enduring truth, wrapped in fable and myth. Her ancestor, the first Artorius, and every ruler since was said to have travelled there to take part in strange rites and mysteries. Few knew how to get there and even fewer tried. Older than the Olympians, older than mortal realms, never invaded or trespassed upon for thousands of years. What could have changed there now?

"Corruption reaches everywhere," he answered, his voice sad. "When the Mother's voice goes unheeded, grief and pain can lead people to evil paths."

"What happened?" Milo asked, his voice full of tension.

"Your mother wants what she cannot have and it has destroyed her reason. She has sealed off the Heart and prepares to welcome the Old Folk. The dream of the Land will be interrupted, or a new one will start, I cannot tell which. All I know is that we are at a crisis point. Whether or not it will survive in its current form is beyond my power to know. I fear that much will be lost, but we must preserve what we can."

Julia listened, uncomprehending. Why must Mages speak in riddles?

"What do we have to do with this? This must be something for the Gods to sort out amongst themselves!"

Emrys shrugged. "Gods, mortals and creatures that are neither one thing nor another. We all have our parts to play."

"And in the meantime?"

"We head south. Grab some breakfast. The sun will be up soon, and I want to be well on our way before then. We have a meeting at the stones in the heart of the mountains."

A faint lightening to the east told her that false dawn was approaching. Julia resigned herself to the journey, meekly trudging along over tussocky grass and through fields, keeping to hedge-lines as much as possible and trying to ignore her damp, smelly shoes. Milo handed her some bread and cheese as they went, but it failed to lift her spirits.

Whatever came to pass, she knew that nothing would ever be the same again.

*

Her vessel was quiet tonight. Then again, Tullia reflected, it was generally that way now. Ever since the 'special envoys' had come aboard and she'd received the order to hunt Admiral Pendragon down, the crew had done everything they could not to attract attention, even from her. They went about their duties with their usual efficiency, but there was little conversation and voices barely reached above a murmur unless they absolutely had to.

Even though Cei had declared against the rightful King, there was little appetite for the chase. The reports she and her fellow Ships received from her father, ensconced in the Royal Court in Londin, told that *Tempest* and her rebellious sisters were heading north – presumably to try and whip up support from the further reaches of Britannia. Tullia knew that it was futile. She listened in as Silvius held a war council in the Great Cabin, her Captain's dry, precise voice enunciating each point in their favour so that there could be no doubt as to the outcome. She would have preferred to join them, but her Captain didn't hold with Ships making contributions to strategy.

Captains order, Ships obey.

That adage had been driven home so firmly that she shuddered at the thought. His disapproval was nothing compared to her father's, but it was bad enough. She remained on the quarterdeck, watching the sunrise with increasing dread and waiting for her next order. To her dexter side she could see the lights of Malvadum, still in the disarray left by their previous visitors. A terrified garrison had been the least of the town's problems and the stench of smoke still drifted about the place. At first, Silvius hadn't believed the reports. A dragon? Ridiculous! But there were too many witnesses and the destruction spoke for itself. Most of the public buildings had burned to the ground.

The tale was a strange one. The fleet anchored, *Blossom* captured and tied to a pole and her Captain killed. Tullia didn't know how she felt about that. She'd heard ripples through the link, but it had been obvious that the rebel Ships, and many others, were blocking her as best they could, whispering amongst themselves. Her time aboard the training Ship hadn't been totally unpleasant, though she felt that she hadn't been treated with the deference due to her rank. It had been enough to get her through the trials (she shuddered at the thought of what she'd been forced to endure), but now she felt more down-trodden than ever.

Regina, do this. *Regina*, do that. Make your report. Take this heading. Send this message.

It was actually worse than she'd thought it would be and she was already sick of it. The chores she'd been forced to do at the Academy seemed easy by comparison. Here there was no rest, no sympathy and little appreciation of her importance.

Tullia spent most of her time dreaming of how it would be when she was finally freed from these shackles and Marcus fulfilled his promise to her. Then, there would be no more servitude ever again.

As for her Captain, she'd insist he be posted to the far reaches of the empire, where hopefully he'd be eaten by a sea-monster.

This happy vision was shattered as he broke into their link.

<*Regina*, make ready. We are to follow the rebel fleet to the north.>

<Aye, sir.>

The reply was automatic. She received the co-ordinates, then felt his attention turn elsewhere as he dismissed her. She could be a machine for all he cared; some great engine clanking away in the bowels of the vessel, fed with coal and only sweating slaves for company. Nobody here truly loved her. Her father said that she'd be worshipped, a being between Gods and mortal, beautiful and unchanging for centuries. Instead, she was treated like some sway-backed old workhorse waiting for the sting of the lash.

Grumbling silently to herself, she relayed the order to her officers and watched them take action. Voices rang around her vessel as the activity ramped up apace.

In the Great Cabin, Silvius was talking to his second-in-command as the three 'envoys' sat silently around the polished table, their sly eyes missing nothing. To the casual observer, they appeared to be three well-dressed middle-aged men with bland features; the sort you'd find in any council chamber in the land. Tullia had been ordered not to observe them in their cabin, and at first she'd been outraged. A Ship was not forbidden any part of her vessel! It wasn't long before she realised that whatever they were, they weren't human. Occasionally their masks slipped. After one glimpse of what lay underneath, she chose not to look.

"How far do you think they'll get, sir?" Pomponianus was an experienced officer, but she saw the moist line around his collar and knew that he felt as uncomfortable as she did around King Marcus's new allies.

Silvius's lips compressed into a thin smile.

"Not far. The waters around Mann are blocked and our allies have secured a beachhead further north. Reinforcements are coming in even as I speak. They'll be forced to turn back. I've heard that they've already sunk one Ship."

Pomponianus was startled. "Which one?"

"Unsure, but it's one less to threaten us."

Up on the quarterdeck, Tullia froze. She'd not heard any distress calls, or anything through the link. This information hadn't come through her lines of communication.

<*Justicia!*> she called.

The Royal acknowledged. <*Justicia* here, *Regina*. What is it?>

<My Captain's just announced that our allies have sunk a Ship to the north.>

She almost heard the intake of breath. <What? There's been nothing on the link and I doubt they could have kept that to themselves!>

<That's what I thought.>

<It can't have been one of us,> the older Ship decided. <We'd know. We always do.>

<Then who?>

<No idea.> *Justicia* didn't sound happy. <Keep your eyes and ears open for anything else and I'll see if anyone knows anything. What's happening now?>

<They're discussing battle strategy.>

<Then we'll get a message through soon. Keep me informed.>

Tullia slid out of the link, glad that she'd had the wit not to alarm the rest of the fleet. The *Justicia* was the oldest of them and she'd know what to do. Unlike some, this Royal had chosen to side with the winners.

Meanwhile, her officers were poring over a large map covering the table, spread out and weighted at each corner. Silvius was still speaking. "I estimate that we'll meet to the north of Mona."

Pomponianus nodded. "Let us hope they surrender."

Silvius raised an eyebrow at his officer's optimism.

"We can hope, but I doubt we'll be that lucky. At the moment, we're evenly matched as far as numbers go, but we have the advantage, thanks to our friends."

He inclined his head to the silent ones. Pomponianus swallowed and cleared his throat.

"Aye, sir. With your permission, I'll return to my post."

Silvius nodded absently.

"Dismissed."

Tullia saw the relief in the man's eyes as he saluted hastily and exited. He would be joining her on deck soon, far away from her strange passengers and their unsettling presences. She'd seen the men clutch at their protective amulets as the latter went past, though none dared speak their fears, even in the darkness of the lower decks. She'd thought of contacting her father over a private channel, but if he reported her breach of protocol to her Captain she'd be in trouble. Nor could she confide in any of the other Ships who were accompanying them. The fleet had swelled to twelve now, though there were only two Royals, *Justicia* and *Dragon* - who was as spiteful as ever. She'd fallen out with the latter almost as soon as she was installed, and they only communicated when they had to. The other Ships had stopped most of their chatter at the news from Malvadum.

Tullia hated to admit it to herself, but she was lonelier now than she'd ever been. Only the thought of what awaited her when this was all over gave her hope.

<*Regina*, report.> Silvius's voice crashed into her mind. Even as she'd daydreamed, she'd been preparing her vessel to make sail as ordered. Her great chains were rattling as they hauled her anchors up to the catheads.

<All is ready, Captain.> She didn't go into details.

<Prepare to Send to the Admiralty.>

<Aye, sir.>

<This is Silvius, aboard *Regina*. I have ordered the fleet north, to intercept the rebel fleet. Awaiting further orders.>

She did as she was bid, opening the link and reaching out with her Potentia to relay the message over the miles. As she'd hoped, her father answered.

<Acknowledged, *Regina*. Your orders are to proceed and engage the enemy on sight, by order of the King. I repeat, engage on sight.>

Tullia heard his words with apprehension, knowing that the rest of the fleet would have the same orders. Engage on sight? So, there would be no surrender, no quarter given. The King intended nothing less than the total destruction of all Ships that stood against him. Part of her quailed, even as she performed her duties. If she'd still been human, she might have been sick to her stomach. She hastily forced her emotions back under control before she could be accused of any lapse, glad for once of the unyielding oak of her Shipbody.

<Understood and acknowledged, Admiral Albanus,> Silvius replied through her link.

She waited for some hint of his emotion, but there was nothing save the sense of his duty. Over the years of command, he'd become adept at hiding his true feelings – that is if he had any in the first place. Sometimes he seemed more automaton than man, like the wind-up figures that were brought out for entertainment in the great houses. They could do repetitive tasks like throwing dice, pretending to read a book or play a musical instrument with as much humanity as he displayed.

<Keep me apprised.> her father continued. <Also, I am happy to inform you that the King has graciously conferred upon me the title of Dux of Britannia Prima.>

Silvius made haste to offer his congratulations, <That is excellent news, Your Grace!>

It was a high honour indeed, making her father the highest lord in the south and Tullia felt a bitter pang that she hadn't been there to witness the ceremony. She'd have been granted a noble title for sure! Then she laughed inwardly at herself. Yes, there would be pain in her future, but those treacherous, false Ships, together with Marcus's cruel uncle, would get the lesson they deserved. It would all be over very soon, and then she could look forward to the life she had always wanted. After all, their vessels could be destroyed but it wasn't as though Ships could be killed!

Mollified and feeling more cheerful than she had been in weeks, she ended the Sending at her Captain's orders and took great delight in informing her sisters of their heading.

*

A southerly wind aided Pendragon's fleet on its way up through the large Bay of Ceredigion and around the Isle of Mona. Maia sailed steadily on, bolstered by her sisters' presences on either side, and allowed herself to hope that all would be for the best.

The plan to get to Abona had been abandoned. Now they aimed to make landfall at the mouth of the River Lon, announce

Marcus's ruse and proclaim Pendragon as the rightful King. There was more talk of troop movements and which commanders could be trusted, but that was for landsmen and the Ships would have little part in that. Their next duty would be to move men and supplies as and when needed, being all the while on the look-out for the enemy, both mortal and Fae.

<It's the best plan he can come up with,> *Leopard* told the others as they talked quietly amongst themselves. <He needs men to deal with Marcus, so he's best to move from the north, gathering them as he goes. I don't think there'll be much help from elsewhere, but you never know. Half of the highland tribes have Fae blood in them and will probably count themselves immune.>

<He'll have to persuade people that Marcus's claim is false first,> *Diadem* answered, <and to do that, the glamour on Excalibur will have to be removed so that all can see it. Has Raven mentioned anything about that?> she asked Maia.

Maia hated to dash her hopes. <No. I don't know if there's anyone in Londin who can do it now. It's thanks to the Gods that we got to know of it at all.>

<Speaking of Gods,> *Farsight* piped up, <Where are they? We need help now!>

Maia heard the sighs through the link. *Farsight*, her old friend Durus's new command was nothing if not practical.

<It's too much to hope that Jupiter intervenes,> *Patience* answered. <You know the Gods work as they will, and not as we want.>

<Still, a few thunderbolts wouldn't go amiss.> *Leopard* grumbled.

<That would be nice, but we must pray and hope for the best.> *Patience* replied and Maia heard the echo of the Priest's daughter in her words. Having met a few Gods, Maia wondered what the Divine Ones were up to.

<Have you sailed this coast before, *Tempest*?> *Diadem* asked.

<I haven't,> she confessed. <I know the east of Britannia better.>

<We'll help,> *Leopard* offered. <It's all rocks and reefs this way, though there are plenty of lighthouses. We tend to hug the coast because we don't want to go too far west.>

She was right. The sea between Britannia and Hibernia was narrow here and nobody wanted to be blown off course.

<I hear the Fae are moving to the north, so we don't want to go up too far,> *Patience* said, adding <I'm not familiar with this route either. I got sent to the Med.>

<Lucky girl,> *Unicorn* sighed. <I wish I was there now, out of this mess!>

<What? And miss all the fun?> *Leopard* growled.

<Well, I do! This isn't going to end well.>

<I wonder where *Persistence* is now?> *Farsight* interjected before the two started trading insults.

<Halfway across the Western Ocean if she's any sense,> *Unicorn* snorted.

<Come, ladies,> *Diadem* said firmly. <All this speculation achieves nothing. We follow our orders and wait for the realm to sort itself out, as it always has. Rulers change, but we endure.>

There were murmurs of agreement.

<We'll be passing Mona shortly,> the Royal continued, <then it won't be far until we drop anchor.>

<And after that?> Maia asked.

<We follow our orders.> the Ship answered. <All will be as the Gods wish it, you'll see. Now, look to your Captains and crews!>

The chatter subsided as each of them withdrew to check their men. On the face of it, Maia decided that if she hadn't known better, it would seem like a normal voyage. Yet, there was a tension in the atmosphere. Her crew went about their work efficiently as always, but there was less banter and conversation. She'd seen men sorting out their sea chests as well and feared that they were making provision for their effects, should the worst happen. Everything was being battened down. It hadn't got to the point of clearing the decks yet, but she knew that everyone was waiting for the word.

She was so absorbed in checking her vessel for the umpteenth time that the awareness of her sister's presence took her by surprise. Pearl was hovering about her deck, unseen, only the freshening of the breeze a sign that she was there. Amphicles, on watch, adjusted his hat.

"The wind's getting up," he remarked.

"It is," she agreed, peering around for the tell-tale hint of the Tempestas' whereabouts. There – a glint, like the flash of sunlight on water.

<Hello, Pearl!> she Sent.

<*Greetings, my sister,*> came the whispered reply in her head. <*Where are you bound?*>

<Northwards, to the mouth of the Lon,> Maia told her.

<*I have been watching to the north,*> Pearl said. <*The ancient race are travelling. I saw their ships. They are smaller than your vessel.*>

Maia heard the news with alarm.

<Could you see how many there were?>

Pearl thought for a moment. <*They were numerous, many more than you. Nor are they alone. They have summoned the* Beisht Kione Dhoo *from their sea caves off Mann.*>

Beisht Kione Dhoo? Maia delved into her memory for any mention of them, riffling through the information her strange brain had stored over the years. Ah, there it was; a note in the *Encyclopaedia of Maritime Monsters*. It had been required reading during her training, even though some of the creatures hadn't been seen or heard of for years.

Just like the sirens that had nearly caused her ruin.

The 'Beasts of Black Head' was what the local folk called the type. They were huge serpents that lived in caves and prowled off the coast of the island, but they tended to keep to themselves. Rumour said that some Fae still lived on Mann and kept them in check. Britannic merchants traded with the population, but the inhabitants of the island remained close to their roots and strangers weren't always welcome. If the Hibernian Fae had entered into a compact with their cousins on Mann, it meant that they were all in danger. Then again, if the creatures remained off the island, it was further north than they were heading and they would have a clear run. Pearl's next words dashed her hopes.

<*They are heading south and are approaching your position.*>

<Have you been sent to warn us?> Maia asked her, knowing that getting information out of her sister was often futile. Pearl belonged to another realm, and one that operated under very different rules.

<Your Gods favour you,> Pearl insisted, *<but they are not the only Powers. The ancient race calls upon different magics.>*

<In other words, we're in trouble.>

<There is danger before and behind you. You cannot escape it.>

Maia's spirits plunged.

<What can I do, then?>

The cool breeze fluttered about her face, billowing her sails to their utmost before falling away again like a sigh.

<Have courage, my sister. I promise you, help will come when you least expect it.>

For a second, the swirling gust settled and a face appeared before her own, airy and translucent. Then it was gone.

<Farewell!>

Pearl's voice faded, replaced by the screeching of a gull overhead as the Tempestas took her leave. Maia took a few moments to collect herself, then opened the link to her Captain.

<Leo, I have information. We have a problem ahead.>

*

They came at dawn, gliding through the mists like half-remembered relics from an earlier age.

Tullia only spotted them when they were almost upon her and found herself staring for several seconds until she had the wit to rouse her Captain.

"How many of them can you see?> he demanded, calling for his servant to bring his clothes.

Tullia extended her Ship senses. <Seven so far, but I think there are more coming. They're paralleling our course.>

<Keep me updated,> he replied. She could see him hurrying to dress and waited for the next order. Her crew had noticed their escort too, muttering to one another and casting glances over her sinistra rail. Some were muttering prayers; none looked happy to see their new escorts.

Pomponianus was speaking to a group of junior officers and midshipmen on her poop deck. They were standing to attention, but she could tell that they wanted to get a better look at the mythical vessels that had appeared from the west.

"King Marcus has summoned allies to deal with the rebels," her second-in-command was saying. "They'll help us defeat them."

One of her junior officers, African by birth, looked puzzled.

"Beg pardon, sir, but who are they?"

Pomponianus turned to him. "Allies, Numidianus. Allies. We obey the Captain's orders, understood?"

"Aye, sir."

Tullia returned her gaze to the sea, staring in wonder at the strangers. The antique appearance of the vessels did nothing to promote confidence. They were small and single masted, with one square sail like galleys in old frescoes she'd seen, though without oars. It was difficult to make out the crew, who seemed to be standing stiffly on the only deck, like so many inanimates. They seemed to carry a haziness with them as if they were barely part of the normal world. Even their clinker-built construction was odd and vaguely unsettling for one used to modern warships.

Despite their size and lack of sail, they slipped in among the larger vessels with ease. Tullia strained to make out more details as they passed, but it was hard to focus, as if her eyes were being jerked away at the last minute. Nor did they make any of the usual sounds. All senses seemed muffled in their presence. She observed two take up position either side of her and had to fight an instinctive urge to pull away and make for open water.

<*Regina*, inform the Admiralty that we have met with our allies.>

Tullia had been so preoccupied that she hadn't noticed Silvius by her side. She complied immediately, relaying the acknowledgement. Away from the Captain's ears, Numidianus had been pulled aside and was being told exactly who their allies were. His friend, Annan, was whispering the truth.

"I tell you, they're the bloody Fae! I'm from the west and I know them when I see them."

Numidianus frowned. "They're legends, right?"

"I wish they were, rot their eyes!" Annan's face was pale under his usual ruddiness, his blue eyes filled with panic. "The Gods know what this new King has done! If he wants to break with Roma fair enough, but this is unconscionable!"

Numidianus moistened his lips, his eyes sliding sideways to the quarterdeck.

"I don't understand any of this. He must have his reasons, right? You heard what Pompey said."

"It stinks," Annan growled, his eyes following Numidianus's. "If this keeps up…"

"You'll what? Jump Ship when we get to port? Don't be stupid. There's no proof of anything. Maybe they've changed. If they give us the advantage, then it's fine by me. Now, my advice is to shut up before we're overheard."

A slight tilt of his head told Tullia that he knew she could be listening in. She deliberately kept her face away to give them the illusion of privacy. She wouldn't be telling on Annan, unless he began to actively preach disaffection. The latter subsided immediately, realising that he'd said too much.

"You must be right," he said in the louder tone of one who knew he'd overstepped the mark. "Our superiors know more than we. It's all good."

"It is," Numidianus agreed. He stepped away. "Time for the first lesson. Let's see how much the middies have remembered from yesterday, shall we?"

Annan nodded. "You go ahead. I'll be down shortly."

Tullia watched as the gaggle of midshipmen assembled for their daily navigation lesson in the day room, chattering amongst themselves as they jostled to see out of the stern windows. They'd be brought to order soon enough. She debated asking Annan what he knew about the Fae. He belonged to an ancient British family from the Silurian tribe and seemed to know what he was talking about. It would also explain the presence of the 'special envoys'. Fae were supposed to be very good at hiding and making things appear other than they were. It was a pity that she loathed the sight of them. Still, if Marcus thought they were potent allies, who was she to argue? She readied herself for the order to communicate with the mystery vessels, but her Captain was silent.

The next few hours were spent sailing carefully northwards around the Octapitarum promontory and across into the waters of Ceredigion Bay. The shrouded vessels maintained their positions among the Britannic Fleet, but their presence had one effect she was grateful for. The Ships were talking again.

Naturally, the first to break the silence was the *Jasper*. Nothing kept her quiet for long.

<All right, girls.> she piped up. <Will someone tell me who in Hades these bilge-suckers are? Have we sailed to the Land of the Dead or what?>

There was a stunned silence, before the *Justicia* snapped back.

<Watch your mouth, *Jasper*! These are allies of King Marcus and that's all you need to know.>

<So you do know who they are?> the irrepressible little Ship continued. <They look like something out of a nightmare yarn told to middies at Saturnalia!>

<Who are they, *Justicia*?> timid *Emerald* joined in. About the same age as *Jasper*, for once she was backing her fellow Jewel.

<Powerful allies!> the older Royal snapped. Tullia thought she sounded defensive. <They'll give us a short battle and a swift victory.>

<That's a good thing, then.> *Emerald* admitted. Some of the others didn't sound so sure.

<That depends what they want in return for their support,> *Dragon* huffed. The younger Royal had chosen to coil her Shipbody up her mainmast, claws gripping the wood as she raised her fanged head. Golden scales gleamed in the late morning sun. <Can't you ninnies see they're Fae?>

Oaths and exclamations erupted through the link.

<Marcus must have lost his mind!> *Gryphon* hissed.

<This stinks to the heavens!> *Londinium* muttered.

Tullia could hear *Prosperity* and *Vanguard* conferring quietly under all the noise.

<I'm not working with the enemy!> *Jasper* announced to any who would listen.

The link had descended into a riot of noise and speculation. Tullia kept her ears open and her mouth shut. Her Captain would want to know of any Ship that might turn traitor, like the *Blossom* and the *Persistence*. The latter had gone silent and disappeared from the shipping lanes since her escape. She would be forever outcast now; no Empire port would give her sanctuary or allow

264

her to reprovision. She would wander the seas alone without hope, or until she submitted herself to justice. Tullia had no intention of ending up like that.

<Enough!> *Justicia* bellowed, forgetting her dignity in the need to silence the arguing Ships. <Remember your oath! This is beneath us!>

<Fighting our sisters with Fae allies is beneath us,> *Dragon* answered. Her great head was swivelling from side to side in agitation. <I can't believe my Captain knows about this.>

<Of course he does!>

<Well, I haven't told him, and neither has anybody else.>

<He's following his orders like a good commander should.>

<There's orders, then there's orders,> *Jasper* chipped in. <I'm going to see what my Captain says about this!>

<Good luck with that,> *Justicia*'s voice was cold. <You're already known as a flighty little gossip and this won't enhance your reputation! It's not as if we can do anything anyway.>

<There's no harm in asking our Captains what's going on,> *Londinium* said. She was a stately Ship, appearing as a wealthy merchant's wife. Her tutela was the arms of the City.

There was a chorus of agreement.

Tullia left them to it and slid quietly out of the link. She had no intention of asking Silvius anything. If Marcus chose to ally himself with the Ancient Enemy, then that was his business and any Ship who protested would be bound to suffer. She'd already made her choice.

It was better to think of happier things, so she focused on her vessel instead. The envoys were closeted with her Mage, Buzzard, another of Kite's acolytes. Now this was more interesting. She hadn't had much dealings with him as he tended to liaise directly with Silvius. He seemed unfazed by her inhuman passengers and she began to get an idea of the depths of Marcus's plan. One of the creatures was speaking, his voice melodic but with an underlying note that grated against her finely tuned Shipsenses.

"…confirmed. The seas have risen and the serpents of Lir are waiting. Should his fleet proceed, they will be attacked."

"Then we fall on them and finish off whatever is left."
Buzzard's face shone with delight. "The Prime Mage will be pleased."

Serpents? Tullia didn't like the sound of that. Hopefully she wouldn't have to face them. It sounded like their allies had planned a special surprise for Pendragon and his rebels.

"The storm is localised, so will not be a danger to us. We will catch the survivors on their return. Inform your Captains to make ready for battle – the enemy is not far distant."

Buzzard rose and bowed respectfully. The three Fae watched him leave, eyes burning with hidden fire that spoke of relish for the imminent slaughter. Suddenly, one tilted its head as if listening and Tullia had the horrible feeling that they knew she was watching…

She tried to pull away, unable to suppress the deep shudder that rippled outwards from her Shipbody.

<Ship! What is amiss?>

Then it was as if her Shipbody was being crushed by the weight of the Fae's malevolent curiosity. She couldn't think, couldn't move, but hung, suspended in a lightless void.

<Stop…them…>

Then the pressure released and the world burst back into her head in a rush of sound and colour.

She could hear Buzzard's voice speaking to the Fae and was dimly aware of Silvius calling to her, joined by other Ships through the link.

<*Regina*! Respond!>

<It was them,> she managed to gasp. Sight returned and she saw her Captain peering into her face, Pomponianus hovering behind him, his expression full of consternation. Every man on deck was looking at her in horror.

Silvius stared at her for a few more seconds, then spoke quietly. "Ask Mage Buzzard to report to me in my cabin, then order the men to battle stations.>

She could only nod wordlessly.

<Do not observe or interact with our guests. I assure you that this will not happen again.>

He turned and strode away, disappearing down the ladder that led to the lower deck. Tullia gathered her scattered thoughts with an effort of will.

"A momentary fault. All is well now."

Pomponianus and others didn't look convinced. She mastered her shock as best she could and gave the order, glad that this would stop any further questions.

"All hands! Battle stations!"

The men jumped to obey, removing bulkheads, securing loose items and piling rolled hammocks in the nets on deck to shield against shot. Many of them knew the realities of war more than she, who had never fired a shot in anger. As she watched them, she felt guilty that part of her hoped the serpents would leave nothing to fire at.

Either way, Tullia prayed her suffering would be over soon.

XII

There was something wrong with the ocean. Maia could feel tremors pulsing through her hull, causing strange vibrations in her keel and rudder as she fought to keep her vessel on track. The waves were mounting higher, slapping roughly against her bow and it was getting harder to maintain headway. To make matters worse, the wind had swung round to blow from the north, hampering the fleet and pushing them back the way they'd come.

Raven was by her side, face into the wind. Heron and Robin had called for the mystery crates to be brought up and were busy assembling their new weapon.

"I don't like it," her Master Mage muttered, knowing that she would hear him. "We can't sail into this and it will be dark soon. Are you sure that Pearl's information is correct?"

"That's what she told me. *Beisht Kione Dhoo*. Have you ever seen one?"

He frowned. "Once, long ago, but my companion was able to talk to it and persuade it to leave us alone. They are ancient creatures and not subject to ordinary mortals. I fear that our enemies have the upper hand here, so I'm going to recommend that we turn back."

Maia heard him with dismay. She'd come to think of Raven as being invulnerable. Anything that scared him as much as this had to be worse than anything she'd yet faced. Even the sirens hadn't been this bad. And now the weather itself had turned against them.

<Captain, Raven thinks we should turn back.>

Leo was with Pendragon in the Great Cabin, poring over a chart.

<The King agrees. We can anchor to the west of Mona.>

She was about to obey, when *Farsight*'s cry rang through the Ship link.

<Serpent sighted, nor' nor' east!>

"All hands! Serpent, nor' nor' east! Guns, stand ready!" Maia bellowed. Below deck, the kraken alarm began its insistent chime.

Osric's shouts mingled with Musca's as both marines and gun crews raced to load their weapons. Simultaneously, Pendragon and Leo appeared on the quarterdeck, together with Sabrinus and Amphicles. Each officer raised telescopes to their eyes to spot their monstrous adversary.

At first, she thought that it was a jagged, black-tipped wave. It was only as it rose higher and higher that Maia could see that it was a huge head on a sinuous neck, surmounted with a spiny crest. It bore a vague resemblance to a horse, but there the similarity ended. Horses didn't have an oily, black sheen to their skin and teeth the length of a man's arm. Huge, lidless eyes glowed with pale fire as the thing reared up, fixing on the nearest Ship.

Patience fired. Smoke erupted from her flank, followed by the crack of gunfire and the boom of cannon as she attacked the serpent with all her power. The creature roared in answer, its mouth agape. Chunks of rubbery flesh and black blood spurted from its neck as her gunners hit it again and again. Purple flashes told of Sandpiper's efforts to keep the thing off, but they seemed to have little effect on the glistening hide.

Pendragon muttered an oath. "*Tempest*! Bring us in closer and support! It's targeting the smaller Ships!"

Maia tried to do as ordered, battling the rising waves and adverse wind to get to her sister even as another head rose to join its fellow, fastening on *Patience*'s stern and thrashing madly. The sound of splintering wood told of its success as the serpent fell away, taking half of the structure with it. Instantly, another hurtled over the rail and seized the mainmast, worrying at it until it gave way with a sickening crack. They attacked like wolves on a deer, Maia thought, destroying vessels rather than targeting their crew, even as *Unicorn* and *Farsight* began to battle more of the monsters. This wasn't hunger, but a concerted attack. Another burst out of the sea ahead of *Blossom* and latched on to her bowsprit which snapped off, sending the monster tumbling back into the foaming waters. Further back, three inanimates were faring just as badly. One was already sinking and two others were following. The serpents were realising that they made easier targets than the living Ships.

"I can't fire without hitting my sisters!" Maia cried.

She tried to keep the creatures in her sights, but it was near impossible. The serpents lived up to their name, writhing and twisting even as the crews fought to keep them back. They seemed intent on causing as much damage to the vessels as possible.

"They know how to sink Ships, damn them to Hades!" Pendragon snarled. "Fire when in range!"

Maia did her best, but musket balls had little effect and cannon shot likewise. For every serpent that sank, gushing its lifeblood, two more appeared to take its place. She could count ten of them now. The one that had damaged *Patience* was methodically demolishing the rest of her stern, whilst *Unicorn* and *Farsight* were also under attack though their men were fighting valiantly. Other creatures were destroying what remained of the damaged inanimates. The inert vessels and their crews didn't stand a chance.

<Mine doesn't seem to know what it's doing.> *Blossom* Sent. <It's attacking the wreckage! I think it's a juvenile!>

The creature was engrossed in chewing on the smashed bowsprit like it was a giant toothpick, allowing *Blossom* to draw alongside and fire at it, point-blank. When the smoke cleared, the serpent was gone, leaving only an oily stain spreading in its wake.

<They're ramming me underwater!> *Farsight* screamed. <I'm trying to reinforce, but it's no use!>

<I'm sinking!> *Patience* cut in.

Maia watched helplessly as her friend tried to lower her boats. One was snatched mid-air and bodies fell like spilled toys, flailing as they hit the water. Other sailors didn't wait, jumping into the churning waves while some clung desperately to the rail, their screams echoing across the water. These creatures were in their home element and centuries of pent-up aggression were being released in a few deadly minutes.

Unicorn had crippled one of the creatures but another replaced it, gnawing at her flanks. Her crew had abandoned their muskets for anything sharp they could find, hacking at whatever part of the creature they could reach. A lucky cannon shot blew a hole in its neck and the serpent screeched in agony, releasing its grip and churning the waves into black-stained foam as it flailed about.

"*Tempest*, order *Patience* and *Farsight* to detach." Pendragon ordered.

The former was already mostly submerged, rigging and sails spreading in piles across the surface of the water and the latter was not much better.

<One second,> *Patience* Sent. She sounded strained, but determined.

<*Patience*! Get out!> Maia called.

<One more – yes!>

Then Maia saw what the Ship was doing. A serpent had come closer to the stricken vessel to feed upon her crew. With the last of her strength, the Ship had thrown her ropes about it, tangling it in the sodden mess of broken spars and sailcloth. The more the creature struggled, the more it managed to trap itself until, with a final roar, it disappeared beneath the surface. Maia spotted the Shipbody dive over the side, her last task accomplished and her Captain clasped to her wooden breast. They had both stayed on deck until the end.

<I'm detached and I have Fabillus with me. The creature will take a while to free itself as it's dragged to the bottom.> *Patience* Sent.

It was a small gesture, but a brave one. The other serpents, seeing the fate of their fellow, gave the wrecks a wide berth, but that meant they could focus on the *Unicorn*. *Farsight* had already disappeared amongst the flotsam and jetsam. Maia strained to see what had become of her friends, but in their shoes she too would be hiding amongst the wreckage. Anyone in open water was fair game for the rapacious serpents. Several had already broken off the attack to snatch up unfortunate sailors and devour them.

Her Mages had joined the fight, throwing battle spells at the enemy with little effect.

<Raven, what can we do?>

<They are creatures of magic,> he told her, grimacing. <I'll have to try something risky!>

271

He stood at her bow, arms raised as he worked. Maia could tell that he was speaking to his fellow Mages, but she couldn't tell what he was saying.

Suddenly, a bright point of light appeared around the wrecks and the badly damaged *Unicorn*, expanding rapidly into translucent spheres, as if an invisible giant were blowing gigantic soap bubbles.

<We can't defeat the serpents, but we can protect our men as best we can.>

Bit by bit, the spheres forced the serpents back. They roared their frustration and turned to the remaining Ships, but protections bloomed about each one. Heron and Robin had joined Raven, adding their Potentia to his.

<Maia, tell all Ships to add their magics,> Raven commanded. <Brace yourself – we're going to draw on yours. Release your Potentia!>

She drew on her training, concentrating and gathering the power within, before thrusting it outwards to race through every part of her vessel, channelling it into a single, shining arrow of force. The flood of magic burst upwards, hitting all three Mages at once. Instantly they convulsed, robes billowing and sparks flying from outstretched fingers as their bodies reacted to the flood of energy she unleashed. Serpents roared as the touch of the spheres burnt their hide and the smell of charring flesh hung in the air.

<Enough!>

Maia seized hold of her power, slamming the metaphysical gates shut and damming the flow. Each sphere was blazing now, pushing the creatures further back away from the fleet. Several had already given up, diving back to the cool depths away from the pain, whilst the remainder contented themselves with grabbing what they could.

With a final roar, the last of them raised its head in defiance, fixing her vessel with its unearthly eyes, before vanishing. Slowly but surely the spheres began to contract, dwindling away until, with a final flash, they dissipated.

All three Mages collapsed.

"Get them below!" Leo ordered.

Maia felt suddenly exhausted, as if her Potentia had been sucked away. She knew that it wasn't possible for her vessel to ache, but it did.

"*Tempest*, contact your sisters. I want status reports. Lower your boats to pick up the survivors."

<*Patience*, *Farsight*! Report!>

The replies were clear, but Maia could feel the grief for their lost crews.

<*Patience*, reporting for duty.>

<*Farsight*, reporting for duty.>

<Where are you?> Maia asked.

<Still with my wreckage,> *Farsight* answered miserably. <There are a lot of bodies. I think I've lost most of my crew, though I have Durus.>

<Same here. Try to save the ones around you and those of the inanimates.> *Patience* answered her, practically.

<*Unicorn*, how are you?>

<Barely afloat, but I'll manage,> came the grim reply, followed by a string of oaths aimed at every monster in the sea.

"*Unicorn*?" Pendragon asked Maia.

"Cursing, Sire."

His mouth twisted. "I'm glad she's still able to. Thank the Gods the monsters decided that Shipbodies were not to their taste! It's a damned shame about the others, though. There were fine crews on those inanimates. *Tempest*, tell *Imperatrix* to co-ordinate the rescues. You need to conserve your energy."

<Will do,> *Imperatrix* answered, when Maia relayed it. <It's a tragedy that Pendragon had his earring taken, but you're doing a good job, *Tempest*! I've only ever done two emergency Potentia releases and they almost finished me off both times. Keep Ship functions to a minimum until you recover.>

<I'd like *Patience* to come to me,> Maia said, knowing that her friend was listening.

<Two Ships in one vessel can be tricky,> *Imperatrix* warned. <We constantly seek to anchor ourselves.>

<What do you do when you're unassigned?> she asked the older Ship.

<We have special anchor points in the buildings, pieces of our former vessels that we bring with us. *Patience*, get someone to collect a spar or some planks to bring with you.>

<Don't worry about me,> *Patience* answered. "One of my boats is almost intact and I can use that."

The other Ships were talking amongst themselves about how best to comfort their bereaved sisters.

<I'll need help,> *Unicorn* stated. <The bloody things chewed on my mizzen-mast so I can't raise much sail. I've lost a lot of crew, though I still have my Captain.>

<We'd have been better off if Marcus hadn't removed our Mages,> *Leopard* said. <Four for the whole fleet aren't enough. *Tempest*, you must share yours. Don't you have three now?>

Maia checked. Robin was still out cold, but Heron and Raven seemed to be recovering.

<I don't know if they'll be any use for a while,> she admitted.

Leopard sighed. <Not surprised. They did well. You gave them a good jolt of Potentia too and that's what swung it.>

<It was a *lot* of Potentia,> *Patience* interjected. <Yes, good for you, *Tempest*!>

Maia was touched by her friend's selflessness. <I'm really sorry that I couldn't save your crew and vessel. Yours too, *Farsight*.>

<You did your best,> the other Ship replied. She sounded resigned. <It happens. Thank the Gods our Captains are safe. *Leopard*, how are you?>

<They didn't attack me.>

<At least you were spared. I felt sure they'd rip you apart too.>

<They wouldn't dare!>

<You're the lucky one.>

It was true. The creatures had gone for the other smaller vessels, but had given *Leopard* a wide berth for some reason. The question niggled at Maia, but she put it aside for another time.

<*Farsight*, finish rescuing as many of your crew as you can, then come to me,> *Diadem* said. Maia was relieved that the experienced Royals were taking over. <You heard what you should do?>

<Get aboard one of my boats.>

<That's right. Do it quickly, before the light goes altogether. You younger Ships don't always know this, but having familiar wood around you is a comfort. Even if it's not your vessel, something remains. It's not something they teach at the Academy,>

There was, Maia decided, lots they didn't teach at the Academy.

*

The envoys were smiling, the setting sun painting their faces with bloody hues.

Tullia tried not to look in their direction, but it was difficult when she'd been summoned to the Great Cabin. Buzzard, too, looked like he'd dropped a copper *as* and found a gold *denarius*. At least her Captain wasn't gloating.

"Two Ships sunk and another damaged, plus several inanimates destroyed. Or so our serpent friends report," one of the Fae said. "They don't know the names, but we got that much out of them."

Buzzard frowned. "Only two?"

The Fae shrugged elegantly. "There was more opposition that we counted on. Apparently, some Mages yet remain with the rebels."

Buzzard was scowling now. "But the *Beisht Kione Dhoo* are impervious to anything human Mages have. How is it possible?"

"There was a Power there. It hurt them, so they withdrew. That is the extent of the information they gave us."

"Could there have been Olympian involvement?" Silvius asked. His tone was mild, but the warning was obvious.

The Fae froze, as if silently conferring.

"Unknown," the first one admitted. "If so, nothing was seen or heard."

Silvius's lips thinned. "Still, gentlemen, we have the advantage. The rebels will be weary and battle-worn."

"The Captain is correct," Buzzard agreed, his expression clearing. "The serpents have softened them up. Now we can deliver the killing blow."

Both men looked to the Fae. It was clear who was in command here. Tullia remained very still and prayed that they would not notice her, wondering which of her sisters had succumbed. Maybe it was *Diadem* or *Imperatrix*? The stuck-up Royals could do with being taken down a peg or two and, as a bonus, it would be something she could remind herself of in the years to come. She'd be sure to drop in lots of serpent references – if she ever met them again.

"We must press on," the Fae said. He seemed to have taken the role of spokesperson for the group. Anyone would have thought him a Northern merchant, with his elaborately decorated tunic and cloak fastened with silver and gold. No iron. Tullia had to fight the sudden urge to push him into a stack of cannonballs and see if he screamed. She'd watched as her crew had moved everything that could harm the Fae to the lower decks, where they never set foot.

Speaking of her crew, she ran an eye over her vessel. The men were working under the stern eyes of their officers, but there was no joy in it. She could feel the fear gnawing at them like shipworms in once-stout timbers. They'd better have some action soon, or they might snap under the strain.

"I agree," Silvius said. "My Lords, I'll order full sail. If the given bearings are correct, we'll sight the enemy around dawn."

"Perfect," Buzzard grinned. "With your permission, my Lords, I'll report back to Kite."

"Very well," the Fae replied. Tullia got the impression that he didn't care what a mere mortal did, Mage or no Mage. "You have your orders, Captain."

Silvius inclined his head, his face impassive. "*Regina*, you have our heading. Make all speed."

He was speaking for *their* benefit, not hers. Come to think of it, he had hardly used their private link at all since the guests came aboard. He'd also put a stop to much of the chatter on her part too, either with him or the other Ships. Did he think the Fae could eavesdrop? It was a frightening thought.

"Aye, Captain," she replied. She kept her eyes on her Silvius's face, though a prickling along her Shipsenses told her she was being scrutinised.

"Dismissed."

Tullia had never been more grateful that she could literally vanish into the woodwork. It was going to be a very long night and she dreaded what the dawn would bring.

*

The clear-up and rescue lasted well into nightfall.

"Commend the bodies to the sea," Pendragon ordered the Priests, who even now were saying prayers for the dead. There was no time to give them a proper burial, as every piece of shot was needed and couldn't be wasted on weighting down corpses. There were fewer than they had been and Maia had the horrible feeling that a lot had vanished, surreptitiously devoured by hungry serpents.

Both Ships insisted on heading the search for survivors, finding half-drowned men clinging to whatever flotsam and jetsam they could find. *Farsight* and *Patience* had recovered one of the former's boats and were directing it in and out of the wreckage as they picked up man after man Their remaining crews, together with those who had survived from the inanimates, were being shared among the fleet.

"We must leave," Pendragon told Leo. "North is out of the question now, so our only option is to try to make for the coast of Mona, or failing that, the coast beyond and one of the harbours there."

"Marcus might have a legion waiting for us," Leo pointed out. "It's what I would do."

"There are some remoter spots," the Admiral said, "and the terrain isn't that forgiving. It could take them some time to get us and meanwhile we could escape into the mountains."

Maia felt Leo's disquiet. It was a bad plan and they all knew it.

"We can then march down the Old Road towards Londinium, picking up reinforcements as we go," Pendragon continued.

That was worse. Unless they could convince the legions that Marcus was a false king, their little band would be trapped and slaughtered.

"We have to get there first," Leo observed.

"Correct, or all this talk is academic."

"You need to eat, Sire."

Pendragon nodded. "I will, as soon as my Ships and men are settled first. *Tempest*, where is *Patience*?"

"Still trying to locate survivors, Sire."

"Tell Fabillus to order her back here. I don't wish to sound harsh, but we must have most of them by now. Men can only last so long in this sea and we have to move."

It was the truth. The cries and screams had stopped. The only sound was hammerings as carpenters mended as much as they could, the slap of the waves against her hull and the gusty wind in her rigging. She didn't envy the *Unicorn*'s crew the task of jury-rigging the damaged mizzen-mast and repairing her flanks. Her crew would have to check below the water line as well. She could only be thankful that, for whatever reason, some of them had escaped unscathed.

The *Unicorn* was talking to *Blossom,* comparing their damage. The old training Ship had become a counsellor to her younger sisters, despite her own grief, and hearing the familiar voice comforted Maia. She left them to it to check on her Mages, and was relieved to see that Robin had woken up. Heron and Raven were conferring in a corner.

"How are you?" she asked her friend.

"I feel like I've been trampled by all four arena chariot teams," Robin replied through a mouthful of cheese and Ship's biscuit. Everyone was on cold rations since her galley fire had been doused for the duration. "That was a massive surge you sent us."

"Happy to help," she told him.

"Better than the alternative. It frightened them off, thank the Gods! What are you doing now?"

"Waiting for *Patience* to come aboard. She's helping *Farsight* now, but my carpenter's rigging up a temporary home for her here, using one of her boats. It's a pity it's not seaworthy, but it can be adapted for now. The Admiral's ordered us to make sail as soon as she arrives. Oh, here she comes!"

Maia watched as the two Ships embraced in *Farsight*'s boat, all that was left of the once mighty vessel, then she set about securing and hoisting her friend's heavy oaken body aboard.

"I'm glad she found Sandpiper. He did a good job."

The Mage was being tended to by Hawthorn for a nasty cut on his forehead, caused by a glancing blow from a falling spar. He had managed to keep his head above water until help arrived, but was still in bad shape.

"I suppose it's the three of you now to maintain all of us." Robin swallowed. "Not a happy prospect, I'm afraid. Heron and I have been working on something to even the odds, but it's not been tested in battle."

"Ah, the mysterious crates!"

"They're the ones! Here's *Patience* now. See to your friend." She left Robin applying himself to his food and glided across the deck to embrace her sister Ship. For a while they just stood together in silent commiseration, as her crew doffed their hats and caps in respect. Fabillus was already on deck, hovering anxiously at his Ship's side.

"Captain Fabillus, *Patience*."

They broke apart at Pendragon's voice.

"I am very sorry for the loss of your crew. Rest assured that all provisions will be made for their safe journey across the Styx. As to the survivors, they will be honoured for their bravery."

"We thank you on their behalf, Your Majesty," Fabillus replied, while his Ship saluted. Maia looked on with admiration. Would she have been so collected if it had happened to her?

"When we reach land, I'll order two inanimates to be outfitted as temporary vessels, so *Patience* and *Farsight* can get back to work as soon as possible.

"Thank you, Your Majesty."

"*Tempest*, make sail and order the fleet to follow. We'll round Mona and make port there. Leo will provide co-ordinates. Now, see to your sister. Captain Fabillus, do come below. I can assure you that your Ship is in good hands."

"Indeed. *Tempest*, my compliments." Fabillus saluted her and followed the Admiral down the ladder and into the Great Cabin. He was very composed she thought, seeing as his vessel had been sunk by ravaging monsters. He and his Ship were truly a matched pair.

Maia made the appropriate adjustments as she led her friend over to where the remains of the Ship's boat were fastened to her deck.

"I'm sorry it isn't much."

Patience smiled at her. "I can always get a new vessel. You just have to give Marcus a good kicking first."

Maia returned her smile. "I'll do my best and hopefully you won't be without a vessel for long. You heard what the King said. Now, get some rest."

The Ship stepped up and Maia could see the relief as her Shipbody touched familiar wood.

"That's better!"

"What does it feel like?" Maia asked, curiously.

"Like I've lost my arms and legs," *Patience* replied. "I feel squashed, somehow. Restricted. It's very strange." She grimaced. "Now, go and do your duty! I can manage. The others all want to talk anyway, so I'll keep them occupied and let you get on with it."

Maia heard the Ship settle into the link and applied herself to making headway against the uncooperative waves, whilst her commanders and most of her crew snatched a few hours of rest. It was still several hours to reach safe harbour on the northern coast of the Isle of Mona but, to her frustration, the wind had veered, blowing strongly from the south-east and hampering their passage. It seemed alive, dodging and darting as if to deliberately obstruct and push them back. She felt like a child again, playing Bulldog in the yard of the Foundling Home and trying to force her way past the opposition.

"I fear we aren't getting anywhere fast."

Raven appeared at her side, seemingly none the worse for his unconsciousness.

"We have to try."

"I suppose we do. We have our orders."

Pendragon had also ordered silent running, so the only light on deck was whatever she caught from the distant lighthouses. Her crew carried dark lanterns, or had to stumble about their tasks by memory and feel.

<Maia, I need to talk to you.>

The words appeared in her mind, red as the thread that connected them both.

<What about?>

He paused and she could tell that he was choosing his words carefully.

<How are you feeling, Potentia-wise? Are you depleted?>

She hadn't really thought about it, but her phantom aches had largely subsided.

<I think so,> she replied, hesitantly. <I felt a bit bruised at first, if a Ship can feel that, but I'm feeling a little better.>

He turned to her, his withered features momentarily outlined in a stray beam that as rapidly left his face shadowed once more.

<That's interesting.>

<Why?>

<Ships are usually totally exhausted for several days afterwards. What I ordered you to do is seen very much as a last resort and in many cases leads to a Pyrrhic victory.>

Maia was puzzled. <Robin said that it was a lot of Potentia.>

He snorted. <It was. More than I've felt from any other Ship, save one.>

<The *Augusta*?>

He shook his head. <The *Britannia*.>

If Maia could have gulped, she would have. Surely she couldn't be ranked alongside the half-legendary progenitor of every Ship? She didn't know how to answer that one.

<I think that there is more at work here than we know. The Gods have shown you favour and you know that they often work through mortals to achieve their ends.>

Unwelcome memory flashed into her mind. An alien voice possessing her body and speaking through her mouth, as Nemesis enacted her revenge upon the Huntress.

<I know they do.>

<Did you feel anything…strange?>

She thought back to the moment. <No. I followed my training. I practised with *Blossom*, but it was different actually being a Ship. Before, I could only do a little.>

Raven leaned on his stick, sucking his teeth thoughtfully. <Then you must have grown into your Potentia. Something's emerging.>

<You make me sound like a beetle crawling from a log!>

He laughed. <No, no. You're full of surprises, that's all.>

<Fancy that.> She decided to deflect the conversation away from herself. <It was a pity your friend the dragon couldn't have helped in the battle.>

Raven's mental voice was tinged with regret. <Alas. He can't fight against creatures of the ocean.>

Another riddle she didn't have the answer to. <I don't suppose you can explain?>

He thought for a moment.

<Let's just say that you and he have something in common.>

Now that was interesting. Maybe she wasn't the only one with Divine blood hereabouts? If that was the case, it was unwise to pursue the topic further.

She'd thought that her days of being a game piece were over, but now she wasn't sure of anything. She stared up at the sky. Clouds were racing past, blown by the same hostile wind and her vessel creaked in protest as she tried to forge ahead. Being watched by Powers she couldn't fathom frightened her.

<Still, you should take it easy after that massive expenditure.> Raven's voice snapped her back to their situation. <Let's hope the dawn brings some good news, eh?>

Maia doubted it.

<My sister told me that there was danger behind as well. Are there any other monsters of the deep I should know about?>

Raven turned to face her.

<It's not monsters I'm worried about.>

*

The rising sun did little to allay Maia's fears. *Patience* had been very quiet during the preceding hours, sinking into a semi-conscious torpor that she'd been warned about when Ships were forced to detach. As she'd told Raven, the lassitude that came with over-expenditure of Potentia hadn't affected Maia for long. She decided to risk checking with *Imperatrix* as to *Farsight*'s state.

<She's the same,> her fellow Royal said. <It's to be expected. She's aboard me now, boat and all. We must let them rest and recover; there's not much they can do as they are now. They'll get new vessels when all this is over.>

282

<As long as we win.>

The older Ship was confident in her answer. <That won't matter! Britannia needs Ships, whatever happens. Trade, diplomacy and defence are our lifeblood. There's no telling how long the treaty with the Alliance will last.>

Maia bit back a sharp retort and withdrew, opening a link to the *Diadem* instead. She didn't feel like treading on eggshells around the other Ship and had far less confidence in their survival. If the Fae got into power, everything could change. Legend said that they'd tried to cloak the land in mists and enslave its people before Artorius had driven them out. Even further back, some tribes had used the Roman Emperors and their Legions to act as a bulwark, and to annexe their neighbours' lands in the process. It had been a savage and bloody time in history and few wanted its return, despite the grumbles for independence from the wider Empire.

<*Diadem*? How are you?>

Her fellow Royal answered promptly.

<Well enough, though I'm having trouble against this wind.>

<Me too,> Maia agreed. <I'll be glad when we reach harbour.>

<Yes. These are horrible times.>

<What can we do?> Maia asked her. <Suppose we're all destroyed?>

<That won't happen,> *Diadem* replied with confidence. <Remember, we serve Britannia and its peoples. Whoever happens to wear the crown, we remain.>

It was a pragmatic view. This was the most they'd ever talked and Maia decided to ask some questions.

<May I ask how old you are, *Diadem*?>

There was a brief silence.

<Let me see,> her sister Ship began. <I was made a Ship when Artorius the Sixth was King, so that makes me... about two hundred and fifty, give or take a few years. To be honest, it's easier to stop counting.>

The sense of the Ship as a human woman was coming through in her words. She could have been somebody's grandmother sitting by the fire and reminiscing, except there were no children at her feet and there was no hearth to sit by.

<And I'm nearly twenty.>

<I can't remember when I was that young. You'll soon settle into this life and then it will be as if you never had any other. Look ahead, do your duty as best you can and know that you are loved and respected.>

Maia knew that *Diadem* was trying to console her.

<Thank you. I was in Portus you know, when you were installed on your vessel.> It seemed a very long time ago since she had been sitting in the parade, her face covered in makeup and throwing sweets to the Foundlings. It was like it had happened to another person in some distant land.

<Of course! You were still a candidate back then,> *Diadem* said. <I forget that you're still learning what it means to be a Ship. These days, you know, we're overstretched. It's not like before, when there were lots of us and we had more time to get to know one another. Now it's all 'sail here, do that,' – orders flying hither and yon. Now, look to your crew and give them the support they need. You are like their mother now and they must know that you'll always be with them.>

Diadem ended the conversation and Maia realised that she did feel a little better. She'd heard so much from some of the other Ships about 'stuck-up Royals', but was starting to realise that most of them were simply very hardworking and couldn't always spend time chatting when everyone wanted them to. It was an interesting revelation and, come to think of it, she'd been busy herself lately. It would be time to worry about the lack of candidates when the current troubles were resolved.

Speaking of work, movement in their cabins told her Pendragon and Leo were waking and being attended to by their servants. The watch was about to change, so she rang her bell to signal hand-over, watching men greet each other as they passed. Some were rousting their exhausted fellows, or rolling their hammocks to stow them away until they were needed again.

A flurry of movement and raised voices in the junior officers' quarters caught her attention. A fight had broken out between two of the midshipmen, fists flying in a tangle of arms and legs, whilst their fellows tried to separate them.

Maia didn't waste time summoning help; she shot through the wood and out of the bulkhead, grabbing the pair of them by their collars and yanking them apart so hard that the seams strained under the pressure.

"You can stop this right now, the pair of you! Do you want a beating?"

They subsided, flushed faces streaked with blood and already swelling where blows had landed.

"He called my father a traitor, because he's in the Senate!" Egnatius spat at his opponent. "His father is commanding an enemy Ship, so who's the traitor now?"

She sighed to herself. She'd seen trouble brewing with this one from the start. The young aristocrat had mostly kept his head down, but his attitude hadn't endeared him to his fellows and there had been small incidents against him, passed off as the usual practical jokes youngsters played on each other, but this time it was more serious. There would be no hiding the mess they'd made of each other.

Honorius was one of the younger Midshipmen, from a proud naval family and usually level-headed. His father was Captain of the *Vanguard*, a well-respected Ship, but one of those caught in port who had declared for Marcus. Both lads were under a lot of strain and it had all come to a head.

"I didn't!" Honorius objected. "I merely said that his father needed to see that Marcus is a usurper –,"

"You implied that he was acting against the King!" Egnatius yelled back. The other boys shrank back against the bulkheads, eager to distance themselves from the argument.

"There's clearly been a misunderstanding," Maia said firmly. "I understand that it's a difficult time for you, but beating each other to a pulp isn't going to solve anything. Do I have to inform Lieutenant Amphicles that his charges are behaving like untutored Northmen, brawling over imagined slights?"

She gave them both an emphatic shake.

"No, Ma'am," they chorused, staring at their shoes.

"Do your duty to this Ship and crew and, while you're at it, pray to the Gods to give you wisdom. Now, you've precisely one minute to clean yourselves up and get on deck before someone comes to see where you are!"

She turned and scowled at the remaining six. "You lot can go, right now!"

They didn't need telling twice, scurrying away like she'd set their breeches afire.

"As for you two, I don't want to see a repeat of this, or I *will* report you both. Mr Honorius, I pray that your father and the *Vanguard* are safe, as is Senator Egnatius. Sort yourselves out and I'll see you up top."

Maia left them to sluice their faces and concoct a suitable story for the appearance of various rapidly purpling bruises, muttering to herself about hot-headed, high-bred idiots. She didn't have this trouble with the boys in the gun crews, who didn't have such lofty opinions of themselves and were looked after by their messmates. She'd rather have been given more like young Sprout, or even Monkey despite his clumsiness. She'd have a word with Drustan to go easy on them, but feared that they would both be put on report and that would probably mean a beating.

And to think that they were the officers of the future! It was a good job that they'd have Ships to keep an eye on them. She chuckled inwardly. After a hundred years maybe she'd know more about what she was doing. As it was, she'd often been given charge of the younger children in the Foundling Home and this wasn't much different.

Once back on deck she scanned to the west, just as the sun emerged from the morning cloud. It didn't look much like anyone's chariot, she thought, more like a disc of glowing copper lifted from Vulcan's forge and radiating heat. The days were getting longer now and summer would be upon them before they realised. Being at sea, she missed the bloom of new green across the countryside as it shook off the chains of winter and burst into life once more. Now all she would see were the nesting sea birds and sometimes catch a brief hint of freshness blowing from the land.

As if summoned by her musings, a delicate touch stroked across her face, as if sent by a loving hand.

"Mother," she whispered. The breeze swirled, growing in intensity, nudging at her from the south-west as if to get her attention. "What is it?" Maia asked aloud.

Another, sharper nudge, almost a poke, then she felt it pass by, sweeping across the surface of the sea to ripple the surface of the waves. She followed its passage to the horizon, pushing herself to as far as it was safe to do in the circumstances.

She also checked the limited Ship link. It was quiet, mostly for fear that there might be eavesdroppers. Maia was ahead, pushing southwards to Mona, the other Ships ranged behind in line. *Unicorn* was having trouble keeping up and was having to use her boats to tow herself, but nothing else seemed amiss.

<*Imperatrix*, *Diadem*, do you see anything to the south-west?>

Having a restricted link was a blasted nuisance. They had to resort to eyes other than their usual wide-ranging Ship senses.

Both Ships acknowledged, running their own scans without question. Then a faint shout echoed across the water from *Diadem*'s look-out.

"Sails ahoy! South-west!"

It had been a warning after all.

<I can see them!> *Diadem* called urgently. <They're moving fast!>

Other Ships agreed.

<Too fast,> *Leopard* said. <They aren't fighting the wind so they'll be upon us within the hour, maybe less!>

<Perhaps they're friendly?>

<We need to know who they are.>

The Ships were all talking at once. They'd never had to fear their own sisters before.

<Quiet!> *Imperatrix* cut through the speculation. <There's only one way to find out. *Tempest*, ask the King if you should hail them.>

At her alerts, Pendragon pushed aside his breakfast and waved for his coat. Leo leapt to his feet.

"What have we got to lose? Friend or foe, they know we're here. Do it."

Maia suddenly wished that someone more experienced could handle this.

"Should I ask *Imperatrix* –,"

"Do it now!"

Maia activated the link, broadcasting as she hadn't done in days.

<This is His Majesty's Royal Ship, *Tempest*! State names and allegiance!>

She held her breath waiting for the reply. When it came, it was no surprise.

<This is His Majesty's Flagship, *Regina*! Heave to and surrender, or you will be fired upon. This is your final warning!>

"It's the *Regina* and the Usurper's Fleet, Sire. They're demanding we surrender."

Anger, determination and sorrow warred on Pendragon's face for a second.

"Tell her that they serve a traitor who has usurped the throne with the help of the Ancient Enemy. Tell them that if they follow him, they too will be damned to Tartarus!"

She did as she was bid, catching his spirit and intonation, even as he cursed at the loss of his earring.

Leo was in her mind already. <Battle stations!>

The Ship link came alive as her sisters followed suit. Musca's voice rang through the gun deck as cannon were prepared for loading. Gear was stowed, living spaces opened up and windows removed in the stern cabins to prevent flying glass. Fighting nets were rigged and guns loaded. Danuco's chanted prayers rang steadily across the deck as Hawthorn and Rowan methodically laid out instruments and cloths in the Adepts' quarters below, ready to receive casualties. In the armoury, marines were breaking out muskets and pistols and checking their supplies of powder and ball, while Sprout and his fellows were rushing back and forth to the magazine with cartridges for the cannon. Through it all, Maia checked and re-checked, crew, machinery, her links. She'd done plenty of drills, but this was different. The men and boys carried out their duties with grim determination. There was no time for fear.

<They can't mean to fire on us?> *Unicorn* was appalled.

<Looks like it,> *Diadem* said. <This is the first time we've ever fought each other.>

<They outnumber us, but we must stand firm.> *Imperatrix* insisted.

<There are other vessels as well, can you see?> *Unicorn* said. <They're hanging back, and they're not Britannic.>

Every Ship strained to see.

<They're not Northmen either,> Leopard observed. <They look like something out of a story book.>

The unpleasant realisation hit them all at once.

<Fae!>

<The puppet masters are here to oversee their handiwork!>

<I hope we can sink a few!>

<How are they tolerated?> *Imperatrix* demanded. <Are our sisters so blind that they can't see what's going on?>

<They're following their Captain's orders,> *Blossom* said. She sounded resigned. <Maybe their minds are clouded, or they're afraid.>

<Is it worth contacting them?> *Patience* had woken from her trance. <We don't stand a chance otherwise.>

<What, and surrender? I'll fight to the death!> *Leopard* snarled. <Come on, ladies. Time to show what we're made of!>

No wonder *Wolf of the Waves* liked her, Maia thought. They had a lot in common.

Pendragon was drawing up his battle strategy.

"They're coming in fast," he told his officers. "We mustn't let them surround us. We'll deploy into two lines at the last minute. With any luck they'll overshoot and we can open fire on their flanks."

"We're heavily outnumbered, Sire," Leo said.

"But we have the Gods on our side, Captain."

The men held each other's gaze for a while, then Leo nodded.

"So we do. *Tempest*, remind the crew of this fact and order the other Ships to do the same. Here's the strategy."

Maia did as ordered, relaying the attack plans and the positioning required of each vessel. Losing two Ships and having another crippled had reduced their little fleet considerably. They were outnumbered almost two to one, not counting the Fae, and some of their number were inanimates.

<Sail ahoy!>

Unicorn called. Two more Ships were approaching from the north, making good progress. Maia stifled a groan. Were they to be surrounded on all sides?

<Yer weren't goin' to start without us Harridans were yer, yer dozy mares?>

289

A familiar voice broke over the link, followed by a stream of cheerful abuse as *Persistence* charged to join her sisters. She was met with glad cries.

<Did yer think I'd miss this? Oh, and I brought a friend, just back from the New World.>

<Ahoy there, me dears!>

Maia didn't recognise the other Ship at first, but the voice brought back a vivid memory. The Admiralty offices at Portus, a shivering and terrified girl and two stately figureheads.

It was the *Swiftsure*.

<Hello, *Swiftsure*. Not seen you for ages,> *Diadem* chimed in. <How are you liking your new vessel?>

<Got mine after you, remember? Settled in nicely for the pull across the Atlantic. So, what are we doing?>

Maia's news was greeted with joy by her officers.

"That's evened the odds more than a little," Pendragon said. "Two very experienced Ships. Give them my compliments, *Tempest* and tell them to make rendezvous with all speed."

He then proceeded to outline the plan and, as she relayed it to her sisters, Maia saw that they had a glimmer of hope after all.

<He's a master tactician,> Leo told her. <I feel better now that we've both Harridans as well. They can be pains in the arse at times, but they don't stand any nonsense.>

<I've not heard them called that,> Maia laughed.

<They've been separated for a few years, that's why. They tend to cause riots when they're together and give senior Admirals earache.>

<They're fighters,> Maia agreed. <It's just horrible that we're fighting our sister Ships.>

Her Captain's face flickered with pain.

<I know. Still, it might not come to that.>

Before she could ask what he meant, Pendragon spoke once more.

"*Tempest*. Relay this to all Ships. All of them, understood?"

"Aye, sir."

"All Ships! This is Cei Pendragon, Son of Artorius, King of the Britons and rightful heir to the throne of Britannia! My son, Marcus, is a liar, a usurper and a traitor. He has allied himself with the Ancient Enemy, who even now control him in order to restore their power over the land. Look about you and see that they are already in our midst! Be warned! The Gods of Olympus have abandoned him! Rise up to protect our people and our way of life before it is swept away forever. Gods save Britannia!"

Maia finished to a wave of silence. It was as if they had all been transformed to inanimates, with no voices but what their crews provided and no will of their own. Then the link erupted.

<Gods save King Cei!>

<A pox on the Fae and all their works!>

<He lies! King Marcus removed the sword!> That was *Regina*, trying to drown everyone else out.

<It was a trick!> Maia yelled back. <A glamour! The sword's still there!>

<We only have your word for that!>

Imperatrix waded in. <It's the truth! Can't you see the Fae Ships around you? You're on the wrong side! Do you want our people to live under Fae rule?>

Doubt, fear and anger rolled through the link like a physical assault, battering at the bonds that held them all together. Blows that would leave worse than bruises, nor would they heal as quickly.

"They're arguing?" Pendragon asked her.

She forced herself to separate his voice from the mental clamour.

"Worse," she said. Leo was grimacing as he caught the backlash.

"Indeed, Sir."

Pendragon's frustration at being out of the link was evident. If he'd been able, Maia thought that he would have ripped Leo's earring from him to hear what was going on.

"This won't help. Order the Ships to break off and listen to their Captains. Raise signals for calm."

Signals were another resort. When Ships were overwrought or not responding, it was a way for Captains to communicate directly. It was the main method used aboard inanimates for centuries. She did as she was bid, ordering Amphicles to select the appropriate pennant. He rushed to obey, attaching the little flag and sending it aloft. Slowly, the Ships responded, breaking

291

off their threats and entreaties until only *Regina* and *Persistence* were left.

<We all saw what yer did to *Blossom* and now she has no Captain. Yer a disgrace to yer name!>

<*Persistence*! That's enough!> *Diadem* interceded as the stream of insults continued.

<You were a raddled old hulk before, and now you're a traitor too!> *Regina* fired back.

<The Gods curse you to rot where you lie!> *Persistence* spat. <Beyond help and beyond hope!>

Audible gasps ripped through the link. It was the most terrible curse anyone could wish on a Ship. Maia beat her brains for something, anything to try and talk sense into her old classmate.

<Tullia!> she called. <What have they promised you?>

Her former friend hesitated.

<You didn't want to be a Ship! You were going to beg your father to let you leave the Academy! *What did they promise you?*>

Regina radiated guilt and fear. Sensing an opening in the Ship's defences. Maia pushed her way in, squeezing through the mental barrier, doing consciously what she'd done unwittingly before. She latched on to the other's thoughts like a lamprey, barbs digging deep.

A jumble of images flashed up. *Beautiful clothes, fine furniture, jewels, a glittering crown. A throne. Marcus smiling at his new consort, first lady of the land.*

Maia almost choked. Of course, so that was it. She hastily relayed everything through the link.

<Look, sisters! We would be abandoned by Queen Tullia Albana! See what I see!>

There was more. *Three men that weren't men, waiting and deadly, cunning and merciless as spiders.* Maia seized the information, channelling it outwards with a strength she didn't know she possessed.

The dead *Livia*'s voice slithered into her brain.

This is my gift to you. Fire and mind!

Images tumbled into the link, unstoppable and damning as the Potentia ripped through her. Past and present swirled together in a maelstrom of emotion, hers and others.

Somewhere, someone was screaming.

The memories were overpowering, sucking her away down a spiralling hole into the cold darkness.

Maia was drowning, burning and freezing, choking on salt water. Blind and deaf, she reached out, desperate to save herself. Then an irresistible summons seized hold and dragged her upwards. She opened her eyes.

Hands gripping her, strong and steady. Raven's blank eyes were wide as he summoned her forth, much as he'd done when her spirit was sealed to her Shipbody. Beneath the cloudiness, she saw a flash of piercing blue.

She wasn't drowning after all. She was on her vessel. She was the *Tempest*. She was a Ship.

Raven heaved a huge sigh. "You're back."

She opened her mouth to gasp, before she remembered that she didn't need to breathe any more.

"You lost control," he explained, sagging a little. "Your Potentia rebounded on you."

She looked around to get her bearings. Pendragon was standing to one side, speaking urgently with Sabrinus and Amphicles. She opened her link to Leo, but there was no answer.

"My Captain –,"

"Unconscious. He was knocked out by the backlash. You've given most of the Fleet a splitting headache, girl!"

It was true. Everyone looked a little green. She realised with a stab of guilt that Leo was in his bed, being tended by Hawthorn. By the Gods, what had she done? Even *Patience* had roused from her stupor and was regarding her with concern.

<Are you all right?>

The Ship's voice was soft, but Maia winced. It seemed she'd given herself a headache too.

<Did you get all that?> she asked. She was just grateful that Shipbodies couldn't be sick.

<We did, and the rest. When you were burned.>

Chagrin and embarrassment made her bow her head. <I'm so sorry.>

<That was somethin' I 'aven't felt in a long time,> *Persistence* rasped. <Yer've got a ghost in yer, girlie.>.

Naturally, most of the Ships here would remember the *Livia* and her special talent, though how often the Ship had used it and when, Maia didn't know.

<Save the questions for later.> *Imperatrix* was firm on the matter. <Many things are now clear. How say you, sisters?>

There were mumbles of agreement and not only from Pendragon's fleet. The *Justicia*, was calling to the *Regina*, but the Ship was silent. Then *Jasper's* voice broke into the link with a sudden warning.

<*Regina's* off course!>

It was true. The huge Ship had veered away from her line. Maia thought she could hear shouts and see figures in her rigging as they desperately tried to regain control of the vessel manually. It wouldn't be easy as she had less than half the crew of an inanimate, and most of those would be marines. Other Ships were calling now, trying to reach their stricken sister, but Maia noticed none of them were on Pendragon's side.

<Acknowledging.>

The reply was faint, but clear. The Ship was waking up. Tiny figures scrambled back to deck as the Ship corrected her heading and regained control of her systems. Meanwhile, orders flew as both sides disposed themselves for battle.

<It's really going to come to blows, then?> *Patience* was staring miserably at the approaching sails.

<No way to stop it now.>

As she watched the ordered tumult about her, relaying commands and preparing herself for battle, distant cries filtered into the link. Many Ships were far away on assignment and their horror was evident. Not one of them could believe what was happening, that the Ships of Britannia were turning against each other after centuries. Some pleaded for them to stop, others had already taken sides but Maia couldn't afford to listen to the cacophony of voices. She had to remain present in this moment, as her crew and the people she loved prepared to do their duty.

Their lives were now in the hands of the Fates.

The two fleets swept into range before she knew it. Pendragon had been right; *Regina* did overshoot, presenting her flank to a broadside before she could veer off. Maia felt her vessel shudder as each cannon fired, propelling bar shot, chain shot and standard cannonballs to do as much damage as possible. Suddenly, a wall of sickly green Potentia sprang up around her adversary and the missiles were deflected harmlessly into the ocean.

"Gods preserve us!" Pendragon cried. "What is this?"

"Fae work!" Raven shouted over the thunderous noise. He was loosing return spells as fast as he could. "They have new defences!"

What use were her armaments if they couldn't penetrate *Regina*'s shields?

Other Ships were firing now, getting the range. Huge columns of water exploded upwards near hulls, but none seemed to hit their marks. It seemed that not many were hitting their intended targets and some were clearly hanging back.

"We need to break off!" she heard Pendragon order.

The *Regina* returned fire even as Maia's Mages did their best to defend her, the vivid purple answering the alien magic. Maia tried to swing herself aside, but she wasn't fast enough. Her shields repelled some enemy fire, but more ripped through her sinistra gun decks, smashing into men and guns and sending lethal shards of oak into flesh and fittings alike. Maia blocked out the screams, working mechanically to shore up her vessel with every procedure she'd been taught, relaying order after order, directing men to take casualties to the Adepts and encouraging the others to salvage what they could.

It was too late. Another devastating blast of Fae power shot from the *Regina*, compounding the previous wounds and weakening her below the waterline. She could only watch helplessly as a cannonball screamed across the deck, passing between Pendragon and Amphicles, and turning Sabrinus into bloody pulp. There wasn't time to mourn, barely to think, as the *Regina* poured barrage upon barrage of rolling emerald fire upon her. This was no natural battle, nor was there any defence against the strange power the enemy Ship had been equipped with.

Raven had been joined by Heron, both men chanting, arms raised and sweat streaming down their faces as they wielded the Potentia to try and break through the Fae defences.

"How are they repelling the iron?" Pendragon muttered, before raising his voice to a shout. "*Tempest*! Tell Robin to proceed!"

295

She could barely answer him, feeling the gushing water flooding into her lower decks as the bilge pumps failed and the sea began to claim her.

"I'm ready" came the reply. The young Mage was on deck. Eight men were lifting a device from one of the crates she'd stored in her hold. It was cylindrical, but with stubby fins on each side, like some sort of metallic fish. Robin was busy turning a wheel on its side and she could hear the ratchetting noise it was making as he wound it up. It seemed more mechanical than magical, the noise settling to a steady hum as he finished and stepped back.

"That should do it. Now!" he told his crew. Grunting with effort, the men thrust the contraption over the rail and into the sea. As it fell, its wings extended, giving it the look of a skate, or ray. She watched it as it sank.

"I don't know how long I can hold out!" she told Pendragon. She could feel herself settling, growing heavier as pieces of her were blasted away, bit by bit. She was about to scream for her Captain, when he appeared, supported by Hyacinthus and Danuco.

<Leo! I'm going down!> He heard her and nodded, though he still looked pale and shaky. She went to his side immediately, clasping him in her arms and taking him to a boat.

"Get the King to safety!" she urged the two men. Relieved of their burden, they obeyed, ushering a reluctant Pendragon to the boats along with the Master Mage. It was all she could do to work her machinery as she was slowly and methodically ripped apart by blast after blast. *Patience*, after helping on deck as much as she could, had gone with the King to protect him as much as she was able. Maia relinquished control of the frail craft to her sister, knowing that she would do everything she could to protect Pendragon.

"Abandon Ship! All hands, abandon Ship!"

Men poured out of the hatches, making for her remaining boats. Crippled, she could only watch as her vessel failed around her, isolating her from her systems and her ability to protect her crew. Rowan, Hawthorn's assistant, dragged a wounded man up the ladder, aided by Big Ajax and Monkey, but she knew that there were many more below who would never see the light of day again. They would be taken to the deeps to face the mercy of Neptune, their spirits one with the Ocean forever.

Her priority now was to save as many as she could. Maia had just managed to launch the last of her boats, when her vessel lurched alarmingly. Men skidded across her decks, some crushed by loose cannon, others toppling over the rail. There was nothing she could do for them now. All her systems were damaged and she felt her awareness drawing from the wood, back into her Shipbody. The *Regina*, unharmed, made sail and left her to founder. Her voice broke into the link as a parting shot to her defeated sister.

<You should have listened to me, *Tempest*! It didn't have to be like this. You brought it on yourself. I'm going to finish this now. None of the other Ships can stand against me!>

Maia didn't give her the satisfaction of a reply, though many other Ships were pouring abuse on their faithless sister. What was the use? Her vessel was done for, and doubtless the *Regina* would pick off the others one by one.

As she clung to the deck for a moment longer, unwilling to abandon her post until the last minute, she noticed a dark shadow heading towards the enemy Ship. The new weapon? It was slowly picking up speed as it moved steadily in the *Regina*'s direction, like a fish caught on a hook being drawn ever closer to its captor. Maia waited for it to be repulsed, as her cannonballs had been, but at the last minute it dipped below the green shimmer of the Fae shield.

Then, without warning, the *Regina* exploded, ripped apart from within. The shockwave swept over both fleets, the dull boom coming a second later, sounding like the voice of Jupiter himself. Where Marcus's Flagship had been, a pillar of fire and thick black smoke roiled into the sky, followed by a hail of deadly fragments.

<*Regina*?>

The other Ships added their voices to hers, calling for their sister irrespective of which side they were on, enmities forgotten in the horror of the moment.

<*Regina*, acknowledge!>

The distant *Victoria*'s plea silenced them all. The other Ships broke off, watching as *Regina*'s masts wavered, then toppled like

297

felled trees, collapsing in a groaning mass of rope, wood and canvas. Her bow and stern folded inwards, water sheeting from her hull as if she'd been cleaved amidships by a mighty axe.

<Can anyone see her?> *Imperatrix* Sent. <Her Shipbody must be there somewhere.>

Maia hadn't time to worry about whether Tullia had escaped the explosion. The *Regina*'s fate was out of her hands now and she had to look after herself. Waves began to wash across her deck as her beautiful vessel succumbed, yet still she clung on like an obstinate limpet, taking a last look around the ruin of her home. It had lasted only a little longer than the *Emerald*'s, before she was destroyed by a kraken. Nobody could have predicted this cruel turn of fate.

<Maia! Detach now!>

She lifted her head and focused on a speck, bobbing on the water. Raven. He was always her anchor wherever she found herself, even more than her Captain. Leo was speaking to her as well, both men's voices overlapping in her head.

"I'm coming," she said aloud, watching as what was left of the *Regina*'s vessel slid beneath the waves to its doom.

Detaching was painful, like ripping off a dried, bloody bandage. No more decks, cabins, sails, rigging, pulleys, capstans. Now she only had her Shipbody. She stared down at herself, remembering what it was like to mould the wood into her desire.

Nobody could ever tell a Ship what she should look like. Maia concentrated and *changed*.

XIII

She swam down, diving further and further from the light with each beat of her powerful tail. It wasn't the deepest of waters, but it would suffice for now and give her a little space alone with her thoughts. There was freedom here in the silent caress of the currents, far from the turbulence and grief. Untroubled fish regarded her curiously. Perhaps they thought she was one of the Mer-People, as that was the form she'd chosen. A sleek, streamlined body and a scaly tail were what she needed now, formed seamlessly from the sacred wood.

Temptation pulsed through her like a siren song. What was to stop her from staying like this, choosing her own path to navigate strange waters where she would? There was no need to eat or breathe, no demands or orders to follow, no vessel to maintain. No need to be human anymore. She could be a strange wooden mermaid, wandering the world with only the denizens of the ocean for company…

<Tempest! Report! Are you all right?>

She was a fool. There were oaths she couldn't break, bindings that were forever, both in the mortal realm and the Divine. Too many people were depending on her now.

<Acknowledged, Captain,> she Sent to Leo. How long had her illusionary freedom lasted? One minute, two? She changed course, heading back towards the surface, feeling her Shipbody respond to the pull of the light and air. It only took a few seconds before she could see the dark shapes of wreckage silhouetted against the sunlight. Reluctantly, she surfaced into chaos.

The desperate cries ceased to be muffled echoes, bursting into her senses with imperative force. She swam to the nearest, to find Hyacinthus and a young lad she didn't know clinging to the remains of a hatch.

"It's me, *Tempest*," she told them, not wishing to add to their fear. "Climb on to my back and I'll get you to safety."

"Thank you, Ma'am," Hyacinthus said through chattering teeth. "This lad was blown off the *Regina*."

The boy must have had some God looking out for him, she thought. There couldn't be many more survivors from that devastation.

They did as she ordered, the older man helping the lad who was shivering with the cold. Maia opened her senses to orient herself, realising that she'd somehow cut herself off from the Ship link ever since detaching. Voices were starting to come through now, but she made a conscious decision to lie low until she knew more about what she was facing.

It was obvious that all firing had stopped. Both sides were riding at anchor, Captains eyeing each other whilst their Ships mourned the loss of one of their own. Speculation flew through the link, along with regrets and contrition. It seemed that orders didn't always outweigh conscience after all.

Privately, Maia thought that the destruction of the Fae creatures on board the *Regina* had something to do with it as well. Their vessels had glided off into mists of their own making and now it felt like everyone was waking from a bad dream into a reality that wasn't much better. Nobody seemed to know what to do.

Pendragon's voice came down the link. They must have finally rigged up a replacement earring for him.

<All Ships! I, Cei Pendragon, order you to stand down! I repeat, stand down! There will be no more loss of life at the behest of our Ancient Enemy! See how they have fled the field now that their commanders have been destroyed by our new weapon. They care nothing for you, as the fate of the *Regina* has amply demonstrated, whereas I care for you all. Be assured that I will find a way to prove my claim to the throne that does not rely on treacherous magic and glamour. Any Captain or Ship who wishes to speak with me privately is free to do so.>

Maia continued to ignore the babble of voices on the link and adjusted her course to take her to the nearest boat, trying to keep herself out of the water as much as possible. The weight left her back as her passengers were hauled up to safety, and she became aware that Leo was directing operations.

<*Tempest*, are you coming aboard?>

She rolled her eyes upwards. He was leaning over her, silhouetted against the sky.

<I'll stay here,> she Sent. <You look overloaded and there may be others I can save.>

<Don't be long,> he told her. <We need to regroup. It seems that many Captains are regretting their choice.>

<Well there's not much else I can do!> she snapped. <I may as well do this!>

<Continue, then,> he replied and she regretted her words immediately.

<I'm sorry.>

<No, forgive me. Damn Marcus and damn this war. Do what you can.>

She swam away, seeking out survivors. The boy from the *Regina* had been fortunate indeed. Bodies were drifting in clusters or tossed like leaves on the uncaring waves, not all of them whole. The water around them was fouled with blood and filth. For a second, she thought she caught a glimpse of someone, or something else, forging effortlessly though the water as she did, pushing men to the surface. Was it Tullia? Then she saw that he was male. One of the Mer-People?

He flashed her a sad smile, then was gone.

Maia forced herself to swim on, but the cries for help had ceased, leaving just the sounds of wind and water. In the background, she could hear the splash of oars, so she raised her head to look.

There was hardly anything left of her vessel in view now. As she watched, the main mast slipped slowly under the waves, its bright pennant with the dragon and eagle waving, as if bidding her farewell.

It's only a vessel, she told herself fiercely. *You will get another.*

Now she truly understood what her friends had been through. It was all part of being a Ship, after all and at least she was still here. And so, presumably, was Tullia, unless her Shipbody had been blown to bits along with her vessel.

A flash of red slipped into her musings. Raven.

<Maia, what are you doing?>

<Looking for survivors.>

<There aren't any left. Come alongside *Imperatrix*. We're all here.>

She felt like crying, but forced back the self-pity instead and headed obediently in his direction.

<*Tempest*, come aboard me. I've secured one of your boats alongside, so you can latch on to that.>

The normally sharp voice was subdued, even sympathetic.

<Thank you, *Imperatrix*.> Maia tried to sound calm and professional, when all she really wanted to do was scream.

She forged on through the water, pushing her way through lingering smoke that she knew would reek of sulphur and death, repressing the strong urge to head out into cleaner seas over the horizon. Had any Ship ever done that, she wondered, just abandoned everything and left?

Maybe one day she'd find out, but now was not the time.

The *Imperatrix* and *Patience* were waiting for her, the latter in Maia's boat which was nestling against the side of the large vessel like an unweaned pup.

<You are both welcome,> *Imperatrix* told them. Her Captain, a grizzled veteran called Cornelius, echoed his Ship's greeting, calling over the side.

"You are indeed, ladies. May I offer my condolences on the loss of your crewmen and thanks for your safe deliverance!"

They thanked him, then their hostess returned to her duties and Maia was left bobbing alongside her sister. It felt good to attach to her familiar wood again, even if it lacked everything she'd become used to over the past months. It felt like home.

"Well, here we are," Maia said. *Patience* smiled, sadly.

"At least everyone's talking. Where did you get to?"

"I went swimming." She'd reverted to her previous appearance on boarding her boat.

"You changed your Shipbody."

"Yes. It's easy. You just have to think of a shape and you can be it."

Patience looked doubtful. "I've never really tried. I more or less came out like this."

She did look like Briseis always had, when Maia thought about it.

"Maybe you should try it one day, when no-one's looking?"

"I think I'll leave it to you," her friend replied.

They fell silent for a few minutes, listening to the noise of the crew on the *Imperatrix* and the chatter over the Ship link.

"What now?" Maia said at last.

"Well, normally we'd be sent back to an Admiralty base, but I suppose that's not an option here. I guess we'll have to stay near one or other of the Ships and make our way to port." Maia decided to change the subject.

"Where do you think *Regina* is now?" She would have called her Tullia and *Patience* by her birth name, but she knew her friend was a stickler for Admiralty protocol.

<Maybe she's back sleeping in the Grove of the Mother,> *Patience* answered silently. Such things could never be spoken aloud.

<If Marcus wins, he can recall her. Do you honestly think he ever intended to marry her?>

Her friend shrugged. <Who knows? It would depend on his supporters and how long he needed Albanus for. Maybe his new allies wouldn't let him.>

"I know he's lost some allies here," Maia said aloud. Several Ships had already declared for Pendragon, including *Jasper*, *Emerald*, *Peridot* and *Dragon*, though some had already left, choosing discretion rather than a side. This war would no longer be fought at sea.

"That new weapon made a difference," *Patience* said. "They think that we all have one. What was it?"

Maia frowned. She remembered seeing it being thrust overboard, but Heron and Robin had kept their secrets close.

"I don't know, but it will change naval warfare. Our shields don't extend too much below the waterline and it smashed right into her hull."

They exchanged a glance of mutual horror.

"It must have somehow ignited her magazine," *Patience* confirmed. "Scary!"

"Very," a familiar voice cut in, "but it stopped the battle."

Raven landed gently in Maia's boat. He seated himself and tucked his hands inside his sleeves as calmly as if he was paying a social call.

"Master Mage," *Patience* said politely. "Do you know what it was?"

He grimaced. "Heron's named it after the torpedo fish, because of the way it looks. It also has the power to send out a shock of sorts that targets certain areas of a creature or vessel. He never thought it would have to be used against a Ship."

"How is he?"

"Oh, he's fine. Saddened at the outcome, but secretly elated that it worked so spectacularly. You know him. He's probably thinking of improvements already. He's asked to be transferred back to *Blossom* and Pendragon's said yes."

"There aren't any more of them, are there?" Maia asked. "I only saw one being launched."

He shook his head slightly. "They went down with your vessel," he muttered, "but the others don't know that. Given time, we can make more."

Patience shuddered. "Would we want to?"

"They cut through Fae power very nicely," he pointed out, "hence their sharp exit. They devised some sort of defence against our more conventional weapons, but not this one, perhaps in part because it's more mechanical than magical."

"It's sad indeed that we had to use it," Maia said, "but what choice did we have? She'd have turned on the rest of us, backed up by the other Fae. Do you think we'll ever see her again?"

"*Regina*? I have the feeling that her Shipbody survived and made it to one of her supporters, but no-one's saying. She wasn't spotted, but I don't think many of her crew survived, including her Captain and his foul allies."

"I picked up one," Maia said, "but there were a lot of bodies."

He nodded. "We have to win this war first and that means moving to land power. The Fae have already established footholds and are gathering their forces. They're unwilling to move yet, but it's only a matter of time. There are certain mystical things that they have to put in place first."

"So we can't do anything," Maia said.

The ancient Mage raised an eyebrow. "I wouldn't say that."

She glared at him. He was being cryptic again.

"We're stuck on two small boats and you're saying we can affect the tide of battle?"

"There is a way."

Maia gritted her wooden teeth. "Please enlighten us, O Great One!"

Patience looked slightly horrified at her disrespectful tone, but she didn't know Raven like Maia did. The old goat had a plan.

"We have other resources, ones that are currently working overtime and don't rely on magic. Well, not very much, anyway. The time of machines is upon us, ladies and you are going to be the start of a new age! After that, you can go back to your vessels. *If* you want."

They both stared at him. "*If* we want?" Maia demanded.

"You might have a taste for something else."

"Such as?"

He grinned broadly.

"Now that would be telling."

Author's Note

Thank you very much, dear Reader, for downloading or buying this book! I hope you enjoyed it. As you have seen, Maia and her fellow Ships are in quite a predicament, as is the whole of Britannia.

The next book will be the culmination of the series, when many things long hidden, lost or forgotten will be revealed. I hope there will be quite a few surprises along the way too.

All the place names in this book are Roman or pre-Roman, except for Malvadum. I couldn't find what Ilfracombe was called, if indeed it was a harbour in our Roman times, so I translated the Anglo-Saxon into Latin. I'm afraid it isn't very complimentary to this lovely part of Devon as 'Mal' means 'bad'. Judging from what happens there in my book, they must have been right!

Now for my usual plea! I would be eternally grateful if you could **leave a review on Amazon**, as it's getting harder and harder these days to stand out from the crowd. There are hundreds of new titles appearing every month and taking the time to leave a review, however short, can make a massive difference to an independent author such as myself. **Many thanks!**

If you haven't already, please sign up to my **monthly no-obligation newsletter** and receive a **FREE Ships of Britannia Novella** and **TWO** short stories!

You can also find me on the **Ships of Britannia Facebook page** and on **Twitter/X** at **@EKkoulla**.

Acknowledgments

Few authors get to the finish line unaided and I'm no exception! Here are a few shout-outs to some incredible people who have supported and encouraged me along the way.

Firstly, I would like to thank my amazing cover artist, Thea Magerand, for translating the vague descriptions I give her into fantastic visual images.

To my wonderful beta-readers, Jane, Robyn and Perry for all their encouragement and for taking the time to peruse my scribblings.

I'm also indebted to my friend Kieran for the great map he created for me, just as I was about to give up on having one!

The manuscript was proofread by my dear friend, Dr. Madeleine Campbell-Jewett, Grammarian Extraordinaire, who found all sorts of mistakes I completely failed to spot despite many readings. I am eternally grateful that her diligence and eagle eyes have spared my blushes! Any errors in the front or end pieces are entirely my own.

My husband, Stephen, who has been a great supporter as always, even though he prefers military history or books about Romans. Real Romans, that is, not my imaginary ones.

Lastly, of course, I would like to thank **you** for choosing to buy or download these books and embarking on these adventures with me.

Until next time!

Printed in Great Britain
by Amazon

37288471R10179